NEW YORK REVIEW BOOKS
CLASSICS

THE LAND BREAKERS

JOHN EHLE (1925–2018) grew up the eldest of five children in the mountains of North Carolina, which would become the setting for many of his novels and several works of nonfiction. Following service in World War II, Ehle received his BA and MA at the University of North Carolina at Chapel Hill, where he met the playwright Paul Green and began writing plays for the NBC radio series *American Adventure*. He taught at the university for ten years before joining the staff of the North Carolina governor Terry Sanford, where Ehle was a "one-man think tank," the governor's "idea man" from 1962 to 1964. (Sanford once said of Ehle: "If I were to write a guidebook for new governors, one of my main suggestions would be that he find a novelist and put him on his staff.") The author of eleven novels, seven of which constitute his celebrated Mountain Novels cycle, and six works of nonfiction, Ehle lived in Winston-Salem, North Carolina, and New York City. He was married to the actress Rosemary Harris, with whom he had one daughter, Jennifer Ehle, also an actress.

LINDA SPALDING was born in Kansas and moved to Canada in 1982. She has written four novels, *Daughters of Captain Cook*, *The Paper Wife*, *Mere* (co-written with her daughter, Esta), and most recently, *The Purchase*, for which she received the Governor General's Award. Among her nonfiction books are *A Dark Place in the Jungle: Science, Orangutans, and Human Nature* and *Who Named the Knife: A True Story of Murder and Memory*. Spalding is an editor of the journal *Brick* and has been awarded the Harbourfront Festival Prize for her contributions to Canadian literature.

THE MOUNTAIN NOVELS

The Land Breakers

The Road

The Journey of August King

Time of Drums

The Winter People

Lion on the Hearth

Last One Home

THE LAND BREAKERS

JOHN EHLE

Introduction by
LINDA SPALDING

NEW YORK REVIEW BOOKS

New York

THIS IS A NEW YORK REVIEW BOOK
PUBLISHED BY THE NEW YORK REVIEW OF BOOKS
435 Hudson Street, New York, NY 10014
www.nyrb.com

Library of Congress Cataloging-in-Publication Data
Ehle, John, 1925–
  The land breakers / John Ehle ; introduction by Linda Spalding.
    pages cm — (New York Review Books classics)
  ISBN 978-1-59017-763-1 (paperback)
  1. Appalachian Region, Southern—Fiction. 2. North Carolina—
History—1775–1865—Fiction. I. Title.
  PS3555.H5L27 2014
  813'.54—dc23

                        2014013613

ISBN 978-1-59017-763-1
Available as an electronic book; 978-1-59017-794-5

Printed in the United States of America on acid-free paper.
10 9 8 7 6 5

INTRODUCTION

John Ehle, born in Asheville, North Carolina, in 1925, can trace his ancestry, through his mother, back to one of the first three families to settle the western mountains of North Carolina in the eighteenth century. The eldest of five children, he was expected to become a preacher and has vivid recollections of his grandmother on her porch swing discussing this with the local preacher. But after fighting in both Germany and Japan during World War II, he came home to enroll at the University of North Carolina at Chapel Hill, where, while working toward a master's degree in drama, he began to write radio plays, half-hour programs about adventurers or heroes for the American Adventure series, which was broadcast on NBC and Radio Europe. Ehle's apprenticeship in drama is evident throughout his subsequent work, in which character emerges most powerfully through the spoken word.

Ehle is the author of seventeen books, perhaps the best known of which is the 1988 nonfiction work, *Trail of Tears*, which tells the searing story of the Cherokee Nation and its eventual removal from North Carolina to Oklahoma. But it wasn't until he embraced the historical novel that he found the subject of his heart and his indelible characters. This cycle of seven novels, dubbed by Ehle the Mountain Novels, follows the lives of several families who settle in the steep mountains of North Carolina, families with names like Wright and Harrison and King, while exploring various eras of Appalachian history, from the first mountain settlement to the Civil War, the building of the first railroad, and the 1920s and '30s.

The first in that series, *The Land Breakers*, was written fifty years ago and stands absolutely on its own. It begins in 1779 with a man and a woman, hungry and young. They have been walking for two or three years looking for land on which to make a home, working their way down the continent, north to south. They were sent from Ireland as children, bonded servants, and now they are married and free with some money saved. When a storekeeper in Morganton, North Carolina, offers them foothold on a faraway mountain, he adds, "I don't want to sell a tiny piece of it, though you look so needful. Have you come far?"

They have come far.

They have come to an almost nonexistent town and they stand looking into the distance at a mountain covered by trees and clouds and the narrow trails of ancient beasts. Nothing lives up there but wolves and panthers and a great, wanton bear. No person has ever made settlement in that high place. But with a horse and a cow, two sows, a boar, four chickens, and a she-dog, Mooney and Imy Wright climb for days, sleeping on the ground at night, until at last they find themselves enraptured and alone above the clouds. Choosing a spot on which to live their lives, they fell trees for a cabin, clear space for a garden, and carry water to make a fireplace of clay. The world is vast and empty around them but, by winter's end, the darkly ambitious Tinkler Harrison arrives with a retinue of slaves and horses and cattle and a new young wife. With him is his daughter, Lorry, who brings two growing sons along with a load of resentment against her controlling father. Lorry's husband has left to find a piece of land in Kentucky. He's been gone two years, but Lorry believes he will return to their old homeplace in Virginia and wonders how he will ever find her now when she's been forced to follow her father to this unknown, wild place.

When Tinkler calls a halt to his kingly procession, he sees Mooney behind a stand of trees digging a narrow grave: Imy has become the mountain's victim. Survival is Ehle's theme. Survival is the constant challenge that each settler must meet. Settlement will come more gradually, as a community is formed through mishap and outburst, through scrupulous plan or devious plot or simple tragedy.

Next to arrive on the mountain is the unseemly family of Ernest Plover, who is dependent on Tinkler and utterly without spine. He brings his unkempt, useless wife and a rabble of singing, barefoot daughters, the eldest of whom is the waiflike Pearlamina, bearing the apple to be bitten or ignored by a grieving Mooney. Bold but strangely innocent, Pearlamina entices Mooney with sudden, unexpected visits. "You build that by yourself?" she says admiringly, on first seeing him by his cabin. And she adds disdainfully, "I knowed a man in Virginia that could throw a horse."

Ehle comes to his characters and their vivid language as naturally as his trees stand rooted to the earth. Of his wife's constant pregnancies, Ernest says, "I don't have to prick her; all I have to do is look at her, and she balloons out." "Ash-looking" is what Lorry does to find potatoes in her fireplace. Imy's coffin is a "bury box," and "cabin-caught" is what they all become in winter and in darkest night. This gift of tongues brings delightful realism to characters who vary greatly one from another in spite of the valley they have all chosen to settle in and defy. The tensions that slowly build between them are ominous and thrilling. "Here we are, come together, and closer will we come."

Mooney must find a wife. But will it be gentle Pearlamina, guileless and seductive, who is creating havoc in his heart?

> He met her on the path one day. She was carrying her youngest sister along the path and was barefooted and held the baby close to her breasts. She walked toward him, her manner grave and serious, but she laughed softly in greeting him, so surprising him that he stopped. When he turned, he saw that she was watching him from farther along the path, and now she took the baby's hand and waved it at him. "Hello. Say hello," she said to the child.

Or will Mooney pursue the older and quieter Lorry, earthbound and sensible, the mother of sons, whose husband may appear at any moment? When Lorry visits Mooney's cabin, she doesn't "think she ought to sit down on the bed. That would be unseemly; also it would be deceptive, for she wasn't anxious in her body yet."

Ehle's women are treated with equal shares of empathy and dispassion. Pliant or unyielding, fretful or persevering, they confront a primitive environment and succumb or thrive. The men, modest or ambitious, gentle or violent, must work toward settlement even during episodes of mortal conflict. Perched on the edge of an uncivilized world, they must decide whether to move on or stay, whether to build of this wood quickly or that wood slowly, whether to sit by a grave or carve out a garden, whether to love and in what fashion to hate. This country will know its torments, most of them human-caused. The wandering husband will appear with a loaded rifle and keen eye; the slave-owning Tinkler will do his utmost to become the mountain's king; and other settlers will rattle and upset whatever compromise is found.

Who better to describe this place than a writer born and raised among its people, a writer who knows their particular language and ingrained habits of intemperance and benevolence. Even his landscape breathes, its plants curled to protect themselves, its rocks pressing hard against feet. There are the predators, too. Snakes and bears. Wolves. Pigs are carried off, sheep and dogs and chickens are killed because they have been brought by man and have no place in the natural world. Snakes inhabit scenes so horrifying, so brimful of detail as to suspend disbelief. Wolves provide the distant chorus behind each puzzlement, and the great bear speaks for the mountain, blessing and damning as he moves among the inheritors of ground and river and trees.

Ehle still lives in these mountains. He has covered enough ground that he sees through its layers, knowing the former forests and the creatures that wandered there and the tools used to destroy what belonged and then build something to take its place. Living people abide in these stories with all their bravery and blemishes. The blemishes were formed long before they set out for the mountain but it is up there that the settlers must look for grace. They have nothing worth keeping, nothing even close to worthy except for their hunger and belief in themselves.

The Land Breakers is a Chaucerian pageant—a pageant of herds and droves and carts and a beautiful woman on horseback and a man who believes himself to be king. It takes place in an early America with nothing to its credit but a people who have created themselves out of whatever it was that made them decide to up and go. It's the something that gets into Mooney and Imy as they make their way south inch by workaday inch. And what a force of new heart they bring to rushing creeks and the apparitional bear and the encroaching neighbors with their own un-quenchable needs. These people will succeed or fail but they will lay down the structure of whatever lasts. They will be followed by their descendants in Ehle's six other chronicles of the mountain and its people. These books revolve around individual crises of faith or pride or class and each one stands entire. Appalachia has found a voice in Ehle's great achievement.

—LINDA SPALDING

THE LAND BREAKERS

*To Betty Smith
and to the memory of Rogers Terrill*

There is America, which at this day
serves for little more than to amuse you
with stories of savage men and uncouth
manners, yet shall . . . show itself equal to
the whole of that commerce which now
attracts the envy of the world.

—EDMUND BURKE to the people of England, 1775

1779

I

It was early summer when the two young people arrived in Morganton, which was little more than a long muddy street with poles stuck in the mudholes, and a few stores here and there. Also there was a place where the court sat in court season, and from the main street one could see far off in the west a blue wall rising from the hilly country, a chain of mountains, the highest in the eastern half of the continent. Mooney and Imy Wright were interested in them, for land was what they wanted, a place for a home, but they were told that nobody lived up there, that the wild animals owned it. There were trails, but no settlements. There was a settlement at Watauga on beyond the mountains, but the Indians were fighting there, making it all bloody ground. In the mountains themselves there was not a clearing, not a house, not a shed, and nobody except an occasional hunter ever entered that wild country.

Mooney and Imy had been married only two or three years, but they had known each other since childhood. They had been sent on the same boat to Philadelphia from Ulster in North Ireland, a land which had been settled by the Scots, so they were Scots, really, and were called Scotch-Irish. They had been apprenticed out at eleven years of age to a family named Martingale, which had six children of its own but which had a lot of land to tend and a mill, which took much work. Imy cooked for the family, and Mooney worked in the mill. The judge who sent them to the Martingales had decreed that "Each child shall receive eighteen months of school except that the girl need have no more than twelve, and proper food and care, and in return for work done, when the child shall have reached the age of twenty-one, he shall receive certain goods. The boy shall be given a horse, a bridle, a saddle, a gun, and three good suits of clothes. The girl shall be given a calf, a bed, an iron pot, and three suits of clothes."

So at the age of twenty-one, they got these possessions and prepared to leave home. Their leaving was disappointing to the Martingales, who looked on Mooney and Imy as their own relatives; in that community the two of them were known and liked by everybody. In spite of that, the young people took their horse, their calf and other possessions and went on toward the south, for it had been their dream for some time to have a place of their own, to make for themselves a proper farm. She, a tall, thin woman with sharp-featured face and clear blue eyes, led the calf, and he, a tall, strong man, handsome and tough of muscles and skin, led the horse.

They had sought good land they could work on their own, but it wasn't so easy to find. Many men had more than they needed, but they wouldn't sell any of it. Mooney and Imy found nothing at all that was rich and promising.

For their keep, and sometimes for a bit of pay, they cut wood fuel, plowed fields, worked crops, grubbed stumps, and Imy cooked and tended house for other women. They harvested apples in Virginia and moved on south. They had worked in a mill that winter and moved on. They worked here and there, for a bag of meal, for new shoe leather, for a pup she-dog. They made slow progress, and their dream kept getting pared down.

They helped a man on the Yadkin—a river in North Carolina—get his crops in, and he let them stay in one room of his two-room house. He told the men of that section that Mooney Wright could lift a four-hundred-pound weight, could fell a bull with a blow, could fit stones together for a fireplace or a river dam.

They had put their young cow to his bull, but the calf was born dead, for the cow was weak from the long road. They had put their dog to a hound, but they got nothing. Nothing had responded to them, and wouldn't, Mooney said, until they had their own land. Even Imy herself didn't warm life-seed into sprouting. So they had no home, no land to work, on which the roots of their lives could grow. There was talk now of fighting going on elsewhere with the English and of a new country being born, but they had no part of it, no stake at all.

"You might consider settling in that mountain land yourself," the Morganton storekeeper told Mooney and Imy. He was a man of thin face and lips and a long nose. "A man come through and give me a map of part of it." He took out a parchment and opened it, studied it with mild interest, ran a dirty forefinger along its marked lines. "He told me this little river here is fresh and fish-filled, with a valley as flat as God's palm on the north side, and then right here a tall mountain rises. The man drawed me this and said no better land is anywhere, but it's not tamed."

They asked how much it cost to buy land there, asking out of courtesy, for they didn't want land so far off. Mooney didn't think of himself as an explorer or adventurer. He was a farmer, and he could build some things with his hands, and Imy could make cloth and sew.

But they asked how much the land was anyway, as they had asked before in Virginia and other places.

"I own all this upper valley," the man said, somewhat baffled by it, as if this were something he had traded for and wasn't sure he should have taken. "I own this hundred thousand acres from the top of the ridge to the top of this'n, and I own from the start of the stream down the stream for ten miles. I traded gunpowder and shot for it to a hunter."

They listened, not particularly interested in owning any of it, but interested that a man would own so much while they, who wanted to own land to tend, had none.

"I got it fer so little I don't know how to charge. How much would you want of it?"

They didn't want any, they said.

"Could you buy it all?"

No, they said, and the thought went through Mooney like a comic theme. Could he buy it all.

"I don't want to sell a tiny piece of it, though you look so needful. Have you come far?"

They had come far, they said.

"I could do this, I could sell you a thousand acres and tell the man I finally sell the whole plot to that you're there, got a cabin on it, and he'll have to accommodate your land within his'n. Most men had rather buy where somebody's gone to open up the territory. I could sell you twelve hundred acres."

Like a comic theme still, even more comic now that the land was closer to them.

Imy asked how much he would charge them, and he scratched his head and worried over it. "Have you got a gun? You'll need one up there?"

They had one, she said.

"Do you have money for powder and shot? I'm told it's land a person will have to fight beasts for."

Imy took what money they had and laid it on the countertop.

The storekeeper looked at it discontentedly, ran a finger through it. "Uh huh," he said. "You'll need a bag of salt and some seed."

"We've got seed," Imy said. "We could use a bag of coffee."

"Uh huh. Coffee's a right smart high. Have you got any tools?"

Imy waited for Mooney to tell what they had, and he didn't mind saying, though he wanted no part of a wilderness. He preferred a settlement; he wasn't an explorer of land way off.

"An ax," he said. "And an auger. A knife."

"Uh huh," the storekeeper said. He was quiet and the storeplace was quiet and musty and smelled of the meal and smoked meat. It was a room stocked with brown and blue linen, stockings and gloves, sheets of glass for sash windows. Looking glasses were lined up along one shelf, reflecting the wall on the other side of the room, where hung sizers and saws and hatchets and chisels, bills, hoes, spades, grubbing hoes, wedges. Near them was a barrel of nails. On the counter was a box of locks for doors. At the back of the room, hanging on wall pegs, were traps of all sorts, but mostly for beaver (though they were called fox traps). There were grindlestones, whetstones, a box of paper, a bottle of ink, a number of saddles, bridles, a piece of leather into which fishhooks had been pushed; there were fans, a necklace made of pearls, a box full of beads strung on thread, three rolls of ribbon, a roll of tape, a small box of thimbles, a box of shoe buckles. Near the back door of the store a heavyset, slow-motioned man was going through a pile of deerskins. There was the odor of tobacco in the place, too, and of firewood that had been burned the previous winter, but the fire was out now in summer.

The storekeeper gazed about the room. He walked down along the counter and came back with an iron wedge. "You'll need that to split logs. You can make a maul, can't ye?"

Mooney nodded. There was a worried expression on his face, which didn't show dismay or pleasure, either; he was waiting mostly, wondering what in the world Imy was up to.

"You ought to have a gouge," the storekeeper said.

Imy took one from a chest and put it on the counter. The storekeeper ran his fingers through the pile of money once more; then he went along the counter and returned with a froe and a foot adz. Behind him on the wall were maul rings, and he took down two of those and put them on the counter. It was still a comic dream to Mooney.

The storekeeper's long fingers moved through the money again, what they had earned and saved. His lips moved as he counted what was still there. "You can get a trace chain at the blacksmith's, and a plowpoint or two," he said. His fingers moved some of the money aside, putting it by for that. "Uh huh," he said, and fell into contemplation again; then his fingers folded as his hands came together, and he said quietly, "For the little money that's left, I'll sell you six hundred forty acres of bottom land."

The answer burst out of Mooney, who for almost three years of wandering had sought a piece of land; even before Imy could speak, he heard himself say, "Yes," say it so suddenly that he stunned the storekeeper. He was surprised himself to think he had said it, and turned away and heard Imy pick up the money for the chain, and went outdoors and sought fresh air, relief coming over him, and he sank down on the porch step and began to chuckle and shake his head. Good land, the storekeeper had said, river-bottom land, he had said.

He went out into the middle of the road and looked off to the west, and there it rose, dark blue, a tall line drawn across the horizon. High up and way off, unknown, untampered with, left but lately by the savages. It lay before him: the mountain world.

———

They had a horse, a cow, two sows and a young boar when they started up there. They had that she-dog and had four chickens. The chickens Mooney put in a cage and strapped to the horse. Imy led the cow. The pigs, of course, followed.

As they climbed the trail out of Old Fort, they entered a misty spot, then walked into a cloud. They were in that cloud all day. The place was damp, and the trail was eerie; the whole place looked like a ghost world to them. That night they lay in each other's arms near the fire and comforted one another, assured one another they had done right in this, and on the second day they went on up, walking as fast as they could manage. At last they came to the top of the climb, to the gap, and they came into sunlight there. Below them was the sea of clouds that covered the lowlands. They were above the clouds, above the world of Old Fort and Morganton, and doubtless of Virginia and Pennsylvania, too. They got caught up in exaltation, thinking about that, for it was all pretty as a picture and as fine as they had ever seen; they got to laughing and joking, hurling pieces of limbs and rocks down into the lowlands. They got to hugging each other, lost in pleasure to be up here and off to themselves, and they sank to the ground together and sought one another in this new place.

They walked along a valley near the small nameless river which foamed downward toward the west—not toward the east at all, as they would expect. That night they made a fire, Mooney using his rifle flint and a speck of powder, and cooked a piece of fish. They let their pigs root for old acorns and for sprouts of green, and the cow and horse grazed contentedly. Then the night came in on them and they felt close, felt like belonging here, as if they had won out at last over the various misfortunes and handicaps of life down there, way off in the lowlands.

The stock was quiet; the dog was cozy and content. The darkness came on deeper; it seemed to be a deeper darkness than the lowlands knew. Then sharply, quiveringly, came a long cry.

Another cry came from another way. It was a creature being tortured, sounded like.

A current of cries began, a babble of screeches, screams, calls.

Mooney built up the fire. Imy gathered wood, too. They were both wide-eyed with wonder and she with fear, and maybe he with fear, for he had never heard such terror-filled noises before. Their pigs got scared and ran off, and the horse squatted down, its legs trembling; the cow came so close to the big fire that she got her head hair singed. The dog threatened and crawled about, dismayed.

The night passed slowly. They hoped for dawn and welcomed it. They gathered up their things quickly, packed the horse. Mooney found where the boar was hiding and led him in to camp. The sows followed, ashamed of their nighttime fears.

Imy was there in the road, waiting, looking off into the woods. "Where was it coming from?" she said.

"Panthers, most likely. Wolves. Lord knows what all."

"There's nothing out there a'tall."

"I wouldn't say so for certain," he said.

"I thought for a while they was going to come on in to congregate at our fire. They was none too welcome-sounding."

"No," he said, and smiled at her. "I'll say not."

They stood in the narrow road that went from Old Fort to Watauga. They could go on, or they could go back. If they went on into the mountain country, however, they might not find it easy to get out again.

What did they expect to accomplish, after all? he wondered. Could they make a settlement back in there? How in the world could they get their crops to market?

They waited. Each was waiting for the other to say, or was waiting for a sound from the woods, which was now as quiet as a Sunday morning. A chicken cackled. The dog got to jumping at a butterfly on a low limb of a bush, snapping at it. When the butterfly went on off, the dog lay down, shamefaced.

Mooney kept waiting. Imy said nothing. So he said finally, "Maybe we can be to our place by evening," and he took the horse reins and led the way along the Watauga road into the west.

The third day they crossed a wide strong river which carried off a sow. Mooney spent the morning downriver looking for her and found her at last, still trembling from her plunge in the rough cold water. So they lost much of that day.

In the evening of the fourth day, at last, at a wide river fording place, they found a hickory tree marked with three deep gashes, as the storekeeper had said they would. This was the sign of the trail that led to their land, and a trail was there, all right, twisting in and out around the trees, a trail made by animals, most likely, or long ago by Indians.

They camped there that night. Next morning they ate cornbread made with meal and river water and drank what milk they could get from the cow. They started up the trail, expecting to be home by nightfall. They reached the top of the ridge by mid-morning, but the trail stayed on the ridge, wound along the crest of it for a far ways.

From here they could see mountains strewn in all directions, and it was awesome to consider the marvels and dens and torrents of this new country, to feel the loneliness of being here, yet at the same time the right of belonging here, for he and Imy were the only people, were the possessors of it. Not even the savage's footprint was on the moss of the forest, not the sight or sound of another person was found anywhere. This was the land of the wolf and the bear, the panther, the snake, the eagle high above them, the buzzards following them—or so it had been until they arrived.

"Our place is just down that next dip," Imy said, limping now, for her shoes had come apart from the walking and her feet were sore.

But the trail stayed on the crest of the ridge, and that night they slept in a damp place, a sort of gap through which the mountain mist poured. They heard the sound of falling water, too, though where it was they didn't know. The sound of water had come to them to be the voice of this new land.

Limping, body-tired, bone-aching, belly-taut, they moved on the next day. At last, as afternoon came, the trail started downward. They moved faster, sensing that they were close. Even the horse seemed to know the trek was near over. Pride swept through them, pride in the long views of new land, in the great trunks of the tall, great trees, some of them as thick as two or three men laid head to foot. The butts rose straight upward for ninety or a hundred feet before the first limb sprang out.

They could see the valley now, down there below them, and beyond it the high mountain they had been told about. They began to run, calling out gleefully. The sow broke loose from the saddle and fell, but followed squealing. "It's right down there," Imy said, running, her broken shoes flapping against the old trail. She held out her hand and Mooney took it and they ran together, side by side, breathing heavily now. They could see below them where the river appeared out of the thickets and treetops. The cow was coming after, lowing. The dog ran ahead of them now. They ran to the valley floor and sank to the ground laughing near the upper springs, at the edge of a cold creek, buried their faces in the water, and he looked up at her then, laughing, water rolling down his cheeks and chin and from his hair onto his torn shirt, he saw her pridefully, loving the sight of her and of this place here, their own, to which they had come, which they had found after their long and fretful journeying.

They could not get enough of walking through that valley and of being with each other in a place of new discoveries. There was one woods where pigeons roosted, came in always at dusk, so thickly settling that Mooney could stand at a certain place and look up into a mass of feathery whiteness. There were vines as thick as a man's body, and Imy liked to climb them and swing out from the big tree trunks, where lizards and squirrels were, and where boomers chattered to her in noisy protestations. She and Mooney did no work. They walked the long lanes between the trees, or lay on the soft ground and made love and slept; they ate berries and bread and marveled at this land and at themselves in it.

They did no work for several days; then one morning Mooney awoke and stretched and yawned; he went off into the woods, and was coming back, flipping spring water from his hands when he saw a great footprint in the ground, one far larger than his own, a reeled print, so it was the print of an old beast. He called Imy, and she came through the woods sleepily.

She put her foot into the track. The track was ankle deep and four times as big as her own. "What in the world?" she said.

. He didn't know, either. How could anybody say what it was, or what might be in this strange world of theirs? "It come nigh to the fire last night," he said, looking cautiously about, sensing the change that had come suddenly to their place.

That very morning he cut a maple sapling and split it open to let the wood dry. He would use that for peg wood for the cabin door and table, he said. That afternoon he selected trees, one oak and the others poplar, that were not too big to be used in building. They were uphill of the cabin site, which was just above the valley floor. At evening he led the way to the oak, which was about two feet thick. She watched as the axhead swung through the air for the first time in that country and struck deeply into the wood.

The sound went out against the face of the mountain and echoed back. They heard it vibrate in the ridge across the river, where it was caught in some of the caves.

He struck with the ax again. The woods trembled. Sap began to seep out of the tree wound and glisten on the axhead. He struck again. The sound carried through that country, a new sound for the wild ears of that place. He struck again, and sap flowed freely from the wounded tree.

They cut the logs into lengths of twenty feet and barked them. Imy moved the fire sometimes, so that they would have light enough at night to skin logs by. He worked day and night and rarely grew tired until late; then his strength would drain out of him swiftly, and he liked at such times to rest limply on the ground near the fire, lay his head back against a tree root and look up at the stars, which he could see through open spaces left by the felled trees. He would talk then about his plans. He wished he had a broadax, he said. He could square the cabin logs if he had a broadax. He wished he had a sled made. He could carry rocks easier from the river bottom if he had a sled.

One day he went to work on the oak, the roof-board tree. He drove the ax into the butt log and set his iron wedge into the crack. He tapped it in, widening the crack until he could get gluts started. They were made of dogwood and were bigger than the wedge. He drove the gluts in deep with the maul he made from a branch of the tree. The maul was as thick as his thigh, and he had whittled it down to a handle at one end.

He quartered the oak tree. He cut off the sap wood, then split off boards with the froe, driving it into the wet wood with a wood mallet. He cut off four thick boards for the door.

As dusk began to settle, he began splitting off boards for the roof.

"Will you have enough for a table left?" Imy asked him. She had been around all day, watching, going after water, helping pile the slabs beside a hickory tree.

"Not enough, if we're to double-thick the door."

"We need a table, and we need bed boards."

"We'll have to make a cabin first," he said, smiling at her. "I'll make you a table later."

"If we had ropes, we could stretch a bed that a way."

"We can make a bed out of saplings or leather or something," he said. "Lord, my muscles is sore, Imy."

"You work harder than anybody ever did afore. You was like that back home, too. You never stopped for long enough to sleep."

"Oh, I sleep. I sleep enough. I like to work. Any water in the pail?"

"No. I'll fetch some."

"I'll get it."

He went down the path to the spring and knelt. The ground was cold to his knees, and the air was chilly there where the water sprang out of the ground. He let the water wash over his hands and wrists. He looked up at the bare sky; the moon was bright tonight. He would need to have his cabin walls up so that he could lay his roof shingles during a failing moon, else they would cup; he would need to move faster with his work.

He leaned far forward and drank, lapping the water into his mouth.

He wiped his mouth with his hand. "Ahhh, Lord," he said deeply. "Lord," he said.

Then he saw the beast. It was across the spring, looking down at him, a great bear, almost twice as tall as a man. Its brown fur was shaggy and torn, and had gray splotches in it. Its eyes were red and rheumy with age. Its mouth was open and its big tongue hung out, dripping wet. The bear was looking down at him as if it had no other thought except him.

Mooney spoke warily, gently to the bear. "We didn't come here to harm you. I know we cut down enough trees for a cabin, and we'll girdle trees to clear a patch for planting crops, but we don't aim to harm you or this place."

The bear's big tongue flopped to the other side of his mouth and he slobbered into the hair of his chest.

Mooney rose slowly. Imy called to him. She was coming down the path. A leap or two of the bear, he thought, and he would be stunned or crushed and Imy would be left alone, out here in the wilderness. "Don't you move, boy," he said softly. He remembered that somebody in Virginia had told him how to charm a bear by humming, and he began to hum.

A dry stick broke behind him. He felt Imy's hand come into his own, and he gripped her fingers tightly. "He stands there as friendly," he said.

But the bear was not friendly. The bear was austere, was a lonely superior figure, the master of the place, of the spring, of the mountain, of the woods, of whatever his red eyes saw. He looked at them with dumb-minded contemplations.

Mooney and Imy began to back away a step at a time up the path. "Can ye sing a song to him?" he asked her.

"I can't recollect one," she said.

"He don't know words. Sing him a song."

She began to sing softly. The great bear watched them, not moving, except that the night breeze waved the long hair of his chest and belly.

When they were far enough away to move quickly, they turned and hurried to the fire and began to stack on wood to make it flare brightly.

They worked more swiftly now. They notched the logs and rolled the base logs into place. They notched smaller logs and lifted them up to form the wall, working patiently, determined to keep the corners straight and even. The moon was still shrinking as they laid the roof boards and fastened them down with saplings, which they pegged at the ends.

Next day he cut two saplings and made runners for a sled. He cut ash saplings, for he knew they would not wear out if dragged on the ground. The horse pulled the sled to the river, where he and Imy loaded it with smooth rocks. Time after time they brought rocks back to the house for the hearth and chimney. They laid them and chinked them with small stones and sticks and handfuls of clay. The rocks cut their hands and the clay shriveled on their skins, but they stayed with the work until it was done.

They were weary then; it was as if the work had sapped them, as if their strength had been absorbed into the house. Imy was weaker than he had ever seen her. She was drained to a softness, had wilted even to the eye. He saw her stop in the woods when she didn't know he was about and stand resting, as if wondering about her weariness, and he was awakened one night by her coughing and restlessness.

I'll take her into the cabin, he thought, and see that she keeps warm this winter and out of the night air. She will be all right.

He cut eighteen holes with the auger into the door boards. He pegged the boards in a double thickness with large pegs, driving the dried wood into the damp wood, which would shrivel around it and grasp it tightly.

They lifted the door into place. It did not fit exactly, but it could be made secure. They fashioned three hickory hinges and swung the door on these, then put leather hinges on, too, and greased them with deer fat to keep them from squeaking. They gathered leaves for the bed. They carried in firewood and stacked it in one corner. He closed the door and propped it shut. She laid a fire, and he brought his flint and powder and lit it. The fire caught and began to crackle.

"Look a there," she said. He turned with her and saw the reflection of the fire on the new logs and on the moist, cold clay around the stones on the hearth, and on the unsmoked stones of the hearth on which the fire lay. They were standing in the center of a glistening womb which they had made.

Like children they began to move about, poking their hands at the solid walls, chuckling at the sturdiness of the place, at the warmth of it, at the safety they felt inside it. Then she got to coughing and had to lie down.

No, she wasn't as well as he wished, but she would come into the fields and help some as he girdled trees, as he would cut gashes around the trunk so that the tree would die. He cleared a patch of land, cutting down small trees, ripping out the bushes, and girdling the big trees. She helped, though not with any heavy work at all.

He made her a bed of saplings and new boards and set it in the cabin across from the fireplace.

As the nights grew more chilly, she coughed all the more. He kept the fire burning high all night, but the night air got into her lungs anyway and stung her. He chinked the house so tightly that very little light could be seen through the walls; even so, the night air always seemed to reach her, and one morning he noticed she was flushed and when he felt of her face, he guessed she had a fever, and nothing in his life had caused him such anguish.

He would pray if he could pray. He would work or slash or kill to spare her, but there was no way to fell the heavy-gripped thing which had a hold of her. He would slash his own body to save her, but that was no good, either. He would walk that valley over, seeking the one who challenged him for her, but even as he stood in the clearing and gazed into the woods, he saw nothing, would see nothing, he knew, out there, except whatever leaves drifted to the newly torn ground.

He wouldn't let her carry water. He let her cook some, but not as much as before. She made a little cornbread; that was about all. She seemed to like cornbread and coffee better than anything else, and he made her use all the coffee beans they had. At night he would sit by the fire and grind up coffee beans for the next day.

One morning he milked; then he drank some of the milk and took the rest to the door of the cabin and set it inside.

The cow followed him. She stuck her nose against him. He pushed her back. "Get on," he said.

He stood there waiting, listening for some word or sound, a word of pleasure, an instruction, question, sigh.

He went inside and stood near the door for a while, before he went to the bed and sat down and took her hand. He leaned far forward and looked into her face. "Imy?" he said.

"What time of day is it?" she said.

"Morning. It's early yet, and it's a cloudy day again."

"I lose track of time."

"You want some milk? I finished the milking."

"I lose track of time and get so scared of dying."

"Oh, listen here, you talk like Mrs. Martingale when she come ill, but she lived for years after that."

"We come so far to here. Way off from where we was. The mountains crowd us in." She shuddered and turned from that thought and held out her hand to him. "See how strong I am," she said.

"Yes," he said, feeling her squeeze his fingers in her hand, but she was not strong at all.

Yet she would be all right, he knew, if she could get through to spring. It was simply that she had overworked, here at a time when winter weather came, for snows were beginning to come down from the high peak; a few whiffs of snow could be felt almost any morning. Lord knows how cold it would get up here.

She had helped him too much. A woman wasn't made to do clearing. She had helped cut trees and pull brush and burn off. Maybe that was it, that in the brush smoke had been the pained spirit of this place, and it had got inside her and was expanding outward, smoldering, stifling her.

It was stealing her away from him at the start of their work and adventure. He was losing her, the body and presence and affection of her, and there was no one else in the place or in his life.

2

A few days later, a large party led by a small bearded man, his head heavy with white hair, was making its way into the valley. Out front three Negro male slaves worked to hack a wider trail for the oxen and carts, sweating in the cold morning air. They never ceased work, their axes never stopped flailing in the sunlight. One of them began to sing, a low-voiced dusky song that seemed more for the lowlands than for this high place, and another answered.

"He's fierce this morning," the first one whispered.

"This morning's no different," the other said.

They got to singing about him, Tinkler Harrison, but in words so sullied and hidden that he couldn't make them out, in meanings so secret he couldn't understand. They were singing about Virginia and the farm there, and about the long road they had traveled since in late summer, once the crops were in, he had told them he had sold the land off and was moving out from there. He never said why, or to where they were going.

Harrison heard them singing but didn't pay much attention. He was not a man of music, or a man who cared about diversion. He watched their axes and knives flash in the mountainside sunlight; he watched the trail as it was being widened, and he paced about in an unsettled way, made discontent by every delay, here on the day of his arrival at the place he had sought out, had driven for over thirty days to reach.

Off in Virginia he had had a plantation, not as good as the best in that country, but one rich enough. It was not the best, however, and he could not command the sort of respect he wanted in a place where other men had a right to as much respect as he, so he had made plans to leave there even before he knew in any clear thought that he would leave.

His plans had started when his two oldest sons had left home, one in flight of a night, one more leisurely. This second boy had married and had brought his wife home to stay, and all went as well as needed to, the old man thought, until one day Avery, the son, came to him and asked for a piece of land of his own. "No," Harrison told him. "I don't want to break up my plantation; it's not as large as the Wilson place now, there down the road." Avery went away to consider that, and a second day he came to him and said he wanted stock so that he could start his own fortune. "No," Harrison told him. "I need the best stock for my own use, and I wouldn't want to give you poor stock to start with." Avery went away and thought about that, and once more he came to his father and asked this time for a wagon, a team of horses, an ax, a plow and a kettle so that he could go away. "No," the father said. "I want you here, you and Grover, for I have lost one son to the West, and God knows where he is now."

The next morning, while the old man stood at the front window of the second floor of this big white house, he saw a sight which stirred him almost to tears. He saw Avery come out of the house, a pack on his shoulders in which no doubt he had rolled up his clothes, and behind him came his wife, she who could not put up with home life any longer; her oldest child toddled along behind her and she carried in her arms the babe she had recently borne. That small troupe of a family walked down the long drive to the road, and not until they were near the end of it did the old man give way to his grief. He threw open the window and shouted to them, shrill in his haste and confusion, called harshly to them: "Go, God damn you, go, God, if you can't stay under me."

That was a stark, clean moment when clearly he saw that in order to save what was left of his family and authority he must get away to a more isolated place. Another and earlier moment, one not so plain, had come when the first son, the oldest, whose name was Joseph, had left, had put on the best saddle on the best horse early of a Sunday morning, had packed up the best clothes he had and a pair of boots he stole from his brother, had taken from his father's room all the money which was hidden there, over four hundred dollars, and had ridden out from home, riding in a dust trail that the father saw and wondered about at the time. "Oh, he has only gone to town to find a girl for tonight," he assured his wife, but when the boy did not return by dinner of the following day, he knew he had fled. He offered a reward for the capture of the horse and the imprisonment of the thief, but by then the boy was far way.

So two of the three sons had left home; only Grover remained, and he was not as fanciful and strong of spirit as the other two. He was handsome; he had a puffy face which seemed to have been molded out of soft clay; it was not an expressive face, except in fear or other negative emotions, which it could display well. His mother, even there at the last days, when she lay sick month after month, kept him near her bedside and had him read to her out of the Bible, mostly from the psalms, which irritated the old man, for he had precious little use for sentiment. This third son he had with him at home, but he was no heir at all; he was not fitted to control, to instruct, to rule with toughness—and it had to be done that way or a plantation would falter within a season. Once the mother at last gave way to the illness and was packed in the Virginia ground, his family was himself, this weak son Grover, and the only daughter, Lorry, who lived nearby.

It had been nine years ago almost to the day that Lorry married Lacey Pollard, a fiery-mannered boy, a courting fool, who had won her heart away, doubtless with slippery words and roving hands. She had been a steady girl, dutiful, the closest one of the children to him. He had never expected her to leave him so impetuously, but first thing he knew, when she was no more than nineteen, still a girl in her father's view, she and Lacey Pollard had gone to take up housekeeping there on the farm Lacey had inherited from his father—a good plantation at that time. He was a man of music and song, with a flashing smile for a pretty woman's face, but no sense for business. He gave Lorry two sons; then, when the boys were scarcely out of swaddling clothes, he went away, leaving the remnants of the old plantation. Some of the land he had lost in trading, some he had lost in gambling, some in folly. "I'm going on to Kentucky to see if I can find a new place there," he told the old man, and he asked for a loan of money to see him through. "Oh, it takes no money at all to ride to Kentucky," the old man said; "there are no toll roads on that way." Lacey Pollard mentioned food he needed. "You can hunt for your food," Harrison said. He was not about to help him, not until Lacey offered to sell what was left of his land, all except the house in which Lorry lived and the yard around it, yes, and the flock of sheep and chickens and two cows, which she was to keep. The old man accepted the land, paying money for it, and watched him leave his daughter.

In this way, she came back under his care to tend.

When four years later he decided to leave that part of the country and seek a place where he could have the reins of all that belonged to him, where he could have certain say in matters of the family and the settlement, she refused to accompany him. He wanted to sell the land he had in Virginia and buy a piece of land many times as large on the frontier, and sell off parts of it as he chose, to settlers he approved of. He could by this means, he was confident, take a river valley off somewhere and build on it a pleasant, well-ordered place that would rival any in the country; he could establish a community of busy, good people and strong families. When he told Grover they were moving, Grover packed up his things. When he told the slaves they were moving, the slaves made ready. When he told Lorry to get her two boys and herself packed up and prepared, she refused. She would not go, she said.

"Why, how will you live here then?" he asked her. "Do you think you can make a living on the two acres of land Lacey Pollard left you?"

"He'll be back in time," she said.

"I'll build you a separate cabin and give you two acres of land at this place we're going," he promised. "I want to go on south this year, to the south and west of here, while I'm able."

"Lacey will most likely be back soon, Papa," she said.

"You burn a sign in the tree outside, or on the door, to tell him where you are going."

Once more she said no. She would stay in Virginia, she said.

He went on home, packed his possessions, and began to make demands far and wide for full payment of all debts owed him. He sold off his land and houses and stock and garnered in to himself his wealth. He made ready to leave, and to leave her, but on the night before he was to go, she came down the drive from the road and came to the porch where he was out sitting, enjoying the breezes, and she said something to him about having heard that he had taken a new wife. "Yes," he said, "I need a woman with me, so I have taken one."

"I hear it's Belle, your own sister's daughter."

"Yes," he said. "I trust my own blood better than another's."

"Belle's only seventeen, Papa, and you're in your late fifties."

"That proves my merit," he said curtly, annoyed that his daughter would bring up private matters. He felt awkward himself climbing into bed with the girl, for she was youthful and a happy person by nature, and always had been a girl of light songs. The first night he had slept with her, she had been reluctant, but he had on the next day given her a room of her own, had given her a red quilt, had given her the clothes of his dead wife, from which Belle could make sashes and skirts and blouses as she chose. He had given her a necklace his wife had worn, a simple thing which the girl liked, and now of a night she was willing to do as he said. But none of this was for his own daughter to ask about.

"She's very pretty," Lorry mentioned wistfully, as if Lorry herself, who was not thirty yet, thought back on her own youthful days with regret and wonder. Then she said she would go with them to the new place, and he wondered if Belle had asked her to go, or if Belle's mother had, or if Lorry was simply going because she knew she could not stay behind and make her own way, for there was no way for her to marry since she was married to Lacey Pollard. Anyway, whatever her reason, he was glad to have her and he struck with her that night a fair price for her passage.

He noticed that the three blacks had got the trail widened for a considerable way. "Drive the carts on down," he called, and the Negro man at once came back up the road to get the oxen, but the oxen moved, even as the old man spoke, and started down the rocky road, the carts creaking and threatening to break apart, here after the long, rough drive.

"Down there's the valley," the old man said, calling back to where Lorry and the two Negro women walked. "Keep the breed stock close," he called to the two Negro boys, who at once began to talk to the heifers and the great hobbled bull, and to the flock of sheep. In one cart rode the noisy stock of pigs, and in another rode the chickens and geese. In a third was a store of sash glass, crocks and other household supplies.

"Keep the horses tame," the old man called back to the boys, and one of them darted to where the horses were shying.

A cart wheel sank into a wet spot of earth and the old man began to curse. He darted forward, calling for the Negroes, alerting everyone to the matter; always he had a way of alerting everybody to whatever problem occupied him. One of the Negro men got a hold on the corner of the cart and lifted it, and the oxen pulled it free from the pit. "Watch more careful," Harrison said, "or we'll lose another wheel, or lose an axle. I don't want delays, for there it lies down there."

Downward they went into the misty place, in the grayness, where the biggest of the trees were, the old man's eyes sharp and his ears listening, seeking challenges to his final, complete authority. They crossed the first creek, then crossed another. At the third creek, the cart on which the sash glass rode got mired down, and Harrison said to leave it where it was and come back later, that they must move on. He ordered one of the Negro boys to stay with it, and the boy, trembling at being left alone in that wilderness, climbed onto the cart and looked after the others longingly.

"Ay, God, we come at last," the old man said. His eyes flashed and his teeth were white and he shook the hair of his head and his beard anxiously, yes, and even in pleasure, for he felt deep pleasure sweep through him. He was home; for the first time in his life, he was home, to a place that was his own completely.

"Ain't that a dog?" a Negro man called to him.

The words drifted in to Harrison's thoughts and brought him up short. A dog sound meant a homestead of some sort, meant human beings on hand. He stood stock still, listening; then he heard the sound of something else, of a thumping, a regular thumping noise. "Hush them up," he said suddenly. A Negro boy struck the geese cart, and the geese, which had been noisy, huddled down and were quiet, and the carts, groaning, stopped.

"Come here, Grover," Harrison said.

Grover came down along the trail, laurel branches slapping at his face, the dew-wetness of the place clinging to his wool clothes and to his body like a chill. Lorry followed him. The child-wife, Belle, stuck her head around a cart and watched, but she didn't follow; she was fearful of anything unknown, for she had discovered that what was known about and explained to her could be fearful enough. She was pretty, with blue eyes which were the color of her bonnet, and a doll-like, round face. She had on a high, frill collar, for Tinkler Harrison liked her to wear frills, he had told her.

"What do you hear, Lorry?" Harrison asked his daughter.

She listened for a moment. The sound came at her from the mountains on all sides. "It's an animal beating apart a tree trunk," she said. She spoke with a soft voice, which had many minor tones in it; she sounded almost like a sad melody. She pushed her brown hair back from her eyes, which were brown, too. She was composed and gentle, seemed like.

Grover said, "I've known a bear to beat apart a tree."

"In the winter?" Tinker Harrison asked flatly, his eyes flashing.

Grover flushed. "No, sir," he said.

"They beat a trunk in breeding time maybe, but that's in spring. And bears is in a hole in the ground this time of year."

Lorry said, "It's a person digging."

Tinkler Harrison grunted. "You say so, do ye?" He gazed off critically, his mouth moistening a piece of tobacco. He concentrated intently now on the sounds, as he always concentrated on whatever it was he did. "It's a piece of metal striking clay," he said finally. He looked at Grover, as if demanding that he deny it if he wanted to. The young man said nothing.

Harrison wiped his hands on his wool pants, then wiped them on the leather shirt he wore. "Where's it coming from, Grover?"

Grover glanced about uneasily, seeking a hint from Lorry. "The east," he said.

"No," Tinker Harrison said flatly. "It's from the west. How far away is it?"

Grover wiped perspiration from his face. "I don't know, Papa."

"You have to learn this country, don't you know it? How far?"

Grover stared at the ground. "I'd say it's nigh," he said.

"Would you?" the old man said. "I'd say it's far." He leaned back on his heels and squinted into the woods. "Not but one reason for a person to be digging this time of year, is there, Grover?"

Grover swallowed. "No, sir."

"What is the reason?"

Grover looked helplessly at Lorry. "It's that man that's maybe here, the one the storekeeper said was up here some'ers; it's him and his wife, most likely."

"Doing what?"

"Digging."

"What?"

"In the ground."

"Of course it's in the ground." He sucked at a tooth and pressed his lips together tightly. "Well, come on." He went down the trail, the Negroes getting out of his way swiftly. He found a break in the laurel and went through it, and Grover followed.

Lorry turned at once and went along the line of carts to one of the larger of them, which she climbed into. Her two sons were huddled inside.

They were only twelve and thirteen years old, and neither of them knew the meaning of this journey, how it was that in the coldest days of January they found themselves riding down rocky paths, fording creeks and rivers, climbing high into mountains along treacherous ledges, under the ominous, black and warted, wrinkled, vine-cloaked trees, rising from sleep in darkness, striking the trail at dawn, driving on under the whip and rule of their grandfather until darkness caught hold once more, this every day for two long weeks. "Is he gone?" the older boy, Fate, asked.

"Yes," she said. "You can climb down now."

The younger boy, whose name was Verlin, climbed down and offered to help her, but she ignored his offer and climbed down herself, then helped Fate down, though he didn't need help. Though older than Verlin, he was not as big-bodied. He was a moody boy, dark of hair and eyes, the only dark member of that family. His full name was Lafayette, which his father had pronounced La-fate, and now he was called Fate. He was unusually handsome, as if he had been molded and fashioned by a French artist.

"You boys stay close by, you hear me?" she said. "Go talk with Belle."

She put on a bonnet and a leather jacket. Quickly she moved down the trail to the same laurel opening her father and Grover had used, and went into the woods, moving slowly.

The dampness of the soft moss got into her shoes, which squished and complained. The leather soles might part from the tops, she thought; this place will need new shoes, new clothes. The bushes snagged at the skirt of her soft, wool dress.

She saw her father down the path and stopped, a wave of resentment going through her as it ordinarily did whenever she saw the old man. He and Grover were kneeling, each on his left knee, near a small gum tree. They were looking at something not far away. Near them, laurel leaves, which had curled to protect themselves from the coldness, tilted in the wind.

She moved quietly toward them. Her father waved her back irritably, but she went on and knelt beside Grover. She held aside a laurel limb and peeked out, and so she saw the clearing for the first time. Toward the far side was a cabin built of barked logs, its roof boards yellow yet, with a single door and no window, with high walls so that perhaps there was a low-ceiling loft above the main room. A stone chimney had been built to the roof peak. There was very little smoke coming from it and nobody was about. But there was the noise, close on her now, of metal on clay and rock, striking.

"You see him?" her father whispered. "There," he said, pointing up the hill toward the top of the clearing. "A big one."

She saw the man then. He stood waist deep in the earth, half buried in the mountainside. The sun, which was beyond the ridge beyond the river, glistened on his massive shoulders and arms as he lifted the ax each time.

He stopped now and studied the woods. His gaze shifted to the cabin; he studied it as if measuring the distance to it, comparing that with the distance to the spot in the woods which bothered him, which was where Lorry hid. She realized he must feel this country and sense its dangers, for he apprehended not only its sounds but its silences.

The man looked once more at the cabin. A dog came to the door and, whimpering, lay down in the sun there. The man shrugged; he lifted his arms and a rifle gun was in his hands. Lorry had not seen the gun before, nor did she know how he had changed the ax for the gun without her knowing. He laid the gun down at the upper side of the hole, took up the ax and began to cut away the earth from around the rock. Then he worked with his hands and later with the pole. All the while she watched him, as her father and brother did. She watched when he gripped the rock from the bottom and hoisted it, a rock as large as a big man's chest, forced it upward to the edge of the hole, then pushed it solidly. The rock bounded down the hill, gathering speed, leaped over a fallen log, and smashed into a tree trunk.

Tinker Harrison sat back on his heels and shook his head in wonder. "He's a strong 'un, ain't he?" He grunted. "Did ye see that?"

Lorry nodded.

"That man you married couldn't lift his shoes off the floor, compared to that'un."

The man climbed out of the hole. He rolled his shoulders, as if feeling the warmth in them, and picked up the gun, shook loose the dirt off of it.

Tinker Harrison rose slowly from his crouch. "I'll speak to him," he said. He entered the clearing, which was as definitely marked off from the forest as if it had been a room, and raised his arm in greeting. "How air ye?" he called.

The man froze in place, stood stock still, looking down at him, the rifle held in his hands.

"I'm a friend. I just come up," Harrison said. "Air ye troubled?"

There was a long pause. "Aye."

"I thought ye might be. You're burying something, ain't ye?"

"Aye."

"I thought so. Not a critter, is it?"

"No."

"I thought not, for I saw nobody at the cabin, so I guessed it was something more than a critter. It's a human, ain't it?"

"Aye."

"I thought so. When I saw nobody come out of the cabin I thought, Well, he's lost his woman right here at the start. It's too bad, I'll say that." He turned his head to the woods. "Grover, go get the men and help him dig a grave."

That evening they were still there, making a coffin. The chatter of their talking got on Mooney's nerves. There was no quiet time for his mind to rest and consider its own thoughts; there was a continual pestering of ideas from other people, and sympathy. Not since the summer had he heard a voice except his own and Imy's, and the two of them were not given to talking much. Even at night when they lay down, they had not talked on and on about their plans, and of a morning when she got up, she rarely said a word, except, "It's morning, might nigh," or something like that to tell him it was coming day. How she knew he didn't know, but always as she got the fire blazing well, dawn began to appear upriver, as if she were the one who had awakened it. But it was not her doing, he knew. The dawn was constant; it was an old thing and come on its own. Not even the will and whispers of the mountain could change it. The truth was not that Imy called it but that she had lived so close to the order of life that she heard it called.

Imy was the one who had shaped and cleared the rocks down here near the spring. She had brushed them clean for sitting. Now he sat on one of them while the busy people up in the clearing made her a grave and a bury box.

The old Negro woman had milked the cow. Mooney would have

milked it himself, but the woman had shooed him off. He would rather do Imy's chores than for a stranger to do them, but these other people had taken over; they had taken the work and all he had left was the worrying. They were working and answering to the old man, who was everywhere, his moist mouth chewing, his tongue spitting out words, orders, questions which he never needed answers to, for he never asked what he didn't already know.

They didn't often come down here, though, not to the spring. The young Negro woman came down once, carrying Imy's pail, which Mooney and Imy had made of maple and bound together with elm bark. The Negro stood at the spring and looked at him with deep feeling, and moaned so sorrowfully he felt uneasy. He had never known Negroes before, and he was surprised this one knew sorrow and sympathy so comfortingly. When she left she walked so swiftly that water sloshed out of the bucket, where ice floated on top.

Mooney heard the old man approaching and saw the white swish of his beard. The old man stopped near the spring and gazed thoughtfully at him, then took up the gourd and filled it and drank deeply. "I suspect we're bound to be neighbors, if you decide to stay on."

"Are they done?" Mooney asked.

"They're pegging up," Harrison answered.

Mooney could hear the mallet on the maple pegs, and after a while the sound stopped.

The old man stirred. "Ahhhh, my," he said, "I buried a woman, too. A man gets to living in a woman's life and it's a sorrow to bury one. It's an emptiness, ain't it? It's not the woman that's noticed; it's the emptiness when the woman ain't there, like as if a man needed his tongue and found it was cut out of his mouth."

Mooney said nothing, though Harrison was waiting for him to comment.

"Ain't that so?"

Mooney said nothing. He walked up past him, entered the clearing and saw the two Negro men and the old man's wife waiting near the cabin door, a coffin near them. One of the Negro men held the lid of the coffin. The big Negro held the mallet and pegs.

Mooney stopped at the cabin door and listened, anxious for the sound of her again, for she always knew what was proper to say and do. What was proper to do now? Would she tell him how to mourn for her?

He went inside. The older Negro woman was standing near the back wall. Lorry was near the fireside, fire sweat on her face. She was calm and watchful, and there was reasonableness and competence about her. She didn't seem to feel sorrow for Imy's death, but she understood his sorrow, that was what she seemed to say to him.

"You want me to carry her for you?" she said.

Imy's body was on the bed; her arms were folded and her face was washed. She had on the same faded brown dress she had worn into this valley. She was a long woman, too long for the bury box, he thought; they should have measured her, for she was longer than most women.

He went closer to her, stood above her, so close he could have heard her breathing if she had had breath left. "Imy," he said, knowing she heard him, knowing she was dead but still could hear him. "It's all over," he said, "and it's lonely here now."

He bent over her. He lifted her easily in his arms and turned with her, but pity welled up in him so thickly that he had to stop, and he cursed for a moment and the older Negro began to moan, but Lorry watched him gently, as if she knew. He stood there in the middle of the cabin he and Imy had made and held her. He started for the door, but his eyes misted over. Lorry took his arm and guided him. Almost at once, it seemed to him, he was in the bright light outside.

He went past where the men were standing and went up the hill to where the bury hole was. Behind him he heard the men dragging the oak casket. The open grave was a cruel mouth, he thought, with teeth of stone and water for spittle, with red clay for gums; the mountain had chilled her and killed her, and now through this mouth it would take her in.

The men left the casket beside the hole. Harrison came up, holding Belle by the arm, and he told the Negro men to drop the casket into the hole. They did as he ordered, then stood back. One of them had the wooden mallet still in his hand. "Put her in it," the old man said.

Mooney, with Imy's body in his arms, sat down at the edge of the hole. He put one leg over the edge of the hole and sought the casket with his foot. He stepped down into the casket; slowly he crouched there, the body in his arms. He and the body were in the casket.

He laid her down, her head on his foot, and he bent her legs so that she would fit in the box. He was done, but he stayed with her, trying not to break to the sorrow he felt.

The old man said, "I'll have a woman strip her, if you want the dress."

"No," he said. He stayed bent over, not wanting to leave her, but knowing Imy would not want him to be so low, would tell him, if she could, to climb out of the hole and stand straight above it, for there was nothing to be done.

He pulled himself from the hole and sat on the edge of it. He crawled away from the hole and stood and turned his back to it as the big Negro man began to peg the box. Then there was the sound of dirt thudding down on the box, and the old Negro woman began to pray.

There would be no more touching her, he knew, no more seeing her by the fire, no more holding her of a night or feeling the softness, then the tightening of her body; they would not plant together the torn rows of their own making. The dirt was closing over her now; the mountain had received them with noisy challenges and now had taken her. The mountain wanted the old way still, and he who changes what is ordered and old and set is a man who grasps the lion's jaw.

He looked down at the hole as the men finished filling it, and he heard the sound of ice breaking on a tree far above them, then the crumbling, rumbling noise of ice sliding from a rock cliff, coming down on tree limbs below it.

The mountain is talking, he thought. It has her in its jaw and it's talking to me now. It sees me here yet, and sees these others who have come here. It hovers over us and tells us that this is only the beginning for those who stay in this valley.

1780

3

Tinkler Harrison found the plot of land he wanted for his house and fields, one near the river, and he and his men undertook day-long toil, working into the night and often through the night. The family slept in and under the carts, but Harrison rarely slept at all. At all hours he sent out orders to the slaves and to the family, except for Belle, who was a silent witness, whose opinion was never asked, whose help was never sought. She was a stranger in her own household, an outsider in her own home who might be told to scat out of the way, even by a slave. She was, by fact of being Harrison's wife, removed from the category of the child, but she had not been admitted to any other, except when for a short while each night Tinkler Harrison would come to her, would crawl into the cart. She would awaken to feel him beside her, his arms around her and his hands on her, impatiently turning and touching her, and then his beard might tickle her face and she would feel the hard appendage of him as he pushed it into place, and she would squirm and move as he had taught her, and groan, for he had taught her to do that, and she would hear with embarrassment the cart creak as it responded to his movements and to hers, and she would think that everybody must hear it, that the sound must go out to where the men were, and where Grover and Lorry were, and to the walls of mountains.

He seemed to like a good deal of groaning, and she supplied that mechanically and would wrap her arms and legs around him as he liked, and feel finally the life flow come from him. At once the cart would stop creaking, and directly he would breathe and grunt his satisfaction, would roll off of her, would drop to the ground, and immediately would begin roaring out his orders to the men and dumping armloads of firewood onto the campfire and feeding the fires which burned night and day at the bases of the huge tree trunks, deadening them.

Her life was lived for these few moments each night, not that she looked forward to them with pleasure but that they were the moments when she fulfilled the purpose her life had come to serve. Beyond this, nothing was asked of her or expected of her or accepted of her. Only the few minutes there in the wiggling, wriggling embrace of Tinkler Harrison—for that she was fed and clothed and given rain-free quarters. In the daytime she would stay near the camp or go into the new-forming cabin. Everywhere she was ignored, except that sometimes Lorry would stop near where she was and would speak to her and might even put her hand on her arm and squeeze her arm, and might even suggest that she sing a song, as in the old days in Virginia.

Lorry felt sorry for the girl in those scanty times when she was not pondering her own predicament. Under the rule and whims of her father, she and her boys were oppressed, and she longed to get into the cabin he had promised to build for her, one off apart from his own place. "There's no time yet," he told her repeatedly, and would not have the matter discussed, but each day she brought it up again and began wearing him down, working her way with him, which she had learned as a girl she could do only with patience and persistence.

———

The snakes and bears were in their holes and caves asleep by now, and only the panthers and wolves among the wild things came near the camp, or near Mooney Wright's lonely cabin. They came with gnawing hunger and cries that frightened the dog under the bed and sent his own blood chilling.

In late January a blizzard from the northwest struck the mountain country, and Mooney brought the cow and one of the horses into the cabin for the night to keep them warm. They stood, thankful statues, huddled together like mates, their heads lowered, looking suspiciously from time to time at the ever-flickering orange fire before which their master squatted and murmured to himself, commenting on the rumble of the wind and the loud shattering sounds, like explosions, of frozen trees bursting on the mountain. The cabin trembled; the wind buffeted it and some of the chinking came out. The snow beat in about them.

For two days he house-fed the animals and milked the cow and drank the milk. He cut off pieces of cured pork and roasted them over the fire. He mixed corn meal, water and a pinch of salt and baked the dough on a rock where it could simmer nicely and finally brown. He would unpeel it from the rock and break it so that the steam would rise from it, and he would eat it with warm milk.

All the while his mind turned on the thoughts of what he was to do, and of the past, coming like mountain mist in morning, leading to this place, to this room, where he huddled with animals in winter. And he would murmur to himself, talking to himself, for he was lonely. Half of me is in the ground, he thought.

When the storm lifted, he went down to the river, which was frozen over, was a gray sheet of ice. He took long walks along the riverbank and saw where the cold water from mountain springs washed down, making indentations in the ice before losing itself underneath. High above, the mountains were white; the world was white and without meaning to him.

Two of the chickens died. The cold and the wolves had preyed on them. The comb of another of them turned black and fell off. The feet of one hen froze and her toes fell off. The snow fell, great flakes of snow half as large as his hand. How soft they are, he thought, and how bitter they sting.

He hunted fresh game in the woods and shot a deer. The boomers chattered at him. Oh, so you want to talk, do you? he said to them. They were the only ones—they and the dog—who spoke to him of late. He saw gray rabbits with big eyes, looking at him wonderingly as they munched on ivy leaves.

He breathed the coldness and the tingling freshness of the pine sap. The air was clean and alive with frozen soundlessness and cleanliness, and it pained the chest to breathe the air for long. He crept back to his fireplace and fed on deer meat and waited for a thought, some idea of what he was to do.

One day a round-faced, lean-bodied hunter came by, leading two pack horses. He was going to Salem, he said. The storm had caught him, but he had holed up for three days and had lasted it out. Mooney, listening to him talk, had for him the same revulsion he had for most of this man's breed. He was animal-like; he could talk now about himself and other people only in animal terms; he had slaughtered a thousand animals or more; his deerskin coat was stained yet with the blood of last season; he considered the functions of the body only in animal terms, and the accomplishments of his days in terms of stalking and trailing and slaughtering and skinning and devouring and stacking of green hides; he could walk the high trail of the mountains and not be much impressed by any cloud or tree or sight, for he was studying the tracks and spore of animals; he knew the marks on the trails but did not much care where the trail started or where it ended, except in late winter when he started home, his horses loaded down with two hundred pounds of hide apiece—deer hide mostly, but beaver, too; about him was the odor of sweat and of animal blood and fat.

He talked of the fog, which he hated, for it made the animals appear bigger than they were, and it hid them too well, and hid even the traps. "It's a deception," he said. "It creeps up from the valley. Anything which creeps up at you is a deception, for what's clean comes from the top, don't you say?"

"Aye," Mooney said at once, wanting him to continue such a show of mind.

"In a man, too, his noblest parts are at the top." He considered that, gazing into the fire. "But I more enjoy the parts that are below," he said finally.

He left one morning early, and Mooney went back into the cabin, shut the door and hovered to himself in his despair.

In February the winged elm grew hazy-brown with bloom, and the ghostlike shade took over the borders of the clearing. In March one morning he awoke to hear a thousand birds, all sorts of birds, a noisy, shrill commotion, and he went outdoors, pushing his long brown hair back from his bearded face, and saw great flocks of robins and bluebirds.

Alders came to budding life and shook out their tassels; small, dark-purple violets appeared. The tops of the maple trees put out red blooms, shading the budded spicebush near his spring. Azure butterflies darted about. The tiger beetles haunted the trails. Lizards moved in frightened dashes here and there. The brown thrasher, the rusty blackbird, the cowbird, the chipping sparrow took their places in a profusion of life awakening, and he would come into the clearing and stare about and listen to the noises, not echoing noises, not fearful either at this season, but vibrant, lively sounds, which were out of sorts with his own distraught temper.

The bears began to shake off the heavy sleep which had occupied them since late December, and emerged nervous and anxious. He watched one of them come from a cave up back of the house and shake himself, peer about critically at the white-lighted world, look up at the trees, which as yet had only flowers and half-grown leaves, which let the sun through. Blinking, shielding his eyes with a paw, growling and woofing at the treacherous light, he waddled into a thick rhododendron slick where the ground was shaded and darker and where he could awaken with less bright-pain.

The sweep of spring crept up the mountain. It moved from the valley's forest of elm, sweet gum, ironwood and sycamore to forests of yellow birch, mountain ash, spruce and fir. Even while snow covered the mountain's top and lay along the ridges that jutted out from its sides high up, trout lilies were gathering strength into their blooms down next to the river. A few days later, near the top of the clearing, he saw trout lilies bloom, and a fortnight later he saw them high on the mountainside and knelt beside them, cupped one in his hand as Imy would have done, and blew gently into the petals.

The mountain country came into life again, slowly, then with a swish of color and action that caught a spark in him, too. He awoke each morning to the first light with a fresh expectancy and lay smelling the newness of the air. A sugar air, he thought; do you smell it, Imy? Sometimes he thought of her as being in the cabin, or as being with him when he milked, or with him as he built the pen to protect the sow and her new litter, and it was to Imy that he talked, as well as to the stock, when he knelt near the hearth and watched eight little biddies run about in early exploration, their ruffled-feathered mama cackling proudly, as if she had brought into the world a mighty brood.

He would take long walks. He would throw a rock at a cuckoo and mock it with his deep voice and name it silly bird, for he knew not one bird name from another. He stalked along the paths thinking that nobody except Tinkler Harrison owned as many birds as he, or animals either, or fish most likely. Creatures slithered away from him as he came by. Nobody owns as many lizards and snakes either, he thought, or spiders or spider webs, and he would chuckle to himself in this mad, busy world. Striding on, he might walk upriver to the breeding places of the creeks, or would stop at the spot where the old man had started his clearing, where the

Negro men worked of a daylight, chopping and burning their way toward a spring planting.

Or he would walk up back of his own small clearing onto the side of the mountain, to where the rock ledges started, and there he would watch the duck hawks rise from their nests and flash silver their wings, and he would often come across a pheasant on the path, its tail feathers spread, neck feathers ruffled, body puffed, strutting up and down before another bird, no doubt his lady, shaking his head now, dipping it almost to the ground.

Or he would walk the boundaries of his holding, which Harrison's men had marked with gashes on the boundary trees. Or he would walk the clearing he and Imy had made, and he would feel softness come back to the earth, a freshness come to it as if it wanted seed, was ready to be done finally with autumn's ripeness and winter's death.

But even in the wealth of spring, he remembered the harshness of this country. It is a cunning place, he thought, a place of dangers, after all.

Rarely in spring would a family move from an established location to a new, untamed one, for they would not have time enough to girdle trees and plant crops for the year. They could ordinarily be counted on to arrive in fall or winter, after they had made their harvest. The family of Ernest Plover, however, had a way of doing most of what it did somewhat differently, and Ernest never quite achieved any schedule, either one which he set for himself or one which others set for him.

He arrived in the valley at planting time, and moved unannounced onto that portion of the land which lay just to the north of Tinkler Harrison's cleared fields and to the east of Mooney's, which lay on the first gentle slope before the mountain increased itself sharply. He settled, then, on poor land to start with, not on flat valley land, and he declared that he would make his fortune there.

His right to be there was that he was Belle Harrison's father.

He arrived in mid-morning of a clear, sunny day, walking at the front of a procession which included a long string of tow-headed children, all of them girls. Immediately behind him waddled a red ox, a weary, heavy-breathing creature even at the start of the day; the ox seemed to be no more securely jointed than the cart it pulled, on which were bundled and stacked the worn-out possessions of this bedraggled band. The cart, warped and swollen from the river crossings, had been made out of twisted wood to start with, out of puncheons and the like, and one wheel had been lost along the way somewhere. A sapling pole had been substituted, and on the pole the cart noisily scraped along.

Behind the cart came a single brood sow, walking slowly, heavily, disdainful of her companions. Behind her came a few small pigs. A dog with dripping tongue and one lame foot was nearby. He stopped often to scratch and to look about disinterestedly at the countryside.

Inez Plover, the sister of Tinkler Harrison, was much larger than her husband. She was a heavy-bodied, big-boned woman, who wore a raggedy linsey-cloth dress which had been dyed blue originally and which now was faded gray from many washings and wearings, and which had holes in it near the hem where she had snagged it on bushes or where she had removed a piece of sound cloth in order to patch a hole that could not with any sense of privacy be left unrepaired. She led by a piece of vine a cow, humble and shriveled, bony of body and inordinately tame and kind, to which had been strapped two boxes, one full of chickens and the other full of geese.

There was in this procession not the slightest sign of human sadness, not, anyway, on Ernest Plover's face. Ernest bounced as he walked and was alert to the ways of birds and beasts and stock, his eyes darting from one study to another with ever-changing interest. He would turn now and then to glance at his long string of daughters, and would comment to them about something he had seen. The girls, too, were alert. All of them were light of coloring and were startlingly, freshly pretty, with sharp, neat features and slender arms, long legs and shiny skin. Their blue eyes seemed always pleased and their mouths were ready to smile and laugh, and there was a playful, devilish look in the face of the largest one, who was sixteen and was named Pearlamina.

To Ernest Plover the arrival was auspicious. Any new start was a golden opportunity. Prior experience had shown that this attitude was deceptive, for he had made many new starts and never achieved fortune of any sort, but he persisted in his faith, until now, poverty-struck, lean and resourceless, he was forced to turn to his wealthy brother-in-law, who was also his son-in-law, for assistance. His associations with Tinkler Harrison in Virginia had been woeful. His farm had been near the Harrison plantation and he had got early in his debt for land and stock and goods and money. He had been unable to pay anything, so he had come near losing the little he had left and would have lost it had not the old man married Belle, the oldest of the burgeoning troupe of daughters. Earlier, the old man had kept Ernest in his bond by many subtle ways. He had, for example, permitted Ernest to borrow bacon in summer, when Ernest invariably exhausted his supply, to borrow salt in winter, when Ernest found he had too little money to purchase it at the store, to borrow tobacco whenever Ernest found his pouch empty, which was often. In bits and little ways the old man had kept Ernest in his debt.

When Harrison left Virginia, Ernest soon found the ways of the independent man were endlessly complicated and full of snares. He encountered the need for planning, which he had no talent for, and before long he lost what was left of his land and house and shed and stock—or all of his stock that anybody else wanted. The loss was his fault, he reasoned, not because he had been unable to make proper plans and allowances, but because his star was unlucky. Fate had for him no helping hand, no smile at all, as it had for other men.

Even so, he received life as a pleasing adventure, deeply saddening but marvelously worthwhile, a miracle spread upon the earth, a mystery which he never sought to solve, for the glory was in its complexities. To him life shimmered brightly as it evolved and slithered out of the future and went on off.

Another explanation for his failure, he announced, was that his wife had borne him nine children, every single one of them a daughter. "My lord," he could be heard to complain whenever he had whiskey enough to drown his happiness. "My lord, I have no one to help me with the plowing and the caring of the stock. My lord, I am inundated with girl-children, ever' one of them with her mouth open, waiting for food. They was born with their mother's appetites, that's certain; they have eat me out of house and home, have robbed my land from me, have filled my house with bellowing and crying and such screechy noises as only a foundry ever heard afore this, and if I make so bold as to touch my wife, or even look at her with any sort of foolish longing, she bears another one. I don't have to prick her; all I have to do is look at her, and she balloons out."

Only when he was drunk did he emote in such fine fashion and declaim his suffering; when sober he was most friendly and evenly disposed toward the features of his life.

He arrived on this certain sunny morning, his brood with him, and set to work making a lean-to shelter. He laid a fire, then waited for Tinkler Harrison to scent the smell of cooking foods or hear the bark of the old dog. Ernest would not even go to see the old man himself; let the old man's curiosity fetch him to the camp.

By mid-afternoon he heard Harrison's horse on the trail, and directly the horse and rider appeared, Harrison peering ahead suspiciously, unhappily sensing who was present, knowing full well from the tracks left on the trail that a busted cart had come up that way, drawn by a lame ox, and that any number of barefooted children had trooped past.

"Lord, help me," Harrison murmured, dismounting, placing his hands firmly on his hips, staring at Ernest and Inez, who was sweaty already from the smoke from the open campfire on which she was trying to cook dinner. "There are eight river crossings to get to this valley, and yet you done it." He seemed to be impressed, but he was irritated, too, for his dream for the valley had not included such men as Ernest Plover, who had sound intent and even harbored a quaint nobility of spirit, but who never succeeded at anything.

Even so, even though Harrison claimed to be disappointed, he was pleased, too, and felt a sort of elation, for he had always liked to have Ernest about, to have him ask for help, which he did often and with a fine wit and manner. He was Belle's father, too, and that had to be considered.

So Harrison gave him a plot of land and told him where his corner markings were. Then he invited him and Inez and children over to his plantation for supper, so that they could eat a good meal, the first good meal of that long journey from Virginia.

To his surprise, however, Ernest refused the invitation. He who had come to beg for land and had accepted it would not come to share supper with the old man. Tinkler went away, unable to figure it all out, not realizing that Ernest Plover never asked for help unless he was in need of it, and never accepted help unless he had first asked.

———

Mooney, from a grove of trees, watched this new, blonde band. He was drawn to them out of curiosity, having heard the old dog howl one night and realizing the howl was not from Harrison's pack. The oldest girl caught his eye at once. She was beginning to fill out nicely; her breasts were poking out under her loose, thin dress so that he gasped on seeing them. She had neat ankles and wrists and was always happy, seemed like, and now and again could be heard singing. It was she who spent much time entertaining the youngest children, and was their favorite sister, he decided. Once or twice he started to go down and say a word to her, but he had known no people-company since the burial and he didn't want any now. He would let his eyes rove over her, his ears listen, his nose smell the odor of cooking food. And when he left their place, sometimes he would stop by Tinkler Harrison's clearing and would squat in the woods and watch the women there move from the cabin to the outdoors fire, which was always burning, day and night. The moving bodies of the women drew his eye. Seldom did he get a glimpse of Belle, but Lorry could be seen often of a day, walking about, working at the fire, boiling clothes or roasting meat, moving a big black pot, shoving her ashes under it, pouring river water into it. One afternoon he watched her pound clothes on a level-topped stump, using a battling stick; her arms would whack the hickory paddle down with a whop, her body moving to the rhythm of the work. He licked the trail dust from his lips and sniffed, smiled with his teeth showing, and stared at her across the wide clearing. He had been a long time without woman care.

Also he watched, fascinated by their strength and the effortlessness of their labor, as the Negro men built a cabin in the northwest corner of the Harrison clearing. It was to this place that Lorry and her two sons moved. He could watch her more easily after that, for the woods came down close to her house, close to the black pot in which she boiled clothes, to her garden spot where she pulled weeds and crushed beetles, to the shanty pen where her chickens were kept of a night, to the shed where her ewes and ram stayed.

But he didn't go near her or say anything to her, or to that young thing at the Plover place, either.

He did little work around his own place. He had not yet made hames for the plowshares, so he had to dig the earth with a stick. He punched holes between the roots here and there, away from the stumps, and put in a patch of corn. He and Imy had planned to clear much land that winter, but he had not done any such work. He burned over a patch below the cabin and put in a bed of flax. Why, he didn't know; who would break it, he didn't know. He wouldn't break it. Or what he needed linen for, except a bit for gun tow, he didn't know, but he planted it. He planted beans in the corn hills and planted sweet potatoes in a long row that wound in and out among the girdled trees. He also put some beans near the stumps, so that they could grow up on them. He planted a few cabbages. He put in three hills of pumpkins. And near Imy's grave he planted four apple seeds and two peach pits, all he had. He guessed they would grow all right there.

He had no hoe, so he took a piece of hickory wood and whittled on it, carved it to an edge at one side and fire-charred the edge to sharpen and harden it. The hoe might split if he hit a rock with it—he didn't know. He could not quite come to terms with work again. He who had worked always, who had liked work more than resting, who had once gone to bed each night thinking of what work he might do tomorrow, who had come to this land with daily plans for it, did little with the land. He had no ambitions for it. He kept the wild things from his stock, for he didn't like to see young life killed, as Imy had been killed, but he had no heart for work.

He was hoeing one morning. It was getting on toward mid-day, for his shadow was short, and he thought he might go cook a piece of meat. The day before he had trapped a wild turkey hen near the river and he had a piece of the white part of it left yet, it was dry meat and made bread, or what passed for bread, for he had no other. He was wondering if there was an egg to be found that the snakes hadn't got. He was thinking in such random fashion when on the ground appeared the shadow of a person. He looked up, startled, and there before him was the oldest of the girls from the Plover clearing. She was smiling, more quizzically than warmly, and had her hands behind her back, so that her small breasts were standing out even more than ordinarily, and she was scratching with the bottom of her foot at a mosquito bite that was bothering her left leg. She had on a plain, patched, linsey dress; a length of vine was tied around her waist; her hair also was tied in a vine.

He scratched at his stubbled face. He hadn't shaved for a while.

"I declare," she said, suddenly, quietly, perfectly at ease, "at least you could say hello."

He nodded slowly. "I—you're quiet when you walk," he said.

"I am, I know. My mama says I can walk up on her and she not know it, and nothing else can do it 'cept a snake." She smiled and seemed to giggle to herself, and she twisted her shoulders so that the dress caught itself tighter around her, and then she looked off at the cabin. "You build that by yourself?"

"Might nigh," he said.

"You must be stronger'n a horse then."

"Huh? I don't know."

"I knowed a man in Virginia that could throw a horse."

He stared at her, intrigued by the guilelessness of her, of her coming on a strange man in a field alone, being unfearful of him, coming through the woods without a gun, and barefoot, too.

"He was a blacksmith for most of his life, and Papa said he could throw an ox, but I never saw him do it, but I was down to his place one day when I was a little girl. He would let me hold the tongs for him as he pounded and struck the shoes or the plowshares or the scythe, whatever it was he was letting me hold, and the sparks would fly up from him and he would be almost covered with sparks. I would blink my eyes and pull back a ways and he would get to laughing at me, bellowing, with those two big hammers pounding down, and one day he was shoeing a horse and the horse kicked him hard, so he turned around and caught that horse with his shoulder under his belly and lifted him off the ground. There was a flying of hoofs for certain, but he dumped the horse onto the water trough. It was a wonder he didn't git hisself kicked again."

She was still staring off at the river valley below, her arms folded, the fingers of her right hand idly scratching at her left arm, and she was smiling with that simple way she had, an unadorned manner that was part of how she spoke and acted. She was bubbling with life and feeling all the while.

"What's your name?" he asked.

"I'm one of the Plover girls that's moved in. We're kin to the Harrisons."

"Who are they?"

"They live in the river bottom. Don't you know a thing? I thought you must a seen them, since they was here all winter, cutting at the woods and burning brush. They burn all the time, and they've got a big place now. He's a rich man, my mama says. He's my mama's youngest brother, and the only one that's 'cumulated riches."

She was quiet again. She would bubble into speech, then simmer down.

When she talked, she was smiling but pensive, and there was a lonely sound in her voice; her voice lilted more than it spoke; it had a singing to it. She was younger than Imy had been when she died; she was smaller and more brittle of body. She was prettier than Imy, too, and maybe had more humor to her.

"What's your first name?" he said.

"Mina. Though I tell you, my name's not that. It's Pearlamina. Nobody's got time for to say it all, though, not around our place, 'cause we got so many youngins you just got to pin the one you want when you want her and not go on talking so much. A person can't do much talking around my house, though you can sing whenever you want to. You almost got to sing to hear yourself, 'cause all those youngins are squalling and bawling and flurrying at one another, and there's always hair-pulling, so you have to make a noise to find yourself. Nobody ever has called me Pearlamina that I know of."

He laughed softly and looked down at the cabin. When he looked back at her she was studying him, trying to make him out.

She looked away quickly and smiled warmly. "You got a pretty laugh," she said. "I expect you'll have a nice wit about you, if you ever learn to talk." For a moment longer she was serious, then she laughed, and he laughed.

All of a sudden she turned and said, "I better get on home and eat my dinner." She started across the clearing, her hips moving under the thin dress cloth.

"Wait there," he said.

She stopped, surprised.

His throat was clogged with wonder at her and his heart was changing inside him and his mind was opening. He looked at her with a hunger for her as a woman and for her as company and most of all for the lightness of her spirit. "You coming back sometime?" he said.

"Law, I reckon so. We just live across the brook run a piece. I expect you can hear us yelling when my mama gets to fussing and saying everybody is too loud and ornery. I'd think you'd a heard us by now, or smelled the pork cooking."

He went closer to her. He thought about touching her, maybe touching her hair, to see what she would do, but he decided it might make her dart away.

"I better go," she said slowly, cautious of the way he was looking at her. She moved down the corn row again, and he watched her, the grace of her, a child not quite a woman yet, or a woman still lingering, part child.

When she was gone, he walked to the cabin and cooked the meat and ate. He had wanted to be alone before, but now he was dissatisfied with the way he was living, and when he was done eating, he took his razor from the shelf and went down to the spring and shaved.

4

He met her on the path one day. She was carrying her youngest sister along the path and was barefooted and held the baby close to her breasts. She walked toward him, her manner grave and serious, but she laughed softly in greeting him, so surprising him that he stopped. When he turned, he saw that she was watching him from farther along the path, and now she took the baby's hand and waved it at him. "Hello. Say hello," she said to the child.

In a flash, as if she remembered something, she turned and hurried up the path.

He found himself growing anxious about her. He would think of her as he worked his land. Whenever his work was done, or even before it was done, he would hurry down the trail to the river and walk along it to where the Harrison clearing was, and he would walk around the edges of it, watching the men work, to the Plover place.

One day at dusk Ernest discovered him, standing on the trail looking on as the little girls played, and invited him to come to visit, so they met that way. They went into the small clearing, where only a few trees had been girdled and none had been cut down. Mooney was introduced to Inez, who stopped her work to smile at him and wonder about him. "You been living here all along?" she asked.

"Yes," he said amiably, sitting down near the fire. Not far away, Mina was showing the children how to sing and dance about. She saw him and smiled, freely and yet wistfully, as if he reminded her of a fond idea.

Ernest took up the ax and coughed importantly, strutted to a huge hickory tree, one fourteen feet through, studied it, considered a gash he had made in it. "You ever felled a bigger tree than this?" he asked.

The tree was the largest on the place, and the most useless, for never could it be made into a house or into furniture or into anything at all.

Better to girdle it and let it dry out. "I never have seen one cut this big afore," Mooney said.

Ernest winked. "I have it to do." He went to work at once, and the girls stopped their playing and gathered around to watch him. He was a slender, wiry man, not strong particularly; he was built something like a spring, and his limber arms sent the ax whiplike into the trunk. Almost with every blow a damp chip fell. The daughters gazed at him worshipfully, and Mina glanced back at Mooney, proud of the marvelous actions of her father, who proved at such times as this that he, like other men, could work.

Inez watched, too, eating corn mush from a bowl, mumbling about the uselessness of such a tree. She counted off her daily chores in time to the chopping, told Mooney that she had to tend the young, make house in the cart and under the cart and under a lean-to, cook the meals on an open hearth, tend to the dog, for Ernest wouldn't do even that, make cornbread for the dog both morning and night, as well as for the family, tend to stock, and mend the clothing as best she could, all while he gave his attention to the tree. "You want some mush?" she asked him.

He accepted a wooden bowlful of it. The Plovers had only a few bowls, he noticed, but enough to make out with, provided everybody didn't eat at the same time.

Ernest Plover's blows got more and more slight. Soon he stopped entirely, and with a deep sigh threw down the ax. He came over to where Mooney was and flopped on the ground.

Mina took up the ax and went to the tree, set one foot in the cut in the trunk, and began to hack. Mooney couldn't help but watch her; with each stroke her dress caught nicely across her body. Not long before she would be fully grown, he thought, and responsive to the proper touch and look and word and whisper. It was all he could do to eat the corn mush for the interest he had in watching her, the way she would set herself just right, the way her hips would swing and her shoulders move.

Ernest picked up his fiddle and began to strum the bow across it. Mina flashed him a smile and the little girls began to prance about. Ernest began to play, and the fiddle music got as hot as the fire before which they sat, near which she cut on the great tree, and it boiled Mooney's temper and made him wary, even of his own thoughts, there in a state of near-starvation for a woman.

Abruptly the music stopped. The end was so sharply done, so unexpected, that he was dizzy from the return to quiet.

Ernest turned to Inez. "Is that the sound of a horse a coming?"

"It's at least two horses. Can't you hear?"

"Oh, hush up," he said. "She's got a mouth on her like a miller's paddle." He turned without rising and tried to see the trail. Inez, with her bowl in her hand, moved toward the cart, where all her things were, the sorry lot of her possessions. The dog, which was lying on its belly on the ground, raised its head and sniffed the air, then lowered its head again.

Riders came in among the trees, there near the fire, and stopped. Inez came back to the fireside, fanning herself with a willow-limb fan.

"It's your brother, ain't it?" Ernest said.

Inez grunted and sat down. Mina leaned on the ax handle, waiting. When she saw her uncle, she let the ax drop and went off through the woods.

The old man stepped into the firelight. He was shorter than Mooney had remembered him being, and was more pixie-like. "Well, air ye never to get cabin trees felled, Inez?" he said.

She shifted her weight and frowned testily. "There's the big tree to work on," she said. "Ernest wants it down."

Harrison looked at the tree speculatively. He shook his head wearily and turned to Mooney. Mooney went on eating, chewing the mush. The old man said, "If you'd married a man with gumption, Inez, you'd have something by now besides a brood of youngins and a dull ax."

"Marry a good man like your own first wife done," Ernest said simply, "and she could be in her grave by now."

A flash of anger crossed Harrison's face, a fierceness appeared there, but quickly he controlled himself and turned to talk to Inez, ignoring Ernest, just as Ernest made a point of ignoring him.

Mooney, feeling ill at ease there, went to take his bowl to the branch and rinse it out. When he got to the wagons he stopped short, for he saw Lorry there, leaning against the cart. She seemed not to be unsettled by his staring at her. "Have you forgot her yet?" she said gently.

"Forgot her?" he said. He realized then what she meant. "Most of what's around the house reminds me of her."

"I thought you might come down to see us sometime in the valley, but you never did."

"The winter closed in. I looked in on you once or twice from beyond the clearing."

She considered that.

"I see you have a house off to yourself now," he said.

"Not much of one. Papa put my cabin so near his I can hear him shouting at the field hands." She smiled wanly. "I guess I'm as much dependent on him now as everybody else."

"That so?" The moonlight fell gently on her face, molding it, and she had a wistfulness about her. He liked the way she looked and talked. She had the lilt in her voice, like Mina. She had a firm body on her, too; he could tell that, for the moonlight fell on her, rounding her, and a flicker of the lights of the fire touched her.

"I never do see a man around your cabin," he said.

"No. He's gone."

"Gone?"

"He left our place in Virginia. I don't know where he is."

A twig broke beyond the wagon, and they stopped talking and waited. "Pearlamina," Lorry said quietly.

Mina came forward out of the shadows.

"Come on into the light where I can see you."

Mina stepped into the light.

"You trying to listen to us talk? Why do you do that?" She touched the girl's face, and a pang of wonder went through Mooney to see Mina, so gentle, so pretty, waiting so close by.

Lorry smiled at her. "Papa brought your mama some more corn meal. It's on his horse, and some bacon is on mine. I sneaked it out of the house for you."

"I won't take the meal, Cousin Lorry, or anything else from him, after he's taken Belle off and made her so sad."

"Let your mama take it then, but you get the bacon right now and hide it till he's gone." She touched her face again, "Go on, Pearlamina."

The girl backed away, still looking at them, first at one, then the other. She turned when she got to the corner of the cart and stepped into the shadows; they heard the horse move as she unstrapped the bacon.

Lorry straightened. "I'd best join him," she said.

He watched her walk to the fire, saw her stop near her father. "Where you been?" the old man said to her.

He stepped around the wagon and went on down to the branch, where he washed out the bowl. He was resting there, waiting for the night to get still and his mind to settle down. After a while he felt he was being watched. He turned and saw her then, standing near the wagon looking down at him. The firelight was behind her, so he could see the outline of her plainly, but he couldn't tell which woman it was.

———

Mina came once more to his place. He was working the corn. He had been so often to her clearing that his own crops were being choked out by weeds, so there he was waist deep in weeds and corn when he sensed somebody was close by. Maybe he smelled the flowers she had crushed in her hands, or crushed against her dress sleeves, for she did it that way sometimes. She smelled most often like flowers; she smelled better than any woman he had ever been close to, that was the truth of it. She came on him softy, appeared near Imy's grave, and commenced to talk, telling him about a pond of water she had found and how good it was to warm in a piece of sunlight now that the summer leaves had blanketed over most everything. Her skin was shiny from the swim, and her hair was wet and was hanging long and loose as she warmed and dried it. She ran her long fingers through it as she talked.

He asked her if she wanted to have a bite of dinner with him.

"I expect I'd better go home to eat my dinner," she said.

"They won't miss you."

"They might not," she said, smiling, "unless they stop to count how many's there."

"I have some turkey meat," he said. "Got that and milk. Got an egg to eat." He was nervous and uneasy, lest she go away. He was concerned about himself, too, for he couldn't tell what he might try to do, what he intended, what he might get himself involved in.

"You can come on over to my place and eat with us," she said, "if you're short."

"No, you stay here." He turned at once and went down the hill to the cabin, where he commenced to stir the fire. Directly when he looked up, she was standing in the doorway watching him. The light was bright behind her, shimmering on the top of her head and shoulders. He got up stiffly, his hands trembling, and went to her and touched her hair. She didn't move away. He took a sheaf of hair in his hand and held it and touched her head, and she smiled at him, warmly and faintly, as if she didn't know why in the world he was doing what he was, but it felt nice to her.

"Don't it make your scalp feel good to be rubbed by somebody?" she said. "My mama used to rub my scalp in Virginia; she had knuckles on her hand hard as ironwood, and she would rub me till I hollered, but it felt so good, and she would tell me to rub her head then, and I would do it, but I didn't have so much strength. Your hands are certainly strong, did you know it? They feel so strong on my head and neck. You want me to show you how my mama done?"

His hand fell away from her and he turned back to the fire, squatted down before it. A child, talking about her mama, he thought.

She came near and knelt beside him and watched him cook the meat on a green-wood skewer. She sniffed the smell of it and smiled wistfully, delighted with it.

He punched the hickory ashes up closer. "I wisht I had a handful of meal, I sure do," he said.

"Why did you run out of meal? I never heard tell of that."

"I didn't care. I had the stock indoors and I give it to the chickens. I didn't care about anything till here lately."

"What you care about now? The crops?"

"I don't care about them too much."

"Don't care about cutting down any more trees, do you? I cut so much on that big tree my back feels sprung like a cracked wheel rung. Now the tree stands there graying, but it's beat us all."

The chunks of meat were dripping now. "You cut pretty well."

"You're the one that cuts well. You can make a chip fly that's dangerous to a body. You can make the ax sound like a crack of ice breaking on the river skim. I've never saw the like."

"A man is stronger than a woman most often."

He took the stick of wood off the fire and she blew on it to cool the meat. She took a chunk of meat off and chewed on it; the juice dripped out of the corners of her mouth and she smiled contentedly. "Law, it's better'n pumpkin on a rainy day."

He burned his hand on a piece of meat and licked his fingers. He didn't like to cook, he wasn't any count at it, but he had it to do.

She pulled off another chunk and plopped it into her mouth. It was a mouthful again, and the juice slipped through her lips.

"You're a funny face," he said to her. "You're getting juice on your dress."

She wiped her dress with her hand. "I like juicy meat better'n anything. I heard a man at the blacksmith shop in Virginia tell me that it wasn't right to eat meat that come off of an animal, that he ate cabbages and collards, and I never felt so low. I wouldn't eat a piece of meat for two, three days after that, and my stomach would growl like a dog's. I got so's I couldn't hardly sleep for the noise it was making, so next chance I got I snuck a bite of meat up to my mouth like I didn't know it was coming up there, and I've not heard it growl much since."

She's a funny one, he thought. She's like a freshet that gushes out of the ground, pure as can be. He touched her hair and felt the fineness of it, and she smiled at him. Suddenly a sway of longing caught him and he took hold of her and drew her close. He looked down at her face and it was tense and her eyes were closed tightly; he felt her body start to tremble, and he held her and leaned over and kissed her left breast through the dress, and suddenly she pulled away from him fiercely and crawled backward over the floor to the cabin corner and sat there, staring at him like a young, wild thing, her hair stringy and in her face now. It was not only in anger that she looked at him, he thought, but in surprise and dismay, too.

He had not expected this. He knew a woman had cares about love-making, about baby birth and being pressed down by a man, but she ought to know that was her lot and not blame a man for it.

He wiped his hands on his pants and crawled over to her. He sat down with his back to the wall near her. Her legs were poked out stiffly in front of her, and he reached over and patted one leg. "I didn't aim to come on ye unawares," he said.

She scrooched up her face and brushed her hair back from her eyes. She seemed to be wary, like a young thing that has been caught.

"I'm stronger'n I need to be, I know. I'm a hard worker when I get to working, like helping your papa; I got to working there for a while and I got to feeling that I ought to do some work here again. I been all to myself here for a long time, except for what company is left in the way it was, in remembering her, and I do. I talk to her, but she's not here. I don't know were she is, but I know within reason she's not here." He glanced at her to see how she was accepting what he said. She was still put out with him, seemed like. "Do you know where they go?"

The big blue eyes of the girl, doe eyes like her father's, turned toward him and her lips pouted out. She was calmer now but was trembling yet.

"She's not in that bury hole," he said. "She was in it, but she wasn't there, neither, and sometimes I think she's in this cabin here, like now she's here and maybe she's madder'n you, mad at me for what I done, grabbing ahold of you. She might be madder'n a rained-on hen, I don't know, for she never saw me go after another woman afore, and the truth is I never done it afore, for Imy and me was growing up about the same time and in the same place."

She was still looking at him with her eyes wide. "You almost busted my collarbone twisting me around," she said.

"I know. I'm stronger'n I ought to be. I know it."

"You took a hold on me that just about broke me in two, twisting me around."

"Well, I know it's something, all right. Imy used to tell me I was too strong. I just got strong like this, and then when it comes over you that you want a woman, strength rises in you, that's all."

"You hurt my arm. Look a there."

It was bruised, he saw. It was swelling now near the elbow. "I was so afeared you'd try to get away I didn't know what to do."

"You had no right to come on me like that. I was eating my piece of meat and you made me swallow if afore it was half chewed." Angrily she swept her hair back from her face. "You almost tore my dress, and it's all in the world I got to wear."

"Oh, hush," he said suddenly, having heard all he wanted to about it.

They sat there, each staring at the far wall. Suddenly she got up, hurt by his abruptness, and stepped over his legs, went to the door, stood there as if waiting for him to say he was sorry for talking so rough to her, but he was quiet.

She swung on him. "You just stay away from me if you got to act like them men in Virginia. If you're like them you stay away."

"Hush up, I told ye."

"A pinching and a pulling, so's I had to fight for ever' breath I took to live by. I like people to be gentle and nice and to smile and be kind to one another, not to be pawing at one another, hair-pulling all the time. You twisted my collarbone so much it's swolled up already."

"God damn it," he said.

She turned.

"Don't you go," he said.

"I'm a going this minute." She started up across the clearing past the shed.

He moved quickly to the door. "Mina, come here, damn ye. What are ye, a little girl that don't know about being growed up, about being in a cabin alone with a man? Now don't go home yet, you hear me?"

She went on.

"Don't you know what it's like for a body to want another'n?"

She went to the corn patch, cut through there.

"Mina!" he shouted at her, but she went on. He turned back into the cabin, frustrated, his throat dry, his hands knotted up. "God damn," he murmured. "God damn," he said and moved about anxiously, breathing deeply. No right, he thought, for she knew; there in the firelight with that fiddle playing, she knew. They all knew. They were born with the seed of knowing in them, and when they got big enough to attract an eye, they knew how to turn their wrists before a man's face, how to walk and how to look at a man, how to giggle and laugh.

He went to the door and glared at the woods where she had gone. Those days of being with her, the nights there with Ernest playing the fiddle, the food meals eaten at her clearing, then she was uppity to a fault. All right for a woman to be private, to let it be known she was not to be taken by a man, but to come into a man's cabin when he was alone and had been alone for all these months, and was so lonely he could taste loneliness, and was too hungry for a person to live without a person any longer.

He went to the fire, where the skewer of meat was, and kicked it away.

She was a woman—don't tell him. She knew.

Yet what could he do? He would not for the world harm her. He would not hurt her at all. He would not cause her arm to bruise. Her mouth he loved. He would not crush her. He would not hold her if she wanted to be gone. He would not tear the sleeve of her dress.

But he had torn her dress and he had bruised her arm, he knew, and it all left him with a worry.

Wearily he took the bucket and went down to the spring to get water. He washed his face and hands, then sat down to let the day grow warm and tired. The dog was with him, and after a while it began to growl.

He looked up and saw Mina standing there near the cabin. She saw him, too, and came on down to stand near where he was. "Mina," he said deeply, "I'm a fool for this world."

She sat down on a rock nearby and calmly folded her hands on her lap. She stirred herself to shrug and said, "I got to worrying about you."

"I was wondering," he said.

"I was nigh to my papa's clearing, but I come back."

There were crickets way off and close by, too, talking to one another. Far down the river valley a fox barked. She's just a girl, he thought. What was I doing to a young girl like that, here in this wild country. "It's the warmest night we've had," he said.

"I told my papa it was so warm I'd spent the morning sitting in a pool of water. I found a pool of water the sun can get to."

"You told me," he said. He wondered what in the world his life was coming to, getting himself mixed up with a young thing. He had had a longing for her, for she was clean and pretty and had such fine bones, and had a nice manner about her. But, Lord, he was worried now about himself as well as her. "You hear the river?" he said.

"You can't help hearing it," she said.

He went to her, touched her shoulder, rested his hand there to comfort her. She stood and his hand stayed on her shoulder. She stood close to him, as if near him was a safe place for her to be. "I'll go on home now," she said.

"I'll walk ye," he said.

She came back whenever she wanted to. Or he went to her place. Or they would meet at the pool she had found, which was high up on the mountain. She sang a good deal to him, songs she had heard her father sing.

> My father and mother were Irish,
> My father and mother were Irish,
> My father and mother were Irish,
> And I am Irish, too.

> We put a pig in the parlor,
> We put a pig in the parlor,
> We put a pig in the parlor,
> And it is Irish, too.

She would sing and nod her pretty head and giggle.

> Oh, the miller boy that tends to the mill,
> He takes the toll with his own free will.
> One hand in the hopper and the other in the sack,
> He takes too much, but never puts back.

They would lie on their backs with their hands behind their heads and look at the passing clouds and consider the words.

> Here we go in mourning,
> In mourning is my cry.
> I have gone and lost my true love,
> And surely I must die.

He didn't get much work done. They would sometimes start in hoeing a few hills of corn, but soon they were singing or carrying on. The girl was like a drug to him. She called him away from what he knew he ought to do. Seemed like she knew whenever he planned to work, and she would come around. He got up before dawn one morning to get a head start on a day's work, but he had no more than struck the first blow before she was standing there. One day he was splitting off floor boards; he had a notion to floor in the loft. He had cut three boards, and he looked up and there she was.

Sometimes he would get off to himself and settle down to wonder about himself, what he was coming to, but he would forget all the worries when she came around. Mina, Pearlamina, little Mina.

They got to fussing more and more often, though, for he couldn't help but be irritated with himself and the way his life was turning out. One night they were cooking supper at his cabin and he began telling her what he and Imy had planned for the cabin, how there was to have been a table built long before this. "We planned to have the loft floored in by now. There's three or four boards split off and nothing else done about it. We planned to have white clay laid on the hearth and baked hard by now. We planned to clear an acre in the early summer for late corn, but it's not done. We planned to have two chairs made. We planned to get flax in, so she could spin threads on cold evenings this winter, but the flax is not worth taking now because of the burs."

She crouched near the fire and watched him, hurt and confused by his complaints. When at last he was done, she glanced about her, as if to see from what direction another unexpected, unwanted wave of worry might come. "My papa says he's going to build his cabin come the first touch of cold weather," she said. "He says he's going to make a two-room cabin with a dog trot. He's not going to use no pine to smell up the place forever, neither. Just going to use nice hard woods like elms. He says he's going to drag the whitest clay from the deepest part of the river to chink the logs. He says there's colored stones in the river, too, that he's going to set in the clay, so's the cabin will show all the colors in the rainbow to a body walking toward it through the woods."

Her papa, her papa. She always was talking about what her papa was going to do, but Ernest didn't do anything except fish, trap a wild turkey or two, and shoot doves out of their roosting trees. "Your papa's going to do all this, is he?"

"Afore cold weather."

"Huh. If words was walls, your papa could make a fortress."

She glared at him. "You think you're the only one that can make plans for building? My family has allus had plans for growing and changing about. My papa would already be a wealthy man 'cept he's got so many youngins, and they's ever' one girls. He's got nobody to help him 'cept me and Fancy, now that Belle's gone."

"Which Belle is that?"

"Uncle Tinkler's wife."

"She your sister?"

"Why, I say she is. She's the oldest."

"I never heard that told," he said, but it was so, he realized; there was a resemblance, though Belle was more round-faced than the other girls, was plumper. He supposed she got more to eat and had even less to do than the average Plover.

"My papa says he's going to make a shed that—"

"Oh, hush that," he said, aggravated.

She left at once, put out with him; she always left when he began talking gruffly to her. He told himself he was glad to be alone for a change, but a few minutes later he was off following after her, intending to show her home. "Mina," he called. It wasn't safe in the woods alone and he worried about her. "Mina!" He stood at the edge of his clearing and shouted for her, but she wouldn't answer.

He came back to the cabin and crouched by the fire. A panther might get her, out there by herself. She had a charmed life, though, all those little blonde girls from that Plover brood did. Ernest Plover never set a guard on his stock, never kept his children in close to the fire, yet he rarely lost anything. Mooney had to bring his pigs into the house on many a night to keep the bears from them, and even so he had lost a few of the spring litters. He should build a stronger pigpen, he knew, but he hadn't, he just hadn't. Lord, he had meant to do so many things.

Damn her, he murmured.

Yet even as he complained about her, he wanted to be near her. He could hardly stand to be away from her. She was a spike driven into his heart, he told himself.

But he had to stop being so free and easy with himself, he thought. He had to work out some plan for his life.

He could go away. He could take her with him. But he wouldn't have more in ten years than he had tonight. He didn't want to leave, anyway. He guessed he couldn't leave. Imy's death had marked this spot for him, and the idea they had had of making a farm here was still his best thought. He could stay and marry Mina, but in ten years he would have nothing more than one pot in the hearth and maybe one in the yard, one horse, one cow—and, no doubt, a brood of children standing in every corner, all tow-headed girls, singing songs and beating on the walls, knocking the chinking out.

He paced and considered. He was occupied in such worry when he heard a beast up on the roof. He crept to the fire and got a small log that was burning at one end. He went to the door, unlatched it, and with a leap he went through the doorway, turned to the roof, the stick raised to throw.

There was nothing up there.

Then behind him, behind the cowshed, he heard Mina giggle.

He threw the log down. "Git," he said to her, exasperated.

She came out from behind the shed, her palm laid aside her face, her tongue flicking over her lips, a comic sigh in her voice. "Why, I never saw the like of a door being opened so fast in my life. It was opened afore I even knowed it was going to be, and if there was a panther standing up there on them roof slabs, he'd a slipped and busted a leg from surprise. If I never see another door opened as long as I live, I'll at least know how it's to be done." She sauntered on down to the house and stopped before him. "I come to be walked home."

He fetched his gun. He put the pigs in the house for safety. He started across the clearing with her. But near the edge of the field he stopped, meditative yet, and looked off across the river valley. "Look at that land," he said. "Think of what can be built there."

The treetops were heavy with leaves, and the moonlight was shining on them as they moved.

"Clear that land. Haul and cut, burn and grub. Make a place here. A big house, spread out like the Martingales'. Another room on that cabin, or two rooms for youngins to sleep in. Floor in the loft besides. Put a kitchen house right where we're standing with a big table. Drag rock down to the spring and build a springhouse. Put a privy in a shady spot. Make pigpens that not even a bear can break into. Get a flock of sheep. Get a big flock of chickens and geese. Have an orchard there above Imy's grave. Have fields down in the river valley, growing hay and corn and such like. You hear me?"

"My papa says he's going to make a springhouse—"

"A mill on the river with two great stones grinding like it did back home, people coming in from all over this valley to get their corn and wheat ground—"

"Coming in from where?"

"Can you see it, Mina?" He turned to her, but she didn't even look at him. He took hold of her shoulders and shook her. "Can you see it?"

She pulled free furiously and stepped away from him. "I don't see nothing," she said. "There's nothing down there 'cept trees."

5

Mooney locked up his place one windy morning, shedded his cow, housed his chickens, tied his dog and left the pigs in the cabin. It was the first cool time of that year, and he went down into the valley, the dog barking after him; he stalked a deer, which wasn't hard to do in a river valley on a windy day, for the wind sounds covered what noise he made.

The hindquarters of the deer had been ruined by insects laying eggs under the hide, but the front quarters were clean. He cut off one quarter, bundled it in the hide and carried it down the valley to where Lorry and her two boys lived.

He felt awkward about taking this present to Lorry Harrison when he had never given a present to Mina at all, but he didn't feel like giving Mina anything, that was the truth of it. She was too much on his mind now as it was. Lord, he guessed she was ready to move into his cabin come spring; to post their bonds on a tree near the trail and claim marriage.

He moved to the door of Lorry's cabin and studied out how he might go about this. He decided to do it simply. He laid the quarter of meat on the step, moving nervously, for he wasn't accustomed to courting; he turned at once and hurried away, but before he even reached the house corner, her door opened and she spoke to him.

He stopped and faced her; he supposed she knew why he had brought her a gift, which made him feel awkward in itself. She said not another word, so at last he spoke up. "I can kill a deer just about any day," he said.

"Is that so?" she said.

"I had that piece of one left."

"I allow," she said vaguely, as if she were still trying to adjust to his presence. "That looks like the best part of the deer to me."

"I noticed that you didn't go often to your father's place, and he never brought you much to eat." He stood stolidly, looking at her wonderingly. He looked out over the great clearing to where, near the spot her father was starting a big house, the Negroes were working, pulling corn ears from the stalks.

She pushed the cabin door open with one foot. "Won't you come inside?"

"I have corn-cropping to do at home," he said, but he didn't move away. He saw one of her boys peek out from behind her skirt. Those two boys gave her an advantage over Mina, he thought, for they soon would be up to grubbing age. "I might come in for a little while," he said. He picked up the quarter of deer by the hoof and carried it past her; he tied it by the meat twang on the rafter. The quarter was long and lean when hung. It was moist, too, and began dripping onto the earthen floor. The two boys stared up at it, their mouths open.

He went back to the door, where she was standing, watching him speculatively. She didn't have the ready burst of smile and humor that Mina had, he would have to admit that. Mina would be talking by now about that deer meat and how hungry she was and how her stomach was growling. Oh, she could talk as naturally as she could splash into a pool of water, but this woman wasn't as ready-witted or as nimble of tongue.

She didn't have much in the way of possessions, either, he saw, not to be a rich man's daughter. She had a table made of hickory. She had a Bible. She had a skillet and a hearth pot. There was a gun hung over the doorway, and her clothes and the boys' clothes were hung on wall pegs. There were bits of yarn and several colored bags of seeds. She had the pieces of a spinning wheel lashed to a rafter, and maybe the metal parts and a few pieces for a loom. There was only one bed, and it was nothing more than rag comforted.

He went outdoors and sat down on the step. She came outside and stood nearby, folded her arms and looked off across the field toward the river. The boys came to the doorway and stood there looking at her. They were handsome boys, and quiet, as if they had been scared by something. He guessed it was their grandfather who had beat down their spirits.

He noticed she was moving her foot idly in the dirt, and even such a small sign of nervousness made him feel more at ease. She had a pretty foot on her; he took note of that. Probably all her joints would be neat. Her foot was big enough, too, not over-small like Mina's, whose feet and ankles were so frail-looking it was a wonder she could walk about all day on them.

"I killed that deer in a short while," he said. "I had a string of dried apples, which I put back after Imy died, and I slipped a piece of apple in my shirt. You boys know about that trick?"

The boys shook their heads.

"It covers your scent, so a deer can't know you're about, for a deer can smell for as far as a boy or a man can see. I put my dog in the house, too, so it wouldn't be smelled, or wouldn't bark and run the game. I knew within reason there'd be a deer down there this morning eating leaves at the canebrake. I went down there, crept onto the valley floor below my cabin, and soon I heard a deer breaking. I crept along and found a pretty buck with two little peaked horns. He had a nice-looking hide on him, so I aimed and fired at his chest, and he leaped into the air like a dancer in a show. There was no corner to the way he moved, it was all smoothed out and curved, and his neck was curved, and he took into the canebrake, knocking down cane. He run like he had lost his senses."

The boys were staring at him, their mouths open, their teeth showing, and Lorry was looking at him now, caught up in the story.

"'Hoa, boy,' I said to him, for he didn't have a chance now. He went on through, knocking down cane as he run. That takes strength out of any creature, especially a creature that won't sneak and cower, won't bend and scrape through. He knocked down. He cleared a path through that cane big enough for two men to walk side by side. He wanted to show how strong he was, how nothing ever born could take him away from there, for a deer thinks that way, as if he's owner of it all, not in a lordly sense like a bear, for a deer can't make other animals leave it be, but he's always able to stay somehow. 'Hoa, boy,' I called to him again, for he was losing blood and I felt sorry for him. I thought, Lie down, boy, lie down; this is the way it is and it's as good a way to go as with wolves biting at your neck, or a big cat waiting for you when you're old. 'Hoa, boy,' I said to him, standing not far away from where he was bleeding down. His eyes were big like buckeye seeds, and were as dark, and he seemed to be so wise and proud, and the red mark was running fiercely on his white chest. 'What have I done to ye, boy?' I said to him. He was weak and was beginning to look weary, like he wanted to lie down. He was sorry for what had happened, I could tell that. I went closer to him and spoke to him, but I stopped that, for what right have I to pity what I'd done, and pity what I'll do again. It's a fool's habit to kill a thing, then act gentle, for it was for myself I shot him and for myself that I acted gentle.

"Then suddenly his eyes changed and I thought I better get out of there. That deer ass-tailed toward me afore I could do more than take one step back, and his sharp hoofs come up, God knows how fast they come at me, and I run tearing down that road he had made. I run, I tell ye."

Lorrie was spellbound, and the boys were caught up, too.

"When I looked back, the deer was standing down at the end of that road it had made, looking at me, its eyes like buckeye seeds again, all the fire and fury gone. He was curved again. His neck was low and his head was almost on the ground. He was dull of mind now, seemed like. I watched him kneel forward on his front legs, and his tail was sticking up in the air like a bunny rabbit's."

The younger boy came closer; his face was solemn as an owl's.

"His eyes wasn't looking at me now, but they was open, and they was open even when he tumbled over on the ground."

He let the words settle in good time, for he was done. The younger boy stood so close now he could be taken hold of, and the older one, Fate, was still holding to the doorpost, staring at him, not sure Mooney could be trusted, but unable to leave him be. Lorry once more was looking out over the fields.

"I weren't in the woods more'n time enough to boil water," he said.

"I declare," she said.

"I can do it most any time."

He said nothing more. He was talked out. He got up directly and brushed off the seat of his pants. When in the world had he talked so much, he wondered. Take that, Mina, she was the one who talked, talked herself clean of air, going on and on about a subject until she killed it deader than a shot boomer. This woman was so quiet she made a man talk, which was all right, he decided, as long as a man had done something of a morning he could tell about. "I'd better go let my stock out," he said.

That night he sat up and tried to whittle Mina a plaything out of holly, keeping his hands clean while he was working on it, for it was a white wood. The plaything was to be a deer, and he had seen the deer clearly in his mind when he started, but his hands didn't carve it right. He found out soon enough that it couldn't have but one antler, and he couldn't get the neck to do like he wanted it to, either. It was all a failure, so he went to bed, made nervous by his little bit of futile labor. He never had been one for doing work on something smaller than his own hands.

Why did he feel he owed her a present, anyway? he wondered. He hadn't wronged her. Taking a quarter of a deer to another woman wasn't a crime. Somebody had to take care of this other woman, for it looked as if her father wasn't doing anything for her.

Next morning he milked the cow, then shedded the stock and went along the mountain, went east to the pond Mina knew about, and he sat down there and waited for her. Mina didn't come; she never did anything she was supposed to, he thought. Nothing was there to occupy him, except the water rippling, and it was a lonely spot without her laughter and singing and fooling around, so he left soon after mid-day.

He went down to her clearing and saw her near the place her father was planning for a cabin. She was tending to the children, clapping her hands, showing them how to dance and prance pretty.

> The jaybird in the sugar tree,
> The sparrow on the ground;
> The jaybird shakes the sugar down,
> The sparrow pass it round.

All those little girls laughing, as if it were the funniest song they had ever heard.

> The jaybird and the sparrow hawk,
> They fly round together;
> Had a fight in a brier patch
> But never lost a feather.

Like a child, like a little girl just now. Not like she was when he held her, for then a look of knowing came on her.

> The jaybird died with the whopping cough,
> The sparrow with the colic.

Along come a terrapin with a fiddle on his back,
Inquiring the way to the frolic.

Laugh, Lord yes, and giggle, jump and dance, youngins, he thought,
learn to sing like she does and sleep in the lean-to tonight, covered over
by the weather.

He went to a branch and rinsed the worry-sweat off his face. I should
have staked the horse out to graze, he thought; the horse could protect
itself. He thought he might have left the cabin door open. He wondered
if he had.

Way off he heard Mina singing.

He went through the woods toward home, but when he approached
Lorry's cabin, he entered the woods again; he decided to stop by there.
He had no story to tell today, but he would like to see her again.

She wasn't in the yard anywhere. He saw that Tinkler Harrison's cattle
were grazing nearby, pulling at dogwood leaves. The two boys were not
about.

The cabin door was closed. The door was latched on the outside, too.

He stepped back, struck by that, as if the latched door in some way
rejected him.

After all, she might have suspected he would visit her again this
afternoon. Maybe she didn't like him as well as he had thought. He got
to worrying about that.

He arrived at his own clearing at dusk, crossed through a patch of
weeds and threw open the horse's shed door. He stopped short, for the
horse was gone.

"Hey," he said aloud, confused for the moment. He hurried down
below the cabin. "Hey," he shouted.

There it was, tied to a bush.

Mina must have stopped by long enough to stake the horse. Well, he
thought, a sweet girl she was and handy to have around.

He came back up to the cabin yard, thinking about the change which
must have come over her to make her do even so mild a form of work.

He stopped short again. There was smoke in the air from somewhere.
There was, he saw with a start, smoke coming out of the chimney.

He hurried to the cabin door. It was fastened. Who had closed and
fastened it? Mina never fastened a door in her life, or closed one.

He pushed it open slowly. A hearth fire lighted the room and a beeswax candle was burning on the shelf, near where his razor was kept.

The hearth had been cleaned that day. The bed boards had been scrubbed with soapy water, for he noticed how white they were, and a fresh supply of leaves had been brought in. The floor was swept clean for the first time in a long spell, and fresh clay had been packed in the worst of the holes. Beside the door was a broom somebody had made. It had been cut out of a hickory sapling; somebody had sliced one end of the sapling to make the strands and had left the other end uncut, to serve as a handle. Beside the hearth was a second broom, this one made of twigs bound with leather.

In the hearth pot, meat was cooking.

He gazed about the renewed place, then backed off from the door and studied the cabin; he had found it easier to consider change if he got away from it and looked back on it; he couldn't judge a change when it was all around him.

The woman had come to visit him, not Mina but the Harrison daughter. She hadn't waited a single day to go by. She must have come early in the morning, too, to have finished so much work. Those boys must have run their legs off to get that much leaves and clay gathered and placed.

She had more advantages with every passing thought. She knew house-tending, that was plain. She had a handy little flock of sheep; it was a foolish notion, maybe, to bring sheep into such wild country, but now that they were here, he might as well get a big sheep flock out of them. Wool and flax together made strong linsey. They could clothe those boys well with that, and clothe her and himself. Linsey never wore out, seemed like. She had no cow, but she had chickens. She had more chickens than he had. She had ten or more. Come a season soon, he might see the chickens hatch, the sheep bear lambs, the hogs bear pigs, see life start in this place.

He felt better all in a moment. He felt like he was winning out at last, finding a proper way. He glanced up at the mountain. "I'll snatch you clean yet; proud, damn you, standing there lording over. How old are you? You older than Mina Plover?"

Yeh, he thought, and quieter than Mina, too.

He milked the cow and took the milk into the cabin and poured it into the clay jug. He had a jugful. Seemed like he hadn't had so much milk in a long while. He set the jug on a bed of coals and peeked into the pot. Deer meat was mushy with herb-cooking and brown gravy.

He took a chunk of meat in his fingers and licked it dry, laid it on his knee. He blew on it, then drank some of the milk.

He would floor in the rest of the loft tomorrow, he thought, and make a chair or two as soon as he could get to it.

Ah, you're dreaming, he told himself. She's a rich man's daughter; she was doing you a favor in return for that quarter of deer, that's all. Do you think she'll come up here and live in this pigsty, with a dirt floor where the chickens peck for food?

The question brought him up short. He gazed disconcertedly at the cabin, and the sapling bed, but also at the bed leaves and at the beeswax candle. No, he assured himself, the woman lit the candle for a reason. He examined the hearth broom she had made. She could have stropped one together unevenly if she had wanted to, but this one was made to last a long while; she had put the strop through the twigs to make them all the tighter and firmer, and she had wound the leather neatly around the handle. It was better than Imy's broom, that was the truth of the matter.

He reached for Imy's broom to compare them and found that it wasn't by the hearth. He looked for it; he searched that entire cabin, but he couldn't find it, and he grew elated then. He got to laughing happily. He went outdoors and breathed in deeply of the fresh air and felt good, for he knew Harrison's daughter had thrown Imy's broom away.

He made a trap and baited it with berries. He caught a hen turkey in it and took it to her. He stood out in the yard and told her how he had trapped it, and she listened attentively and, when he was done, asked him in. It was all as if it had been expected, even rehearsed by the both of them.

He sat down in the only chair. The boys were at the other end of the cabin, and they watched him guardedly. They were awed of him yet, he noticed.

She told the older one, Fate, to get under the bed and find four sweet potatoes. "And watch for snakes," she said. The boy went under and came out with a little fiber-webbed sack, which had only three potatoes in it. "Just need three," she told him quick as anything. "Wipe some grease on them," she told him and he did, but he used the grease in the slut, which was a piece of wood she had gouged out to hold fuel for candle-burning. She scolded him for that and told him to get it out of the grease gourd.

She got the salt herself. She had it hid from the boys in a gourd; she had to break the gourd to get the salt out, for it had caked in there. Mooney's mouth watered at once when he saw it. "I like salt better'n anything on a piece of meat," he told her, speaking up suddenly. He leaned back in the chair, tilted it against the wall. "The Plovers had salt for a while," he said. "Now they're all out of salt, and everything else, seems like. So am I."

"I've got a bit of meal, too," she said, and glanced at him to catch his approval. "If you'll stay for supper, I'll make a bite of bread." Before he could answer, she said, "Here, Fate, you get down to the spring and fetch a pail of water."

Fate was gone at once. He always did what she said, as if he were waiting for instructions from her, and she always seemed to call on him, leaving the other boy to make his own way.

"Hey, boy," Mooney said to him.

The boy's lips pouted out.

"What's your name, boy?"

"Verlin is his name," she told him.

"Does he know his name?"

"Why, I reckon he does," she said, straightening up, surprised.

"Let him answer then. Come here, boy, and I'll show you something." He felt in his belt and got out his piece of a knife. It wasn't much, but it would do to show a boy.

"You do what he says, Verlin," she said.

"Let him be," Mooney said, wishing she would hush. "Come here, fellow." He showed him the knife, but the boy held back. "Huh," Mooney said, studying the knife, as if he saw a stain or a mark on it. "Look a there. Huh. Must a done that when I was off Injun-hunting."

Verlin strained forward. His mother cast a critical glance at Mooney, but held quiet this time.

"Uh huh. Got an Indian hair on it." He held the knife up close to his face.

Verlin inched closer to him, trying to see. He came so close he got his head between Mooney's head and the knife; he was trying to see the Indian hair.

Lorry said, "You ever been Indian-hunting, for a fact?"

He winked at her, but the boy didn't see him, and he didn't pay any attention to her frown. She doesn't have as keen a sense of humor as she ought to, he thought. "I'll get you a knife, Verlin," he said.

The boy's eyes darted up to his. The boy didn't believe him, seemed like, couldn't quite accept it.

"I will, I promise ye."

Fate came inside with the water. Lorry mixed the meal, and soon the cabin was smelling of corn bread baking. She was a busy woman, never wasted a motion of her hand; she never moved except for a reason. She knew exactly what she was doing with every scratch of time, and that little black-headed boy stayed as close to her as her skirt hem. "What's his name?" Mooney asked her.

"Fate," she said.

The other one, the tow-headed boy, was still standing near Mooney, still holding the knife, and now he watched his older brother critically.

"Where's your papa?" Mooney asked. He said it simply. The question came to him and he asked it naturally. He hadn't worried about it, for it was so that the man was gone, and that was the fact of the matter, that was what mattered to him. But Lorry seemed to get cold and taut at once, and she got to stirring the stew in the pot faster than before.

"Ain't he dead?"

"No," she said, stirring faster still.

"Did he get lost?"

"Might a got lost."

Mooney waited for her to go on, but she didn't. "A man can go hunting and something happen he not get back," he suggested, helping her along.

She turned to him. "He left home to go to Kentucky and see what was there in the way of a new chance for us, but he didn't come back, and after a year, Papa sent a man to find him, and the man said Lacey had gone on to Watauga. Papa told me that and I said, 'Well, Papa, Lacey must not a liked me much to have gone so far.'"

She said it simply, but firmly. No, she wasn't evading anything she would be better off to face. "He put in a crop of corn and sorghum afore he left, I'll say that for him. He wasn't a lazy man, but he liked work that didn't delay long to do, not work over the seasons, not to wait like you have to wait for crops and stock. He was always anxious to have it now, so his idea was to take the spring lambs over to Papa's place and bargain with them to get grown sheep." She shook her head in aggravation at that idea. "You ever hear tell of that afore?"

"No," Mooney said.

"He would bet my father with them lambs. He was always trading. When he got home of a night, I never could say whether he'd have an ox or a pig in tow, for he traded for whatever he wanted, regardless of what he needed. He never had the same horse long enough for it to foal. And ride it—he would come down the road, his coat blowing out behind, and jump the gate. He never opened a gate. He could take even an old horse, and it would jump a gate for him, and he would come into the yard yelling and laughing and calling for me."

She had let fondness creep into her voice, and she was pensive when she finished. She realized Mooney was watching her and she got flustered. She went quickly to the door and stepped outside.

Fate started to go after her, but Mooney stopped him, and the boy, resentful of the interference, backed into a cabin corner and glared at him. "Verlin, how long's your papa been gone?" Mooney asked.

Verlin shrugged.

"Can you remember yer father?"

Verlin shook his head, but Fate made a noise, almost like an angry growl.

"Do you remember yer papa, Fate?" Mooney asked him.

Fate stared at him intently, then suddenly nodded, his chin trembling.

Lorry came back inside. "You must be hungry as a bear," she said, and busily went about her work. "I know a man gets hungry." She crouched before the fire and looked to what was there. "I didn't mean to make you think it was all Lacey Pollard's fault for his leaving, or for his having so little accumulated, for my father took full advantage of him. My father is a strong-willed man, and he wants to own it all."

"Uh huh," Mooney said, not caring to hear any more about it. The husband was gone, that was the only important thing. He began to whittle on a stick of firewood, and Verlin came close to watch him.

"I told Papa I would come with him here to this valley, but only if he would build me a cabin, for I had a cabin in Virginia, which was about all I did have left, so he agreed. That was fair, he said. But this was all the cabin he made for me, this place, which he wouldn't sleep in of a night hisself."

Mooney grinned at Verlin, who was trying to see what he was carving.

"I had to come with Papa, for a woman can't stay alone entirely, so I agreed to come, and he said, 'Lorry, what you going to pay me for passage for your goods?' And I said, 'Ain't you my father? Talk about passage!' And he said, 'Nothing's free in this world.'"

Mooney put a sliver of wood in his mouth and chewed on it. The woman could really talk when she got started on something she knew about, he thought, could talk as much as Mina. She was a pretty woman, and quick to work; she was doubtless determined, yet was gentle in her ways.

"He said he would have to bring my two pots, and my wheel and chest, the loom pieces, the table and four chairs, and I asked him what he wanted of it for passage fare, and he said he'd take the chairs. I said, 'Papa, I got to have something to set on,' and he said, 'Well, keep one of them then.' So he took three chairs for the passage fare. I thought he was done, but he come back a second time and he said, 'What ye going to offer me for transporting you and the boys?'"

She looked at Mooney to judge his evaluation of such a question. He grunted unconcernedly; he had heard the like before; it didn't bother him.

"So I give Papa my cherry chest, which was the only thing I had that Lacey had give me, and he took it, and he's got it now down at his place."

"Some men get like that," Mooney said easily, not letting Verlin see what he was whittling, and the boy was trying to. "That bread smells good," he said. "Is it done?"

She glanced at him, mildly annoyed because of his unconcern, but she knelt before the fire and felt of the bread with her fingers. "It's ready to be broke," she said.

"Then you boys move that table over to the bed."

Neither boy moved. Mooney went on carving, and the woman had to tell the boys to move the table. When they had done that, he stood his chair near the fire so that she could use it, and he sat down on the bed and pulled the table in close. He commenced to whittle again, using the table top to brace the wood. Verlin came so near he got his head in the way of Mooney's sight, and Mooney pushed the boy away; then he began talking softly. "Going to try to get some furs to trade for salt. I can trade furs in Morganton, but they don't get thick and worth much till cold weather."

He whittled on the wood and was quiet for a while. "I need salt, if I hope to cure pork next year."

She set a bowl full of turkey meat and the pone of bread on the table. She went back to the fireplace and ash-looked for the sweet potatoes.

"Hope to clear bushes out this winter, get that horse earning its keep. Girdle those trees below the house while the leaves are off. I girdled trees last winter afore Imy died, and I noticed the sap dripped out of them in the spring. It rose like it was pushed up from a sulphur pit and oozed out and coated the ground."

She brought the three potatoes and put them on the table. "I believe that's all we have," she said.

"Here, boy," he said to Verlin, "here's you a knife to hold." He gave him the piece of wood he had whittled on, which was a sort of knife with a long blade that was sharpened and pointed. Verlin took it and seemed well pleased with it, but Mooney saw at once he had made a mistake, for Fate clouded over all the deeper. "I'll make you one later, Fate," he said.

Fate's jaw was stiff, and he glared sternly at him.

"Law, Fate don't need a knife," Lorry said.

The boy kept glaring at Mooney, his feelings hurt.

"I'll get you one, boy. I was only fooling around here with Verlin—"

"You boys stand up here to the table," Lorry said.

The boys came closer, Fate hurt and scowling, Verlin pleased, with his knife in his hand to eat with.

"Here, Fate, you take a potato," Lorry said.

She gave each boy one, and she put the other one before Mooney's place. She had none herself. Such self-sacrificing made Mooney weary whenever he encountered it, for it always created an annoyance. He wiped his knife on the edge of the table, reached far forward, cut a piece off of each potato she had given the boys and slid the pieces into her bowl. She looked up, surprised, and so did the boys, but he acted like he didn't notice; he supposed she was annoyed about his interference, but he paid no mind. She might as well learn now as later that if this was going to be his family, things were going to be done his way.

That night after supper he sat out on the step in the dark. The woman was in the cabin burning sweepings, and he was thinking about how prompt and orderly and generally how pleasant she was. He hoped she was a pleasant woman in bed. It left him a bit uncomfortable to think of marrying a woman he didn't know in any intimate way. He had heard from others that women responded differently. He had been told in Pennsylvania that some women didn't respond at all, and he wouldn't have much use for one of those. He supposed Lorry wasn't like that. He guessed he ought to try to make sure before he committed himself, but it wasn't his way to press in on a person, to make demands. Better to take a risk than press for a judgment which would offend her.

A man couldn't have it all, anyway, he thought. A man could choose a woman who was like a sister to him, which Imy was, or a woman who was like a mistress to him, which Mina might become when she got older, or a woman like Lorry, who would mother the children and comfort him and make a home.

Verlin came outside and was hanging around nearby. "If I had some worn ground," Mooney said to him, "I could grow a patch of wheat. You know how to grow it?"

Verlin shook his head.

"I'm aiming to try to see if tobacco will grow up here, too. What do you think?"

Verlin smiled weakly at him, not daring to state a view.

Lorry came out and stood nearby, looking off at her father's place, where a fire was burning in the yard. "Must be scalding a hog," she said. "I went over there yesterday evening and fetched a side of bacon without Papa knowing it. Belle said they was low on pork."

"It's early in the season for killing pork," Mooney said. He stretched his legs and studied his thonged shoes. It was time, he knew, to mention the matter of marriage to her, but it wasn't the easiest subject in the world to catch hold of.

"It's a wet-breathed night," she said.

"It is," he said. There was no church and no preacher up here, but they could post their bonds and could hold a service when a preacher came through. "Is that your black pot there in the yard?" he asked her.

She said it was.

"Verlin, you go get your clothes out of the cabin and put them in that pot."

Verlin stared at him incredulously, then at his mother, who gazed off at her father's house, no doubt as surprised as Verlin. Slowly Verlin went into the cabin, Fate glaring at him, and slowly he came back out, carrying his clothes. He went to the black pot and stood there considering his mission. He looked back at Mooney. Mooney nodded encouragingly. He looked at his mother, but she was stiff and solemn and acted as if she hadn't noticed he was anywhere about.

Verlin shrugged, stepped up to the pot and threw the clothes into it, then stood stiffly still, waiting for the rebuke he was sure would come.

"Fate, you go get your clothes now," Mooney said, "and put them in the pot."

Fate held his place there at the cabin door; he didn't budge. Lorry stared off at her papa's house.

"Very well. Verlin," Mooney said, "get the bags of seeds off the wall pegs and put them in the pot."

Verlin fetched the bags of seeds, went straight to the pot and dropped them in.

"The yarn," Mooney said to him.

Verlin got it and put it in the pot.

"The bowls and trenchers," Mooney said.

Verlin put them in the pot.

"Fate," Mooney said, turning once more to him, "get that quilt off the bed and bundle it so's you can carry it."

Fate didn't move.

Mooney waited, then got up slowly. He moved past the boy and went to where the quilt was. He folded it into a square, then folded that. Fate was standing near the door, watching him. Mooney laid the quilt by, then in a single motion brought his hand around and slapped the boy on the face, and the boy, knocked back, stunned, stared at him, hurt and frightened and angry.

Mooney saw Lorry in the yard; she almost cried out, but she stayed quiet.

"Next time I send you for something, go get it," Mooney said. He went outside, confused, unnerved by the boy, who was crying. He could hear him. "Verlin, get that wheel down from the rafters," he said, feeling miserable, and he went off to the lambing pens and locked the sheep in for the night.

When he got back, he said, "We'll fetch the stock and the table in the morning." He saw that Verlin had the wheel, and Lorry had the fireplace pot and her own rifle and spare clothes; Fate had nothing. Mooney considered him briefly. "We'll leave the quilt till morning, too," he said, and, lifting the big pot, led the way up the path toward his own home.

His dog began to bark before they got to the cabin, and he went inside alone and collared it and led it down to the dogwood tree below the house, where he tied it for the night. It could keep watch over the stock better from there, anyway. When he got back to the house, Lorry was building up the fire, and the boys were huddled on the edge of the bed, glaring at Mooney and their mother, evidently none too secure in this new place. "I finished up most of the loft by now," Mooney said, "but I don't have a ladder made yet."

"They can climb up that far," Lorry said. She crouched near the fire and peeked about at the room, which was not furnished at all well, which was no better than the shack her father had made her. This room was a long way poorer than what she had known in Virginia.

She glanced at Mooney, wondering about him. He was a big-bodied man and seemed to be a proud person. The previous winter she had sensed his grief for his first wife, so she knew he had loved her; maybe now that same love would stand between them like a wall, or maybe it would be given to her instead. Was he gruff or patient as a person, she wondered.

"If you boys got to go outside afore you go to sleep, now's the time to do it," he said.

"Where we go?" Verlin asked.

"Out in the woods."

Verlin got off the bed and went to the door. As he opened it, a panther up on the mountain cried, and the boy shut the door and put his back against it. Lorry almost cried out, yet almost laughed, to see the terror on his face. "Here now," she said, "it's not close. You can tell that it's not close."

Verlin sought assurance from Mooney, too, who nodded. Even so, the boy hesitated until Fate came forward, opened the door and stepped outside.

Verlin followed and pulled the door shut. Through a place where the chinking was gone, Lorry could see that they were standing near the door, and she suspected they wouldn't go as far into the woods as they ought to. "Are the bears a nuisance up here?" she said, seeking a subject to talk about.

"They come by now and then. The dog lets us know."

"Does she ever fight one?"

"No. I never let her. I keep her housed up."

Lorry crouched near the fire near him and stared into the fire, as he did. She glanced at him and tried to record in her mind the way he looked, how his features were and what his manner was.

The boys knocked on the door, so she moved the lock poles to let them in. She went outside then, and the boys locked the door, then sat down on the bed and stared before them.

"We got work to do tomorrow," Mooney said to them. "While I drive those sheep up here, you boys can tend what stock I got and hoe the corn."

The boys gazed unhappily at the bare, smoky walls of the room.

"Not any leaves or straw in the loft to sleep on, and that last loft board's not pegged yet, so you better let it be. Find a warm place and curl up and you'll fall asleep, I'll warrant ye."

The boys looked up at the loft, then looked back disconsolately at the fire.

"Your mama and me will sleep down here." He could sense the stiffness come into both of them, especially into Fate, but neither boy said a word. "If there's many beasts tonight, you'll want to jump down here in the night and build up the fire. One night a panther got on the roof and tried to get the boards loose so it could get in. I could see its paw working at them, and it got its paw through, and it was working at getting its arm inside."

The boys were listening attentively now.

"That night I had to keep the fire going bright to keep from having him come down the chimney on me."

"Did he come inside?" Verlin asked.

"No. He might a managed it, but I got a lighted piece of wood and held it up to his paw, and he got his paw singed. Of a day you can see the hole he made or see it even of a night if you sight a star through it. When you get up in the loft, it'll be easy to see it."

Lorry knocked on the door and he let her in; then he went outside and she propped the door closed and took what water was left in the pail and moistened a scrap of cloth and told the boys to wash their faces. She started to have them wash their hands, but on seeing how dirty they were, she gave up on that. "Soon as I can, I'm going to make soap," she said. "Then we'll get that grime out of your finger skin. My goodness, look at how dirty you are. Maybe I can get some from Belle, sneak it out of the house without your grandpa knowing it." She considered that. "Of course, when he finds out where I'm living, he's going to be even more upset than before." She sighed wearily, as if the thought troubled her deeply. "Well, you boys get on up there to bed."

She helped them up to the loft.

"If there's a snake about, you call down," she said. "Do you see one?"

Neither boy answered.

"Fate?"

"No'm," he said.

"All right then, go to sleep now, and don't worry. I hope this is the last time you'll need to move to a new house."

She waited by the door until Mooney knocked; she let him in and locked the door for the night. "I checked the stock," he said, "and it's all right. There was a weasel out there, but it run."

"They're a nuisance," she said. She crouched by the fire, for she didn't know where to sit; she didn't think she ought to sit down on the bed. That would be unseemly; also it would be deceptive, for she wasn't anxious in her body yet. She had come to the place not for body affection so much as a need to have father care given her boys, to find a protected place for a family again, which is what she craved deeply.

She heard him taking off his clothes. Upstairs she guessed the boys were watching through cracks in the loft floor, and no doubt they were in a toil of wonder about what was going on tonight. Fate, more than the other, would be concerned, for he had been given a blow and a command already; that wouldn't set well with him. Fate had the fiery spirit of his father, a high-walking pride that set him apart from others and made him special somehow, as his father had been, even in his own eyes.

She began to take off her clothes. She took her dress off and found a wall peg near the fire and hung it up. She went over to the bed, wearing her undergown, which was thin and body-clinging. He was glancing at her; she wasn't surprised at that. She wasn't ashamed, either, for she had been well made from the start, and the bearing of two boys had cost her only slightly of her shape.

He was undressed now and was standing over in the corner of the room, beyond the table.

She could hear the boys breathing upstairs. She wished she could assure them that she wasn't afraid. She was uneasy, though, for the place was new to her, and he, standing over near the corner, didn't seem to be at ease himself, and she didn't know him at all well.

She crawled onto the bed and pulled the ragged quilt over herself. She didn't look at him when he went to the fire. She heard him pick up the pail of water and she heard the water splash onto the fire. There came a hissing, a sizzling, a roar of steam up the chimney, and she heard the boys gasp. Then the room was dark except for the gray smoke that the chimney was sucking up, and except for the few bright coals that were left.

"How you going to start another fire?" she said softly.

"I have the gun flint," he said. He didn't move that she could tell, and she said no more in criticism, for she was grateful for the darkness, too.

She heard nothing now, except the fire. She saw his outline as he crossed before the fireplace. He stopped near the table, and she could make out the figure of his body, the strong lines of it, the bigness of him and the upright manner he had and the set of his head. He stood there naked by the table, as if thinking about what he was to do. She saw him move toward her. He became part of the shadows around her, then she felt his hand grope along the bed and touch her shoulder. It moved along her shoulder to her neck, and his hand, coarse and hard as shoe leather, touched her face, her cheek and chin, and his fingers moved along the outline of her chin.

He sat down on the bed and leaned forward and his chin touched her forehead. He rested his head on her head, and she felt his hands seek to hold her.

She remembered the times before in the years before when Lacey Pollard had been with her in their room, in the house his father had left him, and how the trees were wind-shaken outdoors that night and the grate fire was warming, and how he, a young lord and master of that country, sought, touched her and awakened her; so quietly he would speak to her and confidently come to her with gentleness and firmness, seeking her in the darkened room.

He knelt beside her on the floor and his hands moved over her breasts and shoulders, and he spoke to her, and his voice was deeper than Lacey's, and she was trembling and waiting. Then he was lying beside her, and he came to her, and it was the most natural act in the world, seemed like, to take him unto herself and into her own body and seek with him the moment of longing and the planting of the birth of their own kind, here in their own house.

6

Tinkler Harrison rode out into the fields the next morning to see how the night fires had burned, to judge how many old trunks had been pared down by the heat. He was out there talking to one of the Negro men, a huge-bodied man named Suckly, when he saw the deserted cabin with the door left open, with the black kettle gone. He stopped talking in the middle of a thought and spurred his horse sharply, so that it almost bolted from under him, and drove hard to the cabin. It was empty as a robbed room, except that a folded quilt lay on the plank bed.

He went outdoors, panicked with the thought of her absence, by the loss he suspected, which he was not sure about yet. He called to the big Negro, who came hurrying across the field.

Then he saw Mooney Wright, walking down the path from the trail, his long strides carrying him confidently, and he knew then, he figured out where she was, for once before she had tricked him proper, had gone off with a man. Seemed like she was quiet-tempered in public, but was subject to sudden foolishness and man needs.

He watched as Mooney let the sheep out of the pen and began to gather them into a flock.

Suddenly Harrison turned roughly from him, mounted and rode off, kicking at the horse.

Lorry was waiting for him outdoors, bonneted and composed. "Well, have you lost your senses?" he demanded of her.

"No, Papa, I have not," she said.

"You've got one husband a'ready."

"He's not about of late, Papa. He's gone, and I suspect he's dead."

"You don't know he is. Can't ye live without a man to pester ye?" She said nothing to that, and he stared angrily about the clearing. He looked critically at the shed. He looked at the cabin, which had been made of green wood and had warped; the door was closed, and since he saw no chickens about, he suspected they were housed in there to keep them out of mischief for the moment. "If you have to have man care, at least you can get the man to come to you," he said.

She moved away from him, furious and hurt, but he didn't care. He handed the reins to Fate and walked up into the clearing. It was all rough, coarse work, and the grave was a proper marking for it.

"He's barely got enough to call it something," he called to her. He looked about, shading his eyes from the low, early-morning sun. "You had best come home with me afore he gets back."

She shook her head and walked down toward the cabin and stood there near the closed door.

He went down to where she was. "Where's his other cow?" he said.

"He has only the one," she answered.

"What'll he do for milk when it's dry?"

"She's likely to bear a calf in the spring if you let us put her to your bull."

"You'll need another one for milk while she's bearing and nursing, won't you?" He was trying to be reasonable, but anger was cruelly troubling him. He moved abruptly past her to the closed cabin, went inside, swinging the door back. Chickens flew up all around him, and he stopped, stiff and frightened, as they came out of the room.

He heard Lorry call out, "Now we'll never get them caught again." She came inside, her face flushed from anger.

"Dirt floor," he said bluntly, turning to her. "Where's the comfort in this place? Where you going to weave at?"

"Now you listen to me," she said, pushing the boys outside, closing the door, shoving the door rock against it. "You come up here running down what we've got, now you hush, Papa. I know you want us down there in that valley, but we're up here, and I'm not hearing another word."

He sank down on the bed, for he saw no chairs, and stared up at her, his eyes bewildered. A chicken which hadn't got out the door came close to him and pecked at seeds that had dew-stuck to his boots.

"If you'd be willing, you could help us," she said more gently.

He grunted again.

"But no, you have a price for everything. You killed my mama with your price on everything."

His sharp eyes glistened, a warning to her.

"And ever' boy you got has left you, except that one that hushes when you say hush and sleeps when you say sleep and works when you say work, and is around you waiting till you die so he can take the possessions and sell the land and be gone."

"You talk, you talk," he said, hurt and baffled by her. "Just live up here then. Live on this dirt floor, cook in that fireplace, in that skillet there. Make a stew. Yea, put a piece of deer in it and cook it with a potato and call it a meal, with a piece of pone and a glass of milk, if the cow ain't bearing. You go on with your ways, and you raise them boys to be a sight on a hillside."

"You started no better—"

"God damn it, you don't have to start where I started; that's what one generation does, is to build on another, but you won't. Well, start where I started. Start over in a pigsty for all I care, start so low you can't never get your fingers clean of cow dung and your mind clean of worry of a night; stay up here and be an animal by fighting them, and put your chickens in the cabin to protect them from the weasels and the snakes, and shake your bed of a night to be sure there are no snakes in it to lie with you, or with your boys. What do you think goes on inside my mind when I see my grandsons here and you here, for you're the only one I ever felt affection for, the only one since I was a boy I ever give a care for, the only one like me, with gumption to her. Not like your mother." He glared at her out of his anger and hurt. He moved irritably to the loft hole and looked at the wall logs, which the boys climbed to go to bed of a night. "His first woman died here, right here, working for him."

"It was a croup she got of a wintertime."

"No, it wasn't a croup. It was a frontier fever, a doubt that started small and grew to fester and wouldn't come out, like a goiter on the throat. It comes from the work, and from asking what's it for, what's it all to come to, for there's easier places." He shook his head in aggravation. "It's got no cure that I know of."

"You're talking wild," she said, watching him for a sign of weakness.

"Your mama got it, had it all her life, after it contacted her back when we was poor—"

"Leave my mama be—"

"The truth is that she never—"

"Let her lie in the grave at least. Let her have some peace now."

He fell silent. Helplessly he shrugged and looked about the room, his habit disconsolate and worn through. "My lord," he said. "If I had knowed you was going to take up with him, I would have stopped it, for you're not a common woman."

"Don't talk to him, Papa," she said.

"I won't talk to him, not now or ever. If I was to, though, I could remind him that you are a reader, that you can write a letter to anybody in the country, that your husband is a proper man with schooling, that you are used to having a servant to care for you. I could tell him you are above the pack and herd."

"I ask you not to talk with him at all."

"Who are you to ask about something which festers in me. I care, don't you know that? Don't tell me I don't have the right to care, for what a man's mind broods on, he can't knife out. His feelings ain't like a wart on his thumb, to be took off with ashes."

He scratched at his bony chest and waited for a reply. He belched and went to the door and opened it and the sunlight struck his face. She was close to him and could see his face, and he was close to tears. She had not thought he would ever cry. She saw the boys standing just outside, looking up at him. He seemed not to notice them at all. Before him lay the raw and ragged hillside where the dead trees stood, and scattered over the cabin yard now were the chickens eating.

"I—" he began, but his throat closed on him. Muscles in his face and neck were working spasmodically. "I've come to the end of my life, Lorry, and all I've got is half a dozen slaves." He closed his eyes. "I wanted this valley done proper."

She felt sorrow for him, but she knew him well, especially the hardness of him, and she fought against pitying him. He had ruled always with a swayless will; he had always been tough in his heart. Maybe he did have a softness there for her; he often had said it and sometimes had shown it, but he was not soft by kind, or dependable about it.

"A pack of slaves," he murmured again, "is all I have."

"I know it, Papa," she said quietly, "but I'm not coming back down to the valley to join them." She watched him as he understood, and with a shudder he went quickly through the door and to his horse and moved away.

There was one other visitor Lorry knew to expect that day. She propped the door open and went to work, sweeping out and straightening, waiting for her. Not long had passed before her shadow appeared on the floor. It was Mina, and she gasped as if she had been struck by a sharp surprise. When Lorry looked up at her, Mina's face was drawn and she appeared old—the girl only sixteen or seventeen, youthful beyond price; she seemed for a passing moment to be an old woman in her soul.

"Why, law, I never have been so surprised in my life as to see you standing there, Cousin Lorry. Where in the world is Mooney at?"

Lorry set the broom by the hearth. In her mind she sought a way to say it all, but none occurred to her, then she said, "Are the boys outside anywheres?"

"I didn't see the boys."

Mina suspected, Lorry realized, but she wouldn't accept what she knew until she had to. "They must be down watching the horse and cow. Mooney's gone to fetch my flock now. We're house-tending together, Mina."

Mina accepted what she heard as if not a word had been said, and as if nothing now needed to be said by either of them. She swayed slightly, standing there in the doorway. "I'll help you sweep," she said. She moved quickly to the hearth, seeking something to do, anxious to hide her hurt. She took the broom and began to sweep, but abruptly she sat down on the bed. "I never have been so taken by anything," she said.

"Mina, he's older than you."

"Why, I hope your husband don't come back and find you here with him."

"Oh, Lacey's gone by now, Mina."

"He's not dead."

"How do you know he's not, dear? He went up to Kentucky, and most of those first settlers got killed there. I expect he's covered over by leaf mold by now."

"I never thought with a man wedded to you that you could take another'n—"

"Five years is long enough to wait. Five years is most of my youth, but look at you—you have your entire youth, and afore long a handsome young man will ride through this valley and tell you he wants you to be his wife and tend his house."

"Law," Mina said, "I got a startled feeling when I saw you here."

First chance she got she went down to the spring for water, and she was gone quite a long while. When she returned she set the pail just inside the open doorway and was gone before Lorry could speak to her. Lorry felt like weeping to think of the hurt heart of the girl. Life seemed to fashion such painful shapes sometimes.

Later that morning, Mooney got back. He didn't ask about Mina, but Lorry told him the girl had come by and had gone for water. He said nothing. In the afternoon he returned to the valley house to get the table; he could use the planks for shelves, he had said. While he was gone, Mina visited the cabin again and brought a sheaf of wild flowers which she set in water in a clay jug just outside the door. She sat on the stone near the doorstep and talked for a while, watching the path to be sure Mooney didn't come back and find her, for she wasn't able to face him yet. She said she was never so pleased as that morning when she went to the pool of water she knew about up on the mountain and found that the sun was already warming it for her and was waiting for her.

———

Theirs was such a little cabin that it seemed like there wasn't room for everything to have its place. They made a ladder to the loft and put some of the goods up there, and Lorry got to pestering things, sweeping and cleaning and adjusting and asking him for new wall pegs, which he provided by boring into the dried wood with the auger and whittling locust pegs and jamming them in. She hung up her clothes and the boys' things, too. She had strings of dried apples which she put up, and strings of beans and peppers. She had bunches of herbs she had gathered in Virginia, and little cotton bags full of seeds. The bags she had made herself years before, even before she married Lacey Pollard, and she had dyed them different colors. One was for wheat and another for rye; one was for flax and another for cotton; one was for peas and another for beans; one was for pumpkin and others were for marigold, bleeding heart, and zinnias. She hung up Mooney's shot bag, powder horn, and wiping tow.

She had two skeins of linen thread, one scarlet and the other black; she had a skein of wool just waiting for the needle. She hung all that up, and when she was done, Mooney was astonished at the place, for it was colorful as a flower and smelled of seeds and cloth and of the beans cooking in the iron pot. It had the odor of wood burning and of good leather; it had the odor of corn bread baking in the skillet.

She was up before the break of day, fixing the fire. Then she sat by it and washed herself and combed her hair. Mooney lay in bed and watched her and wondered about her. He still didn't know her well, not the different ways she had and various smiles and frowns and sighs. She flitted away from his knowing about what she was thinking; with a smile she avoided his knowing. Always working, and good work, too. Never tired, until maybe at night, when she would sit by the fire and moan just once or twice, or sigh. This was after the boys were bedded down in the straw ticks in the loft and he and she were alone. Alone and quiet, listening to the cabin mostly.

Once her hair was rolled into a knot, she would wash, then go to the spring and bring a pail of water. She would put the water on to boil, and as she did that, she would tell Mooney what sort of day it was, whether clear or cloudy, warm or cool. Then she would go out again and directly she would start milking; he would hear the milk striking the sides of the pail.

Soon he would say, "All right, boys, get up now." He would hear them start to move about.

She cooked meat for breakfast, and whatever eggs they had from the chicken flock. They had no bread, and there was no salt, but nobody complained, though sometimes he would start talking about what they would have to eat as soon as he could get a proper start on that farm.

She parched coffee beans better than anybody Mooney had ever known. She had made for herself a little rock oven in the fireplace, over to one side, and inside that oven she parched the beans until they were brown as chestnuts. She would grind them on a block, just as she did the corn, and would boil them to get all the best strength out, and serve the coffee black and hot.

The family would sit down on logs, for they had only the one chair as yet, and Mooney would break the sweet potatoes, if there were fewer than four, and would serve the food to each person.

They rarely talked, except about the work that was being done or was yet to do, about the need for a spring house to keep milk in and a smokehouse to keep meat in, about the need for furniture and shelves, about the need for getting a stronger pen to keep the sheep in, for the wolves came closer, seemed like, every night, and howled their hungry-bellied sounds, and one night Lorry thought she heard a panther moving about, slinking around the outside of the house, and the dog began growling deep in its throat, fearfully.

In the evening, after the dishes were put away, she would take to the paths and find sallet greens, find poke, cut young green shoots from the wild grape vines, pick leaves of herbs she knew were safe, blue root and dock, for example, and mix them together and cook them with meat in the pot.

She was a good hand to wash clothes, too. Mooney swore a man could hear her using the battling block in the next valley. He made her a place under a laurel tree for her boiling pot, which he had hung on a stout pole. She would make a fire under it, fan the fire until the steam came up; after a while she would lift the clothes from the boiling water and lay them on a half log he had smoothed for her. She would take hold of a poplar paddle he had cut and whittled for her, and steadily beat them clean. Then she would wash them again and spread them on bushes to dry in the sun. She would come back to the cabin, the dried clothes in a wicker basket she had made one night out of hickory splints he and she had whittled out, sometimes carrying the clothes basket on her head, come into the house smelling of hickory smoke.

It never did rain whenever she was washing or drying out clothes, Mooney noticed. She had nature in her control, too, he guessed, and he told her that one night and commenced to laugh. She frowned faintly, not understanding, he guessed, for work came natural to her; she and the work she did were part of the same thing. She smiled finally; she had to, for he insisted on laughing about it. She smiled and went back to crushing corn into meal with the hominy block and pestle.

When they found a ewe dead one morning, killed by a wildcat and the meat mostly eaten, she knelt by Mooney without him saying a word to her, and they cut and tore the skin off and together washed it in the branch; then they cut the wool from the skin. Death wasn't natural to anybody and picking a skin that had been torn by a cat wasn't natural, either; Mooney didn't like to do it, but they did it together. Then they sheared the other sheep and got a nice pile of wool, and she called the boys and they went down to the brook and made a little dam out of rock, so that they had a place to wash the wool. She came back up to the cabin with the wool and emptied it into the tanning trough, a half log which Mooney had hollowed out. She carried water and filled it and put a handful of soap in it, and she put the boys in the trough and told them to tromp the wool.

Every morning and afternoon for an hour or two, they tromped the wool, cleaning it for three days, changing the water each day. And no sooner was the wool dry than she was making dye. She said wool should be dyed before it was spun. She mixed indigo, bran, madder and lye, boiled them in the iron pot, and she set the pot beside the hearth to keep warm—but not get too hot—until the dye was ready to come. Then she dipped the wool time after time, until she had a deep blue color.

"If I had bay leaves and some dye flowers dried out, I could make yellow and green colors," she told Mooney, apologizing for making only the one. But she knew blue was as pretty a color as there was. When she had most of the color out of the dye, she hung the wool on pegs to dry, and it was soft, ready to be spun. She put it on a shelf he made for her, to be kept until winter, which was the weaving time.

One night he told her how he felt about all this, not in words that endear themselves to a woman's heart, but quietly he said he didn't know what he would do without her.

"I hope you won't have reason to change your mind," she said. "You say you'd miss the boys if anything happened to them, or might miss me, but I've a right to thank you for your work and what you've done for them and me."

"I've not done much," he said.

"I never saw a stronger man. And I've never known you frightened. At night when the wolves howl out in the woods or even in the clearing, you stay steady."

"They're scared animals," he said.

"The boys would get pained with fright down at the valley cabin, but up here they're calm now, and I've got so I rest more, too. I lie quiet in bed because you lie quiet, and I know if anything goes wrong you'll know it."

As white as could be, her fingers were, he noticed, as she clutched her hands. "I'll do what I can anyway," he said.

The cold weather came, but the work continued. He broke the helve of one of their two axes, and he went about making another one. He found a piece of wood he liked, one which would have the staying power he needed. Some said ash was the best, but a man in Virginia had told him hickory wouldn't snap like ash when a man swung it into a tree. They had always used ash in Pennsylvania, but he got a hickory sapling six inches through the middle, and found a length of it that was free of catfaces or snerles.

He worked with the grain, sharpening his knife on a stone time after time, whittling down from the big wood to the narrow helve, smoothing it out, taking his time.

When it was smoothed right to fit his hands, he fitted on the axhead. Then he cut a wedge of pine. The pine would catch hold, he knew; no wedge was better than pine.

The boys needed shoes, so he made them shoes. He had a piece of leather, which was big enough for the two boys. He traced out each boy's foot on the cabin floor and carved a last out of poplar, one for each foot. He cut soles to fit the marks on the floor, then cut top leather for the tops and, using the poplar last, he was able to peg the two pieces together properly, using maple pegs, which would go into leather easily but, once the leather was soaked and swelled, wouldn't come out. A man would have to split the leather to get one of them out.

He used whang leather to sew the uppers together; he had a piece which he had made out of the hide of a groundhog. He cut thick threads of it and waxed them well. Then he cut leather insoles to fit into the shoes. "You'll need these shoes, boys, when we go up on the mountain hunting or to pick berries." So he told them. They didn't need them around the house at all, and they wouldn't need them on the paths, but they would need them at places where the paths ran out.

Out of the remainder of the piece of hickory he had used for the handle, he made a chair. He cut the posts out of the green wood carefully, keeping the posts back from the fire so as not to dry them out; then he cut rungs out of a dry piece of oak and pushed them into holes in the posts. The posts drying out would shrink tightly around the rungs so that they never would come out. He did the back slats the same way. Once the chair was driven together, he put little pegs through the posts and tenons; then he and Lorry went into the woods and cut hickory bark. They split out long withes, shaped them carefully, and wove a bottom for the chair. "We'll make another'n come spring," he said, "when the hickory bark slips easier than now."

7

C old weather came with a sudden snow and caught Ernest Plover unprepared. The great tree on which he had spent some time hacking away stood yet, and his rickety camp huddled nearby, water-sloshed and mud-mired. An array of children, geese, the red ox, the weary dog exasperated with the folly of human beings, all these had various living, sleeping, eating, working habits. The cart had disassembled itself, claiming finally its right to rest, but the children were continually active, yelling, singing, crying and laughing.

Except now that it was cold, there were grumpy dispositions, and questions were asked even by the children concerning why they had no cabin. The lean-to which Ernest and Inez had made the previous summer fell in on them the first night of snow.

Ernest, faced with catastrophe, moved to meet it in a straightforward way. He sent out word by Mina that a house-raising was to be held at his place forthwith. Mina raced to her uncle Tinkler's place, but she didn't get more than half the message said before he asked how many logs had been cut and skinned for such a house. She had to admit to him that there were too few for even a small place. In truth there were sixteen, she said, which Mina and Inez had cut themselves.

"My Lord in Heaven," Tinkler complained, impressed by the dimensions of the failure. He told two of his Negro men to let his own house-building be, for he was putting up walls on his big place now, and to get on to Ernest Plover's place. For every tree Ernest personally cut down, they were to cut down two. If Ernest didn't cut steadily, they were to come on back home. "Cut the logs to sixteen-foot lengths," he instructed them, "and don't bother to square them up. We'll need to get the Plovers into some sort of shelter afore the youngins die in the weather."

It hurt Mina's spirit to hear him talk so freely and bluntly about her folks. She had rather live in her father's house, even if it didn't have a roof on it, or even walls to hold a roof up, even if it were a lean-to and that caved in, than to live in his cabin, or in that fancy mansion he was making now, which was nothing more than a prison to put poor Belle in.

She hung around the Harrison cabin site, there near the river, and hoped to get a glimpse of Belle, but Belle stayed inside in the dark. Those that had seen her—and Mina's sister Fancy claimed she had—said she was pale as fresh milk in a white-clay pot.

There was the sound of chopping by the time she got back to the road, and she felt good listening to the thudding sounds as they bounced back from the far mountain, muffled somewhat by the snow, which was on everything and made the tree limbs droopy, and covered the little bushes and the flower places. She started up toward Mooney Wright's place to ask him for help, an eagerness alerting her, as it did most ordinarily when she knew she would see him soon. She longed for his presence. Maybe that was love, she didn't know. She had heard love sung about often, and told about in the passages her father sometimes would read in the Bible, but she didn't know what was love and what was longing, and what was the wanting not to be lonely, which she had now and had often.

She went up to his cabin and saw him out chopping wood. She stood patiently nearby, even though the snow frosted her toes, and waited, wondering when he would see her. When he did, he smiled so readily that she was pleased more than she wanted to show. "I never saw in my life a man maul pieces of wood so sturdily," she said. "It's as if the devil was hiding in ever' one and you was bound to cut his head off. You got so many logs stacked up there to burn that you'll char the house to a piece of wood coal afore you come into spring again. It's a wonder there's a tree standing on this lot."

"You come on me quietly, Mina."

"The snow don't talk back to a person when you walk on it, didn't you know that? It's not like twigs and dry grass. I come to tell you that my papa is having a house-raising."

The smile changed on his face to a look of wonder. He gazed perplexedly about him, then tried to look as if he thought Ernest was doing the most natural thing in the world. "When's it to be, Mina?" he said.

"It's this morning," she said.

He moved his feet about in the snow to keep them from freezing, for he wore nothing on them except deerskin, and that was little better than parchment. "This morning?" he said, considering that. He took the ax up again and stood there thinking about the matter. "I won't be long," he said, and went toward his cabin.

Fate came close to her and watched her. She knew him better than the other boy, for sometimes Fate would go off into the woods, go down by the river, and she would come across him there, listening to the water, which he said reminded him of a long time ago, which was, Mina guessed, the thought-empty sound of days he had forgotten. The river spoke to him as it did to her of what she couldn't remember.

And maybe it spoke to him about his real father, whom he probably couldn't remember except as a shadow in his mind.

"What you want?" Fate said.

"I come for help," she said. "My papa is going to give a house-raising."

Fate accepted that information without show of interest.

"You look so solemn it's a wonder you don't turn into a bullfrog, Fate. I never thought I'd see anything so sad in my life as you, except maybe an owl in a tree that's been foot-tied to a branch. You got such dark eyes and black hair, you're at least half an Indian."

He frowned at her suspiciously, then shrugged.

"You're like your papa, I expect." She said that knowing it would bring him to terms, for she had twice before mentioned his father to him, and both times she had seen him start. He did so now, too, and looked at her so piercingly that she felt surprised at her own power. "I saw him yesterday," she said casually, and the startled look on his face grew deeper and sharper, and she felt a pang of wonder in herself to have lied so blatantly; she was joking, that was all, fooling around. "He was upriver at the springs, near the webbing of the river waters."

"It's not so," he said.

"He was riding a white horse. Did he have a white horse when you saw him last?"

"Yes," Fate said.

"He had on a black leather jacket, like my mama says he always wore. He had on black homespun trousers, and his boots was cobbler-made."

The boy was in an agony of wonder that was strange to see, and she felt a pounding in her own heart to think she had such powers to confuse him. She wished she had indeed seen Lacey Pollard, that he would take Lorry back, take her to that valley cabin and leave the Mooney Wright place free again. "He was at a spring drinking water, and I got a long look at him. Black-haired, like you, and black-eyed. Is that the way he was when you saw him?"

The boy's anxious breath was moving in mist puffs from his mouth.

"And there was a hawk come near to him, and I saw your papa smile, and his smile was white-teethed, of the prettiest teeth I ever saw. Do you remember how he would smile?"

"Yes," Fate said.

"And his teeth was white?"

"Yes."

"That was him then. And he said to the hawk, 'Come get you a drink, too,' and his voice was like a soft music string, and lo, the bird done it."

"No," Fate said, biting his lip, wanting to believe but not believing yet.

"I tell you it's so," Mina said, awed by her own words.

Suddenly the boy moved to her, strongly lashed out at her, struck her, tried to strike her again in the face. She fell back, anger sweeping up in her. She turned from him, then swung back, pointed down the hill toward the laurel stand. "There he is, there, you see?"

The boy turned. "Where?"

"Did ye see him? There he goes through there," she said, and began to run and slip and slide through the snow. She heard Fate start after her. "I see him," she called, angry with Fate for striking her, which he had no business doing in this world, for she hadn't meant to hurt him. "Through those trees through there," she called.

She heard the boy fall down. When she looked back, she saw him scrambling up again. Barefooted, he came running after her, eyes teared to overflowing, and she felt so sorry for him that she stopped and, when he came running up, took him in her arms and held him tightly to her. "I didn't really see him, Fate," she said. "Don't tell your mama," she said, ashamed of herself. "Will you promise?"

His crying eyes stared at her, but he was not crying.

"Fate?"

He said nothing.

"Don't tell your mama Lacey Pollard's back," she said, and backed away from him, then moved around him, not going close to him, and hurried up the path to where she saw Mooney waiting.

It took several days to cut enough logs for a cabin. They were of poplar mostly, for it was softer and easier to cut than other woods, and on the first clear day after the snow was melted, when the sun had warmed the ground and made it firm for working, the families met at Ernest and Inez Plover's clearing.

The men laid a pile of stones at each corner in order to put the house a few inches off the ground. The open space around the bottom could be stuffed with rock and clay easily enough, and would have to be until a floor could be made. They worked laying on the logs, worked at will, some of them moving from one corner to another, wherever the need took them. They built fast now. "It's all right, it's all right," Harrison said. He stopped at the corner where Mooney and the boys were working. "My, my, look at that," he said to the boys. "Look at the clinch work on that. It's dovetailed might nigh perfect."

Mooney moistened his lips and stared off at the woods, none too trustful of the old man's praise.

Harrison moved on around the cabin corner, nodding, clucking his tongue whenever he saw a place where the logs had not been fitted well. "It's good work, though, all in all," he said.

The men had built the walls up to head height by the time the sun shadows of the girdled trees were short and pointed directly away from the river. Inez, Mina and Lorry called the men to noon dinner then, and the group met around a table which had been made of saplings laid between two piles of logs. Inez had killed a pig and had boiled chunks of the hams. She had used the washtub, which would hold ten gallons; she had made it half full of pork, cabbage and pot likker, which she dished up in wooden bowls and clay cups—in everything she had and everything Lorry had brought to the house-raising with her.

The bread had been baked until it was brown as a pony, and when Lorry broke it apart, the steam swept up into her face, dampening it in a second.

The men were hungry. They tore at the bread and drank the pot likker, tore at the pieces of ham in their bowls. A jug of milk was passed around;

those who wanted milk drank from the jug. There was a wooden bucket full of spring water set at one end of the table with a gourd by it.

That afternoon the work continued, and when the roof boards were overlapped properly and butting poles had been pegged in place to hold them, the cheerfulness that had been building up all day broke free. Everybody was happy, was smiling now at this glistening house, slick and fat, like a solid toy, for it was a small thing, especially when compared to the lofty trees around it. The children jumped with joy before the miracle of such a place. Almost at once there was music in the yard. Ernest had his fiddle and his strident tenor voice sang out.

> Come, Father, come, Mother, come riddle us both,
> Come riddle us both as one,
> And tell me whether to marry fair Ellen
> Or bring me the brown girl home.

He was singing out, his voice carrying into the woods, and Inez went to the door opening and saw him clogging as he played and sang, and Tinkler was clapping his hands to the music and patting his foot.

That's one thing about Ernest; he could sing and clog as good as anybody. He could cut the pigeon wing and ride a short loper with the best. She had married him partly for that reason. Her father had said a man with that much music in him was the devil's own, so Ernest promised her father that he would smash apart his fiddle and live a life of righteousness, but it wasn't more than two nights after they were married before some of his friends came by to party. They came right on into the cabin and called them out of bed. It was embarrassing for her, but Ernest got up at once and told them to turn to the wall while his wife dressed. That done, he took a bucket of bran and threw it on the cabin floor to make it smooth, and they commenced to dance.

They danced for hours, seemed like.

She saw Grover out dancing now with Lorry, and Mooney was flinging Mina around, and Mina was laughing. Inez wished she could join in, but she knew she was too big for carrying on that way herself.

She propped a piece of a log up and sat down on it. She sat just inside the door because it was such a comfort to be indoors at last. One of the Negroes had a barrel he had turned upside down, and he was beating on it, and Ernest was still singing and calling out. It was a thumping music more than anything, and she bet it carried over this whole country, up to the very top of the mountain. There were probably elks up there right now wondering what on earth was happening.

There went Harrison, trying to clog. Why, he was too old for it. And now he had the hand of Fancy and was pulling her into the fray. Why, law goodness, Inez thought, he was making a fool of himself.

Her own foot patted with the music, and her body moved in time and tempo with it.

Then over the sound of the music came a new sound, one to chill the blood, to stop the singing and dancing, a tremulous woman's voice, a creature voice close by, crying in heart terror.

All got silent in the clearing.

"My Lord in Heaven," she heard Grover say. She saw Fancy kneel down, awed and watchful.

There was such quiet now that Inez could hear her own breathing. Even the wind was still. The men squatted on their haunches, their lips pressed tight, their eyes squinting as they watched the full shadows. Then once more the beast cried, and far off across the river another of its kind answered.

One by one the men turned from the sound, embarrassed by their show of fright. Ernest laid his fiddle aside. One by one the family groups, the men with their rifles and the women carrying pine torches, went off toward home in the night.

———

Harrison was building his big house now; that was the work he had set aside for winter. It was to have three chambers, one opening off another, for Harrison didn't like hallways.

At Mooney's place, the main work was clearing more land. Mooney's brush fires were now as big and steady as Harrison's. Some of the logs burned for weeks. "Haul in the limbs and stack them between the logs," he would tell Verlin and Fate. They knew what was expected of them now, and what could be expected of the work horse and of the chain and of the fires and ax, of all the tools and stock they used. The family was a machine of matching, meshed cogs.

It was not that the family was making a machine that they could use;

the family was the machine. The family and the clearing and the crops and the stock and the tools were part of the same thing. The family and the place were the same thing and could not be separated one from the other. One could not understand the family without knowing about the land and their work on it and plans for it, and one could not know the land with any real understanding without knowing this family of people. They were dusty with the land; the grit of the land was in them. Their work, which was done together, was the chief meaning of their family lives.

"We're making way here," Mooney said. "Going to do well afore it's over." He talked often about the place they were making. And he rarely left that place. "Work to do," he would say to the boys. "Let's stay with it now." Work to do—that was the same as saying there was living to do, and planning to do, and birthing to watch over.

The winter passed this way, with working and building, with the making of a plow of an evening, with the clearing of land, even as snow lay around the brush and atop the laurel bushes. "Wrap them strops around your shoes to make them warm, boys," Mooney would say, and go on working.

They made a lambing shed up back of the cabin. They cut logs for a corn crib, which they would need the following summer. They cleared land and burned brush and kept the fires blazing and generally made ready for a big planting in the spring. They suffered losses of stock, but none that new birth in the spring wouldn't replace, until one morning when Fate found the dog dead, slit open in the night by a bear.

The ground was so cold they could not bury it deep, but they did as best they could. They put the dog near Imy's grave, and marked the place with a rock. The dog had not been a brave one; the noises and threats of the wilderness had frightened it from the start, but it had been friendly and had given warning to them countless times. It would be more difficult to get along in this wild country without the dog to scent and hear and see for them.

1781

8

He turned the earth that next spring, earth that had never been turned before by a plow. It turned black with humus, but it was rocky, too, and the tree roots were damp and tough and protective.

He taught the boys to plow. Both of them had big bodies, and Verlin, who was big-boned, was strong as a young ox. They were able to weight the plow sufficiently if they worked together, so that was the way he taught them, and they managed, hanging to the plow handles, almost riding on the plow to hold it down and in the row, pushing and grunting and fighting forward, helping the horse all they could.

The four ewes bore lambs that spring. Lorry brought the lambs into the cabin and tended them there until the weather warmed. There were six in all, and they were awkward with youth, but as pretty as a song, Lorry said, and she made a shepherd's crook from a piece of water-soaked maple and often tended them herself, letting them romp about in the yard and play, or go into the woods at the valley edge of the clearing and eat green shoots, the ewes with them, the ram leading the way. But of a night they were locked up securely, for the foxes liked them, and they were the favorite food of the wolves.

The hens hatched three nests of eggs and marched their broods about the cabin yard, the mother hens puffed up with pride and anxious to oppose dangers, the small yellow biddies darting to their mother when called, slipping under her full wings as she squatted over them to protect them. But the weasels and snakes began to get them, anyway, and each of the three shaggy mother hens was worried frantic, trying to save her brood. One afternoon a weasel attacked a hen. A cry went up, a squawk that startled everyone, and Lorry, who was the closest to the cabin, took a gun and ran fast as she could and found the weasel tearing at the bird. Lorry shot, and the weasel, spurting blood, rolled over and over on the ground.

She and the boys tried to round up the biddies, for they had fled in all directions. The boys came back with a biddy in each hand, the creatures trembling yet from the shock of the warning squawk their mother had made. There had been eight of them that morning; they found six by nightfall. They put them in a chicken coop and fed them crushed seeds and water.

Mooney had brought two bearing sows into the valley, and the previous year they had borne fourteen pigs. They had crushed four by accident, bears and other animals had taken four, and a bear had killed one sow, so there had been only eight swine in the herd at breeding time. The sows were young, so they bore small litters this spring, but they were active in defending them. Also of help this year was a strong log pen just below the house, downhill of the spring, where they were able to protect themselves very well. However, twice soon after the spring births there came fierce squeals, and Lorry and Mooney arrived at the pen only to see a black bear leaving with a pig. At night, too, almost every night, they would hear the squeal of the hogs or the baas of the sheep, and Mooney, complaining about the loss of their dog, would go outside with his rifle in one hand and a pine torch in the other to scare off whatever creature was bothering the stock. He would come back to the cabin, often with a tale of loss, but he never complained about trying to start farming in the place.

When the earth was warm, one night he got out what corn had been put by for seed, and the boys counted it. Lorry had taught the boys in Virginia to count and write their names, and they could make out most words and could figure, given time to do so. She used the counting of the corn seed to test their learning. Mooney that day had begun marking rows in the ground, cutting roots out of the way with the ax, he and Verlin working the rows past the stark, girdled trees which dropped dead limbs from time to time. He had cleared land enough for forty rows, and the question Lorry gave the boys was how many hills must go in each row to use all the 3,255 corn seed. The boys tried to work out that puzzle, and they could not, though they squinted and frowned and looked mind-heavy about it. Lorry got weary talking to them. "Just go on up to bed," she told them. "I don't know how either one of you can farm or carry on trading at a store if you can't figure better'n you can. I told you in Virginia you were going to need to know figuring, but it appears you can't do more'n look at one another and admit confusion. You've counted up thirty-two piles of a hundred seeds each. Now two seeds are going in a hill, so you're going to need exactly half that many hills. Now you just go to bed and see if a dream tells you how many hills are needed for a row."

She sent them to bed, then she and Mooney sat by the fire and solved the problem themselves.

The next day they worked the ground up loose for each hill. Into each hill they put two corn seeds and one bean seed. At one place in every other row they put a pumpkin hill.

This field lay above the house, not far from where the apple trees were growing.

Below the cornfield they planted two long rows of cabbages. Below these they put in two rows of sweet potatoes. Below the cabin, in the place corn had been planted the year before, they plowed a patch of land for flax, and they harrowed it, using tree boughs, dragging them over the land. They cast the flax seeds one mid-afternoon before the evening rain.

They planted eight rows of sorghum. Lorry had a few flower seeds, and she planted these near the lambing pen. Then, on the east side of the house, where the plants would get the morning sun but be shaded during the heat of the day, she planted gourd seed, and she and Fate cut grape vines in the woods and made runners for them so that they could grow up the side of the cabin.

New ground wouldn't produce wheat, oats, barley or rye. Only corn of all the grains would grow well in new land. Corn was the crop they both respected and taught the boys to respect. Corn grew better in new land than in any other, and was able to protect itself. Beetles couldn't strip its tough leaves. Birds couldn't peck the grain from inside the shucks. Water wouldn't beat it down or flood it out or rot it. Wild turkeys couldn't reach the ears, nor could chipmunks, groundhogs and squirrels get to it.

Corn served as food for family and stock both. Even the cow and horse would eat it and grow fat on it, and the leaves of the corn plant made fodder for winter stock feeding; the stalks were cut for rough fodder.

The corn crop was the major hope they had, and as soon as the plants broke ground, the family got busy pulling weeds, protecting the light-green shoots. At the start of each day, they would walk through the corn patch to see if it had suffered damage in the night, and at evening it was the last place they checked before Lorry went inside the cabin to take up supper. They would often talk about the corn, about having bread to eat once more, about what they would do when they had corn in the crib.

"I'm going to pen two hogs and fatten them in the fall," he told her. "At least two. It'll take more'n a thousand ears to get the wild masty taste out of two, for they'll need to be penned two months apiece, but we'll just have to use it, that's all."

"I wish we could fatten three hogs," she said.

"Might do a third one this time next year, if we've got corn left. I've got to trade somehow for a bushel of salt as it is, to cure the two. I hate to ride all the way to Morganton for no more'n that. You reckon your papa would trade me a bushel of salt?"

She stared off at the tall trees down below the cabin. She didn't move and she didn't say anything. There was a gentle wind there in the cornfield, fluffing up the leaves, and it was as if the wind had caught her ear.

"Or had you rather I not ask him?" he said.

"I wish the corn was already grown," she said, "and I could get some watery meal and fix a pudding. I can taste corn pudding right now, as if I had a bite in my mouth. I've not had corn pudding for two year, if it's a day."

"No," he said, looking at the green leaves turning, listening to the slight noises of the wind and the cooling noise of the river. "It'll take me four days going, four days getting back, but I can leave soon as the corn plants are well started. It won't matter when I go, if you're not afraid to keep the place."

"I declare," she said, "I kept a place in Virginia for years. It wasn't on a wild mountain, but I know how to protect myself from strangers. I'm not new-made at all."

"I won't ask him for help then," he said.

9

Belle was sitting in her new house at one of the windows, looking out at the falling rain, so she was the first one in the valley to see the Germans, who came up along the valley road on a summer day with rain splashing down on them and on the horse cart which was behind them, and on the man, the two children and the little wife, all of them walking against the wind. Even from the parlor window, some hundred yards away, Belle could tell they were new settlers, and she called out excitedly to Tinkler Harrison, who hurried in from the bedroom, fastening his clothes in place. He rushed into the wet yard and, shielding himself with his hands, began to call to them to come on into his place if they were aiming to settle.

The Germans came up the path, through the fields. The son, who was about fifteen, ran on ahead, then stopped, gazing suspiciously at the watchful old man.

"I been a hoping for settlers," Harrison said to them when they were close. "Did ye want land?"

The German grunted and nodded and came on, covering his head with his arms as best he could, trying to protect himself from the washes of water. As he neared the house, he began to complain in German, and it was then that Harrison realized he was of foreign stock. He might have shut the door had not Belle been standing in the way.

The German, Nicholas Bentz, reached the door and stopped, rain dripping from his black hair. His dark eyes surveyed quickly the people before him, the long house and the sheds, and nearby the Negroes. He watched as the elderly, bearded man came close to him, looked closely at him.

"Well, come on inside," Harrison said, "afore ye melt from the water."

Nicholas stood there yet. His wife and two children waited near the cart. "I saw your notice," he said.

Harrison chewed on his lip and considered that. He had sent Grover a month before to Morganton with a parchment to be posted at the store. The sign advertised free land. "Come on inside and set," Harrison said evasively.

"Where is the free land?" Nicholas asked.

"Up that a way," Harrison said, making a vague gesture toward the mountain behind them.

The German turned. He studied the mountain for a long while; then he looked at his wife, who was shawl-cloaked and dripping water; then he looked at his two children. Heavily, wearily, he turned back to the old man. "It can't be farmed," he said.

"No," Harrison said. He looked off at the rainy sky, vaguely unhappy to be questioned about the notice. He had not known anybody would take such a generous offer seriously.

Nicholas Bentz that morning purchased from Tinkler Harrison three hundred twenty acres of valley land at the head of the river, where the creeks webbed and joined. He paid half of the cost at the time, and signed a debt to Tinkler Harrison for the remainder. He had no alternative. He had left his home on the Yadkin River two weeks before, having been ordered from his home by his younger brothers.

The situation had come about largely as a consequence of his own actions, Nicholas admitted. He was the oldest son of a wealthy planter, a stern, strict Lutheran gentleman who had come from the Ruhr valley when young, fleeing religious intolerance and persecution, and had cleared land and built an estate, much of it with his own hands. In this family, in a stone house in which two fireplaces were large enough for a grown person to walk into, in which an organ was installed, in which only the German language was spoken, Nicholas grew up, working hard.

As he matured, he sought ways to rebel against the tough rule of his father. At the age of sixteen he began to run away from the house at night and seek out new friends. When he was eighteen, he had a mistress, whom he supported by stealing goods from his father's chests and cupboards. When he was nineteen, he was beaten by his father with a horse whip for being found in the home of a married female cousin. By the time he was twenty, he discovered that he preferred the company of non-German women. All in all, the situation became so aggravating that his father locked him in the cellar of the house for a week. There the young man drank all the beer he could hold and sang ribald songs in a bellowing voice which astonished his younger brothers. When he was released from the cellar, the servants found that he had broken every bottle down there, and had smashed every barrel as well.

He was placed in the custody of his uncle, a pastor, and he submitted to a series of lessons intended to elevate him and make him more noble. He respected his uncle, a strong and benevolent man who was not averse to moderate drinking in the privacy of the parish house. They became close friends, and the relationship might have proved beneficial, had his uncle not revealed one evening that he was infatuated with Nicholas; his advances so repulsed the young man that he left the parsonage at once and was found a few days later in the embrace of an unattractive whore.

He was returned to his father. No explanation for the failure of the uncle's good services was made, at least none was made by Nicholas. The father assumed the boy was beyond salvation and made preparations to marry him to a reliable girl.

Her name was Anna. She was plain and straight; there was no protuberance at all where Nicholas had always believed protuberances would be found on women. She was most serious of manner and speech. He agreed to the wedding because Anna had a pensive quality he liked, a solemnness which indicated that perhaps she understood what he was suffering.

They were married in the Lutheran church, and he took her to a small, new house built for him by his father and brothers. There he lived with her a year before she conceived a child. The child was a boy and was named Felix. Four years later, a girl was born. There were no more children, and Nicholas rarely desired further intimacies with his wife; their infrequent and unsatisfying encounters had led him into deeper despair.

Soon after the birth of the daughter, whom he named Sally in spite of his father's objections, he began to seek out other women. His father knew of this; his brothers knew of it, too, and lost no chance to mention it. Each of the seven brothers had a wife and children, had a happy home so far as could be told from the outside of their stone-and-log walls; each of them had plenty of stock and had fields cleared and grain-bearing. Only Nicholas was a blight on the plantation; his part of the plantation alone was weed-choked and unproductive.

Tiring finally of old age, the father grew sick, accepted death and was buried. Three days later his will was read. Nicholas didn't bother to go to hear it, but Anna came home more drained of energy than heretofore, and in her small, slight voice, which was no more than the husky sound of the frailty of herself, told him what the lawyer had read.

> *And to my eldest son, Nicholas, because he, when he reached an age of discretion, did forsake the teachings of his parents and his church, and when he reached his majority did receive a colt, a cow, and calf, but shamefully lost them by gambling and drinking and entered upon a very godless life, indeed even cursed his father and laid hands upon him and one time threw him to the ground, who took unto himself women not of wedlock, and did even after marriage in the church forsake his wife for other women, to him I leave one shilling sterling and exclude him from everything else.*

Two days later, even before his father's waxen, white face had vanished from the brightness of Nicholas' mind, his seven brothers came to Nicholas' door and asked him to leave the farm, the land, the house. They gave him a horse to pull his cart, and in the cart they put a few belongings and a sow.

"You can put you a house over there on that little rise," Tinkler advised him. The rain had stopped and they were standing out near the biggest of the Harrison fields. "There's creeks nigh there, and springs. I know how the Germans has always been ones for creeks and springs."

"And trees," Nicholas said, looking up at the great willows which shaded the river.

"I cut down most all I could on my place. Where my father come from, he said you could look across thousands of acres and not see ary tree."

"A pity," Nicholas said. He reflected on the sight of the trees along the river and said, "Silly things, aren't they, each one standing on one leg, silly creatures. No man, if given the mission to make a cover for the land, would ever dare to make so funny-looking a thing as a tree."

Harrison frowned at him, wondering how strange a man he was to talk so whimsically, without reason in what he said.

———

When Mooney left to go to Morganton, he took a few skins of deer with him and the horse to carry them and to bring back the salt and other supplies he needed. While he was away, another new family came into the valley, came to Mooney's place. Lorry had never seen a dustier pair than they were when they stopped at the edge of the clearing, these two young people and a huge ox, which had been pulling a narrow sled on which possessions had been packed and tied, what possessions were not on the man's back. He was blond, of sturdy build, with a handsome face and ready smile.

The girl was pretty, a blonde with good coloring, not too tanned of face. Lorry could see that what they had on the sled—a few bags of salt, gunpowder and corn meal, a few tool heads—would not put them in good stead here.

"We had a wagon," he said, "but two wheels busted, so we made a sled."

They ought to go back to wherever they had come from, Lorry suspected. How in the world could two people with no more experience than these make out up here, when they had brought so little.

"We had a plenty of furniture," the girl said, "but we had to leave it along the way. We've got chairs and chests scattered all the way down the mountain road. We couldn't get up the mountain with so much of a load."

"Not with one steer, I wouldn't think you could," Lorry said.

"We had two," the boy said, "but one stepped in a woodchuck hole and broke a leg. We had seven hundred pounds of possessions when we left home."

He spoke about his loss without a ripple of worry, Lorry noticed, so maybe they could make out up here, for endurance in spite of losses was mostly what was needed. "You come on in and eat your dinner," she said to them.

"We have no money," the girl said.

"I've got no food worth money," Lorry said, and led the way through the clearing to the house.

On the way she heard the young man commenting to his wife about the way the trees were deeply girdled and at the right height for later cutting, about how the corn was over twelve feet high, about how the crib and lambing pens were solid, how the shed was built low, so as to be all the sturdier. When they got to the cabin door, they both stopped and admired what they saw so thoroughly that Lorry came to wonder if they were playacting, though she knew they were not and that was all part of their own young dream.

They toured the walls, looking at the possessions. To the girl every piece of color and piece of cloth was a marvel, and the trappings, bags, the comfort of the place were signs of wealth, though no doubt at the home she had left, these would be thought of as poverty items. The strangers ate fast and said they hadn't had any greens to eat for a long while, except for one patch of water cress. They had eaten mostly bread and meat and the breast of a turkey he had shot, which they had broiled on a spit over a fire. To hear them tell it, they had attracted plenty of wild animals.

It was all a cheerful game to them, Lorry realized; they had not yet come to terms with the hardness of it. Maybe on the long journey they had told themselves that an end would come to it and they would be at their destination soon; then life would take on a brighter hue. Now the end had come to the journey, and hardness had only begun. It would go on and on and on, but she would not tell them that. Let them enjoy their springtime thoughts while they could. She had enjoyed hers, back when first she had married a man she loved and settled in her own cabin in Virginia.

After eating, the two new settlers, whose names were Paul and Nancy Larkins, carried a load of goods along the path toward down-river. They walked along, heavy-shouldered under the loads they had, but laughing and joking with one another, helping each other endure for a few steps farther.

"Look out for that snake," Paul said suddenly. The girl threw down the pack she was carrying and scampered out of the way. He laid down his pack and commenced to laugh, for there was no snake. She was so provoked she chased him, and they ended up far down the path, their goods, except for his rifle, strewn behind. He let her catch him, and they fell into each other's arms there in a quiet place and rested, breathing deeply, laughing and waiting, not waiting for any sound or action or arrival or anything at all, but letting their lives stay suspended for the moment.

"We can build our place right here, if you want to," he said after a while. "Or up there on that rock."

"I never heard tell of a house on a rock," she said.

"Never heard tell about you and me, either, until we met. Never knew there was a girl pretty as you, and eager as you to have love made to her."

"You be quiet with talk like that."

"What you blushing for?"

"Am I?"

"I think you are."

"I'm ashamed, that's the reason, for it's partly true."

He laughed softly and squeezed her tightly. He kissed her.

"You better go get them things," she whispered, but she didn't let him leave.

They walked up on the path to the rock he had mentioned, climbed up on it, and from the top, where there was a flat place, they could see all the way up the river valley. "We'll put our cabin here; we'll be different, you and me," he said. "We'll open our door and see all that way, see those mountains back in there at the hind end of the cove."

"Maybe when the leaves are off the trees, we can see the river from up here," she said.

"It must be down there near where those beech trees are."

"We'll be up above the mist here."

"Look," he said, grasping her arm. "See," he said, whispering.

She saw it then, a black bear waddling along far away, studying the tracks on the ground before it, wondering what sort of intruders had come up this way. She saw Paul raise his gun, and she whispered to him not to annoy the bear, knowing when she said it that he had never known a moment of fear in his life.

The sound of the shot burst across them and swept up onto the mountain; immediately came a roar of outrage from the annoyed beast.

She was aware then of three ever-changing actions, each of life importance to her. One was the action of the bear as it sought a reason for the red gushes that were trickling out of its stomach. Annoyed, pained, it must have sensed that the two people somehow were robbing it of itself, so it started toward them, moving at a gallop.

The second action was the face of Paul, where she saw a greedy confidence, a love of sport and adventure; he welcomed the acceptance of his challenge by the beast; he relished it. She was at once terrified of him, and immensely surprised, and in a way pleased by him, accepting his confidence as her own.

The third action was the loading of the gun. While the bear moved toward them, Paul took the ramrod, took from his hunting bag a piece of tow, rammed the tow into the barrel, took his powder horn and pulled out the stopper with his teeth, poured powder into the muzzle until he was sure he had enough, took a piece of deerskin, which he put over the muzzle; into this he centered a bullet. With the ramrod he pushed the bullet down into place. All this he did while the bear was charging up the path toward them, was nearing the rock on which they stood.

Paul's hands moved swiftly to the firing pin. He shook the gun, trying to get a few grains of powder to fall through. The bear was coming up the rock on which they stood, slobber slopping from its mouth. Its teeth were white and shiny, its eyes were fierce with hatred. With a roar it was before them. Paul raised the rifle. Nancy saw his hand close in on the trigger. Even as the first drops of blood from the bear touched the stock of the rifle, she saw the flint strike the fizzen steel. A spark leaped out. There was a crash of sound, then a thud as the bullet landed in the bulky mass of fur before them.

Paul dropped the rifle. His hand appeared a moment later, a knife in it. The knife was about to strike out when the bear fell off the rock, tumbling backward to the soft earth, where it landed dead.

Nancy sank down on the rock, realizing fully for the first time what they had done.

———

Mooney wasn't back even at the close of the tenth day. Lorry spent every hour of that day and the next one wondering where he could be, rehearsing in her mind what she would do if he did not come back at all, what she would say to her father, what he would likely say to her, what she would tell the boys. She remembered afresh how it had been when first she had begun waiting for Lacey years before. She had learned waiting then, as if it were a trade, as if it were like cobbling or basket-weaving. Don't tell her about waiting. It was harder than other work, she thought, for it lingered longer. One could finish other work; one could come to the end of cooking a meal, for example, and know it was done, whether good or not, but waiting lingered. There was a lot more painful to a woman, but waiting got into the mind and got to be a part of every thought and even of sleep at night, so that nothing was restful. And after a while the waiting throb was all she knew; it was the first thing she knew of a day, and the last one of a night.

On the twelfth day she was milking. The sun was quite low, just barely visible to the eye, and his shadow fell on the ground near where she sat. She looked up, wondering if she dared show all the pleasure she felt on seeing him again, knowing she would not, for it was not her manner to show her feelings openly.

Quickly, awkward in haste, trying not to appear to be overanxious, she brushed her hair back from her face and drew her dress closer around her throat. "I declare," she said, "I've been wondering when you would come back."

He smiled down at her for a moment more, considering her fondly; then he sat down on the milking log beside her. He glanced around, then looked at the cabin door. "Somebody here?"

"A young thing and his wife has been staying here nights. They're sleeping yet."

"I bet you give them your bed."

"It's less trouble to make a pallet on the floor for one than for two."

"Did you hear any corn shucks rattle in the night, over where they lay?"

Lorry gazed straight ahead. "I never listened."

"You didn't?" he said, laughing softly. "Look here," he said. She saw it was a gourd which had been notched, and inside it two tiny trees were growing.

"What in the world is that?" she said. "I never saw the like."

"I never did, either, but I needed a way to carry two peach trees."

Lorry took the gourd. They were nicely formed little trees and she was pleased beyond reason to have them.

Verlin came outside, solemnly looking at Mooney. He came over and sat down beside him. "You got back?" he said.

"Why? You didn't think I could go so far and come again?"

"It took longer than you allowed it would."

"Did it now?"

"Took three days more."

"Listen to him, he can add figures so long as they don't go past ten."

"Mama was worried."

"I was worried? I wasn't the one mooning about this clearing, stumbling over ever' stob and stump in it."

She planted the two trees, then went down to the cabin. Mooney was inside by then, talking with Paul and Nancy Larkins. They were sitting before the fire, and Mooney was telling about his plans for this place. They liked him, she could tell, and were a bit awed by his size and friendliness. She started cooking the eggs and meat, and it was along about then that she thought she heard a yapping noise from somewhere in the room. She wondered if a fox pup had got inside, but she knew that was unlikely.

She heard the sound again, and this time Fate heard it, too. "I heard something yapping," she said.

"Whereabouts?" Mooney said.

"A little dog noise," she said.

"Did you hear a noise, Verlin?" Mooney asked.

Verlin shook his head, but Fate said he had and began to search under the bed.

"I tell you this," Mooney said, continuing his conversation, "it'll all open up in time. The settlers are down there seeking land, but the land's up here. They don't trust the mountains now, and they don't like the roads. How can they get their stock to market over such roads as these, they say. But I told them a way would be found. A way is always found."

"I believe it," Paul said.

"We can grow might nigh all we need right here, and what we manage to drive down to market will more than buy the rest. Within two year I want to drive my stock down there and let others see it can be done. I told them to be looking for me and Verlin coming down the road, driving pigs and sheep."

Strength seemed to radiate out from him as he talked. It bound the others to him, brought them all, except for Fate, into a close communion there by the fire.

"Already Harrison's place is looking like a rich plantation. He's making progress. I'm making out here."

"I'm going to clear soon," Paul said.

"Yeh, tame it down and we'll have a good place, don't you think so?"

"I do," Paul said. He meant it, too. He understood. Maybe Ernest Plover didn't see it yet. But here was a neighbor who would be of help; the two families could help each other.

Lorry served breakfast, and even as they started eating, once more she heard the yapping noise. Mooney, smiling, reached into his hunting shirt and drew his hands out. He held a small furry animal. Two shiny, bright, dark eyes looked up at them.

Both boys held out their hands for it, but Mooney reached across the table and gave it to Lorry. "It's for you," he said, "to help watch the place. I worked three days cutting cordwood to earn her."

It was soft as down and light as a feather, a tan pup with liver spots on its fur. Lorry got misty-eyed looking down at it and was speechless, for she never had known how to thank anybody for a present.

———

Mooney helped Paul Larkins cut trees for a cabin. The young man was a hard worker and followed suggestions well, but he was surprised to find it took so long to get a tree cut. A tree didn't yield to his strength of will or daring, but only to the continual cutting of his ax. Sometimes half a morning would pass and he would still be cutting on the same tree; he was forever and a day being surprised by that.

Mooney also visited the other settlers and kept up with what was happening. He never went to Tinkler Harrison's house, but he walked along the river one day, in the grove of trees that had been left standing along the bank, and examined its features. He saw Belle come outdoors and water a few pansy plants that were growing near the river-side door.

The house was long and low, unlike any he had seen in Pennsylvania or Virginia. Its river-side door must have been eight feet high and four feet wide. It was, to his way of thinking, foolish to build such a big door, better to have a small opening, but the old man had made what he wanted. The house had two great stone chimneys, large roof shakes, and ten shimmering panes of glass. Mooney was impressed with it, in spite of his animosity toward Harrison.

Another day he walked to the German's clearing, he and Verlin, and they watched Nicholas and his boy start digging a hole. Better for the family to get trees cut, Mooney thought, so that the logs could dry out; better to get solid walls up than to worry about a cellar. "I think I'd get a cabin built," he said, being careful about making a suggestion to strangers. "I'd put four thick walls and a solid roof around me, for they're up there." He said the last referring to the mountain, the wild things there.

Nicholas studied him thoughtfully, and said nothing.

"They've probably been gathering in close from other valleys, too," Mooney said. "Maybe they know in such mind as they've got that we're unfriendly to them."

Nicholas was not in any way convinced, Mooney realized. Not many people considered the dangers of the mountain in the same way he did. To him the beasts up there were part of a single mind, which encompassed the mountain, the vines and patches and rocks and caves and snakes and buzzards and hawks and eagles and all the rest. The single mind must realize now that a tide of change was happening, and it would come to resent and fear that more and more. But Nicholas Bentz and his wife didn't understand.

They talked a while longer, mostly about which trees might be girdled now and which ones should be left until the leaves had fallen.

Come dusk, Mooney and Verlin went on down the road, and they were no sooner halfway along that path than they heard the German woman begin talking stridently. When they looked back, they saw Nicholas climb down into the hole and begin grubbing out dirt.

"Going to put geese down there, Verlin," Mooney said, smiling. "Nail them to a board and fatten them." Verlin looked up, surprised. "That's the way they do it, then eat their livers. Got to have a place to store sauerkraut, too. Lord, I'd dig a pit for a privy afore I'd dig one for a cellar for kraut, but nobody who's not a German has ever figured out a German's mind."

But he liked Nicholas very well. He and Nicholas and Paul could work together, he decided.

Of the three, he was the only one who had crops planted, and he worked his fields every day, wondering what success he would have come harvest time. He had cabbage in two short rows, but rabbits had got to much of them. Seemed like he and Lorry couldn't make a fence that would keep rabbits out. Even one paled in brush and chinked wouldn't keep them out, he suspected.

They had the field of flax, but the bull nettles had troubled it, growing faster than the crop, so they had had to make paths through the patch in order to get to the weeds and pull them up. A crop would be made, but it would take much cleaning to get the food fiber out of it.

The sweet potatoes were in such rich soil that they were vine-growing faster than a proper pace. The roots were not as large as they should be; they were dry-typed, too, and fibery and tough. A sow bear and cub had got into one of the rows a few nights before and had eaten their fill, breaking up the hills and laying about destructively. In the cornfield, the pumpkin vines were forming large pumpkins. The bean vines hung profusely from the corn stalks, and on the stalks were large ears of corn. The corn was their best crop. The corn was the miracle that would save them, be their bread and stock feed and stored food. Even after all the loss from insects and animals, Mooney hoped to have four thousand ears of corn in all. If he had not had trouble, he might have had three times that much, but he was not going to fret about that. Half of the four thousand he would save to feed the family and to make bread occasionally for the dog. The other half he would use for seed, and to feed the chickens and to fatten, come fall, two pigs.

He walked through his corn patch often, studying it, picking insects off the tasseled ears and hoping he would not have bad luck with it, that it would hold true and be sufficient. He worried about the chance of some late ailment striking it, a flock of locust or other blight. Lorry would relieve his worries as best she could. "I can taste corn pudding right now, as if I had some in my mouth," she would say. "I'm going to make a pan of gritted bread tonight." She would touch the big ears, encased in their protective covering. "It does seem like it's all right," she would say. "Are those sapling logs going to be enough for the crib?"

He had skinned a hundred sapling logs, each about six inches through. He had cut some of them into eight-foot lengths and some into twelve-foot lengths, and they were well seasoned by now, and were notched. He planned to build walls of sixteen logs each. He had cut a few roof boards and he had a length of oak to split for shingles. The crib would hold the crop, or that part of it he would need to carry through the winter.

It took a world of work and cutting of wood to build anything, he knew that. It took a hunger for work and a cold will, even to cut saplings on the edge of the clearing and stack them for fences or for field fires, though that was easy labor when compared with hacking away at two-foot trees in order to get sun room for a bigger crop next year, or with the work of grubbing rocks, rolling them down the hill toward the spring, where in time he hoped to put a springhouse. Lorry needed one to keep meat from spoiling and to keep the milk and cool it so that she could churn butter, once he had made her a churn.

Work, that was the secret of it. Work cutting and splitting until your strength was ebbing, then go down to the river bottom to trail the cow and horse, drive them home to the clearing, put them in the stable and lower the night log across the door. Go into the house and eat your supper, deer meat usually, a reminder always that the wilderness was close by, and bread made of new corn, and, of late, a piece of boiled cabbage.

IO

I f he had a crock he might make vinegar out of the wild grapes, he thought. With vinegar, Lorry could make pickled beans. But he had no crock or barrel, and no time to make one, so he took a length of buckeye log, which was soft and pliable, and into one end of it gouged a deep trough. He put it inside the cabin, and the boys filled it with muscadine grapes they gathered and crushed. By the next morning, fermentation had started; there was a creamy bead of suds on top of the mass. There would be a weak wine in a few weeks and vinegar soon after.

They went out to find bee honey one day. They left as soon as the sun was warm; Mooney told Verlin to be in charge of the sweetening pot, into which he had put some of the wine. "Set the pot out in the sun, boys, and when it gets warm, you'll see the bees start to gather."

So they did, and Mooney, taking his ax and gun with him, moved the pot to the top of the clearing and waited nearby for the bees to gather again, to find it and feed on it. "When you boys see a bee leave, try to follow it. See, there—there goes one, Verlin, up that way."

Verlin took off running.

"Stay with him now," he called.

The boys followed the bees as best they could. Mooney would move the sweetening pot always to the farthest point the boys had reached and set it down. Then would come a spell of waiting and talking, while bees fed again.

It was Verlin who called out, after an hour's chase, that he had come to the bee tree.

It was so, an old, rotted trunk. "I can taste that honey now, can't you?" Mooney said, looking about proudly. "Nothing better'n honey to me. Let's fill this pot and get home, ain't that what you say, Verlin? Get home and have hot bread and honey tonight." He whistled and shook his head. "Can you taste it?"

Both boys nodded. They were chewing on their tongues hungrily. They had not had a taste of honey since they had lived in Virginia.

Mooney stuck a wad of grass in the hive's entrance hole; then he knocked a hole in the base of the trunk. He knelt nearby and studied the hole. He cut a piece of bark and on the bark laid a pile of twigs and leaves. He lighted them and put the fire, bark and all, into the hole of the tree. He covered the fire with green grass, so that smoke began to billow up.

"You watch out for them bees that are arriving," he told the boys.

"They want in," Verlin said.

"They must like a smoky house then," he said.

The boys squatted near him on their haunches and considered the bee tree.

"Look at them red squirrels. See them?" He pointed toward a chestnut tree. "See there?"

"We've seen squirrels afore," Fate said, pretending he wasn't interested in common sights.

"Hump," Mooney said. "I tell you what, those squirrels have a good year ahead. There's going to be mast for everybody this year—nuts and acorns aplenty. Up in Pennsylvania one year the mast failed and the wild things got to fighting for their lives. It's mean; nature has a mean streak in her."

The boys stared before them, considering that.

"But it's good," he said, and winked at Verlin. "Honey's the best food to have. We're going to have honey and hot corn bread tonight. I tell you, Verlin, I started to buy your mama some wheat flour when I was down in Morganton. I come within a breath of doing it. At least I could get her enough to thicken gravy with, I thought. But I found I had no means. I had to have salt to cure meat, for I'm sick and tired of deer, ain't you?"

Both boys nodded.

"They tell me an Injun won't eat deer, he's so tired of it. I'm like he is. No, I've had my fill of deer and turkey both. But listen, I can see the time coming when we pull chairs up to the table and there before us is wheat bread, honey and cured ham—all three. Think of that. Make you drool?

My mouth waters like a baby's that's been shown a nipple. Oh my." He shook his head and moaned. and the boys moaned, too.

"Won't eat much pork, though," he said, "not this year, because we don't have a big hog drove yet. We'll kill two hogs, that's all. That's not much pork, but it'll give us more'n we ever had afore in this valley. And by next year, we'll have a drove. We'll have hogs enough to drive off to sell. A man can get easy money for hogs."

"Where?" Verlin said.

Mooney was brought up short by the question. He looked at Verlin suspiciously, then glanced off through the woods. "You can always sell hogs in Morganton," he said.

"How you going to get them there?"

Mooney swatted at a bee. "Huh," he said. "You don't know the first thing about it, I can see that. Drive them down there in a drove."

"All that way?"

"All that way, that's it. Cross the rivers. Have to."

The boys looked dubious.

"You're like those men in Morganton, Verlin. That's all they know to ask—how can ye get the pigs down here? I say there's a way. A man's nothing in this world but hempen rope and will. A man don't break. A man can find an answer to such as that. A man can come up here and make a big farm, get a big drove of hogs, get a flock of sheep—my lord, don't tell me he can do that and then can't get them to market." He scowled at the boys.

"We're going to do it, you and me, and these others in this valley." He grumbled and complained to himself about the doubters of this world, and the boys listened patiently.

The bees were more numerous now, and were more angry. They were charging into the smoky bath, trying to enter the hive. Somebody had to go into that smoke and break that hollow log all the way open, Mooney knew. It was not a task he particularly wanted for himself. In Pennsylvania a boy always had to do it, though he almost always had to be tricked into it.

"I tell you, Fate," Mooney said, whispering to him so softly Verlin couldn't hear, "I wish you was big enough to split that hive open yourself."

Fate studied him critically.

"If you was older and stronger, you could go in there with the ax and land a blow at the side of that trunk that would knock it open. I sure wish you was eager and strong."

Mooney casually went over to a tree and contemplated the woods, and directly he heard the ax smack into the tree. He looked back, and the hive was opened and Fate was running for all he was worth, several bees flying after him.

Mooney quickly pulled the black pot in close to the opened hive and scooped out honey by the handfuls. "Honey and hot bread, Verlin," he said enthusiastically.

Verlin got his hands into the gooey mass, too, and helped fill the pot.

Fate came limping back and tried to pry himself a place before the hive. Mooney gave him room. "What you do that for, Fate?" Mooney said. "You might a got yourself stung, if you hadn't been such a fast runner. I expect you outrun those slow bees, though."

Fate scrunched up his face and said nothing about his aches.

"You boys come on now, afore we all get in trouble." He picked up his rifle and the black pot and started down the hill. He looked back and saw Fate coming, both hands full of honey, eating honey as he ran. "You boys trip and you'll get left," Mooney called to them.

They ran until they reached a brook, where they stopped to rinse off their hands.

They went on through the high woods then, drunk with the sweetness of the honey, talking confidently, arguing, hurrying faster as they neared home.

———

On the morning when the first witch hazel flowers appeared, at a time when they often heard the thumping of the pheasants in the woods, both signs of coming frost, Mooney told the boys to pull the blades from the sorghum cane, and he went down the rows himself and selected from the tallest canes the best of the big brown tassels of seeds, which he took to the house and put in a gourd, to be saved until the future planting time.

The boys pulled the blades, then cut armloads of the stalks near the ground and brought them to Mooney, who was busy contriving a press out of two oak boards. In the bottom one of the two he had cut grooves so that the sorghum juice would drip drown into the iron pot.

There had been so much rain during the last part of the growing season that the yield wasn't as large as he had hoped it would be, and his press wasn't as good as a geared press, but the stalks gave up their sweetness, nonetheless; the sirup dripped into the pot in spurts as he crushed and turned and crushed again each hand of cane. The bees and flies and wasps gathered, coated themselves with juice; they fell onto the ground from heaviness, and into the pot of green liquid.

When the pot was two-thirds full, he helped Lorry carry it to the fire. One of the boys fetched a long pole, and she stirred the sirup as it thickened. A green skim formed and she removed it, brushing it onto the ground. When the green skim stopped forming, she reduced the heat, and after a while a white foam gathered to the top. This she ladled off carefully and put into a bowl, to be twisted later into candy.

"I declare, if I get the molasses too thick," she told Mooney, "they'll clabber on me and sour." It was a complaint, a gentle complaint, for it was a pleasure to make sirup and she didn't intend to get it too thin. Better to have it too thick, even though it might be gummy. The steam rose about her, dampening her face and dress. The bees buzzed everywhere, infesting the bath of stream, toppling into it as often as not, to boil in the sirup.

She made two gallons of the molasses that day, and more the next, and put it in gourds to keep.

On the third night of the molasses-making, which brought them to the end of their cane crop, they were in the cabin working with the pot of white foam, working it until it was thick enough to be cut. They were doing this when the pup began to growl and nose about the door. Almost every night the pup had barked, later to be answered by wolves from the edge of the clearing, or by a fox, but her growl tonight was not for wolves. She had come to have a rather casual growl for wolves, for she had found that Mooney was not much concerned about them, only annoyed with them. This was a different growl, and it indicated that a more dangerous animal was near the clearing.

Mooney unlatched the door. He saw in the moonlight two good-size black bears, one of them moving around the black pot, trying to get the last bit of molasses out of it, the other licking molasses from the ground, licking even the two boards which Mooney had used for a press.

He watched them as they tasted the green waste which had been scattered about. It had a bitter taste, Mooney knew, and addled the brain for a time. He watched curiously as the bears began to waddle about, seeking more of it.

They found all there was. Then, either because of the effect of the herb or, more likely, because of their disappointment at having found so little molasses, they began to fight one another. They fought for several minutes, knocking each other down, rolling over on the ground, before one went away, walking off in a rambling manner. The other licked the pot again, then left in a different direction.

The chestnut trees had released their harvest of nuts; the pigs filled their bellies with them, and the boys gathered them for the winter and fed them by handfuls to the two fattening hogs. Acorns, beechnuts and chinkapins rattled always across the forest floor, and the chipmunks and whistle-pigs gorged themselves until they were fat and wobbly.

When the first warblers and thrashers stopped at the valley on their way south, Lorry and the boys pulled the main harvest of gourds from the vines, cleaned them out and set them to dry. On a dry day the flax was pulled and laid out on the ground; the weeds were sorted out of it, the flax was tied, and the boys stacked it in the loft of the cabin, near the loom and wheel.

By now the frost had touched the mountain peak and was moving down the mountainside. The balsam forest didn't change, nor did the slicks of rhododendron, but the trees below them took on tones of red and yellow.

The wash of color flowed down toward the clearing, reached it in the sharpness of an early morning. And about them now the woods were changed into a fairyland of color. The buckeye turned yellow and dropped its eye-shaped seeds. The box elder near the spring turned into a bank of yellow leaves and pods; the maple in the valley just to the edge of the clearing got red as fire and beside it a white oak turned into the color of old wine; the sourwood was a rich red, the red oak was orange, and the possums climbed higher every night into the persimmon trees.

The salamander laid her eggs in the stream. The poplars finally turned from green to shades of yellow and gold.

Mooney and Lorry pulled the corn. The boys hauled it to the newly made crib and stacked it away. It was safe now; it was stored beyond bears or seasons, and all that day the warmest elation possessed them.

They pulled the corn leaves from the stalks and stacked them. Mooney uprooted the corn stalks, cut them into pieces with the ax and stacked them near the stable.

The sun set blood-red each day, and rose as brilliantly from upriver every morning. Autumn, Lorry thought, in these lush, water-fed lands, was more colorful than springtime. And the air was clear; there was no haze at all. One afternoon she was able to make out high on the mountain an elk standing near the crest of a rock, and on another day she pointed out to Mooney a herd of deer. Often of a day she would see ravens leaving the mountain peaks in dizzying flights, fleeing winter, swooping down from the high rocks where they had their summer nests. The crows were dismayed by their arrival and argued with them about it, but the ravens, as if to show their right to nest where they pleased, would fly in mated pairs into the air and do acrobatic stunts that ended in the clouds. Then from the clouds they would appear, and dip and twist, tumble, plunge, roll sideways in the air, and finally land near where the crows unhappily were perched on tree limbs, trembling.

The winter wren moved down to the valley, too, and the white-throated sparrow came back to the valley. Winter was in the woods, but suddenly the coolness left and it was warm of a day. The violets bloomed again. Streamers of gossamers, woven by spiders and set loose on the wind, waved from the trees.

At night the foxes barked at the moon. The owl sometimes kept them awake, too, and the wolves had gathered into packs and could be heard high on the mountain chasing down elk and deer. The trees dropped their leaves, and the streams were glutted with them, and the water in the streams would disappear under them, then appear again near the rocks, and would sometimes flow over a bed of them. A family of pheasants could sometimes be seen, Fate said, lying on colored leaves not far beyond the spring.

Paul and Nancy Larkins worked on their cabin. Mooney helped them chop and cut, and Mina helped the boys gather rock for the chimney and hearth. A chill returned to the air, suggesting approaching bitterness. The groundhog sniffed the wind and went back to his den, there to stay until spring.

"It's time to kill the hogs," Mooney said one night. He was sitting by the fire talking and waiting for that utter weariness which came to him before sleep. The boys had been quiet, listening to the wind and playing with the dog. "Which one you want first, Lorry?"

"It seems to me like the red one is the fattest."

"I think so," he said. "Might as well do the hard one now. You boys get poles and separate those two hogs in the pen tomorrow morning."

The boys watched him expectantly.

"And don't feed that red hog tomorrow, but give it water."

The boys nodded.

"And don't feel sorry for it," Mooney said. "I've told you afore about making pets out of stock."

The boys pressed their lips together and stared at the fire.

"They told me up in Pennsylvania that it's a sign of bad luck to have pity on what you've got to kill. It's not right to the hog, or sheep, or whatever. So drag saplings tomorrow morning and separate them two and just feed one, you hear?"

He went outdoors and went down to the fattening pen, where the two hogs were. The boar heard him coming and began to grunt, so he spoke to him and the boar got quiet again.

He looked down at the two big hogs, lying on their sides on the ground, too fat to want to rise. "How you, Poppy?" he said to the big red one, then turned away. It didn't do to pity them, he knew that.

Two mornings later he took his ax and went down to the pen. He removed the roof logs from the place where the big red one was.

The hog got to his feet and looked up at him.

"You boys go get the horse and chain," he said.

He spat on his hands and lifted the ax. Swiftly he brought the ax down, striking the hog between the eye and the ear, and the hog crumpled to the ground.

He took the side logs out of the pen, hooked the chain onto the hog and dragged the carcass out. He bled the hog, then pulled it on up to the black pot, where Lorry was heating water.

The water was steaming but not boiling. He tested the water the way he had learned in Pennsylvania: he dipped his finger into it quickly several times in succession, to see how many times it took before the water scalded his skin. It scalded him slightly on the third time, so it was all right, as he told Lorry. If it burned on the first or second time, it was too hot for hog-singeing and might cause the hair and bristles on the hog's skin to set.

He and Verlin lifted the hog and set its rear end into the water. He had a smile at the sight, for the hog seemed to be resting there, taking a bath, its front hoofs poking out.

When the rear half was steamed hot, they put the head-half in; then he and the boys scraped the skin while Lorry emptied the pot.

He cut through the skin and cleanly cut off the hams and shoulders. He cut out the spare ribs and side meat, and Lorry took each section as he gave it to her and laid it in the rinsed-out pot, which was set on the ground and was cool. He cut off the leaf fat and she put that into the pot. It came off easily, for the carcass was still warm. He gave Lorry the heart and she put that into the pot.

He pulled the hide off the carcass, what was left of it, and told the boys to grain it before it hardened, then he went up on the side of the hill and sat down near the grave and rested, for he was tired. He hated worse than anything slaughtering stock.

When he got back to the cabin, there was the smell of fresh pork coming from the hearth pot, and Lorry had a bowl of honey on the table. She had taken some of the dried corn and had milled it. A pone of bread was on the heat rock, and the promise of the place, of the farm and of the valley and of the family, came to him, and he welcomed it. They fell to eating and ate all that was cooked, and talked in pleasure about what they had.

That afternoon they tended the stock, and it was evening when they carried the pieces of pork up the loft steps and laid them out on a board. Salt was rubbed into the hams and shoulders until the meat sweated and caked the salt. The slabs of bacon, which weighed forty pounds apiece, were cut into three parts each and were salted and stacked. The hams, which weighted over twenty pounds apiece, were placed skin side down next to the shoulders.

When this was done, at the last light of day, they stood back and looked on at the sight, at the white meat which had pink in it and which looked gray because of the whiteness of the salt. "It makes you feel wealthy," Lorry said.

"Those hams and shoulders look like little animals cuddled down for the winter," Mooney said.

"How long will they stay like that?" Verlin asked.

"Forty, fifty days," Mooney said. "The colder it is, the longer they stay. They get the salt in them to the bone, then they can't spoil."

"Not ever?" the boy said.

"For years, anyway, especially if you smoke them when they're cured."

"I like it smoked might nigh as well as plain," Lorry said.

"No need," he said, "no need to smoke them here, though smoking keeps the flies off."

"It's a pretty sight," she said. They stood there looking at the store of meat, until at last they went down the ladder and ate another meal of fresh meat, field beans and hot bread.

That night a bear came to the clearing and ate the scraps that were left. The boys had hung the pigskin on the side of the crib, and the bear sniffed about that. Mooney shouted at it from the door, trying to scare it away, and the bear turned toward the cabin, bewildered by what he saw— a yellow-lighted doorway, open like the mouth of a giant animal, and in the mouth a creature as thin and sharp as a snake's tongue.

The bear growled and tore at the pigskin.

"Get gone, get gone," Mooney said angrily.

The bear woofed and ignored him.

"Hold that dog," Mooney told the boys. "Don't let her get free." Both boys had ahold of her.

The bear waddled off to the side of the crib and stopped there, but it looked back at the cabin, then began to sniff around the crib.

"He's still hungry for meat," Mooney said. "You boys bury what we have left of that other hog tomorrow, you hear?"

"The bears will still smell it," Verlin said.

"I don't need advice right now," Mooney said.

The bear backed away from the crib, then went close to it again, struck it a mighty blow with his paw, and the sound of the blow echoed back from across the river. He sucked at his paw, then struck the crib again, and the side of the crib trembled.

The horses began to move about inside the shed, frightened now, and to press against the shed door. The sheep moved in their pen, seeking a way out.

Mooney raised his rifle to his shoulder, braced his arm against the doorjam, and fired.

He closed the door and Lorry bolted it with a pole. He went to the bed quickly and began to load. The bear struck the door with his paw, and the door trembled in its holds.

The bear struck the door again. Chinking fell from behind the logs on that side of the cabin and the door flew open. The bear started forward and Mooney fired from beside the bed. The bear hurtled backward, for the shot hit a bone. At the same moment the young dog tore loose from the boys and moved toward the bear, leaped against it, trying to grab hold of its jaw with her mouth. There was a heap of bear and dog tumbling about in the yard. The bear got up and started back for the house, but Lorry threw a lighted piece of firewood at it, and the bear turned and started across the clearing, the dog snapping at it. Mooney took up the ax and ran after them, calling to the dog, but the dog went on.

Mooney stumbled over a piece of a sapling log and fell heavily to the ground. He got up, feeling of his shin, which was paining. Far off he heard his dog, baying.

He limped back to the house. "Where's the gun?"

Lorry handed it to him and he loaded it. "You stay here," he said to the boys, and turned and ran up through the clearing. Verlin moved to the door, but Lorry caught hold of him and held him. "You do what he told you," she ordered.

Verlin pulled free of her. "I'm going," he said, and fleet as a small animal, he dashed away.

Way off they heard the dog and moved toward it, seeking to stay on the trail in the darkness. "That bear'll tear my dog up," Mooney said.

Verlin was huffing for breath. "Will he kill her?"

"If she's got no better sense than she's shown so far, he will. I didn't know she would go chasing after a bear. She's not even of full size yet."

"I tried to hold her."

"A female's not usually so prompt to fight."

The path was steep. He moved with heavy breathing. Prickly limbs of bushes slashed at him, but that only made him more determined.

High on the mountain he stopped at the laurel slicks, a matted jungle of rhododendron bushes. The bear had gone into it.

He looked off to the right, up above the slick, toward where the dog was still baying. "I'm going through it," he said. "You want to come?"

"I think so," Verlin said.

"Stay close then."

The trails twisted and turned, and all he could see were the tall, stiff bushes around him, closing in even the sky above him, closing out the moon and stars. Now he was in the world of mountain secrets, of lost ways and weasels.

The dog's voice came from uphill, so he went that way. He reached the end of a path, had to back up and find another way. "Get in these hells and can't get out," he said. "Can't see a speck of light even."

Verlin was holding to his shirt now, for he couldn't see to follow. Mooney was stumbling over bush roots and sticks, and the loose rocks slipped under his feet sometimes.

He walked until he had little strength left. His breathing was coming hard, for he was tense as well as weary, and he was angry at all that was wrong. "You ever want to kill something, boy?" he said.

The boy's teeth were chattering from fear and the cold.

"I'd kill these bushes. They're pretty when they bloom, but they're hells all year along. What's pretty is not allus safe, I tell you."

"Are we going on?"

"Yes. I'm just listening. That dog has moved, ain't she?"

"I don't know. Maybe we moved."

"But that dog moved across the ridge there, didn't she?"

"I don't know."

"She must have, for she's not within sound of us now."

The wind felt noisily of the rocks, but in the limbs of the bushes not even a whisper was made. "There's a big open space at the top of this slick," he said.

"The mountaintop, it's clear."

"Uh huh," Mooney said. "I'm going on up there."

He pushed his way along the narrowing path, moving until the bushes stopped him. He braced himself and pushed hard and the bushes let him advance a short way. He moved on, but the bushes began to come lower over his head, so that they had to bend to get through. He fell to his hands and knees and, pushing his gun ahead of him, began to crawl. "Don't you ever come alone in one of these, you hear me?"

"Yes," Verlin said breathlessly.

"Come in here and not be able to get out by yourself." The bushes began to close tighter around him. Branches poked at his face and eyes and throat. His body was aching. "We're almost to the top of it."

"How you know?"

"I know when I get to the top of a laurel slick, don't you worry about that." He rubbed his torn skin with his fingers. "Huh," he said, grunting. "I'll tan that dog's hide if I ever catch her."

He crawled until the bush limbs pressed down so tightly he had to lie on his belly. He slithered through, pushing the gun ahead, pulling himself forward by grasping at bush trunks. He tried to get back on his hands and knees, but the limbs wouldn't let him.

He stopped. He lay there on his belly on the ground, panting for breath. He wanted to start fighting the slicks, try to break through, but he knew that wouldn't do any good.

Something moved in the bushes. It went away, breaking through the bushes. Some beast or other.

"We're about at the top," he said to the boy. "Not far to go." He began creeping forward, pulling at the bushes. He grasped at a bush, and something damp moved from his fingers, went away, and he froze on the ground. A small beast he guessed. A rat, maybe.

He forced himself to reach for the bush trunk once more. He pulled himself forward. He tried to push himself to his hands and knees but couldn't. He reached out and grasped a trunk and pulled himself forward. He forced himself to grasp another trunk, and another, until he stopped thinking about it, and he went on until there was no trunk to grab hold of.

His mind returned to thought and he asked himself what had happened. He lay there wondering. He reached out, feeling, seeking. There was no bush to grasp. He turned his head, looked up and saw the stars near where the mountain stopped.

"I told you we was near the top," he said.

They lay there side by side until they had their breath. The boy got up slowly. "I lost my shirt," he said.

"Huh?" Mooney said. He sniffed the chilly air. "Law, that was something."

"I'm bleeding some."

"Don't never go into one of those slicks," he said. Painfully he took a few steps toward the gap.

They were on a rock shelf and there was light now, drifting down from the moon. The rock shelf was near the mountaintop, which was a deer and elk pasture; the moonlight reflected on the rock and the pasture. Being here was like being small in a great land. Here a man was no bigger than a gnat on the belly of a horse, he thought.

They came to the balsam woods and stopped, awed by the utter darkness before them. They moved into them slowly. The wind whined; the trees moaned and solemnly honed their limbs.

He heard the dog again, far off. The hound note held, then shifted in a changing breeze.

"She's some'ers on beyond the mountain."

He backed away from the great trees and moved into the open once again. Clouds were racing by, not far above their heads.

Verlin was close enough to brush against him. Mooney put his hand on the boy's head. A boy was like a pup, he thought, a friendly pup and it whining. "Your mama's down there worried about us. We go tearing off like crazy men, chasing a bear. Look a there, you tore your shirt off your back, Verlin."

"I told you I done it."

"Look at you. You got no pants on, either. Verlin, you ain't got a stitch left on yer back."

Verlin looked solemn. He had been scared nigh to death in that slick, and there was no humor in any of it to him.

"Your mama's going to skin you alive. My Lord in Heaven, boy."

"I didn't mean to," Verlin said grumpily.

"Well, we've going to get you out of the cold." He found a crevice which he poked about in for snakes; he crept into it and Verlin followed. Mooney gave him his hunting shirt to put on. "Verlin, don't you tell your mama we went in a laurel slick, you hear?" he said.

"What am I going to say?"

"You think of a way to explain it. Look a there," he said, pointing toward the top of the mountain where now white clouds were passing. "Huh," he said. He huddled against the rock. "You see the settlement? See down there. One cabin is sending up sparks. Might be Paul Larkins', or maybe the German's." He rubbed his arms to warm them. "We'll stay here safe," he said, "until we warm; then we'll go find the dog."

They moved along the side of the mountain, high up near the peak. They followed the sound, hurrying, slapping into tree limbs, moving fast. They came to another, smaller laurel slick and stopped, then sighed, moved on, seeking an opening. He found one and went into it, holding the rifle before him.

He crashed his way along, the boy behind him. The barking had a closer sound to it now.

They came to the end of the slick, and before them was a great rock. He climbed the slope of it, tapping the gun stock against it to warn the snakes. He got to the top, the boy following, and stopped to rest. The barking was close by.

They moved quickly and quietly until they saw the dog sitting near the trunk of a hickory tree. She saw him approach, but no change came into her howl. Like music, it was very much like music, he thought.

He crept close. He saw nothing above; then abruptly high up he saw two eyes sparkle as the bear looked down. He aimed and fired.

There was a grunt. Nothing more.

He took out tow, took off the ramrod and was ramming home the shot when there came a sound of cracking limbs above. The bear was coming down. The bear fell, fell on his stomach and didn't move.

The dog came over to the mound of fur, her tongue hanging out. She sat down near the bear's head and considered it speculatively. She stretched out on her stomach, so tired she could scarcely move, and with a lazy, weary motion, fastened her mouth to the bear's neck.

"I'll tell you this," Mooney said quietly to Verlin, "we've got us a good dog there."

Small pieces of pigskin, fat and cracklin's, which had been put back, Lorry boiled outdoors in the pot, then left to cool. By evening there was a layer of white grease on the top of the pot, and she ladled that off to keep.

She emptied the pot and put lye water in it, water which she had let soak through hickory ashes overnight. She boiled the lye water until it would float an egg. She put the grease into it and stirred it with a sassafras stick.

When the bark on the stick began to get stringy, she set the grease to cool.

Mooney put the boys to work on a log, scooping it out. He and the boys lifted it onto the pile of wood next to the door of the cabin. That done, he went over to where she was. "I'll say this," he said, "you stay with your work."

"I do no mor'n I have to."

"You don't lose a day, and act like every one is a race to sunset," he said.

"I don't know why you tell me that," she said, pleased.

She helped Mooney on another day tan the leather he had made. The tanning trough was where oak bark had been soaked in water for most of the year, the bark being changed from time to time. On the tanning day she brought ashes from the hearth, dumped them into it for lye, and stirred the mixture.

He fetched the pigskins and the bear hide, and two deerskins. He left them in the trough until the hair would slip, then laid them over a barked log and worked them until they were pliable. "I'm going to cut new harness from the best of this bearskin," he told her. "I'll need new harness if I'm to clear more land this winter."

"You need you a good pair of boots," she told him.

"I'd like to have a pair of boots," he admitted.

"Verlin is still nigh about naked," she said.

He glanced at her to see how angry she was with him. "We can cut him a pair of pants out of a deerskin."

"If you cut one boy's pants, you've got to cut the other'n a pair."

He thought about that. He needed leather; he needed twangs and slings, harness and shoes.

"I can make them a linen shirt apiece this winter," she said, "or one of linsey, if we use part of the wool."

"We'll get them clothed," he said. "Cut each boy deerskin pants, and we'll use the hogskins for a shirt apiece. Maybe we can split them."

"What about yourself?" she said. "You need a shirt."

"I'll kill a deer or two when I can."

It would be well to shear the lambs, yes, and shear the ewes again, Lorry thought. She had put off mentioning it earlier. Her mother had told her that no lamb's fleece should be cut without the woman saying what the fleece would be used for. Lorry was waiting, hoping she could have a baby started in her womb before lamb-shearing had to be done.

There was herb-gathering yet to do, too, even though late fall was not as good a time as spring for it. Any number of illnesses and afflictions might strike them during the winter, however, and they needed to do what they could to prepare. She had learned from her mother how to cure the agues, which chill and fever a body, the cahexia, diarrhea, dysentery; she knew how to tonic a colic or a cholera morbus, how to stop convulsions or web-treat a wound; she knew the symptoms of ringworm and whooping cough; she had cures for rashes, prickly heats and the itch. Her mind was busy with information about cures, spells, roots and bark. "We've got herbs to gather soon," she had said many a night since summer, but there had always been something else Mooney wanted to do first. "We ought to get the herbs afore all the leaves fall," she told him many times. He would nod and promise her a day, but it all went by somehow. Then one night she said they must gather the herbs next morning if they planned to do so at all, and Mooney didn't say any different.

So she brought baskets from the loft and shook them out. She got gourds ready, too. She came to the fire and sat down, and quietly but firmly said, "Verlin, you stay here tomorrow; Fate, you come with us."

Mooney looked up sharply, startled by her interference, but she returned his gaze firmly. After all, herb-gathering was a woman's task and she should be able to choose the child she wanted to help her.

Mooney turned from her. He studied the birch flames on the hearth, aware that both boys were waiting for his view. "Verlin, tomorrow while you're stock-watching, you can weave me a trap for coons," he said. "Get some canes and split them into twos and fours."

Boneset they found in the valley near the roots of a chestnut tree. Boneset tea was good for colds. Lorry told Mooney they needed tar of the pine, ooze of the sweet gum, and spirit of the beech, so he tapped three trees and fastened half-gourds to their bark. Pennyroyal, the best thing in the world for pneumonia, they found in plenty. They came upon a bed of galax and Fate bundled a hundred waxen leaves with honeysuckle vine. Mooney noticed a stand of ginseng and Lorry dug them up carefully so as not to break the roots.

They looked for pokeroot, which was needed for the itch, and red alder, which could be made into a tea for hives. They gathered dock leaves, which would make a poultice to draw the soreness out of boils.

She needed belladonna for lessening pain, so they sought the deadly night-shade plant. She needed leopard's bane. She needed acid from the prickly ash and the roots of the blackberry brier.

They walked on up the mountain, gathering and discussing and thinking about where they might eat the lunch Lorry had brought. Now and then they would stop to rest, or to gather a kind of leaf or bark. "I declare, I thought I saw a flash of cloth through the woods over there," Lorry said at one point, looking off toward a stand of tulip trees.

Mooney looked in that direction. So did Fate. "What do you suppose it might be, Fate?" he asked him.

The boy's big dark eyes turned up to him questioningly.

"Looked like a swish of colored cloth," Lorry said.

It might be Mina, Mooney thought. "Mina, you over there?" he called. There was no answer. "She's probably hiding out from us," he said.

They cut a length of wild-cherry bark and wound it into a roll. They climbed higher on the mountain, cutting a patch of seneca along the way. They stopped to rest near the balsam grove high up. Balsam was the best herb for kidney ailments, he knew, and he cut bark from a tree on the edge of the woods. He didn't want to go into the woods, if he could help it, for such places were houses of spirits and the devil. Only a few shafts of light filtered through the heavy branches. On the floor were no bushes or shrubs, only moss and ferns, which had moisture clinging to them. A balsam woods was a coffin, he thought; there was no way for a beast to live in there, or even for a flower to bloom. It was the place old beasts most likely went to die, when they had lorded over the wilderness as long as they cared to and were weary of warding off death, when they were ready to find death and say to him: Do what you have in mind to do. Then the moss would cushion them on itself. Perhaps a buzzard would find a way down along one of the shafts of light to tear away the flesh. The moss someday would cover the bones.

There was a ledge nearby with a path leading up to it. As they climbed the path, they caught glimpses of the valley below them. Past limbs of beech trees, they saw the Harrison clearing, a patch of brown in a thickly green sea. Mooney saw his own smaller place, with a smoky chimney, a shed, a lambing pen, and below the house the pigpens. He could see Verlin and the dog walking across the lower part of the clearing. From the last bend on the path, he could see the German's clearing.

Still looking and talking, they went on up the little path, and from the top of the ledge they could see it all, see every clearing, see the river, see the trail in the valley and decide where the trail must be that went along the mountainside, and where the valley trail, which was becoming a road, it was used so often. He was caught up in wondering at the sights, in marveling at the sense of accomplishment it gave him, when he noticed Fate's eyes widen with surprise. Mooney turned, and there, sitting at the back of the ledge, was Mina Plover, a big smile on her face. She began to giggle at the looks on the faces of the three people who were so startled to see her.

She walked home with them, and helped them cut aspen bark, for it would relieve muscle pain. They cut a root from an elm tree and peeled off the bark. The bark could be beaten into a pulp and dried in the cabin chimney; it would heal wounds, Lorry said.

From the edge of their clearing, they collected holly berries, which could be used to purge with—eight or ten berries for a single dose, Lorry said. They cut sassafras bark and sassafras roots, which would make a strengthening tea.

They arrived home and dumped down their store of supplies in the far fireplace corner, and at once the cabin smelled richly of sap and bark, of roots and moldy earth. A person could feel safe to live here now, Mina said, with such herb smells to drive away sickness.

Even Fate was pleased. Normally he was shy and reticent about anything Mooney did, but he was happy with the store of herbs and even smiled at Mooney now and was pleasant to him. After Mina was gone, Mooney asked Fate a good many questions about their tour of the mountains, and the boy answered them and told Verlin, often with enthusiasm, about what they had done and where they had gone. The change in the boy pleased Mooney and surprised him.

After supper he went outdoors and stood near the lambing pen, where he often went to listen to the night creatures, and directly Fate came outside, too, and began to walk about, waiting for Mooney to speak to him. Mooney went on up to Imy's grave and sat down there on a rock, and he began to talk, not to the boy, who was a fair distance away, but to the grave. He had done so before once in a while, telling Imy what had happened of a day; and Lorry, though she always frowned when she saw him sitting up there, had never objected.

He told Imy what had happened gathering the herbs. He was talking along that way when he saw Fate move up along the west border of the clearing, stopping from time to time as if he were listening for something.

"Imy, we been out gathering herbs," Mooney said quietly. Out of the corner of his eye he saw that Fate had heard him talking. "One spring you and me got a few, but today we harvested a stock that will carry us for a long while, mor'n a year, though we'll collect others along in the spring when sap comes easier."

The boy was trying to hear him.

"Verlin stayed home and tried to make a trap. He fashioned a piece of one. It's not going to do, but we'll weave it again tonight or tomorrow night. A boy learns by trying, and when he's tried and not done well, he can be taught easier. A man can't teach a boy much that the boy's not tried to do for himself."

He heard Fate moving slowly up behind him in the bushes.

"Fate was with us today, Imy. We don't ordinarily say more'n a dozen words to each other in a day, and they're not words that pry into a matter, but we got along today without argument."

Down below, the doorway of the cabin was yellowing from firelight. He could see Lorry moving about inside, putting the herbs away. Below the cabin, Verlin was leading the ram up toward the pen.

"I can't talk to Fate about some matters. I can't tell him why it is his mama needed to marry again, for that's something a person grows up to know in feeling more than in mind. I can't tell him why his papa left and didn't come back, for I don't know. Lord, it's not something I can figure out, for it's unlikely that a man would do something like that. Fate and me can't sit down and reason out these matters, not yet, and maybe not ever, for it's chancey to talk about another person."

He was quiet and listening.

"I can see some matters we might discuss, him and me. I'm thinking of such as my coming into his house down there in the valley and making things over my way, when he had been taking care of his mama right along. I couldn't a been more plain and blunt than I was, and he had a right to play an angry part with me for it. He had a nice farm there for his mama. He had sheep and chickens, and there I come and changed it all around, took everything off to my place, without talking it over, showing him and his mama and Verlin my place, how it all was bigger here and better. I went in there and whacked my way through. A man can do that.

A man as big as me is accustomed to doing his work that way, accustomed to telling stock what to do, to wade in on anything and lash out, moving whatever is in his way, cutting down or plowing up. A man works that way, but I needed to show a difference here, for the boy wasn't a piece of stock or land. He was a man, not grown yet, but accustomed to his own way, and I wish I had gone about it differently."

He was silent and waiting. He could hear the boy breathing, that was all. Then he heard a catch in the boy's breathing and that tiny sound went through him like a shaft of pain. He closed his eyes tightly, hoping the boy would not sob, would not give in to the pity inside him.

The breathing steadied. Mooney was grateful for that. "I saw where some of the chinking has come out near the chimney, Imy," he said simply. "We need to put little rocks in there and some wet clay. I suppose we can use that clay out of the branch, that of it which is gray, and there's plenty of rocks about." He let the words settle and the night sounds sweep over him. He stood, brushed the dirt off his pants. "It would be a big help to get that chinking done," he said quietly, then went down the path, walking slowly, went to the lambing pen, where Verlin was working. He glanced back only once and saw the huddled figure of the boy, there just above Imy's grave.

On the next afternoon, in the cool of the day, when he was free for a little while from sheep-tending, Fate went down to the creek and brought back rocks and some of the light-gray clay, and mended the chimney.

The family got the sheep into the pen and one by one Mooney and Lorry hobbled and sheared the ewes. When it came time for the lambs, Lorry hesitated for a moment before cutting on the first one; then quietly, firmly, she said, "The wool's to be used for a baby's things." She noticed the barest flicker of a glance which revealed that Mooney had heard her.

"When's it to be?" he said.

"It's not far along," she said.

"Summer then, is that it?" he said.

"Summer might be," she said. Yes, he was pleased, she could tell, and so was she, for this was another way to hold the family together, and was an answer to any question of their right to live together.

"These lambs are going to be cold as a bare-bottomed baby in the snow," he said, suddenly cheerful. "But they don't have as much feeling as a man for coldness, anyhow. Not much feeling or sense, either. A lamb is a fool-stunted thing, and so is a ram."

"I don't know as they are," she said, gently patting the head of the frightened, shivering animal.

"They're pretty, I'll admit that, and cute as a pearl button, but they're not sensey."

He's talking about sheep, she thought, but he's wondering about the baby, what it will be in kind, how it will grow, how he will tend to it and I will tend to it.

They washed the wool in the pool below the spring. The next day they washed it again. On the third day she sent the boys to the top of the cabin with it, to spread it out on the roof boards in the sun.

There it lay, drying and growing fluffy, setting off the cabin prettily, she thought. She walked up the hill a ways and looked down at it and at the boys, scampering about, chasing the naked sheep off to the grazing places in the woods.

Mooney came up the hill to where she was. "I've not seen such a sight in years," he said.

"Nor I," she said.

He gazed down at the house, proud and comfortable to see everything so well done.

After supper they sat at the fire and he whittled at pegs, which he would need to put together the wheel and the loom. He listened to Lorry as she read to the boys a story about David and the giant, who met in a battle in the great valley of Elah long ago. She taught the boys to read some of the words, those they didn't already know. Then she went with them up the ladder to the loft and snaked the pallets for them and came back down and brought the chair up close to the fire.

She folded her hands on her lap. "It's so pleasant of an evening," she said. And the fire was so pretty, yellow and white, burning scarcely at all, so that the place was almost dark, even at the fireside. She looked over at him longingly, languidly, and he looked at her.

She got up sleepily and went to the shadowed corner across from the fire. She took off her dress and hung it on a wall peg, took off her other things, climbed into the bed and covered up to her chin. She lay looking at the loft floor above her, so safe and content, feeling like that.

He sat by the fire, whittling on pegs, setting them aside as he finished each one. When he was done, he got up and stretched. He came over to the bed and looked down at her. It pleased her, the way he looked at her. She heard him taking off his things and soon his body was close to her, and she turned herself into his arms.

She lay there, weary and comfortable, listening to the fire burn; she knew that far above them the tree limbs moved in the moon-lighted wind. They had come to be a family, she thought, more here than in Virginia, more here than she had known a family could be part of itself, safe unto itself, in a house that smelled of cooking and herbs and wool and wine vinegar, each one in its special season, as the family made for itself comfort and protection. All that lies about us is foreign to us yet, she thought, but here we are, come together, and closer will we come.

II

E rnest Plover, when the first bitter cold snap fell upon the valley, took to the bed sick. Inez tended to him, made boneset tea for him, which did him good, but he didn't like the taste, so she used what ginger she had and such sage as she could borrow form Anna Bentz and made a better-tasting tea for him. Also, she did as Nicholas advised and fed him kraut juice of a morning.

On seeing how much attention a cold could gain, some of the smaller children came down sick, too, and before long the Germans claimed they had no more boneset, and Inez felt called upon to send Mina to the woods to find some.

Mina did poorly at the task. She didn't like to tromp about looking for herbs with snow on the ground and all the leaves gone off the plants. What in the world could she find? She pulled up a few roots and went home with them, said they were boneset roots, and her mama made tea. It was so powerful a tonic that Ernest and the children were panicked into thinking they had rather be well than to suffer such medicine.

They were too bleak—the woods of a wintertime, Mina thought. The laurel was green, but the leaves curled to protect themselves from coldness; the bushes looked ill. The woods were bare and hateful-looking; every thorn and thicket stood out plain. Dotted underfoot were the patches of galax, which was always pretty and waxen, and there was wintergreen, which she liked, and sometimes overhead in an oak would be a ball of mistletoe. But these specks of green only set off the greater colorlessness and coldness.

When the forest floor was snow-covered, she couldn't walk far, for the snow bit at her feet like an animal. She would see where the bouncy rabbits had been through, crossing one another's paths, and she wondered how in the world they could stand the sting of it, and how they lived in the winter anyhow, and why they didn't do like the bears and go to dens and cuddle up and sleep for the cold time. Even the bats were asleep in the caves. Sometimes she saw a raccoon track, but even they were snoozing longer than the night each day. Frogs and toads were quiet, too, and for all she knew they and the bees and hornets were asleep.

But the rabbits were about, they and the foxes and wolves. The wolves were coming closer, seemed to her. They had been up on the mountaintop for a while, but now their lonely howls were close by. And the foxes were slick and hungry. They had got into her father's chicken lot and done much damage. They would tunnel, leap, tear, bark—somehow they would make a way through. It had been every morning's work to fix the fences back, until the German came by and cut saplings and vines and leather and made the fences so that they held.

Mina liked the German very well. He was a strong and handsome body of a man, and was friendly. She sometimes managed to go to his house to get juice or herbs, or to return a jar. The first time she went, she told him about walking through the woods alone, even up on the mountain, and he had cautioned her against that. He talked so nice to her. He was gentle in everything he did and said and seemed to like her, and when she was about to leave, she said she didn't know how in the world she was going to get back home through the woods, it being so dangerous and all, and he said he would walk her.

A look had come over his wife's face that would have frozen a thought, and the young German, Felix, had quickly offered to walk her home himself, but Nicholas said he would go, that he wanted to talk with Ernest about something, anyway.

They walked along the trail together. They walked side by side, for she liked to walk that way, until it narrowed to a path, and then she walked ahead. She guessed he was watching her walk. She had seen a keenness come into his eyes once or twice before when he had been looking at her. Wasn't it strange about the way a man would look at a woman sometimes, she thought, at least the way they looked at her, and had since she was a girl. Her dress was so tight and thin, she knew he had a view, all right.

————

At night, when the boys were fretful with their lessons, Lorry would have them shell corn into a basket, and from the shelled grain take out the colored grains. Every ear, seemed like, was speckled with blue and red. She would have them select the best of the white grains, and these, when they had enough of them, she would boil in water in which she had put a little of the lye from the ash hopper, enough to yellow the corn hulls. She would boil this until the corn was no more than half done, then she would dip the corn out and pour it into a basket, from which the water ran out. She would carry the basket of steaming corn to the spring and wash it, shaking the corn and rubbing it, freeing the kernel from the hulls.

She would then walk the basket back to the pot, carry more water from the spring, and boil the grain again. Later she dipped it out as before and washed it. Then she boiled it until it was tender.

The boys liked this hominy, so she made some every week. It would keep for two days if put in the kitchen or for three or four days if put in the loft.

The rest of the shelled corn would be ground into meal. The finer bits would be sifted out for bread, and the coarser ones would be stored for grits. She did most of this work herself, though the baby was taking on size within her and sapped her strength.

She carded the wool and spun it on the wheel, and she spun the flax. She could relax as she made cloth. She could sit there at the loom and listen to the boys talk and watch Mooney work on wood and leather. The shuttle murmured under her hand, and there was the steady thud of the batten striking the web, sounds which settled in nicely with the fire sounds. She would tramp the treadles, all without conscious thought, for she had done it in many winters before this one, had made cloth for her boys before this time, and cloth for a husband before this one. The flax was on the loom, dyed light tan from the black walnut bark, and she threw the shuttle, carrying yarn of undyed lamb's wool, through it, and the cloth inch by inch came from the loom night by night. It was a loosely woven cloth, but once she had put it in the dye pot and the dye had struck the lamb's wool, once the new wool soaked it up, it would shrink around the linen with a tight grip.

She had all too little of the lamb's wool for her needs, and half of it she would weave not with linen at all, but into itself, to make soft cloth for the baby. Later, from the flax, she would make a piece of cloth for the baby, too, as well as tow for the gun barrel and dress cloth for herself.

But from the linsey cloth, the strongest of all, she would make a shirt apiece for the boys, and a shirt for Mooney.

He was making a pack saddle while she worked. He had cut a forked limb out of white oak; he had looked for two days in the woods for just the right one, and he had had to climb high in the tree just to get it. He had whittled it down to fit the horse's back, and to each fork of the prong he pegged a board into which he had drilled holes, and into each hole he inserted and bound a wooden ring.

They worked until late most nights, and liked to work. Toward the end of evening he might put a log of birch on the fire, for it threw such pretty flames to talk about. She could see faces in the flames; it was if other people were there in the room, people long since forgotten, or old ancestors never known, who had come to keep them company.

He would talk of plans, and of what he had heard. The German had told him his wife made a yellow dye from crushed chestnut hulls and a bit of alum. Also he had heard that old man Harrison had gone to ride, to see that everything on his farm was set for the wintertime, and his shoes had frozen to the wooden stirrups. There was no way for him to get off his horse except to get out of his boots, which took some doing. Ernest Plover had seen it, or said he had.

Or had made up the story, Lorry said.

The boys might mention a chipmunk which stayed not far from the spring and could be found on almost any warm winter morning, waiting there.

"The laurel buds are big," Lorry said. "The dogwood buttons are almost off their stems from being so fat. It's going to be an opening out for certain, come spring." And she said, "The cardinals are so frigid with the cold, I give them a handful of bread this morning when I milked. That's why I put that little piece of bread atop the door lintel tonight, to save it for them. They're such pretty birds to stay here through such a wintertime…"

They talked so softly that not a sound got through the chinked walls of their place.

And down the valley road, Inez would be talking to her brood, getting them bedded down on the floor for the night, for as yet they had no loft.

And farther along the Germans were doing their firelight work, and the fire threw shadows into the lines of Nicholas Bentz's somber face as he carved on a small wooden toy, which he was going to give Mina Plover. As he sat there near his wife, he thought about Mina and wondered if ever he would dare touch her, hold her, love her.

We are set in the world, Nicholas thought, we are set not adrift as on a sea, for the sea supports whatever floats on it; we are adrift in the air and move like dried leaves whisked about, subject any moment to the falling to the ground, to age-olding, to the open grave or leaf-molding.

Anna, rocking back and forth on a small stool, spoke to Felix, asked him if he was sleepy yet. She looked deeply into Nicholas' face, wondering what thoughts were in his mind now, for he had been moody for several days.

At first, coming to this new place had been a help to him, and to them all. Work had healed many of his worries, and the climate had set well with him. Not long after their arrival she had been surprised one night to awake to find him clutching her, seeking her passionately. She had yielded to his needs and she had felt again ever so completely the craving of him, as if he were seeking life, were trying to free himself into life. She thought as she wrestled with him that he was wrestling with life itself, and the thought came to her that he would surely kill himself before he found comfort complete enough to satisfy himself.

"What are you carving?" she asked him.

"A doll," he said.

"For the girl?" she said, meaning her daughter.

"Yes, for the girl," he said.

Paul and Nancy Larkins fastened their door for the night, which meant that three stiff poles were lowered into place. Mooney Wright's experience with bears had shown that only the thickest and best-guarded door would offer protection.

Paul stooped before the big fireplace and piled wood into it. His chimney had a good drawing power, and fire-steam and smoke swelled up with a roar.

"What do you suppose the bears think of that noise when they hear it?" Nancy asked, yawning sleepily.

"They probably think this house is a beast of some sort," he said.

"They don't have much mind, no doubt, though I've seen clever dogs and such afore."

"They're not clever like you and me," he said, winking at her.

She looked at him with half-closed eyes. "You're crazy as a bird," she said.

"You and me are," he said. "A bird in a birdhouse that's all tight and newly made." He poked his hand against the wall. "Solid as can be. Nothing can get in here, unless it can break down that door. Look how that roof is tight and it's weighed down, too. Hardly can a noise get in this place."

"Or out of it, either," she said. "We can sit here by the fire and say whatever we please and it won't be heard by anything else."

He sat on a piece of a log which was nearby. "What shall we say?"

"We can talk about what we'll name the baby."

"What sort of secret is that?"

"A nice secret, I think."

"I'd rather talk about how babies get made."

"I would rather name the baby."

"I remember the first time I was ever alone with you, at the place your wagon broke down near a creek and your father had gone on down the road to get help. I said to myself then, even before I spoke to you: 'I will marry her someday.' It was the best thought I ever had, up to that time."

"Have you had better ones since?"

"About you I have."

The hissing of wood sap started as the log began to thaw out well and drip onto the coals. He began to scrape the ashes out from under the logs and scrape them into a small hole in the rock floor. He had built the fireplace near that hole for just that purpose, though Nancy had never used the hole for such, nor had he until now. They had been saving their ashes for the ash hopper to make lye.

"We will get warm as bread in here afore we go to bed," he said.

"You better put those stones nearer the fire to warm."

"They're warm now. You want them in the bed?"

"I suppose it's almost time." She carried them to the bed and tucked them under the quilt. She took off her dress and stood for a moment in her shift, watching him. She took off her shoes, untying the leather twangs and unwinding them, and she got into the bed and moved close to the wall. She stretched lazily, relaxing her muscles, and was aware vaguely that he was watching her.

He came over to the bed and sat down on the edge of it. He grasped her tightly and held her close to himself, so close she was almost hurt by him. He got up and undressed and hung his leather shirt and pants on wall pegs. He pulled off his moccasins.

He got under the quilt beside her.

They were quiet and content for a while. He said something about the gusts of wind which were sweeping down from the woods. "Maybe we'll have a storm," he said. "The roof boards will hold, though."

She murmured about the fire, which was dying down faster than usual, for ashes helped to hold a fire. "It misses its bed of ashes," she said.

"Yes, but it'll make another one soon," he said.

The fire got low and he fell asleep. She lay awake wondering about her love for him, about how deep love was and how much deeper it would be someday. She remembered what her mother had said once, that a woman could show her love for a man in so many ways, in the cooking and sewing and stock-tending and helping in the fields and comforting that she does, but a man couldn't express it so easily, for he had fewer ways.

The cabin grew dark. She got sleepy and moved closer to him and fitted her body to his and soon she dozed off.

She awoke to feel his hand moving across her hip. She lay quiet for a moment, then whispered to him, asked if he was awake.

He didn't answer. He was still breathing deeply, very much as if he were asleep.

She nudged him. The steady breathing stopped. He had awakened now, she knew, but he made no sudden move; he awakened as a hunter awakes, with few motions or signs.

The hand was moving still, or whatever creature it might be that touched her.

"What is it?" he said, speaking not to her so much as to the thing itself. He rose slightly in the bed. "Go on, get," he said suddenly.

There was no answering squeal or sound. She could feel the creature move across the bed still. It had no breath or voice.

"What is it?" he said.

In a choked voice she said she didn't know.

"I'll have to make firelight," he said. He threw the quilt back.

"There's some pine by the hearth," she said, "and resin sticks are in the basket."

He left the bed and had started for the fireplace when something bit him. He kicked at it angrily. "What the devil," he said. He took another step and was bit again. He leaped to the fireplace and dumped on the pine sticks. The fire flared up at once. It lighted the room, and he turned to see that the floor was alive with snakes. Still other snakes were slithering from the hole in the rock where the hearth ashes had been thrown. The warmth of the ashes had awakened them from their winter sleep.

He cried out in weakness, here in the first moment of fear he had ever known. "No," he said deeply. "No, God," he said. He saw her on the bed, and knew she was beyond his help now.

A pain pierced him. He felt behind him for a stick of wood and started beating at a snake.

He saw that she was standing in the corner, on the bed, the quilt held up around her. She had thrown the snakes off the quilt.

A pain came to him from his legs and struck through him. He felt his own heart suddenly leap inside him. He crawled to the woodpile and from there put more wood on the fire and on the hearth itself. She must see. She must be able to see, he thought.

With a log he covered the hole from which the snakes had come. He took a stick of wood and began to beat the snakes that were in the room, flailing about at them, feeling the stick crush in on their heads as he struck them, but the floor was wriggly with them. He beat at them and waded in among them, being bit but moving in among them, and he heard her begin to scream.

Pain throbbed and coursed through him. He wanted to touch his wife again, to touch her, but the pain swept so high he could not even hear her scream as the pain carried him away. He turned to hide himself from her and from the fear in her face, and went through the mass of snakes to the fireplace. He tried to build the fire higher so that it would hold through the night until light came in through the cracks in the roof and walls.

He could feel his heart beating, trying to escape from his injured body. He thought he must go to the door and open it, but he could not move. She must be heard down in the valley, but the door was closed; he must open the door, but he could not.

Firmly, gritting his teeth, he began to move to the door. His hands were swollen to twice their size, his body was bloated; his blood was about to be pushed out of his body through his fingers and toes, he thought. He reached the door. With pained hands he threw off one of the poles that held it shut. He tried to throw off another, but the pain engulfed him and he crumpled to the floor.

They must hear her, he thought. If he could open the door, they might hear her.

He forced his body to move. He touched the second pole. With pain he touched it, and with greater pain he threw it away from the door.

He must stand erect to reach the other pole. He stood. He stood up straight and touched it, and with pain he grasped it and threw it off. He clutched the door, opened it, threw it open and fell dead onto the stone floor of the room. She saw him fall in the fire-lighted room and she screamed, and her voice went out through the open door into the great valley.

Lorry, lying awake in her bed, nudged Mooney. He lay still for a moment, then sat up, listening. "It's only the wind," he said.

"Or a panther," she said.

He went to the door and stepped out into the yard. The air was cold and crisp tonight, more so than usual. The wind blew heavily, then relaxed for a moment, and he heard the voice, a scream of terror, not like a panther's scream, not exactly like it.

He went inside, sat down on the bed and lashed his shoes. The dog was whining, not barking but whining, as if it sensed some uncustomary dread.

He took his gun from the wall pegs. Once more the wind died down and he heard the screams. "It's a strange, fierce sound," he said. He went out into the yard and stood there listening, trying to determine which way the sound was coming from. It might be from Inez Plover's house, from Harrison's, or from Paul Larkins'. If it was from the first two, there were neighbors closer than he. If it was from the Larkins' place, he was the one who should be of help first.

"I'll go to Paul Larkins'," he told Lorry.

He had to tear two roof boards off the cabin to get to her. He had to lift her out through these. She knew only to hold to his arms and let him help her. Otherwise, her mind was in a dream of fear; it would not snap out of the dream, seemed like. She could not talk or walk, though she had not been bit, so far as he could tell.

He carried her home, and even as he walked, the mountain, as if it knew, as if it had seen the horror and had feeling and responded to emotion, the mountain and the wilderness unleashed a storm, struck with it even as he carried Nancy up the river road.

He laid her down on the bed, but she turned away from the quilt and cried out in fear of it, and left the bed, afraid of the bed, and turned wide-eyed with horror from the hearth, for he had died on a hearth, and turned with anguish from the door, for he had thrown open their door, and then sank down to the earthen floor of the cabin, weeping, then felt around her for the snakes on the floor, and all this while Mooney and Lorry were helplessly watching.

"Her people will need to come for her, as soon as they can," he said.

Above them, the mountain itself seemed to erupt, the sky broke with sounds. The wind and even the fire in the hearth groaned and roared.

The storm held bitter sway for two days; then the temperature dropped considerably and the mountain world was frozen into place. Mooney could not even get word down to the Plover house about the tragedy which had taken place, or go back to the Larkins' house to shut the door and save Paul's body from the beasts. He stalked his cabin, unsettled by the brutal ways, the wildness of the place.

For four days the world was frozen; then the sun came out and the ice began to sparkle and melt; the creeks began to break free of their bounds. There was by afternoon frequently the sound of ice breaking, of ice falling from trees and from the cabin and shed roof. There was underfoot in the yard the sound of water running off down the hill, beneath the mounds of snow. Mooney led the demented woman to Harrison's house, where a room could be provided for her and proper attention given her.

He returned home and spent the day tightening his pens, for he said a beast attack would surely come. "They've been up on that mountain waiting," he said, "and they'll be down here directly." He knew this without knowing quite how he knew it. He took the dry wood from inside the cabin and laid two fires in the farmyard and covered them to keep them dry. He moved more wood into the cabin to dry.

No sooner was it dark than they heard the howls of a great pack of wolves. The sound came from up at the Larkins' house, where the corpse was.

When the sound became a yapping more than a yowl, Mooney told the boys to light the yard fires. "Don't hurry," he said, "or you'll do worse than you ought to. We have time yet." But not much, he thought, not much.

The boys hurried to the stacks of wood, one of them near the sheds and the other near the pigpens, and lighted them.

When they were back, Mooney took his gun, went to the crib and climbed to the roof. "Go get me your gun, too," he told Lorry.

Now the sound of the wolf pack began to beat down from the rocks nearby. It reverberated and echoed and built upon itself. It seemed to cover everything, as if a flood of water were moving over them.

Lorry pushed the boys into the house and shut the door, even as the pack of wolves broke from the woods and came bounding forward. The first ones began to hurl themselves at the pigpens. The others came sweeping up the hill toward the cow and horse shed. Mooney's frightened stock set up a bedlam of cries and tried to break loose.

The gray lead wolf raced toward the shed and hurled itself at the door. The door held, but the horse began to kick, trying to free itself so it could flee.

Mooney shot the gray wolf, and at once two wolves began to rip it apart and feed on it. Mooney with the other rifle fired at a wolf which had hurled itself at the door of the lambing pen. Two other wolves leaped at the door which broke open. Mooney left the shed, ran to the door and with the butt of the rifle began to strike at the wolves, driving them back.

The fires were growing bright now; the wolves were disconcerted by the light and the crackling, roaring noise. Standing in the doorway of the lambing pen, he fought them off, until at last the fires so frightened them that they drew back. He began shouting and waving his arms at them, and abruptly the pack, as if working from a single mind, turned from him and went on, baying out their threatening challenges, moving toward Tinkler Harrison's place.

That night they did much damage there, and later destroyed the stock of the Germans', and laid waste as they chose in most of the valley.

1782

12

Three men and a woman—she the wife of one of them—arrived in February and at once began to debate whether to stay or go on to Watauga, where they had heard the best land was taken, or to the Cumberland, where they had heard the Indians were burning all that the settlers built, and were carrying off the stock and corn, too, so that a man who was rich with goods of an evening might find he had nothing by noonday of the morrow.

As it happened, the four adults arrived on a day when the monstrous bear, hungry after a period of hibernation, killed a hog of Harrison's. The following night the bear, the same one, came into their camp, waded through their pack of four dogs, and took a pig. The men were so drunk and confused they ran down the road half naked, shouting out about their loss and astonishment. Ernest Plover, dressed in his nightgown, joined them and soon others were in the road. The new men said the bear was twice as big as a barn door. They had never been as impressed in their lives, they said, and at once they released their four dogs to trail him.

Harrison came riding up to see what was the matter. There was a loud discussion, which was interrupted when over at his place his pack of dogs began running. They were loose now, too, and the valley was in an uproar of baying and excitement. Grover came up on a horse and told his father the pack had got out some way.

"Some way you had something to do with, I warrant," Harrison said.

That night the newly arrived woman, Mildred, stayed in camp alone, while her three companions were on the mountain singing songs and hunting the big bear. The wolves came around, and she chunked pieces of firewood at them; they wanted the cow and Mildred was bound not to let them have her. All night she was up, swinging firewood and calling for help. She had not so much as a pen to hide in, so she chunked firewood and prayed until dawn, when the wolves faded back into the laurel growth. Then she dropped exhausted to the ground, either fainted or died (she said later she thought she must have died), and when she awoke the sun was high up and the men were back, trooping into the settlement, drunk with whiskey and disappointment because the big bear had evaded them. They brought back their dogs, or what was left of them, for one had been killed and another had been carried off and the other two, one of them a big mongrel named London, were cut up and were far wiser than they had been.

When Mildred's husband, Amos, his brother, Frank, and their friend, Charley Turpin, got to the camp, they asked what had happened to all the firewood. She lashed into them, told them to cut some more and get ready to throw it all night, and if they wanted to stay here in this Godforsaken country, they could do so, but she wanted to go on to the Cumberland.

She might as well have been talking to the cow, for they were talking among themselves about the bear and hunting bears and what a wealth of animals there was in this place and how lucky they were to find it.

"They got more wolves here than anything else," she told them, but it didn't make any difference what she said.

That night she let them worry about the wolf pack, which came back at sundown and howled and attacked. The men were up all night laughing and drinking and shooting at the wolves, and they got a contest going about who could shoot the most of them. The wolves sang prettier than the men did, as she told them, and she vowed she wished she hadn't been the woman to agree to come along and cook for them—and she wouldn't have, except Charley Turpin had been so pleasant to her when he had asked her.

They were fiery men by nature, all right, known to be that, and if Charley hadn't injured that man at the Yadkin, they wouldn't have had to leave in the dead of night. It wasn't the court which he feared so much as the man's family—though he feared the court, too, the possibility of a trial, the stern, eyeless judge, the sentencing, the sermon, maybe even the hanging. Lord, she had seen a hanging when she was a girl, and it was pitiful, was a sight to lodge in the mind.

Charley had injured a man, had almost killed him, then had come to Mildred's husband, who was a friend and who had often idly talked of going west for better land. The two of them had got Frank into it and all three had left that night, bringing her along and the cow, which followed up the long road through Old Fort and along the Swannanoa, the road which went to Watauga.

Charley had got her into this, but he was so handsome and was such a happy man that she never could grow as angry with him as he deserved. He had been in trouble before and had got out of it, trouble with both women and men. All his life he had gone his own way like a stallion that wouldn't be tamed, and behind him was a trail of incidents to make a body's head swim with wonder, but he showed no scars. He sat on one of the best horses south of Virginia, carried a rifle with inlay on the stock, had a knife first honed in Philadelphia, and on his belt was a Cherokee tomahawk (he who had never seen an Indian in his life). The leggings, boots, pants and hunting shirt he wore were made by different women and that little hat he wore aside his head, where his black hair curled, was made for him by this latest girl, and it was her brother he had wounded in a knife fight.

The three men had fallen in line for this valley; they liked it well and had said so, but Tinkler Harrison didn't take to them. He complained about their drinking and the shooting and said he didn't think he would sell any land just then to anybody. He was angry for a fact, and stayed angry even when Charley Turpin showed he carried cash money and offered to buy a thousand acres, said he, Amos and Frank would pay one hundred dollars for it. Cash money seemed to catch Mr. Harrison's eye, all right, but even so he said he wouldn't sell to them, that he wanted the settlement to be more orderly than they had proved to be.

Mildred told him she had two daughters and four sons back in the Yadkin Valley and that Frank was a family man. Charley was the only one who didn't have a family, she said. "We're going to bring all our youngins and stock up here soon's we get cabins," she said.

When Harrison remained adamant, Charley started talking about what a pretty horse Mr. Harrison rode and how they had heard about him all the way to the Yadkin Valley and about Harristown—though they had never heard a thing, except that there was a knotty little settlement starting far up near the top of a river—and how they had traveled all this way and felt at home here. Harrison remained unimpressed, so Charley said wouldn't it be a shame if the reputation of the place should be hurt by somebody passing the word that Harristown was so sick with diseases that nobody could safely live there.

Harrison listened to that more attentively, Mildred saw, and thought about it. Charley smiled graciously and began talking about how the settlement looked like it needed a pastor. He said he could preach and had preached many times on the Yadkin, which surprised everybody (Mildred had seen him walk girls home from meetings but had never seen him inside a church). He told about how he had a way of curing sickness with prayer without the use of herbs at all. Harrison listened, thinking deeply now. Charley said he taught school on the Yadkin, too (Mildred didn't think he could read). And every once in a while he would return to the idea about the reputation of the valley. Finally, when everything had been said, Charley told Mr. Harrison, "Why don't you go on home and pray over it," and he led Mr. Harrison's horse out of the campsite onto the road, and there was nothing for Tinkler Harrison to do except ride home.

That night the three men shot at wolves and sang all night. When morning came, they ate everything Mildred cooked; then Charley got on his coal-black horse and rode down the trail to the Harrison place, the hundred dollars in cash money in his belt. When he got back, after visiting the cabins in the settlement and making himself at home, he was talking about where his cabin was to go. Also he talked about a clearing off to the side of the road where there were more pretty girls in one family than he had ever seen before, and one of them had been hanging around the Mooney Wright cabin that morning, the one who went by the name of Pearlamina, and he said he told her he would bring her a horse to ride home on that night, for he wouldn't want pretty legs to have to walk so far.

He sat down by Mildred's fire, took out a piece of deer meat he had brought back with him, which the German's wife, Anna, had given him, and warmed it on a stick, turning it frequently. He hunched over toward the blaze, talking all the while about how he wanted his cabin near the river where he could fish from his front door, and how he didn't want much land cleared near his place for he wanted to fight wolves every night, and how he would eat bear meat and deer meat and coon and cross the river for loving, as well as when he wanted to teach school or preach.

"You're a fool, Charley," Mildred told him. "You're so promising a man, and you fool your life away."

"Got to keep moving, honey," he said.

"Yes, you have, or the law will get you, or any one of half a dozen husbands."

"Hush, hush," he said, whispering to her and glancing awkwardly at Amos, which made her laugh.

"You fool," she told him, laughing at him.

"I told that Harrison I was going to clear land and settle down." He nodded emphatically. "I am, too. I'm going to cut down a tree." He propped the broiling stick with rocks and went around looking for an ax; he found one in a cart and started roving about the campsite studying trees. He stopped near the biggest one he could find, walked up to it and hit it a mighty blow, sunk the axhead well into it. Then he couldn't get it out. He looked at the ax, then up at the tree.

He backed off a ways, studying the tree. He went back to his steak and turned it. "I better stay with preaching," he said.

Mildred laughed. Amos asked him what he was going to use as a text for his first sermon. He thought about that and a big grin came over his face. He stood and looked down at them as if they were his congregation. "Friends," he said. "Dearly beloved. My text today comes from the pages of the Holy Writ and was selected with brother Harrison in mind. It reads: 'He was a stranger and I took him in.'"

That night he saddled his own horse and Amos', too, tied Mildred's blue ribbon to the saddle of Amos', and rode off with a great clatter, dashing down the trail as if the world wouldn't wait until he got to wherever it was he was going. He didn't get back until late and he was singing out at the top of his voice a song Mildred had never in all her life heard him sing:

> Oh, for a glance of heavenly day
> To take this stubborn stone away,
> And thaw with beams of love divine
> This heart, this frozen heart of mine.

He dismounted and swung around by the fire and didn't seem to pay any attention to Amos, who was waking up unhappily. He had been smitten, Mildred decided, as much as ever in his life before, if looks would tell.

"Found that pretty girl," Charley said. "I promised to take her to see the old country." He nodded emphatically. "But I didn't say when."

"What did you tell her, Charley?" Mildred asked, jealousy going through her, as it always did whenever he talked of his women friends.

"Lord, she's pretty, and she can run. Ran all the way home, and I almost killed myself trying to catch her."

"Well, doesn't sound right to me," Mildred said.

"She led me on. I thought everything was ready. Then she said something about having seen one baby born, and she commenced to run. I couldn't catch her and fell in a brook trying." He laughed out loud and kicked at the burning logs. "Hell, she's all right. You remember that Thompson girl down at the Yadkin, Amos?"

Amos glanced uneasily at Mildred. "I saw her around," he said.

Saw her around, Mildred thought. He saw her around, all right.

"Well, this one's as pretty, but she's not had as much experience, the best I can judge, except in running."

"Her father'll get hold of you with a gun," Mildred said.

"I don't think he's got one," Charley said, and laughed again. Then slowly the smile went off his face. "But Mooney Wright, he's got one, and he was there at the cabin where Mina was hanging out. He was standing by the sheep pen when I got there."

"Which man is he?" Amos asked.

"That big one. This girl's not his'n, but I don't know for sure just what their history is. He told me clear as a bell that he expected the girl to get home speedily and safe, and I thought right then the wise thing to do was give her one horse and let her go one way and me go the other, for that man must be eight foot tall when he's leaning over." He laughed and smiled at Mildred. "But I saw Pearlamina. She come to the door of that cabin up there, and she was like a tamed wild thing, all pretty, even in her faded dress, and she had a smile that flirted with her face, not sure it wanted to show itself. She looked up at me as if this was her first date and she had been thinking about it all day long. There she was, barefoot, and I'll bet you with nothing on under that dress except her natural hair."

"The way you talk," Mildred said. "You ought to be beat with a stick."

"She looked up at me as if she had been memorizing my face. I got off and helped her mount her horse, and held her ankle in my hand until that big man cleared his throat. So I got on my horse and we rode down the path, my shoulders hunched over waiting for that gun blast, but it never come, and I said to her, 'Pearlamina, you told him you was coming out with me?' And she said yes, and that he didn't want her to come, neither. And I said, 'Why did you decide to come—is it because you like me?' And she said it was because she liked to ride horses and didn't have one." He commenced to laugh, and Mildred laughed, too, and grinned at Amos and Frank.

"Sounds like she's got wit," Mildred said.

"I said, 'I'll get you a horse to keep.'" He ground his boot heel in the ground. "'Get you one when I next go to Morganton,' I said, and she said she wanted a white one." He laughed again, his laughter rolling out through the woods. "My Lord, I was done out a horse and we wasn't out of sight of the chimney sparks. I said, 'What you going to pay for it with?' And before she could answer, I said, 'The best way to pay is with loving,' and she said it would take too much loving to pay for a horse, and she kicked her mount in the flanks and rode on a ways. I waited for a while, then rode up beside her again, reached over and caught her hand, and she let me hold it. I said, 'I'll give you the horse for nothing,' and she seemed to know what she was supposed to say then, about giving me her love free. She blushed and kicked her horse on ahead again, and after a while she stopped the horse by a brook and sat there on it while the horse drank. 'It's thirsty,' she told me. I let my horse drink and got off my horse and hitched it to wait. She got off hers after a while and tied her horse and sat down on a mossy patch. I went to her and began to talk about the owl hooting nearby, and she talked about the music in the woods and commenced to sing me a song, and I sang one, and we sang and I kissed her lightly a time or two, and pretty soon I was getting warm as a hearth bug, and she was still singing and letting me put my arm around her, so I got a grip on her and got around to seeking a closer understanding. Right when I was damn near overcome, she got up, leaving me lying on the ground, and said about how she had once witnessed a baby being born, and took off running. I was so surprised I couldn't think. I ran, too, as best I could, but a man's not swift in such a season, and she knew the path and I didn't, and she left me behind. So I went back and found the horses and come home." He sat there, staring at the men and nodding, as if he had never had such a yarn to tell. He crossed his arms and rocked back and forth slowly, letting the fire warm him. "I never knew but one other that would go so far and wouldn't go no further," he said.

A wave of anger suddenly came over him. "She had no right to lead me on like that." He got up and stomped off, but the anger left him soon, and he went over to Amos' horse and patted it gently. "Do you remember her?" he asked the horse.

Mildred went to the horse, too, jealousy bubbling in her yet. "Where's my ribbon, Charley?" she said.

"She's wearing it in her hair," he said. "It looks pretty on her, Mildred." He went back to the fire and stood looking down at it. "I tell you men the truth. I'd do well to forget that girl."

Soon there was a world of building going on in the settlement. Three cabins were put up on the unsettled side of the river, and a bench was put across it. The bench, or bridge, was no more than a series of sawhorses that Harrison and the other men built; there were four of them, and planks were laid across them. The span was only one plank wide, and Mina wouldn't dare go across it for a long while. When she learned to use it, she didn't dare stay on the other side because of Charley, who was always chasing her.

Even so, in spite of his temperament, she liked him and sometimes when she heard him singing, she would come down to her side of the river and sing songs across the water to him. She would even go to walk with him on short occasions, and in traveled places, but she was afraid of him and of herself when she was with him, lest she lose out on such a future as she had. The German boy had perked up interest in her and often of late would come by her father's clearing, when he had a spell off from work. Grover, too, would ride up on one of his father's big bay horses and talk and laugh about something, and listen to her sing. So it wasn't as it had been the year before, when she hadn't seen a hope in the world of a family of her own, but she wasn't certain of anything, for Grover never so much as touched her hand, and the German boy was moody.

As for Charley Turpin, so far as she could tell, he was like the song person, Black Jack Davie, that's what he was exactly, and he wouldn't ever have anything except a bed to lie on. But she guessed it would be a right nice bed.

She thought about lying in it more than she wanted to. She sang Charley the Black Jack Davie ballad sometimes when she went down to the river. But she wished he wasn't so footloose and free.

One night when he came to visit her at Lorry's house, she even went so far as to show him all that Mooney had done, and to talk about family ways. He nodded seriously and acted impressed, but at the last he let his snickering get the better of him. "Nobody's going to hog-tie me," he said, and laughed until she thought he was a fool for certain—as if he had a right in this world to think she was trying to get him to change his ways so that she could get a hold on him and marry him.

She told him she planned to stay that night at Lorry's house, that he needn't think about seeing her home, and went off, riding darkly out of the clearing without looking back. She went inside the cabin, curled up before the fireplace and gave way to the disappointment that was in her.

It was Lorry, who had so many work cares, who took the patience to comfort her with talk about how a woman gets her heart tangled up in cords of care, and how a woman can't ever be free of them entirely and has to learn to live with them. Mina guessed she had so many cords on her heart she could hardly breathe, with the German boy and Grover, and Charley calling to her from across the water, and the German looking like he would die whenever she came near him. He had even left her a comb. She had broken it in two and put it back on the gift rock. A week later, when she went to walk, she found another comb. She broke it, too, and stomped in into the ground. A week later, she fell asleep in the woods, and when she awoke, beside her was a comb. She left it there and went home.

Mooney Wright, she thought about him, too, and would creep up near his clearing of a daytime and watch him, listen to him talk with his family, and she remembered him often of a day and night both, and felt angry with herself for longing for the man that had married her cousin.

So there were currents moving at her from every way. She had no place to stand in that stream she was in, she thought; she was pushed here and there, and she couldn't see any real hope at all. The more men who came around, and the more she filled out in body and filled out in her mind with thoughts about herself and them, the more her father got to fussing with her and nagging at her and carrying on about her. Charley was the only man visitor he didn't seem to object to, and the only reason in the world for that, she had decided, was that Charley usually had whiskey with him. Ernest swore at Charley until he got drunk; then he would praise the boy and stagger up and down before the outdoors fire, speaking at length about Charley's exploits, confusing them with his own.

When Ernest was sober again, he would curse Charley's name. But later he would tell Mina to go down to the river and invite Charley over. When she wouldn't, he would tell Fancy. Fancy would go to this side of the bridge and call over that her father wanted Charley to come by. She always took her little sister with her and held her hand.

13

One day that spring, Tinkler Harrison took a chair down to the river and set it near a beech tree, but apart from the shade so that he could get the full warmth of the early-year sun. He enjoyed sitting of a late afternoon in the sun, sweating, feeling the fat of his body dissolve out into pure water. He had a theory which he had perhaps too often expressed to Grover that not only was it healthy to sit in the sun and lose fat, but, if one sat near the river, which was bubbling and noisy, the sound and presence of the river water would assist the fats of the body in seeking a way out, in order to join the greater body of its own kind.

Also, he liked to sit by the river because the turbulence of its waters responded to the turbulence of his mind. He had an orderly mind, but an active one. It was always busy with plans, either for the valley or for his kin and neighbors. He could not let his ideas about the settlement rest, could not sleep except that he dreamed of his planning, so that day and night he was planning always.

He could envision great open fields rich with corn and later on with wheat and rye. He could imagine that a mill could be set not far from his house on the river. He could hear the blacksmith hammers ringing out, and tinkers coming by with their wares, and a potter making jugs. He could see in his imagination a little church with a four-sided steeple, set near a big hickory tree over near the road. He had heard it said that a church should not be set under a nut tree, for the falling of nuts would disrupt the services, but he had always found diversions during religious observances welcome, and should the church also be used as a school, the nut tree would help the scholars master their powers of concentration.

He could imagine all these measures of progress for the settlement, but he knew they were no nearer realization this spring than they had been last. In fact, the settlement was in worse shape.

The pack of wolves had scattered the stock, costing him in cattle and oxen and hogs, costing the German the hog he had, costing Mooney Wright some of the best of his swine. The wolves had even cost Harrison one of his horses, which had run down to the river, had found itself on ice, had slid on the ice, still standing on its hoofs, and had skated across it. Nobody saw the sight, but the marks were on the ice next day. The horse had ended up in the twisted limbs of overhanging trees on the water's other side, where it smashed itself beyond repair.

Chickens were lost, geese were scattered, except for Ernest Plover's, whom even the wolves had ignored, and for days the populace had been out seeking and driving home what was their own, what was left, for the wolves continued to prey on the defenseless animals.

Small and poor was the settlement now, but Grover need not talk about that in Morganton next time he went to advertise the place, Harrison thought. They need not know in Morganton that Ernest Plover had done little to clear his land, that he was not a settler but a stream fisherman and would be of little asset to the community. It bothered Harrison no end to think any man would be so lazy a being, so profitless, and for the wolves to pass Ernest by, not to touch a single hair on his underfed stock's back, even so much as to take a chicken from his mangy flock, was the final note of irony. It seemed that there were devils placed around the land of lazy men which guarded them. A pestilence; Ernest's presence in the valley was a pestilence.

But Grover need not say that in Morganton.

Nor need he talk in length about the German family. Nicholas Bentz's losses had taken the gumption out of him and had made him into a hunter, a wood rover, a man who was rarely home. He had no hogs at all now, and no sheep or beef cattle; he had no hope, he said, of a crop, unless he harvested hides, or unless he kept a flock of turkeys.

It was enough to drive a strong man down to see the way he let his clearing go and piddled about with wild turkey eggs he had taken from woods nests.

Nor need Grover talk in Morganton about that group of inbreds beyond the river, which kept bringing up more and more goods from the lowlands, and more and more children, so that the woods across the river was infested with youngins and odors. With that many children, a hole should be dug and a privy built; the woods could not absorb so much daily contribution. And consider the weak-seamed quality of the men. Charley

Turpin was a big talking fool, as Tinkler saw him, a wastrel. Amos, who was Mildred's husband, was the laziest man Harrison had ever seen; Amos was lazier than Ernest Plover, for he was not alert in any way, not even in his laziness. He could not discuss, as Ernest could, the advantages of idleness. The other man, Frank, was not able to do more than clear a little land now and then, for his wife was thin and easily tired, and he had to think about the welfare of all that big, husky, whiskey-drinking brood. He was, however, a more secure person than the others, and was as reasonable in his manner and direct in his statements as the others were unreasonable and unkempt. He did much work, though not nearly enough to stem the tide of chaos around him.

The only one in the valley who was working was Mooney Wright.

Harrison leaned over and kneaded his hands roughly. He was wary of Mooney. Mooney was a strong one, not subject to weakness at all. He had done only one grievous act, in Harrison's mind. He had taken Lorry and the boys from him.

For a man to be jealous of his daughter was a damnable thing, Harrison thought, though he realized he had been jealous of Lorry for years. It was to her that he had let his heart go out, yes, back when she was a small thing.

If a man could keep a daughter small, he thought, could halt her growth, it would be possible for father and daughter to maintain contact with family affection. But such could not be. Lorry grew up, married that unbridled man, who had what Harrison called a singing in the heart. He had little interest in daily work there, Tinkler knew that; he might as well have filled it with singing.

. But fortunately the man went away and did not come home. Drowned, shot, beast-killed, Indian-slaughtered, who could say?

He had written home only once. He had asked Lorry if she could find a way to Watauga with a party, or if he should come for her. Harrison had held the letter secret for two days. He had it within his power to deliver the letter or destroy it. He thought it all through. A weak man, he decided, would deliver the letter and lose his daughter; a strong man would destroy it.

It was painful to destroy it, for it would pain his daughter, the one he loved. Always he had found it difficult when she had been little to bring himself to lick her with a switch, and he had not done it but twice in his life, for it hurt him so, and hurt him for days, but look here, what sort of licking would it be to a woman's heart to destroy this letter? How many days would that hurt her, and hurt Harrison? How many years, remembering what he had done?

And what if she found out?

No, he thought, that mattered not so much as her leaving now for a far-off place. And if she found out, she would forgive him for destroying it. A woman forgave any man, even her father, for an act of love.

The big fireplace in the Virginia house was at the end of the dark-wood parlor. He tore the letter up and put the pieces in the red ashes. It was all simply done, and she was standing not more than five feet away, talking with her mother, saying that she wondered if Lacey would be back by spring.

So it was done. He had done it, suffered it all, gone through the fire to do it, had done it for love.

He had suffered for many months, even years for it. Only the strong knew what suffering was. The weak never found themselves in the strong webs; the strong man was the one who found himself day and night bound and struggling, so that the work he did, the plotting and the owning and the buying, the decisions he made—and in a large family there had been many to make—were often hard-fibered. Yes, hard, like old roof boards that were cupped, bowed at the edges. But that was the way of life, wasn't it? Did anybody who had lived with the land and grubbed tree stumps in his youth, who had traded close and won out and in the end had come to be a rich man, did anybody who had made his way by his own craft, fighting against nature, which was the tough antagonist, and against other men and women, did he see the sweetness in gentleness? Gentleness was an unkindness, often as not.

He stared heavily at the current. He clasped his hands tightly, lowered his head until his jaw rested on his chest. His lean, thin arms twitched with mosquito bites that he did not feel, would not feel, for the pain of the flesh was not a deep pain to him.

Mooney had built new doors on his stable, Harrison had noticed. The horse would never be able to knock it down. That door he had built was half a foot thick. He had six leather hinges holding it, and he had three sapling poles to put across it of a night. It was made of white oak and was pegged, the German said, twenty-eight times.

Think of that. Think of the work. But think also of the passion of the man. A man can be judged by his passion, Harrison felt.

Mooney had brought his ewes into the house to bear that spring, had brought his two big sows into the house to bear—had swine in the house, but he had told the German he could not afford to lose a single piece of stock now.

Yes, he was in danger of being a pauper, like the rest, in spite of his work. Maybe they would all go down before these mountains. Destitute. A pestilence of sickness might come on them next, for they were ill prepared to heal themselves. And not a new hardworking settler had arrived all that spring, no good additions to help fight back the beasts, no buyers to pay for land, no leaders newly arrived to give hope and direction to the wearying enterprise.

He worried about his vanishing dreams for this valley. He sweated in the sun, his pure watery sweat dropping to the ground to seep from there, he knew, into the greater body of pure water flowing by.

He rode that same morning up the river trail to the end of the settlement and surveyed the broad, flat lands, wood-coated, deep-earthed. Strong men could clear it, year by year they could dig it out, work it into trade. He rode on up the ridge a ways to see what shape the trail was in. The winter had dealt unkindly with it, but it would do; it would have to do. Disuse had merely hampered its smoothness.

He came back into the valley, past the creeks which fed into the headwaters of the river, and on down to the valley floor. He stopped at the German's house, hopeful that the man had changed his ways and was cutting brush and stubble from his fields. He saw the woman chopping in the cornfield, the boy working in a nearby row, the little girl kneeling in the earth pulling up weeds. "Where's your man?" he called.

The boy turned aside, as if the question had burned him; he went to chopping harder at the ground. He was a good worker, a strong boy with big thighs and rounded shoulders on him. Muscles were there, but the boy's eyes reflected inward more than outward; he thought on what he saw more than he saw of it, and he thought on what he did more than he did of it, as if the world that was outside himself were not as real or consequential as the world inside his own skin.

"Is he about?" Harrison asked again, moving his horse closer.

The woman pulled her bonnet lower over her face. "He's off hunting,"

John Ehle

she said, and said no more. He could not get another word out of her.

At Plover's house he tied his horse and went close to the cabin. There was odor of family living about it, of sweat and the smell of the pigpen close by. The corn needed hoeing, he noticed. He saw the children everywhere. Mina was standing at the other side of the woodpile.

She came around the woodpile toward him.

"Where's your mama?" he asked.

"In the house," she said.

It was strange for her to come to meet him, he realized, for usually she went the other way whenever she saw him approaching. On impulse he moved past the woodpile to see what it might be hiding, and so he came upon the startled German, Nicholas.

Nicholas stood awkwardly.

"You owe me on your land," Harrison said, "for you've not met a payment since you bought it. Are you earning it?"

"I've been out hunting deer," Nicholas said. "I stopped by here."

"I see, I see," Harrison said curtly, not fooled by that. Impetuously his mind moved on, now that he had light to see by, and solved some of the riddles of the settlement. "There's not a family that has as much stock now as they had when they first come here," he said, "and yet you've been courting, have you?"

"Watch what you say!" Nicholas said.

"I'm not afeared to say what I think, never have been. I say courting, do you want me to say more?" He glanced at the girl, who was standing self-consciously to one side, scratching at her leg with her bare foot. "Ernest," he shouted. He walked to the door of the cabin, but he would not go into the dark place and risk disease. "Ernest!"

"He's fishing," one of the children said.

"Inez!" he shouted.

She came from the back of the cabin, hurrying, clutching her dress in her hand to hold its hem out of the way. "I didn't know you was here," she said.

"Inez, are you going to rear your children to go sleeping with every man who moves about them?"

"What you mean?" she said, glancing uneasily at Nicholas and Mina.

"I want that girl to get herself to my place and stay there. If you won't care for her and protect her, I'll see that she's properly protected, both from herself and others. I'll not have my kin go common."

"No," Inez said sharply, "she's not yours, so let her alone."

"Inez, you've asked me to save your family many a time, and I've done it."

"You've been more than kind—"

"Because you're kin and I respect blood ties, I've done it. But I'll not permit that girl to stay here with that man. Do you hear?"

Ernest came through the woods. He came running up the path as hard as he was able, and stopped at the edge of the clearing. He had heard some of the talk, and he surmised at once what it was about. He stood there licking his lips, glancing at Mina, then at his wife, then at Harrison.

There was a spell of quiet; even the birds were silent. Then it was Ernest who spoke. "You've got her sister over to your house now. I think you've made her your wife. Well, you'll not get another'n. I'd rather have her sleeping with the stock."

"You are a common sort of animal," Harrison said sternly.

"Common is as common thinks he is."

"Well, what do you think you are?"

"I think my own thoughts, never fear," he said.

"I want you to remember I have done more for you than any man alive."

"And look how we've prospered. You've helped me to stay and suffer." He moved closer to Harrison, spoke directly into his face. "I'm in your debt for making me a pauper, for I remember yet when I had land of my own, and stock, and a place of my own, and it was you who took it from me."

"You couldn't pay. Later I sold you this land. Do you want it, or do you want me to take it from you now?"

"Why, it makes no difference what I say to that; you wouldn't have me gone. I'm the only one left with life enough to squirm when you step on me."

They stared at each other until Harrison turned away, moved past Inez and went to the place where he had tied his horse. He looked back, looked over toward the German, who turned, embarrassed and humbled, and stumbled away into the woods.

A weak man, Harrison thought. He mounted, and without glancing again at the family, rode out of the clearing.

For a moment the spell of his anger held sway over them all. Then Inez began to weep. Long sobs came from her, and Ernest looked at her with tenderness, but he didn't move to her or say anything to her. Mina came over to her and put her arm around her.

What to do, what to do, Ernest wondered. Had he done right or not? He didn't know, but he had pride left, surely, and pride would have its say. He supposed he had not been wise, but how was he to be wise when he was in a country strange to him? This was not his proper place.

What was his place? he wondered. Where was his world? He had sometimes stood on the riverbank and told himself: Deep down in the cold water is your world; a rock lashed to your feet is your clothing for that world. To enter it you need only to climb to the place above the rapids, where the pool is, where it is always calm, so it must be deep, and there bury yourself and leave a world that is not your own and find a garden, long fields already cleared and cribs already filled, a new place in which a weakness in a man is a matter for a word or chide, not a break through which the terrors of the world flow in.

14

She was never so surprised in her life. It was a sight to think of him standing there outside their house and talking so fierce, and shouting at her mother as if her mother didn't have but one ear in her head, and scaring the pants off the children. He had done more harm to her soul in one morning than had been done by anybody in twenty years—or seventeen years old, she guessed she was. It was so bitter to think back on it that she couldn't hardly walk straight down the road. It was as if the weight of the whole sorry morning was squared on her shoulders.

Her father had told him off, though. She hadn't thought he had a courageous bone in his body, and she guessed he didn't have but that one, the one he saved for old man Harrison.

Come prancing around, sneaking past her to the woodpile. And that German man had gone off into the woods, so shamed he probably wouldn't come back that way again.

For noon dinner that day they had some fish and rabbit cooked in the same stew. It was enough to turn a body's stomach. She ate a rabbit leg, then got her things together, which was nothing at all, and walked off down the road, for she knew well and good she wouldn't find no worse place to live at. Except old man Harrison's.

But even if she had to go live there, he wouldn't dare touch her. She'd cut his head off with a knife if he come around her. She'd tromp him silly. He'd think he'd got a hold of a wildcat that'd been eating green berries.

She walked past his field without paying so much attention as to count the cattle out pasturing. She walked past the German's place and didn't look up that way either, for she could see out the corner of her eyes that the German woman was there, leaning on the doorpost, staring. Mina walked right on out of the settlement and up the trail, patches of dust rising from around her with every step. "'Oh, for a glance of heavenly day,'" she sang, kicking at the dust with her naked toes, "'To take this stubborn stone away.'"

Birds rose around her from the trees. She guessed she had scared them off their nests. "'And thaw,'" she sang, even louder, "'with beams of love divine/This heart, this frozen heart of mine.'"

Going to leave the valley, going to leave them all behind, and probably not see them again till judgment time.

Well, her father had so many children he wouldn't know she'd gone away till sometime when he was in a counting mood. He'd have to count two or three times to make sure, and he'd look around and say, "Inez, one's missing." Her mother would stick her head out of the cabin, which wasn't nothing but a children's trough, and she would say, "What size is it that's gone?" And he'd say, "Lord knows." They'd line them all up by the cabin door and figure out that the one missing was the one named Pearlamina. "Why, where you reckon she is?" her mother would say. "I thought I saw her just the other day." "I thought I saw her," her father would say, "walking up the road, singing 'Heavenly Day.'"

They'd know she was gone inside a week, but they'd never know what happened to her.

> I had a piece of pie
> And I had a piece of puddin'.
> I gave it all away
> To hug Sally Goodin.

That tickled her.

> I went on a hillside,
> Saw my Sally comin'.
> Thought to my soul
> I'd kill myself a runnin'.

She giggled. That little song was nice, though "Black Jack Davie" was the best.

> Black Jack Davie came ridin' through the woods,
> Singin' so loud and merry

That the green hills all around him rang,
And he charmed the heart of a lady,
And he charmed the heart of a lady.

"How old are you, my pretty little miss,
How old are you, my lady?"
She answered him with a "Hee, he, he.
I'll be sixteen next summer,
I'll be sixteen next summer."

"Come go with me, my pretty little miss,
Come go with me, my lady.
I'll take you across the deep blue sea,
Where you never shall want for money,
Where you never shall want for money."

She stopped in the road and listened, just in case he was that very minute coming along on a horse, a big black horse and him black-haired hisself. She wished he would stop that horse and ask her to go off across the deep blue sea with him.

She'd go. She'd like more than anything to get back over there where her grandpa had been. Why he ever left over there she didn't know.

She kicked at a pack of dust and found that it was a turtle. "Well, I say to my soul," she said, grabbing her toe and frowning. "You find you a place to lie that ain't in the middle of the road, afore you get tromped."

She climbed on up the trail toward the gap, fussing and singing. She stopped once and looked back, and the valley was so pretty she thought about going on home, but she didn't, and soon she came to the top of the high ridge.

It got dark on the trail. The trail was still soft and dusty, but rocks were present, too, and they got to pressing on her feet; she got bruises on the arches and soles, and got her toes stumped. It was getting chilly, too, and still she wasn't nowhere. And hungry—law, she reckoned she could eat elm bark if she could get it busted up to chew on.

Somewhere off to the side there was sometimes a breaking of bushes, like the sound of an animal making its way on unknown ground. She had to sing to keep her courage up. She sang the whole story of Black Jack Davie, up to where the woman was sorry she'd gone off with Black Jack because she didn't have nothing finally but him and an old straw pad to lie on. Seemed like she had aged past sixteen, and she had come to regret not having stayed at home with a rich husband, who would give her velvet shoes and a gold ring.

Well, a body couldn't have it all, Mina thought.

Now there it went, that moving through brush. Something was in there. Must be a big animal. She knew the animals at home; they doubtless knew her, anyway, for she had walked through the woods so much. But this was strange country. She guessed if she sang, the animals would leave her alone, but she was tired of singing. She had sung all the verses she was going to, and if it was a beast, she would have to let it take her. Everybody had to die sometime; might as well be soon as late.

It was so dark she couldn't see the trail at all well.

That sound again. Something was behind her now, out on the trail.

She turned slowly and saw him standing in the road, down the hill. "Why, I declare, you following me all this way?" she said, her voice trembling.

He looked black as night in the darkness, and his eyes shone. A bear's eyes always shone so brightly, anyway. He was the big bear from the valley, she suspected.

"Want me to whistle a tune? I'll sing you a song. You want me to?"

He stood without moving, listening.

"You want me to sing 'Heavenly Day'?" she said, and hummed the music of it. The bear stood motionless, listening. Then abruptly he left the trail, went off into the woods.

Mina waited, fearful and lonely. "I don't know," she said softly. A person could hardly think of what to do.

She went limping up the road, moving slowly and listening from time to time. A wolf howled off to her right and was answered by another. Her teeth started chattering and she clamped her jaw shut. She kept climbing. Seemed like when she got to the top she'd be somewhere, to heaven if nowheres else. She'd never walked such a long distance upwards in her life.

The moon appeared, and it was close to where she was. A cloud was passing, and the cloud closed off the moonlight. She had to stop, for she couldn't see the trail.

She stood looking up at that big cloud. My, it was something. It was like a living thing; it was so close and it moved so fast. It was going faster than a horse trottin', right across the top of that mountain range. The moon was somewhere back up there, now so dim she couldn't see it. Suddenly it was there again; then it was covered over by the cloud, which looked exactly like a pearl that a man had showed her once in Virginia.

She watched the cloud go on by; then the moon was clear again. "Law, that's something," she whispered, and realized she could see the trail and went on.

Farther along she saw below her in the left, the east valley, a body of clouds, going off to the shoulders of far-off mountains, and she stopped to consider it. The scene was like a picture, and she loved to look at it.

She stood there long enough to realize how cold she was, though. It was chilly up there, she'd say that, cold as a baby's tail when it had wet itself in a cold loft. She clutched her arms around herself and wished she had a fire.

She should move on, she knew, but she liked the sight too well. It was all rolling clouds, billowing and changing as if a giant were underneath them, blowing them around. He was lying on his back in the valley, she thought, breathing in big gasps of air, and when he had his fourteen lungs full, he blew and the clouds rolled as the breaths came through.

He had a family of giants down there with him, and he just did it to pleasure the little giants. He just did it of a night afore they had to go to sleep. He told them stories and blew, so they'd have big notions in their heads by the time of sleep.

And those little mountain peaks jutting up here and there in the clouds were his toes.

He was snoring now. She laughed at the idea of that.

The clouds began billowing differently, and the sight beat the feather stuffin' out of anything she had ever seen, or that anybody had seen, she guessed, for she'd never heard tell of anything like this in her life.

The light went away and she looked up and another one of those racing clouds was going across the moon. Law, it was almost within touch. What a wonder to be up here on this high place tonight. Where in all this country could a body be to equal it, with the clouds putting on a show, and the moon hiding and coming out again, and the tall, black pine-sap trees jutting up so high. It was more'n a person could stand to think about.

A rumble came louder than before. A bolt of lightning struck and she stared, her eyes wide, for the lightning was below her. It had come out of that sea of clouds in the valley and had struck downward toward the ground. She was standing up there above the storm, and the storm below was brewing like pot likker over an oak fire, and she shouted out. She shouted as loud as she could. She was up there above the storm and she wanted somebody to know it afore she got carried off. She had never been above a storm before in her life. There was nobody she knew who had ever done it. There went more lightning, and thunder rolled down and up and around her; it caught her and shook her; it scared her heart and made her hold herself tight as a bear hug. It was seething and roaring down on that giant down there. It was bubbling with fury.

She laughed. She'd tell about it someday, if she could. "The rocks can rend"—the words went through her mind suddenly—"the earth can quake;/The seas can roar, the mountains shake...

> Of feeling, all things show some sign,
> But this unfeeling heart of mine.

She awoke in daylight. She lay without moving for a moment, for she had awakened strangely, she knew, and she thought at first she was up high on the mountain in back of her cabin and that it was afternoon, that on a walk she had bathed herself and had gone to sleep.

She remembered about the giant and looked down into the valley, but there was a thick mist, so that she couldn't see far in it. There was the trail, not dusty but settled down with dew, and maybe a rain had fallen.

She felt her dress. Yes, a little rain had fallen.

She jumped up, agile and lithe, stretched her arms and yawned. She rubbed her nose. She was hungry as a bear. She yawned again, not even wanting to, and sniffed in the cool, pine-scented air. She rubbed her eyes.

Law, it was morning.

She ran her hand through her hair. She rolled her hair up, pinched it tight and fastened it with a vine, but the vine broke, so she let it hang loose.

She guessed she was ready to go, but where she was going she didn't know. As far as she could see through the mist there was no clearing.

Nothing but the tall trees and endless land her grandpa had got her into.

She brushed her hair back out of her face. Didn't even have a comb. Here she was seventeen years old and her dowry was a length of broken vine. She didn't have a sheep to her name, much less a calf. A man marrying her would just have her and a bed, like that Black Jack gave his girl. He wouldn't have a gold ring from her hand, that was for certain, and not much food, either.

Her stomach growled. "Hush," she said. It was going to be growling loud as her father's fiddle playing by noon, she suspected.

Her mind stopped on a thought. Surprised as anything, she looked down at the road beside her. There in the soft earth were the tracks of a bear.

Her gaze moved along the tracks. They led to a dry place about the size of a huge bear's body, not more than ten feet from where she had slept. There were tracks that led from that place into the forest, that had been made since the rain.

She rubbed her stomach and looked about reflectively. "Well, I'm obliged," she said aloud. "You staying out here in the cold and keeping watch was the nicest thing you could a done for me."

There was not an answering sign in that great forest, except the green, heavy leaves blowing on the hardwood trees and the evergreens bowing their limbs slowly up and down.

She found a berry patch in mid-morning and ate berries until she guessed her stomach was surprised as anything. She was still in the berry patch when she heard a horse coming, and she knew at once her Uncle Tinkler had sent someone to bring her back, or had come himself.

She hid behind a tree. Soon she saw a horse loom out of the fog, Grover on it. She wanted to laugh right out, she was so pleased to see a living body.

Grover came past where she was, no more than ten feet from her, and his head was high and his back was stiff and straight, and his horse was so pretty with the fog billowing around him.

"Grover," she said, but not loud enough for him to hear her. She had meant to be loud enough, but she had stopped her own voice.

She crouched behind the tree until the last thud of his horse's hoofs was gone; then she came out onto the road, feeling more lonely than ever. She was so far from humankind that if she had a need to cry out, no one would hear her or give her help; if she needed care, no one would tend her; if she needed meat, no one would serve her. There was no tray with a bread loaf in it, no pen with a pig in it, no coop with a chicken in it, no field with a lamb in it, no stall with a horse in it to take her far away.

She walked until her feet were so sore she had to sit down. She hadn't known her feet could ever get sore. She had thought they were like a muscle in a horse's side. She hadn't even known she had feeling in her feet, except for fire. It was her stomach that ought to be hurting more than her feet, she thought, and her stomach did complain right smart.

It was weakening to her, that was the trouble, weakening not to have more'n berries, which went straight through the stomach like a pack of wolves in a race with a ewe. She wished this were chestnut time. In chestnut time she could stuff herself with nuts till she was fat as a gourd.

She started walking again, and her feet hurt worse than before, in spite of her rubbing them. It was like that with the children at home, she'd noticed, particularly with that little Frances. When you petted her, she got to needing more and more petting. 'Course, that was all right if a person didn't have anything else to do all day and night except pet Frances, but if a person wanted to have variety for her life, she had to put Frances aside. And it broke her heart. If you didn't pet Frances at all, she would only pout, but if you petted her, she would bawl when you stopped, so which was better, Mina wanted to know—to have her pout or to have her bawl?

She stopped on the trail. Frowning, she looked back the way she had come, then off to the sides into the woods. She was closed in by trees and couldn't see a sight, and couldn't see any hope, either. Rising about her to the right she saw a mountain, black as pitch on the top, and beyond it several more peaks, all black on the top, as if the rocks or trees were painted black; they held up the sky, she thought.

The fog came in around her again and she couldn't see a thing. Why, I ain't sung all day, she remembered suddenly.

She decided to sing, but nothing came to mind, nothing she really wanted to sing in that foggy place, and thunder rumbled way off somewhere.

She went walking along, walking on the outsides of her feet, and she got to humming; then she sang softly. "'To hear the sorrows thou has felt, O Lord, the stern of mind would melt.'"

She hoped that maybe around this bend there would be the road.

"'But I can read each moving line / And nothing moves this heart of mine.'"

The trail was going down now, heading down the hill, looked like. A spring dashed from a rock to her left and she stopped and drank. She rubbed her nose and scratched with her fingers at her thighs where she itched from bites and walked on. It felt better to scratch than not to, she thought. Let the bites get red and itch all the more; it didn't look like she was ever going to come to a road, anyway.

A wolf howled close and she stopped. It was just to her left a short ways. She'd never known a wolf to be so close when it howled.

A wisp of wind broke through the fog. Lightning flashed and thunder answered. It was above her somewhere now. All she needed was a bath of rain to bury her spirit deep down, she thought.

The wolf howled and she stopped again on the trail, for it was right on her, so that she could almost feel its breath. She was startled by another sound, for from the other side of the road there came the trembling, clear breaking cry of a panther. She couldn't move because of that sound, it was so full of warning and fog and terror; danger was caught prisoner in it like thunder was caught in the air.

Then came a gruff sound, a growl more than anything else. It was not as far-carrying or ominous as the cry of the panther had been, but it had more strength in it. She turned slowly and saw the great bear lumbering up the trail toward her, hurrying. As he came toward her, she heard bushes breaking in the woods to each side, for the wolves and the panther were leaving, and the bear stopped not far from her and growled again, as if clearing his great throat, and one of his paws came up to wipe slobber from his face. He gruffly spoke again.

"I appreciate your help," she said. She sniffed nervously and self-consciously. She wished she could do some kindness for him, to occupy his mind in gentleness. "You want me to sing 'Black Jack Davie' for you? I would, but I'm so tired I can't remember the verses. I got to walking and forgot even to bring a handful of bread, and it's so high and cold up here, all day walking in the fogginess, why it burdens me down." She suddenly laughed softly, pleased by an idea. "You got four feet, and I'm the one that's worrying. You got four feet to pain you."

The bear stood close by now. Slowly, without hurry or any quareness, it stretched out on the ground.

It smelled sweaty, she noticed, and musty and musky, like a fur rug that had got dank.

Far above them a bolt of lightning broke and thunder rolled across the top of the range. The bear sniffed the air. Unconcernedly it lay its head down on the road.

The air abruptly, shatteringly was filled with light; then a crash came as the thunder sounded, and soon rain splattered down, cold on her skin. The bear didn't seem to notice the rain. Ordinarily the tree limbs would have saved her from the worst of it, she knew, but look at them being harshly blown about, as if the wind intended to tear them off and whip them into the valleys. She huddled down, soggy and cold and tired and fretful, near the bear.

She heard the wagon before she ever heard the voices. It's the giant's wagon, she thought. She looked up and saw that the sun was looking at her, and she smiled. She liked the sun so much of a day. The fog yesterday had shrouded her down. "Somebody's coming," she said, and looked toward the big bear, but it was gone.

She crawled over to where it had slept and felt the dry dust there.

That wagon was way off yet, but it was coming toward her from one direction or another. Maybe it was her uncle coming out in his wagon to gather her in.

She sneaked into the woods and sat down behind a laurel bush.

Soon she heard people talking, and her uncle's wasn't among the voices. The people were coming up the rise, so they were coming in from the Watauga road direction, too. She craned her neck forward to get a sight of them.

She saw a man first of all. He was walking in front, a big man of fifty-five or sixty years, so big she had not seen anybody to measure up to him. He was like a fifty-gallon barrel with legs and arms stuck on it, she thought. He carried a rifle in one hand and held his horse's reins with the other. He had a beautiful bay horse, no more than six years old, with a white streak on its forehead, a long mane and silken tail, and it wore a saddle made of pigskin and a saddle blanket made of lamb's fur.

Behind the horse came a small, narrow little sled being drawn by a great ox, and the sled was packed almost to overflowing with goods, some of them under leather sheets and some in the open. Next came a strong, fine-looking old boar and two small new sows. Then a woman came along. She was old and lined, and her skin was leathery and shiny, and she was leading a cow by a piece of rope. Near her was an old dog.

The man stopped, for he had got well ahead of the ox. He waited for the sled and the woman to catch up and he said, speaking out in a voice that rumbled in the hills everywhere, "Air ye comin'? I say, air ye comin'?"

"Don't you see when you got sight?" she said sternly.

"Yesterday we made sorry time, carrying them pigs across the ford, but we're going to do poorer today, with that ox not moving faster than a man can crawl through a laurel slick. Come on, come on." He took out a twist of cured tobacco, unsheathed his knife and cut off a piece. He was about to put the tobacco in his mouth when he froze in place, stood staring at the road. Mina could see him plainly now; he stood there staring down at the bear's tracks. Slowly he looked up the road and to the side, without so much as moving his head.

Then he shook his head as if to clear it. He robbed his eyes with his tobacco hand, and he commenced to chew on the tobacco. "Well, I declare," he murmured, still chewing to loosen the twist. "Huh," he said, grunting.

"What ye stopped fer?" the old woman called to him.

"You hesh," he said. He set his jaw and peered about. Suddenly he moved, and he moved swiftly; he seemed to deny when he moved that he was an old man at all, for he was at the edge of the woods before Mina got a breath in her chest. His rifle was to his shoulder and his finger was on the trigger.

"No, you don't! No, you don't!" She came out from behind the laurel bush and moved toward him, and he turned to her, startled, and backed off until the brush was against him. "You leave him alone!" she said fiercely. "Don't you kill him!" Out the corner of her eye she saw the horse rare back; the woman grabbed hold of the dog and was trying to calm it, and the pigs had run. Mina knew she must have scared that big man out of his wits, too, for he was shaking in his shoes. She guessed she was enough to frighten anybody the way she had come down from the bushes, not dressed in more than two yards of cloth and it old and thin and torn, her hair strangely roustled, too.

A smile began to work at the corners of the man's mouth, as if he had decided the worst of it was over. He licked his lips, then looked back at his wife, who had let the cow go and had come up beside the ox, where she could see the girl better. "Air ye daft?" the old woman asked the girl.

Mina glared at her.

"I say, air ye daft?"

"No, I ain't daft."

The woman looked about her, lest another witch-child come roaring out of the thickets.

The man chuckled low. "She give me a fright, Florence," he said.

"She give me one, too. And you've got your pigs scattered down the mountainside."

"I never seed the like afore," he said. "I was aimin' at an old bear, and from my backside come this unseasonable attack. I nigh shot myself getting turned around."

"Well, I wish you had," the woman said. "You told me you was taking me back to civilization, and this ain't goin' there." She was still considering Mina critically, not even glancing at the man when she talked. "I don't know what you're a doin' up here," she said.

"I'm walking," Mina said.

The man spat out the tobacco, reached into his shirt and took out a piece of boiled lean meat and bit off a chew. Just the sight of him eating made Mina's stomach growl. He heard it, too, and so did the old woman.

"Give her a bite," the woman said.

"You hush and go find them hogs," he said.

"And get et by the bear?"

The man was still looking at the girl, an incredulous smile on his face.

"If you'd a been such a good hunter," Mina said, wanting to escape blame, "you'd a saw where I'd walked. But you just had eyes for the bear's tracks."

"I saw where you walked," he said, "but I couldn't figure it all out." He glanced at the tracks on the road, then over where the bear had slept. "And ain't yet," he said. His face moved gently as he chewed the meat. "But that's the biggest bear I've ever saw, I'll say that."

He offered her the piece of pork, but she wouldn't take it. He came closer to her, moving slowly, and held the pork out, held it so close she could smell it, but she shook her head. Her stomach growled, and he held the pork right under her nose and whiffed it about. "Air ye hungry?" he said.

He put the pork at her lips and gently pushed it into her mouth. She bit off a little piece. And all the while the woman was standing there by that great ox, her arms crossed, looking on with a speculative smile.

"There's bread in the wagon," she said.

"Give her a bite," he said. "But you'll have to put it in her mouth for her." From his shirt he took out a handful of corn and scattered it on the road. "Sou, sou, sou," he called, and started looking for his pigs.

They had bacon frying a little while later. Mina found a soft place beside the road and lay there thinking about how good it was to be with other people, not to have the world to herself. She yawned and scratched her itch bites and yawned again, and stretched.

The old woman was complaining. "You said you'd take me to civilization again."

"Naw, I said I'd take you where the Indians wasn't. It was the Indians you was afeared of."

"You're too old to fight Indians is what I said."

"You don't know what you're talking about."

"I can't lie asleep no longer in Indian country. And you said you'd take me out of it and to a civilized place."

"Hush and let me think," he said. "Your talking gets to sound like a mill wheel after a freshet. You ought to know I'd be a lost soul back in tame country, where the most excitement that happens in a year's time is that the ducks fly overhead. I ain't going to go there, but to a place where I can hunt and spend my time, some'ers away from the Indians, fer I admit them and the wolves is the pests of this country."

"I'd be pesty, too, if that bunch of you from Watauga kept a shooting at me all the time. If you'd let them Injuns alone, you might a come out better."

He cursed in soft, easy language, as if the idea were beneath thoughtful reply.

Mina sat cuddled up beside the road, near the sled. They had quite a few possessions, she noticed. They had two chests that probably were full of cloth and bowls; they had a spinning wheel that had been broken down into its parts; they had the pieces for a loom; they had two iron pots, one stuck down inside the other, and a set of plowshares and axheads. They had coffee beans and a bagged ham. They had a show of side meat.

"I've not got much longer," the man said, "and I want to spend it the way I like."

"You always have had your way."

"I aim to hunt and farm a little and rest easy, fer I know that I'll come to a halt soon."

"You've got as long as me," she said.

"Florence, I've not got as long as you, and you know it, so hush."

"You're the one that's talking." Then they were quiet, and the bird songs were heard clearly. The woods were full of birds asking who these people were, where they came from, where they were going, why they had left and why they had traveled this trail north from the Watauga road.

"What you reckon we've come into with that girl?" the woman asked, her voice so whispery that Mina could scarcely hear her.

"Come into a wildcat," the man said. "The last time I was so scared was by a wildcat, that whiny cry a wildcat's got. Not much in a wildcat's cry at all except open terror. Well, that's the way her voice was."

Mina twisted anxiously. It wasn't entirely so, she told herself.

"Well, is she daft?"

"She don't appear to be. Her eyes are clear."

"She's in need of care and teaching," the woman said. "She's starved and she's most naked. She could at least put some flax cloth on if she's got no wool, and she could stop scratching so much."

"She's dressed all right to suit me. I wish I was young agin and saw her coming across a meadow. She's got keeness to her a young man needs, and she's got right pretty features."

"Some woman ought to take her to hand and put her in cloth and comb out her hair, might even fit shoes on her, teach her to do woman work, to make cloth and such." Her voice had got so low it cracked as she spoke.

He cleared his throat. "I don't object," he said simply. "Do as you please." Then he said, "Henry, get off that hunting shirt. I told you afore not to lie on my shirt. Here, give me that."

"Don't stir the dog up. He's old enough—"

"Now let me temper the dog. I've told him not to get on my things."

"Well, he likes you so much. He just likes you, that's all. And why shouldn't he? He sees more of you in your hunting than I see of you to home."

"Well, I don't want my dog lying on my things." He cleared his throat. "Air ye finished with cooking the supper, or air ye going to take the rest of the night?"

"I'm not finished. The bread's not browned. I ain't served brownless bread yet, and I'm not going to take up shiftless ways."

"Lord, I've eat bread so mildly cooked it was mealy white. And I've spent about twenty years of my fifty-seven waiting for your bread to get brown enough to suit ye. I don't care how brown it is, so long as it's hot."

"You'd eat the meal raw, I think."

"I've done it. I've done it out in the woods. I've took a piece of raw meat and beat berries into it, then soaked meal in water and eat a meal, fer I had no fire."

"Anybody that would eat raw meat ain't worth cooking for."

"It's tasty with berries in it," he said, and Mina had to smile.

It was funny to listen to them, for they talked so grand to one another, fussing all the time but not getting angry with one another, talking fierce with easy pleasure.

"Henry, if you get your nose in that fire, you're going to have no whiskers left on yer mouth," he said.

"Here, Henry, you want a piece of pork?"

"Now damn it, don't feed my dog afore I get a bite."

"Here, Henry, I'll break ye off a crust of bread—"

"You'll let the steam out of the loaf."

"I thought you liked raw meal and water."

"I say, here we are, with the dog eating and me hungry. It's something to write a letter about."

"You got nobody to write one to, except one might be taken to your boy if you can get something wild to deliver it to him."

The man grumbled. He complained in murmured oaths. Then he said, "I hope I have time to see some more country." It was like a prayer, a little song to heaven, seemed to Mina, and the old woman didn't say anything.

The man raised his voice. "Hey, bear girl," he called out, "hey, you with the strange pets, come on over here and get your food."

He certainly can talk loud, Mina thought.

"Come on over here and tell us where in tarnation we air. I met a rider at the Watauga road who told me there was a settlement back in here called Harristown."

Mina sat up. "Harristown?" she said, surprised. She hadn't heard that name before.

The big man appeared above her. "What's the settlement's name if it's not that?"

"It's—named for my papa."

"That's what that man on the horse told, that it was named for his papa. What's your papa's name?"

"Ernest Plover."

"Uh huh. Florence," he said, looking over toward the cook fire, "we're going to live in Plovertown."

The woman grunted.

"How many people you got living there now?" he asked.

"It's got more'n I can count," Mina said.

"Has it got twenty?"

"It's got more'n ten in my family," she said. "And it's four in the German's family, and four in the Mooney Wright family, and ole man Harrison has three in his family and six more hands to work for him, and there was two nice new people last autumn, but they got et by snakes come cold weather, one of them did and the other one lost her senses and had to be come for from the lowlands."

"Et by snakes?" he said.

She had to tell him the story, which always made her shiver for part of a day. The old woman's teeth got to chattering as she listened, and the old man's eyes got big and bright, and he kept clucking his tongue and shaking his head. "Snakebit seven times, you say? Listen to that, Florence."

Mina told about the wolves attacking that past winter, too, and how Tinkler Harrison's horse had got so scared it had gone skidding across the ice. With every story, as the valley began to appear to be crammed full of marvels, the old woman trembled all the more, and the man got gleeful as a boy with his own pup. "Hey, Henry," he said at one point, "sounds like we've come to the right place, don't hit?"

When Mina was quiet enough to give him a chance to talk, he told stories about his own experiences. He told about Indians and the way they had of coming down on a place and burning every cabin and taking the corn from the crib, the stock from the pens, taking the youngins away to raise for their own needs or to trade for Indian children at the trading places, or trade for salt or whiskey, and how it was a time getting the children sorted and rationed out to their parents, for sometimes their parents had been scalped or shot, or had moved on to the Cumberland or somewhere, and sometimes the youngins didn't know their own parents, and sometimes they had come to live like the Indians and cried when they were left behind with the white folks.

"A child ain't to blame," the old woman said. "A child is only a small thing that needs light to grow." She punched a stick into the fire and spread the coals about. "I've seen many a child grow," she said, "though not but one was mine."

He took out a pipe and a pack of tobacco and lighted it with a coal stem. "That boy of ourn grew up straight."

"I vow," she said.

"They won't never get him," he said quietly. "Neither the critters nor the Indians. He's bigger'n me, even."

"Is that the truth?" Mina said, surprised.

"That's right smart, ain't it?" he said, and winked at her.

"You look strong as an ox, all right," she said.

"I'm stronger'n that. I'm as strong as my boy, and he once't killed a bear with his hands." When he saw her shake her head in disbelief, he said, "It weren't but a yearling, but it was a bear. I had shot its mama, and this 'un come down out of a tree almost on top of me, and Josh caught it and carried it to the pine needles with him, wrestled with it." He pushed the lighted wood deeper into the bed of tobacco in his pipe and puffed it to smoking.

"Did Josh choke him to death with his bare hands?"

"You'd never choke a bear with your hands. His paws would flail you afore you got it done. He's got claws on each paw that'll tear flesh open to the bone. And his claws won't come in like a cat's; they're fastened stiff. He can cut bark off a tree, can split a tree trunk with them claws. And he's got more strength than a man has got."

"How did Josh do it then, if'n a bear's so smart?"

"You mean did he plan out a fancy scheme?"

"I'm only asking how he done it. You claim to know."

"He did it natural. As I recall, he got one foot on the bear's flank and a knee on his throat, and he had his hands free to try to pin the bear's arms down. That's how."

Mina sniffed and poked a stick into the fire. "What did he do then?" she said.

"Nothing to do. The bear died."

"Well, law me, he sure must be a good hunter," she said suddenly. "I never heard such big talk afore." She looked proudly at the woman, but the woman wasn't listening. Her thoughts appeared to be a long way off, and after a while she sighed and blinked, as if coming back to the place she was in, and then, without even looking at Mina, she took a comb from her hair and handed it to her.

"Why, I can't take a present," Mina said.

The woman put it on Mina's lap. "Them as are poor can't allus be proud," she said.

"I never took no present in my life," Mina said defiantly.

"Take it, and you're welcome," the old woman said. "I own two more combs. What you reckon I could do with three combs?"

Mina looked down at the comb. It was bone and pretty and she wanted it. She picked it up, held it gently in her hand. She had never had a bone comb. "I never had nobody give me a present afore," she said. "I don't rightly know what to tell you."

The old woman went on looking at the fire and rocking gently back and forth.

"I'm obliged," Mina said, and the old woman nodded.

Mina started combing her hair. She combed it, trying to get the burs and thistles out of it, and a rich warmth came into her scalp. The old woman got up and went to the cart, looked into it, then went over to one side and looked off into the woods. The man didn't do more than watch her. She came to the cart once more and looked in, and she put her hands on her hips. "Jacob," she said.

He chewed on the pipe stem, but after a moment he got up, rising slowly but with power.

"I need that chest," she said.

He cleared his throat. "We'll be unpacking tomorrow, Mama."

"I was just looking at her there by the fire and thinking back and wondering, and I got the idea..." She hesitated.

"Uh huh," he said quietly. He chewed on the pipe stem; then he touched her arm, almost as if brushing past it, and climbed into the cart. He began to shove some of the stuff around.

Mina combed at her hair and made faces at the dog, but she had to smile at him, too, for he was ugly. She didn't notice what the others were doing until the woman came back over to the fire. She had a dress in her hand. It was a blue cotton dress with scarlet-thread handwork around the throat and hem, and it had a belt. It had not been worn much.

Mina stood up slowly and backed off from it. The old woman sort of crumpled it into a wad and pushed it at her. "I don't know what to do with this old dress, and you need covering."

"Why, I couldn't take no dress from a stranger person," Mina said.

"I've got so many dresses, and some I've saved from way back. I've got so many."

"I couldn't take no dress. No person ever give me a thing, till that piece of meat this morning, then that comb, and now you're pushing a dress at me. You must think I'm a beggar woman."

From beside the ox cart the old man spoke up in his deep voice. "She wants you to take it, girl, don't you know that?"

The woman stooped by the fire and poked a stick into it and studied the fire as the smoke swelled up from it. The man went to the side of the road and started talking to his horse, and Mina was left with the dress in her hand. The cloth was so soft, so much softer than flax linen or linsey, and was so light, so much lighter than wool, and was so nicely dyed that she knew she would have to keep it. "Cotton certainly does take the dye well," she said softly.

"Don't it?" the woman said. "It can't be beat for colors. I've brought a bag of cotton with me. I've got enough wool cloth to last me for a spell, but I brought some balls of cotton and cottonseed, as well as flax. If I can find the right spot, I'll grow a little field of cotton next year."

"Yes'm," Mina said softly. The dress was dear to her already. It was as close to her now as it would be if it were put on her body, for it was pressed against her so tightly.

"Why, I have so much goods," the woman said. "He's such a fine hunter and farmer, and he's prospered. We've accumulated. When you're my age you'll be surprised how many things you've accumulated. I left a house full of goods at Watauga, just in case my boy comes back that way from the Cumberland one day. I bore two boys, but the other'n died when a baby of a coldness; it seemed to fell him in a day and night. I kept that dress and another'n might nigh like it, expecting Josh to need 'em someday if he found a woman to suit him. But Josh ain't even looking, and he's going more to the west all the time."

"Yes, ma'am," Mina said, holding the dress close to her.

"I'd be blessed if you'd take it," the woman said.

Mina stood there by the fire, lingering, not knowing what to say. Then she said, "I'm obliged." She stood there for a while longer, then went up the road.

Henry came with her, watching her. He wanted to see what she would look like in the dress, she guessed. She took off the old one and washed her arms and stomach in spring water. The dog lay down on the road and watched, cocked his head and growled in his throat once or twice, as if he sensed that an animal was close by.

The old woman waited by the fire, feeling nervous enough to complain. She hadn't given away much in her life and didn't know how to do it casually. She had given away firelight to a neighbor whose hearth had run cold; she had given away meat when Jacob had killed a beef; she had given away wild deer, turkey and the like, but not before had she given away something pretty to a girl. But it was an act of kindness she had often thought about.

Jacob came back to the fire and said the ox was all right, that he had done well on this journey and hadn't lamed up much. "Not many settlers will find their way back into here, though," he said. "It's too rough a trail, nigh too rough for oxen, but I like this, Florence, this country. I like the new feel of it. It's not been spoiled yet by traffic. It's better'n Watauga."

"I wish we'd go to Morganton and get shet of these mountains entirely," she said. "I'd like to have people around to talk to and a place to go to worship."

"Naw," he said deeply, "I can't go down there. It's all finished there. They've got their answers. But this is new. I've got to be where there's the start of things."

"You've always followed from too far away, and what do you say when your strength goes? Like an old bear looking for an animal that's done been wounded by another beast—"

"You talk too plain," he said, aggravated with her.

"You and me has been around a long time, and I know what you think because I think it the same time you do. So I know your strength's started failing. And I know when you're in pain."

"Do you? Well, do you know a man never stops, no matter what his trouble is? Do you know that?"

"I know you ought to rest more than you do."

"Naw. Did you know the best way to rest is to start over? There's always a place to start over some'ers. And only the old don't know it."

She stared at him across the firelight. She frowned and leaned back on her stiff arms and looked at the blaze. "It's in your chest, ain't it, that it bothers you?"

"I know what life is and death, too," he said, "for I've seen it come and go in stock and wild things. And I know how an old bear is, but I tell myself it ain't the same with me."

"Well, let's not say no more," she said.

"Maybe I'm wrong, but I've not been proved wrong yet." He reached out with the toe of his shoe and kicked at the wood. He took out his tobacco pouch, but he shoved it once more inside his hunting shirt.

"Out of tobacco?" she asked.

"No, but I soon will be, so I'll save what I've got."

She nodded, then said slowly, "Was it because of the pain you come east, or was it because you couldn't keep up with Josh no more?"

"You like to talk, don't you? You ask more questions than you ought to, even for an old woman."

"I was only asking out of interest," she said quietly.

They watched the fire burn, and he glanced off in the direction the girl had gone. "She takes her time."

"She's getting prettied up. Got her hair to roll and all. You think she'll be willing to come with us tomorrow?"

"Henry's coming back," he said.

Mina stopped down the trail a piece. The dog stopped, too, and waited for her. She came closer by only a step and stopped, as if afraid to show herself. The old people looked at the fire, so she came closer still, and when she was standing close enough, they looked up and saw her, a girl of medium height, full made of body, with long, flax-colored hair rolled up in a bun and caught by a bone comb, a pretty girl wearing a clean blue cotton dress with scarlet thread woven into it. And for some reason she was crying.

15

Mina lay awake that night thinking she might go back to the valley with Jacob and Florence. She would like more than anything to be back home and to be their friends in that place, to go home leading the big ox, with Jacob walking out front. But she knew she had her father's own deep pride, that she would not go back at all, now that she was a wayfarer.

She ate breakfast with Jacob and Florence, and when they asked her to accompany them, she thanked them very much and said she would stay up on the ridge a while longer and for them to go on ahead. When they were out of sight, she turned toward the Watauga road, toward the broad river, and hurried on.

Soon, though, she was tired, not from a body weariness, but from a mind weariness, for she wished she had been able to go home. She sat down on a big boulder and let time drizzle past; then she walked a little piece, then sat down again and pondered her predicament, caught like a prisoner between two worlds.

She was sitting there considering her thoughts when she heard a horse; it was the second time in two days she had encountered travelers on this tiny trail coming from the lowland direction.

It's Black Jack, surely, she told herself, smiling at the notion.

Around a curve the rider came, and she saw him, black-haired and black-eyed, dressed in black leather and fine white cotton, riding a great black horse that seemed to breathe smoke from its nose. "Law, I never thought I'd see you a riding on this ridge on such a day as this," Mina said.

The horse reared up. The man reined in, startled, and frowned at her from his twisting, stomping steed. "Hey, whoa there, whoa, whoa," he said. "Whoa, boy." The horse was stomping at the dust wisps, smoke spouting from his nose, and the rider stared down at her. He leaned toward her and smiled. "What say there?" he said.

She felt awkward as could be. "I was all alone up here," she said, "and so pleased to see a body come along."

He studied the eerie air about him, the twisted trees heavy with wetness and grayness.

"I've been a picking berries," she said.

"I see ye have," he said. "You have juice on your mouth yet."

She wiped at her mouth with her hand. "Where you a going?"

He winked ever so quickly. "I rode the night thinking to myself, Now, if I keep going and watching, along sometime tomorrow I'll likely come upon a pretty girl standing by the roadside with blackberry juice on her face and a little smile, and she'll have a voice soft as flower dew."

"Huh. I never."

"I was thinking as I rode up that rise back there, Well, it's high time for her to show herself." He studied her. "You're so high up, I imagine you're an angel child."

"You got the wrong person in mind, I imagine, for I'm not aiming that way here lately."

He dismounted, watching her all the while, and, folding his arms, seemed to rest at ease, but, as she could tell, he was aware of the road and the woods, of everything that moved. She watched him, interested in his face and the steadiness of his dark eyes. He was not a big man; he was not as big as Mooney Wright. He was about the size of the German and was slender and tough of body. He was handsome and reminded her of a picture of a knight.

"I was singing about Black Jack and then along you come, black as the inside of a keg."

"You figure yourself for that little girl he went off with, do ye?"

"Law, I never thought no such a thing. I was singing that song for enjoyment and there you come, and you're black-haired."

"Uh huh. And you're sixteen."

"I'm older'n that by far."

"You might be at that, for you've got a right smart of shape on ye."

"I guess I've got all I'm going to get," she said simply.

"Might be sixteen and a half," he said, winking at her.

"I'm older'n that," she said heatedly. "I'm older'n you think, if it's any mind of yours."

He chuckled and shook his head. "You must be awful anxious to find a beau to come this far."

"I was a picking berries, that's all," she said.

"Come up here to find somebody to carry ye off, make love to ye on a straw pallet."

"I never heard such talk in my life—"

"Hold ye tight, make ye soft and cuddly—"

"You hush your mouth, talking to me like that—"

"And there I come, here I am."

"No, sir, there you're not, neither, and don't you come nigh me."

He sat down on a rock, a big smile on his face. "I think this way—a girl that'll come all that way to find me won't mind crossing the few feet more to where I'm resting on a stone." He glanced at her, but she didn't move and appeared none too favorably inclined toward him. Suddenly he closed his eyes tightly. "I been riding all day and night, ma'am," he said simply. "My horse was following a trail I couldn't see. All night I rode, not sleeping, and I rode through mist all day, and now and then I heard a cat cry or a fox bark, and I said to myself, Where in the world are you, where you going, boy? And I said, Up ahead."

She sniffed. "Huh," she said.

"I wonder how close I am," he said.

"Close to what is it?"

"To where I'm going."

"You talk so funny. While ago you was a pretty talker, but now you talk so strange."

He smiled at her. "No need of that." He studied her. "You're a pretty little thing. Do you have a name?"

"Pearlamina," she said. She wondered why she had told him all of it. It was so formal to say it all.

"That's pretty. Like you, like a song. Pearlamina. I once knew someone who had a little girl with that name."

He was one of the most likable persons she had known, but he was so foreign, like a Spaniard or a Frenchman—she didn't know exactly, for she had never known one of them. "What got to be your name?" she said.

"Lacey," he said.

She was so close to him she didn't dare gasp aloud. She held her breath instead, and the breath almost stifled her to death. Maybe he didn't even know she was startled, or that a weakness had come over her. Her stomach was nigh turned about from nervousness. "You going where?" she asked in a hushed voice.

"To the end of this trail, Pearlamina."

No, go back down that road, she thought. You ride away, ride away fast. Get on that black horse and let it take you away from here.

His gaze came to her and was steady and boyish. "Where does the trail go, Pearlamina?"

"Law, how do I know?"

He smiled, as if he knew they were playing a game. He began to whistle softly. "Sing me a song."

"No, sir, I'm not a going to do any such of a thing."

He stood up, reached out easily and gently took her arm. She watched his face as he drew her closer. His arm went around her waist. His face touched her hair and she never wanted to think another thought or know what to do. "Sing something for me, Pearlamina."

"No, I won't." She felt like a child, the way he was and the way he held her close to him and nuzzled his chin into her hair. "I can't think of nothing," she said.

"'He came all so still,'" he said softly, not singing as much as talking kindly, "'to his mother's bower, as dew in April that falleth on the flower.'"

He stood there, his head resting against her head. He laughed softly, then his arm was gone from around her and she heard him move away and when a while later she looked up, he was standing at his horse, his hand on the saddle, his head lowered.

As she watched him, he lifted his head, sighed quietly, deeply. He looked over at her. "I asked where does this road go, Pearlamina?"

"On until it comes to a river."

"Who lives there? Do you know a woman of brown hair who has a blond-haired and a black-haired son?"

Mina knelt down before the fire and looked into its red heart. "Nobody lives there a'tall," she said.

"You lived there, didn't you, Pearlamina?"

"No, I lived another place."

"Then my horse, where was she a going?"

"I don't know. I'm not able to know nothing about your horse."

He came to her. He stooped and his head was near hers. He touched her chin and turned her face so that she was looking at him.

"We can ride out to the Watauga road," she said softly. "We can go out of this country, Lacey Pollard."

"Lacey Pollard?" he said quietly. "You know me?" He smiled gently at her. "Who lives in the valley?"

"I don't know," she said.

"Is her father there, too? I remember him, for he knew hisself so well. A man that knows hisself is so simple to get to know. The world to her father was the place where he breathed in air and ate of food and set to rest or lay to sleep; beyond that it didn't matter much to him. He didn't see how a man could get lost, how a man likes to get lost, has to, yes, in a woods afore he knows the woods, in a road afore he knows the road, in his love of a woman afore he knows a woman."

She stared at him, strained and strangely.

"I want to see her again, Pearlamina. I've been lost so long. I'm traveled out, Pearlamina. I've seen the long fields and the tall woods. I've hunted all I want to. I've killed so much. God help us all."

"Yes," she said.

He was somber, but the boyish, playful glint was in his eyes yet. His hand came up slowly and he laid his palm alongside her face. "I remember so fondly now how it was with her, how gentle and pleasant in Virginia, back afore I went off looking. I've looked so far and deep. Is she well?"

"Why, I reckon she is."

"Is she living with her father?"

"Why—no, she's not."

"Is she living alone?"

"Why, don't ye know she's married?"

It was evening when they reached the ledge that overlooked the valley. Below them, not far away, was the fire Jacob and Florence had made. On beyond that, far below, was the river. They could see the cabins and sheds. They could make out a Negro man working in the big Harrison field, and nearby a Negro woman was pulling beans. Beyond them a herd of long-horned cattle stood in a pasture. On this side of the river was the rolling sea of trees, with three little cabins spewing smoke, and beyond the river were six cabins, placed as if they had been set out by children.

Lacey surveyed it all. His expression was steady and plain, but directly he closed his eyes and irritation seemed to come over him; he trembled and was older all in a moment, and he made an angry noise deep in his throat.

"That cabin beyond Uncle Tinkler's plantation house is where once she was living," Mina said, "but it's empty now, for he come and took her off."

"Where's his place?" Lacey said.

"That one, with the two sheds in the yard and the pig pens below."

He saw a boy making his way through a flock of sheep. Verlin, his own boy, was walking there.

He saw Verlin sit down near the cabin.

"The man walking on the valley trail is the German," Mina said, pointing. She went on to tell how he had lost his stock to the wolves and about how he pined away. Lacey let her talk, for she did it naturally, but his mind was roving across his own worries, and before long he commenced to pace fretfully.

By now it was growing dark, so Mina made a fire. He saw her take meal and salt from his saddlebag, and he said nothing. She began to pile damp wood near the fire to dry. "I guess they're looking at us from the valley by now," she said.

"Are they?" he said.

"I saw once afore a fire up here, and ever'body was worrying about Injuns."

They saw somebody come out of the woods at the top of the Mooney Wright clearing. A woman. It was Lorry, he saw. He moved to the edge of the ledge. Then came a boy, Fate it must be. When he had last seen Fate, the boy had been a child holding to his hand, crying like his heart would break.

Now he saw the man with them. He was walking with ease, taking long steps.

Lorry stopped in the cornfield. Verlin walked toward her, peeked into a basket that she carried.

God help me, Lacey thought, regret sweeping through him. After six years he had come home to find he was the stranger in his own family.

He watched Lorry and Fate walk down from the corn patch, taking their time, enjoying the day. She went into the cabin. The man and Verlin walked along the path toward the pens. moving confidently, and went off into the woods together.

Lacey stared at the deserted clearing; then meekly, wearily he crept to the fire and crouched there.

"They've gone inside?" Mina asked.

"Yes," he said. "Is he fond of her, Pearlamina? Tell me that."

"I ain't saying nothing about it."

"Now you tell me what I want to know. Is he fond of her?"

"I ain't—"

"Is he fond of her?"

She glared at him, shocked by the sternness of his voice. "Yes," she said. "He's more fond of her than he might be of another."

"What do you mean? What other?" He moved around the fire to get close to her. "Look at me, Pearlamina."

"I said he's fond of her."

"Pearlamina—"

"I ain't a going to look at nothing I don't want to."

"If you lie to me, I'll skin you. Now here, put your hand on mine."

"I will not."

"Put your hand on mine."

She laid her hand on his palm.

"Does he have a deep fondness for her?"

"Yes," she said.

Lacey, still watching her, crept back around the fire and stretched out on the cold stone. "And she of him?" he asked.

"Yes," Mina said.

It grew dark and he lay there still.

"They can see our fire as clear as a star by now," Mina said. She huddled near the back of the big rock they were on, shivering in spite of the fire heat. "They're wondering who you are."

"Maybe they know."

"The German probably thinks it's his own kin come to fetch him home to his big house. Uncle Tinkler maybe thinks it's a blood son come back to him, for he talks of that. He wants to see a son of his agin, he says."

"Grover is there aside him."

"He don't like Grover. He don't like the way Grover never does a thing, except look moo eyes at Belle."

"Who's Belle?"

"My sister, and the one that's married to Uncle Tinkler now."

"Lord in Heaven," Lacey said quietly.

"He talks about his sons a coming home to him, though he's the one that driv them ever' one away by his cussedness."

"Does Lorry know it's me up here? Does she know who I am?"

"She's probably not noticed. She has worries enough with that there baby she's a carrying."

The words shook Lacey to trembling.

"It'll be born this summer, I expect," Mina said.

He tightly closed his eyes.

A while later he began to hum a sad song to himself, a lonely sound up there where they were; then he started talking softly, rambling on. "She wasn't so much sought after as you might think, Pearlamina. Most boys didn't like her papa well enough to ask for her hand, and she was an aloof woman by nature. I married her in late summer in seventy-two at a little church, the Presbyterian church. We was married by a preacher. Nigh a year later Fate was born; then a year or two more and there was Verlin a living. I was so proud I damn near busted. I said to myself, Lacey Pollard, you've found out the meaning of life; you'll never need to run off agin; here you got it all, a woman handy, a baby to work for, to teach something to, aplenty of land, and all the comfort you need. Live and die here, I said, don't go nowheres more. So I told myself, but Lord, I kept strewing my thoughts, and one evening I couldn't hold off any longer and I left, not meaning to be gone long."

"You was gone for many a year. I remember when you left."

"I left in seventy-seven, started to Kentucky to find better land, but on the Wilderness Road I met settlers coming back, black-socketed in fear, scrawny of fat. The savages had cut them down, captured some, driv them out. Not a one wanted to stay in that wild place, and they said to get away, that nothing civilized could live up there. So I decided to go some'ers else to find a place for Lorry and the boys. I rode south and found nothing worth more'n what I'd left. I crossed the long trail to Watauga and found many a fugitive living there. It was not the place I wanted, and the best land was gone, anyway. There was a group of settlers in Watauga organizing to go where no settlers had ever gone, to cross the

Cumberland Mountains and pitch their tents near French Lick. I offered to go with them. That was in seventy-nine. I went and helped them fight Injuns and beasts, and then I come back to Watauga for salt, and the word come to us about the war and I went with the Watauga men back across the big mountains to fight at Kings Mountain, some'ers south of Morganton. I aimed then to go back to Virginia and get Lorry and take her to the Cumberland, even though it was still a bloody place to fight Injuns in, but on the way to Virginia I went up the Wilderness Road to see how Kentucky was getting on, and I found it had all been tamed and was owned, all the blue-grass country, by speculator men. The Cumberland would be tamed the same way, I knew, and soon enough, so I went to my farm in Virginia to get Lorry, and I found it was owned by a man I never saw afore. He said he didn't even know a woman by the name of Lorry Pollard. Lord, I was tired then. I had been so far and had come to nothing. I took up and wandered south again, looking for my own people. Over a year I traveled lonely; then a man in Morganton in the hotel told me old man Harrison now owned a valley, and to reach it a man must ride the Watauga road to the fourth fording of the broad river, then ride up a narrow, ridgy trail marked by a locust post. I thanked the man and went out to the livery stable, paid my horse board, and I rode lathery that night. The next day I come to the mountains. I clum them and on I rode, and I kept thinking, Lorry, I'm coming closer. I rode on until on the proper crossing I saw the ridge trail and my horse seemed to know it, and we went on into the dark. All that night I rode. And that was just last night. Think o' that. Last night."

She considered him solemnly. "She might be thinking of you this minute as strong as you're thinking of her. Was she fond of you?"

"She was. I'll say that. She wasn't never a loving person by type, but she took to me foolish."

"She ain't likely to have forgot you. Law, if you ain't forgot, why should she? A woman has a better memory for love feelings than a man, don't she?"

"I think so," he said hopefully. "I think she does."

"She's probably down there pining away, expecting you'll come back."

"Do ye think so, Pearlamina?" He lay there, his eyes tightly closed, the firelight fluttering on his face. "Pearlamina, I been lost so long," he said.

"You go on to sleep," she said. "Tomorrow you can ride down there, and more'n likely she'll meet you on the road. I'm bound she'll come to you. You can live in that empty cabin, for it's yours, the cabin she was using. And there's plenty of furs to be trapped in these parts. No trouble making a living. I wouldn't worry another minute about her or them boys."

He went to the edge of the cliff and stood for a long while, his back to the fire, looking down at the valley. There was nothing to be seen down there now, Mina guessed, except a few sparks coming up from the chimneys. Suddenly he turned and went toward his horse, not hurrying but going there directly.

"Are you a leaving here?" she called out, but he didn't answer, and directly she heard the hoofs of his horse on the trail.

She ran away from the light of the fire in order to see him, but he was gone, was out of sight. She couldn't even tell which direction he was taking, for the sound of the horse's hoofs came at her from all directions and splattered on the rocks around her, and she was too far away.

Then she heard him singing. He was singing quietly, keeping himself company on the dark, steep trail below her.

> He came all so still
> To his mother's bower,
> As dew in April
> That falleth on the flower.

16

Lacey Quincy Pollard moved like a secret-minded beast in the valley. He turned up at the German's house, stepped out of the woods while Nicholas was woodcutting, smiled and said, "I wonder if you know the way to Lorry Harrison's new cabin?"

The German, who didn't have any idea who he was, told him the way. Still Lacey lingered, showed no interest in going there. He sat down on a stump and let the hot sun trouble him. "You like it here?"

The German sat down on a stump, too. "I have lost more than I've gained," he said simply.

"That's the way I used to do when I farmed," Lacey said. They talked for a long while about the losses one could encounter in farming; then Lacey told about his travels in the west and how the endless trails were like the patterns of a man's life, always progressing but not going anywhere that could be predicted, yet pleasant. It was almost dusk when he started up the path, not toward Lorry's cabin at all, but away from it.

The next night he came by the Plover place. Ernest, who was preparing himself to go across the river in search of replenishment, thought he was a ghost. He came close to him and gazed deeply into his eyes. "Lord help us," he said. "You have your own true features yet."

"Looks like you been breeding well," Lacey said, looking approvingly at the string of little blonde girls.

"Lacey, is it you in the flesh?" Ernest said.

Lacey said it was, and he started to joke and talk. He visited for the evening, entertaining the girls, giving them songs he had heard in Watauga, the Cumberland and Kentucky, holding two little girls on his lap and bouncing them up and down as he sang to them.

Then, when the party was no more than sighing along toward a close, he disappeared into the black woods, his black horse following.

By morning it was known throughout that valley that he was

somewhere about. It was known everywhere except at Lorry's place. Nobody went there, for they were certain Lacey had gone there. All day Ernest kept looking for Lorry to return to her valley cabin to take up housekeeping with Lacey again, and he was surprised there was no chimney smoke or other sign of life there by sunset.

That evening Tinkler Harrison, who had looked the day through for a sight of Lacey, prepared a feast. He had a pig and a chicken killed, and he cooked everything over a yard fire, all the better to fetch him. He told Belle to put on her best most frilly clothes, and he and Grover put on clean clothes and fastened their brass-buckle belts in place. All three of them had taken their places near the fire and Belle had begun nervously fluttering a fan before her face when they heard horse's hoofs striking the path, and directly they heard a man dismount. Lacey walked in close to the fire.

"I knowed pork and chicken would fetch you," Harrison said jubilantly.

"Either one would have fetched me," Lacey said, smiling. He laughed softly, not at what he had said but at the good feeling he had at being there. "You the young wife?" he said to Belle.

She was too speechless to do more than nod, for her mind was dizzy with the sight of him.

"I believe I'll stay to eat," he said, and sat down not far from her and winked at her, so quickly and easily that she wasn't certain he had winked at all; then he smiled, disarmingly and simply. "My, it's cool tonight." He reached over and patted her hand. "How you like it here in this valley?"

He and Harrison talked well into the late night about the valley's hopes, and they saw visions of the settlement that would surely develop. "A thousand houses and two thousand sheds," Lacey prophesied. He made glowing predictions for the region, one flowing after another, and along at the time when the fire waned, he got up to go. "Which way is Lorry's cabin?" he asked.

"Why, have ye not been there?" Tinkler Harrison said, astounded.

"No, not yet," Lacey said solemnly. Lacey left, and Harrison stood as if in a trance listening to the walking of his horse. When the sound had entirely gone, he suddenly turned to Belle. "He's not going there now, is he?"

"It doesn't sound like it," she said.

Harrison moved past her, and called to one of the men to bring him a horse.

He rode toward Lorry's place, exultation rising in him, carrying him forward, making him spur the horse faster. He rode into the clearing. "Lacey's home!" he shouted. "Lacey's come back!"

The house door stayed shut. Not an answer came from within. Once more he called the news, but there was no answer to him, not even an added spark came from the chimney.

He sat on the horse, looking at the night cabin, animosity and resentment and affection coursing through him.

Inside the cabin there was quiet so deep Lorry could hear her own heartbeat. The cry of her father had awakened her, and even before she had oriented herself to wakefulness or knew who had spoken, she knew what had been said. The meaning had come to her, as if her skin had absorbed it, her flesh had heard it.

Beside her she heard Mooney breathe softly. He was awake and waiting. He knew, too, now.

She could not decide what to do or say. After years of waiting, caring for the belief that he would return, she was ill prepared for the announcement of his arrival. A tide of wanting, hating, fearing unloosed itself in her.

She heard the boys stir upstairs. What were they thinking now? What reaction did they have to the announcement so starkly given. Surely for them the security of the place was shaken more certainly than if her father had called out the presence of a dozen bears, or a pack of wolves, than if he had announced a pestilence to attack their summer crops.

After a while she said, "It won't matter a bit in this world."

"No," Mooney said. He lay there reviewing every thought his mind had ever held about her and the boys, and the farm they were making. He had not felt so lonely, not felt so thrown away from his life moorings since he had been put out of his mother's care when a boy, put on a ship and sent to sea. This land is like the sea, he thought, untamed like it, rolling high like it, curling in heavy waves like it, and he knew his life here had now come crashing down, like the sea, shattering about him. "It won't matter to me at all," he said. "He won't come nigh here."

"He might come nigh. They are his boys. He has a right to talk to them."

"No, he won't come here."

"He's not a dangerous man by type," she said.

"Does he know you're bearing?"

"I don't know."

"Has he been watching us, do you suppose?"

"I don't know." She touched his arm lightly, comfortingly. "There's nothing to be done now," she said.

She got out of bed before the break of day. She stirred the fire and put on wood. She combed her hair, aware that Mooney was watching her, and she knew he was wondering if she would show signs of nervousness, reveal that the night news had affected her. She rolled up her hair as calmly and firmly as she could and went to the door. She took down the poles, wondering all the while if on the other side of that door Lacey Pollard stood. Or maybe up the hill he would be sitting, waiting.

She threw open the door. All she saw that moved was the cow pushing against the side of the stall.

She let her breath escape easily. She stepped outside and pulled the door closed behind her.

On the way to the spring, she kept looking to see if he was anywhere about. She reached the spring, had even started to kneel, when she saw his footprints in the damp earth.

She swung toward the woods. "Lacey," she said.

The woods were bare and lifeless; there was not even any motion in the trees.

She turned and knelt by the spring, moving carefully and awkwardly because of the bulky unborn baby inside her. She filled the pail, then pushed herself back to her feet. All the while she knew he was watching.

Without glancing at the woods, she walked up the hill to the cabin.

As she poured the water into the fireplace pot, she said, "He was at the spring this morning."

Mooney got out of bed at once and took his rifle from the wall.

"He's the boys' father," she said.

He stared at her, seeking some sign of her deepest thoughts, then set the gun aside.

She put a handful of beans into the water, then took the pail and went out to milk the cow. All the while she milked, she watched the woods, wondering where Lacey was and when he would show himself.

She was working in the field when his shadow fell on the ground before her; slowly she straightened. She was as firm as flinted stone, he saw. Age had toughened her. Her eyes were a darker blue than he had remembered them to be. Her lips were thin now, and not as red as sometimes they got to be near the fire heat. Her hands holding the hoe were rough.

Beside her Verlin stared fearfully, his mouth partway open, his teeth showing.

Lacey smiled. He bowed in a courtly way, and said, his voice light and deceiving, showing none of the secret dark currents within him, "I was walking by and I dropped in to see how you are, and I see you're getting on well." His gaze scanned the hillside to where the cabin was. The big man was somewhere down there, but was not in sight now.

"You've been gone a long while," Lorry said.

"Yes. How are you, Lorry?"

"I'm working yet."

"I see you are. And this is Verlin, is it?"

"Yes. Say hello to him, Verlin."

"Hello," Verlin said, whispering.

"You look like your uncle Grover, did ye know it?"

The boy replied but so softly the words couldn't be made out.

Lacey, embarrassed by his staring, turned to look at the crops. He looked about approvingly, speculatively at what he saw. "My, you got a nice place here, Lorry." He started on down the hill. "I tell you," he said, "you got a world of work already done on this homestead." He stopped to gaze at the crib, as if he had never seen a crib before. "Why, it's bold enough to hold corn for two families." He turned to Verlin. "You make that, boy?"

Verlin stared at him, still unable to adjust to his presence.

"And look a there," Lacey said, turning to gaze at the cabin. "It's a house sturdy enough to withstand any sort of weather." He moved to it, stopped at the door, stood there reflecting on the contents of it, this poverty home of his own wife and sons.

He turned suddenly, was about to speak when he saw the warning look on Lorry's face.

"Why did you come here, Lacey?" she said.

"Is the man about?" he asked.

"I don't know where he is. Maybe watching from the woods, where I expect you've been all morning. Maybe now you're here and he's watching. Or maybe he's gone down to the river." She walked past him and entered the cabin. She went to the fire and stared down at the hot-burning coals. "You'd best get away from here," she said.

"It's not so easy to leave, Lorry."

"Go on and let us be."

"You was fond of me once—"

She swung on him. "No, not now—"

"Maybe you'll be again."

"Lacey, for God sake—"

"I come to dinner," he said. "You going to ask me to stay?"

A shadow fell on the floor and they both swung around.

"He can stay," Mooney said.

17

The family sat at the table in the cabin, and Lacey told about a white bear he had seen near Watauga, which he and others had sought after for part of one winter, had trailed through cold and snow and ice and fog. When he finished the story, he commenced to tell about a creek beside an Indian village in Kentucky that rolled uphill. He told how the fallen leaves floated up hill in it, told it all with a light manner yet an honest voice, winking now and then at the boys, remembering for them every detail of the stories he had told about, even the color of the leaves in Kentucky and the ways the Indians talked.

The boys were caught up in his recitations as if they were prisoners to him, but Lorry looked on sternly. She wasn't even eating; she was sitting there watching Lacey, remaining solemn when Lacey laughed, then looking at Mooney, who was cautious now and severe.

Lacey seemed to notice neither of them; his eyes were on the boys, his smile was flashing at them as he told them about an Indian he had known in the Cumberland who had carried three rifles with him wherever he went, and could shoot a pine cone off a tree from forty paces. He talked about the Watauga settlement, told them how the houses were located near the road, and where the two mills were, and how the men took to Indian fighting. He told about the food parties they gave, and how the pies were stacked one on top of another. A buxom woman would slice through the whole stack, take out a piece as tall as a man's hand and put it on a tray, to be eaten by anybody who had a taste for pastry. This was after the chicken and turkey were gone, and the hams, which were eaten either cooked or raw, for he said cured hams could be eaten raw, and after the deer meat was eaten or fed to the dogs, and after the corn bread was cold. He told it all, and about the coffee steaming in his throat and gurgling in his stomach. He told about the white whiskey they drank, too, and the wine made from wild grapes, and remembered everything about a hunt he had gone on into Indian country.

Mooney sat across the table from him, eating little, watching him, and now and then noticing anxiously the way the two boys leaned expectantly toward him. Now and then Lacey would laugh, and Mooney would listen to the laughter as if seeking to identify it in his mind, as if trying to find out what reasoning there was in it or behind it.

"You boys go outdoors," Mooney said suddenly, interrupting Lacey.

The boys looked up at once, surprised and baffled. Lorry stared down suddenly at the table top. Lacey, who had been stopped in the middle of a sentence, had his mouth open yet. A half-laugh started, and he said, speaking softer and more apologetically than before, "I'm not quite done with my story."

"Go outdoors," Mooney said.

The boys, still confused, backed away from the table. Suddenly Lacey reached out, caught Fate's hand, held it as if he couldn't afford to be parted from the boy just then, and Fate, not having been touched by his father before in his own memory, seemed to consent to be held.

"Go outdoors," Mooney said, and when Lacey seemed about to object again, Mooney brought his hand down on the table, struck it a blow that scattered two bowls to the floor and so startled Lacey and frightened Fate that he ran out the cabin door.

Lorry awkwardly knelt and picked up the bowls, and without a word set them down near the hearth. She stood at the fireplace, looking down at the coals, her back to the two men at the table.

Lacey cleared his throat uneasily. He smiled. "I've not had a better meal in some time," he said. He took a piece of meat from his bowl and chewed on it, the juice dripping down along his fingers. He licked his fingers. "You can cook just like always, Lorry," he said in a relaxed, friendly way.

Lorry didn't know how he could remain so calm in a situation swelled by animosities, one so complicated in relationships that she could sense a dozen currents. She wondered about Mooney, about what he might do, whether he could control himself for long. She wondered about herself, too, for, seeing Lacey again, she knew she cared for him, not in the full-hearted, girlhood way of years ago, but she loved him yet. Each man was the father of the two boys, each in a way, and each one mattered to her.

The baby inside her began to move, as if seeking life of its own now, as if reminding her of itself and its needs.

"You hunt much?" Lacey said.

"I stay here at the place," Mooney said.

"You have a fine place," Lacey said, glancing about at the uneven walls. Above them the loft floor had warped and had many cracks, and from above the loft, light filtered down through the roof boards, which had cupped, too.

"This is only the start," Mooney said.

"Oh, it's got prospects, I see that," Lacey said. "It should be worth a lot of money. I was thinking about that while I was eating." He took another piece of meat out of his bowl and chewed on it. "I have some land in the Cumberland, there near the bend of the river where there's a place called French Lick, which was a buffalo stand once, where there was thousands of white buffalo bones when I first come there, back when the place was Indian land."

Mooney listened, not moving even in gesture.

"I have a piece of land there that's flat as this table top, have a section of land bordering on the river. A man can float his goods down that river to the French trading places, the Indians say. It has big possibilities for development. I bought it from a man in Morganton and have it in my mind to move out there permanently with my family."

He waited. Not a word was said. Lorry didn't even whisper an answer.

"I was thinking yesterday that I could buy a work horse from old man Harrison, and a little cart, and I could put on it all the things that are needed for my family, and start out. The first night we would stop up on the ridge and make a fire and cook our supper, and the next morning we would walk on down to the river. We would cross that maybe afore sundown, then go on west, following its banks, not often leaving the banks until we got to Watauga. I know so many men there I could trade easily for stock. Then, after resting, we could move on to the Cumberland, to where the settlement is starting, where it's well under way, where the land is rich and so deep a plow can never touch the bottom of it. We could be there in five or six days."

Once more he waited. Nobody said anything.

"I went away to find such a place," he said patiently, "and I wrote a letter once I found it." He hesitated, for Lorry looked up at him, surprised. "Did you ever get it?" he asked.

"No," she said.

"I thought maybe you'd not, for I had no answer. I asked in the letter if there was need to come fetch you and the boys or if you could bring them on out there. I got no answer, so I came here to claim what's mine."

Again, as if resting to a stop, he paused. Mooney sat still and sullen, waiting.

The shadows of the boys came closer to the door. The fire burned lower in the hearth. Lorry stood nearby, glancing now and then at Lacey, but revealing no personal commitment at all.

"Mountain land can be good land," Lacey said simply. "The trouble is that getting one's stock to market is not the easiest journey in the world. A man can have a fortune in stock up here, but have it closed off from markets by the hills and by the wild things and by the rivers. So no matter what a man owns, he's not wealthy, for a man can never hope to free himself from the place he's in, from what the place is."

"I'll get the stock out when the time comes," Mooney said.

"How many days of stock-driving, do you suppose?"

"I'll get through," Mooney repeated.

"They tell me that the piece of land I have on the Cumberland is the best one in the west. A new country is going to spring up out there, one far off from the old one."

"We're far off from the old one," Mooney said.

Lacey studied the shadows near the door where the boys were, then looked up at Lorry, who gazed back at him unyieldingly. He grunted, showing slightly the irritation he felt. "Nothing better than sitting in a cabin thinking," he said. He lapsed into quiet, and seemed to be considering deeply some friendly matter. "Would you care to swap?" he said, speaking so softly that the others could scarcely hear what he said. He leaned farther across the table. "I was thinking I could stay here and work this place, with old man Harrison once more close by. It's not what I planned on, but I would rather be back within his shadow than off alone. And you could take my place alone."

"I'm not anxious to move," Mooney said.

"No, I thought not," Lacey said. His fingers began tapping on the table top. His gaze moved about the room, from the gun to the powder horn to the shot pouch to the yarn to the bags of seeds, to Lorry standing at the fireplace. "Is there any other trade that might be made?" he said.

"No," Mooney said.

The incident here in this cabin, with her standing so straight and unrelenting, closed off his hopes for the coming days, Lacey knew, and even ruined, like wine turns sour, his memories of the family, of the Virginia times spent with them. He felt a helplessness, as if his past were being robbed from him and his own future altered, and in a way denied him. He had lost his history, his children, his wife, his home, his hope, all gently gone, all taken by the orderly minded man before him and by his own and the man's silent wife. "What are the boys to be? Farmers, too?" Lacey asked.

"So I intend."

"In this country?"

"Yes."

Lacey thought on that. "I'll give you my farm on the Cumberland. Take them both there, and take Lorry. There's more of a chance there."

"I don't accept. I'll not take favors."

"Favors for my own? Do I do favors for my own? I don't do a favor for you, but let me do a favor for them."

"We'll keep this land," Mooney said. "You work your own."

"Work it for what? I have no need of it. Nobody farms for himself; it's a family way to do."

"You keep it."

"I'll give it to her, or I'll give it to them—I don't care. But let them have a chance at it."

"No," Mooney said, "we're well set here."

"Well set?" Lacey said, dismay rising swiftly, but he controlled it and said no more. A helplessness seemed to come over him, and after a moment he got up. He stopped before Lorry briefly, then went out the door, and the bright sunlight dazed him.

His boys stepped back against the cabin wall and stared at him.

"You all right?" he said, not expecting them to answer, wanting to speak to them, that was all.

When he was near Imy's grave, he turned to look back at the cabin. He saw that Fate had come partway up the hill and was standing near the lambing pens, watching him. Lorry had come to the door and was standing in the shade. Suddenly anger came over him because of her, for not a word had she said in his behalf in all that brutal conference.

"My God," he whispered, viciously angry with them, with her. "My

God," he said aloud, and turned and went up the hill and out of the clearing, and on up the rocky path to where his horse was. He mounted it and started along the path which went above the clearing, anger rising in him thickly.

Suddenly he stopped his horse and sat there, trying to get control of himself. When he felt calm once more, he nudged the horse forward, fighting to control his bitterness, uncertain what he would do to relieve it.

18

To Lorry the falling of the rain, the growth and drying and breaking of green things, the cooking and eating and washing of the arms and hands and necks of the boys, the laughter in the firelight, the growth of the baby inside her were part of a pattern, as routinely and consistently drawn as the daytime light cast on the cabin floor through the summer-open door. Birth was natural. She had no worries about it. The birthing would be a day or a night of pain, with the old Negro woman tending her, as she had helped with the other births in Virginia.

The work—digging and cutting away, lengthening the open spaces, felling trees and skinning logs, chopping bark for the tanning trough, the daily chores—helped take up her mind so that the baby due to arrive was a relaxing thought.

The lambs were gentle in the field, she thought, but no more gentle than the baby would be, clutching at her breast, enfeebled by youngness and the efforts of being born.

Waiting for the bread to brown was a time she liked to think about the baby, or waiting for the boys to climb the ladder to go to sleep, late of a night when weariness came over her, or the time when she lay in the bed and waited for the wolves to hush, or waited for the distant crow of her father's rooster and the answering sound of the German's rooster from farther off. She would listen to the cabin creak and listen to Mooney breathe, listen to the boys turn on their pallets upstairs, and think about the baby.

Only when she thought about Lacey Pollard did she sense a tightening of the nerves. She and Mooney had not seen him in the weeks that followed their meeting. They did not talk about him, but he was in her thoughts, and in Mooney's; she could tell from a tenseness and wariness in him, and the way he watched the woods around the clearing. Tinkler Harrison had come to Lorry's cabin to tell her that there were those who said Lacey had gone away, to Watauga or the Cumberland, and others claimed to have seen him in the forest. Harrison added with full anger that she was setting all that valley out of joint. "When you choose the wrong man, you send the other man limp," he said.

Harrison's visit had been a brutal time. Mooney had come stalking down the hill, asking in a hard voice what Harrison had come to say, what he meant to try to do. Harrison mounted and left, frightened as she had not known him to be frightened for years past.

Mooney would put up with no hesitation; firmly he held the family unto himself, refusing to consider a contrary way. He had no patience with the idea that the law required her to go with Lacey; the law had sent him into a slavehood for twelve childhood years, he told her; what did he care about the law? There was no law here, anyway, except the ways of justice. The notion that the boys belonged to Lacey did not deter him either, for they were his by choice, by rights stronger than the happenings of an act of passion on a distant night. And wasn't she bearing now a child of his own?

She was grateful for his sureness; she wanted him to decide the issue and to permit no doubts to arise. And now in the birth she must bear well, she knew, and permit no doubt there, either.

At the first series of sharp pains, Fate rode to his grandfather's place. Harrison came outside, swatting at flies and cursing the heat. "Is she ready for the test?" he said.

"Yes," Fate said.

"Ay, God," he said. He sniffed of the sultry air. "She should a chose a nighttime, when it's cool."

"Aye," the boy said at once, anxious to get back and help her.

"I'll tell the woman," Harrison said. He went into the kitchen house and told the old Negro there to let the fire be as it lay and to get a clean length of cloth and her herbs.

Quickly she went out of the kitchen and to the slaves' cabin, where she kicked pallets aside and into a far dark corner. Fate could barely see the pallets on the floor, the work clothes hanging on pegs, the gourds tied on the walls.

He looked down into a gourd near the doorway and saw a dry, leafy substance, which he touched with his finger.

"No, no," the scrawny woman said, and charged toward him, shaking her head anxiously. "No."

He backed away, examining his fingers to see if they had been burned or hurt.

"Leave the red alder be," she said. Certain he was impressed by her, she went back to the far corner, where she began putting things into a shawl. "Them are red alder leaves."

Fate watched her, not wanting to be closer to her than he was, not wanting to go nearer that store of herbs, either, for with them and with her he associated pain and sickness and the mysterious attitude which was death, and with her, too, he associated spooks and witches and unnaturalness.

When she approached the door, he backed off a ways. She came outside, the shawl tied with a big knot in her hand. She walked toward the stable, where Tinkler Harrison was saddling her a horse. "Air ye ready?" he called as she approached.

She said nothing. In the kitchen she had been attentive to him, but now she was a person apart, equipped with her bag of cures for pain and trouble; she had taken on a different air. She was above him and apart from him; not a slave woman at all, but the healer.

She mounted the horse, sat sidesaddle on it, the bag on her lap.

"She won't go to a birthing without going on a horse," Harrison complained to Fate. "She gets so quare when she's called on to heal or deliver that she don't hear what's said. You can wave your hand in front of her face, but if she don't want to see it, she won't, and there's nothing to be done, for she's the only one here abouts with power to heal."

She sat on the horse and seemed not to hear him. Harrison gave the reins to the boy and told him to lead the horse to the clearing, that he would be along directly. "These things always take longer'n the woman predicts," he said.

Fate ran part of the way. The horse jogged, and the old Negro didn't tell him to go slower, not until they were halfway home. Then she almost fell off and awoke from the trance she was in. "Stop it, stop the horse," she said.

He stopped it, and he stood well away from her when he she got off, too.

"I'm older'n you think," she said, and sat down on a rock to rest.

When she didn't move for a long time, he said, "Mama needs help."
The old woman moaned to herself.

"Ain't ye coming?" he said.

She moaned again.

He licked his lips and studied about what to do. He thought about picking up a stick and hitting her with it, but he didn't want to hurt her, or to delay her, either. "You tended many birthings?" he asked. He got no answer. "I help with the lambs sometimes," he said. "We get twin lambs right often."

The old woman moaned. Maybe she didn't hear, he thought, or maybe she was interested in something else. "Where did you learn medicine?" he asked her.

She opened her eyes. She gazed at him as if out of a distant fog of thought. "Your grandmamma taught me," she said. "Your grandmamma knew all the herbs in the woods, all the barks and roots and leaves, too."

The boy had never heard much about his grandmother, except that she was sickly. "Is Mama going to hurt?" he asked. He didn't know how a baby was born. He knew about sheep and sows, and Mooney had told him the dog might bear soon, for he had bred her to the German's dog. But the boy didn't know about people.

"She'll pain," the old woman said.

"More'n a ewe?" he asked.

"More. More than a mare."

"Why?" he said.

"Because God twisted the woman. Don't you know that?"

"No'm," he said.

"The devil come on her one evening and told her to eat of the fruit of a tree, and she done it, though God had told her not to, and God come down in a chariot and hitched it at the garden gate, and he strolled down the lane and found the woman naked with Adam, both without a stitch on and loving shamelessly, and he commenced to gather in his holy wrath, and he said to git, git out of this holy place, and he pointed at them and lightning struck from his fingers and thunder rolled and broke from his nose and mouth, and the man run, but the woman fell, and God went to her and said, 'Eve, I've done twisted you up.' It was like a stick had been poked into her body to rupture her. 'It's a reminder whenever you're birthing,' God told her. Then he went back to the gate, walking slow, pained to have seen such sin."

The boy couldn't follow all of it, but it seemed like a firm truth. "Mama's sin?" he asked.

"Your mama suffers for it. Your grandmamma did, bless her sweet soul. God bless her," she said fervently, "Jesus bless her." She stared off, remembering then. "The pain's as deep as God's punishment," she said.

When they reached the house, he saw that Mina was there, and he felt better at once. She had been on her way home from Paul Larkins' deserted cabin, where Jacob and his wife, Florence, had set up housekeeping, when she saw Mooney up by the lambing shed, clutching his hands and looking distraught. She had found Lorry sitting on a chair near the open doorway, a thick sweat on her face and an anxiousness about her.

Mooney followed the Negro midwife indoors, but he came outside again directly, anxious to stand away from the pain, but not to leave altogether. He stood near the cabin door for a while and looked at Lorry with compassion, then critically studied the midwife, contemplated the seriousness of her, the way she had of looking at Lorry as if making an accusation against her, condemning her for the plight she was in.

Fate understood that look better than Mooney, for the old woman had told him about what the pain meant, and why it had to be, about the fierce anger God had had one morning. He understood well enough, but he didn't like her slowness. She had taken too long on the trail, and now that she had arrived, she didn't tell Lorry what to do or what to expect. From her dirty shawl, she began to take out herbs, which she laid on one corner of the table. She took out a few pieces of roots, too, and a copy of the Bible, which was old and had pages folded and torn and torn out. She took out a sharp knife and wiped it on the skin of her forearm, cleaning it. She took out a length of linen string. She took out three pods of red pepper.

Lorry sat by the fire, waiting. When she saw that the woman was ready, she rose. Her face got older and grayer as she stood there, her back to the door light.

The old woman began mumbling. She knelt on the hearth, took water from the pot and poured it into a jug. She took the red peppers and broke them, then split them with her fingernail to free the seeds; she fed the seeds into the jug, then broke the pod skins into pieces and dropped them into the jug. She set the jug in among the hot coals, so that the brew could steep.

She returned to the table, took one of the herbs and cut it with the knife into tiny parts and mashed them in her palm with the tip of the knife blade. Mumbling, she went to the fireplace once more and dropped the herb mash into the jar. She came back to the table and took up the closed Bible.

It was then, after all this, that she told Lorry to go to the bed. Lorry sat down on the edge of it, sat there breathing deeply, as if the few steps of walking had caused her a loss of breath. Fate pressed himself back into a dark corner of the room and watched fearfully.

Lorry threw the covers back from the bed and stretched out on the fresh straw matting.

The midwife had opened the Bible and was reading from it, but she wasn't reading, either, the boy knew; she couldn't read. She was reciting but not reading, and the words made no sense, but since the Bible was in her hands and open, the words she said took on the strength of the Bible and its history. She read and turned pages. Some of the pages were torn off at the top, but she didn't seem to notice; she read where the page was gone, then her eyes would move on down to where the page was left.

Lorry watched her, a sweat heavy on her face and body so that her dress clung to her. A pain gripped her and she moaned, and the midwife nodded heavily, accepting the sound as if she recognized it and had expected it, as if she had been reading about the sound in the Bible from that early page.

Fate moved from the corner slowly and sought the ladder to the loft, for he could not stay there any longer. He didn't want to leave his mother, but he needed the safety of his bed above. He needed that, the place he slept, but on the ladder he stopped. He couldn't bring himself to leave her.

Where was Mooney? he wondered. Where was Mina? Mina had been here and now was gone. Where was Ernest Plover? Where was his grandfather, or the new man, Jacob? Or his wife, Florence? Fate could run to Jacob's house and ask him and Florence to come. He could be there, if he ran, in a few minutes, and they would come surely. But he would have to leave his mother.

The midwife laid the open Bible on the table. She bent over it and touched it; then with trembling hands she tore off the top of a page. She balled it in her hand, touched it with bear grease from the slut on the table, moved to the fireplace and knelt down. She held the jug in her right hand and the ball of paper and Bible words in her left, and she put the ball in the ashes, set the jug down squarely on top of it, held it there, breathing deeply of the smoke that swelled up around it from the paper.

Once the smoke stopped, she came back to the table, carrying the jar of tea. She poured some of it into a cup and sniffed the odor of it. She tasted it and her face wrinkle and her mouth pursed with sourness. She made a sound deep in her throat, then went to the bed and gave the cup to Lorry.

Lorry drank what was there. It was bitter, Fate could tell from her expression. He wanted to go to her and throw himself on the bed and help her, do for her whatever he could, take for her whatever pain he could, drink the tea for her, bear for her whatever child needed to be born, save her from this midwifey creature.

The old woman brought the cup back to the table. She drank the last scalding drops of it, and her loose mouth chomped against itself. She shook her head in the throes of its bitterness.

Lorry moaned, and Fate watched as, under the dress, her body stiffened.

"Air they hard yet?" the old lady asked.

When the pain stopped, broke loose like a branch snaps on a dry tree, Lorry relaxed and nodded.

"Sit up," the old woman said.

Lorry shook her head.

"Sit up," the midwife said firmly, irritated by the delay.

"It's not needed," Lorry said.

"I have a way I do. Sit up."

With a sigh, Lorry pulled herself up and sat with her back against the side of the cabin. She began to murmur a prayer, or a plea, Fate didn't know, as the next pain increased inside her. Tears formed in her eyes; then her face seemed to freeze in place. The pain mounted and her body grew stiff and unyielding, sweat came out of the skin of her forehead and neck and throat, and the old woman behind the table leaned closer, closer as the pain mounted, murmuring, watching the pain as if the pain were sighted, could be seen walking toward her along the valley, as if the pain were coming to meet her from out of the garden, making the footprints God had made; the pain mounted as footsteps approach, the pain throbbed with the feet of old pages, with God's words falling as footsteps, mounted to the present place, this cabin, came on as the old woman bent closer and closer, God arriving, listening, listening for what sound the boy did not know, came into the cabin—

She screamed. Lorry screamed. She screamed and it dazed him, blinded him. He bolted forward, away from the wall, toward her, and it seemed he was fighting his way to her through a drifting stream that pulled him back and wanted to carry him to the wall again. He reached her and grasped her hand, and he felt then a heavy hand on his shoulder, and a hand on his chest, and caught a glimpse of the old woman as she pulled him away and forced him to the door, hurled him through it. Behind him the door slammed and the wooden poles slid into place.

Fate saw Mooney standing in the yard near the lambing shed, staring at the cabin door. Mooney didn't appear to notice him. He sat down on the ground near the cabin door; he was trembling so much he didn't dare try to walk. He wanted to walk, to go get Jacob, but he couldn't.

Verlin stood nearby. Fate said, "Go get Jacob, why don't ye?"

"Mina's gone to get him," Verlin said.

Fate closed his eyes tightly. Mina, he thought. Yes, Mina, hurry, hurry, Mina, hurry, he thought. He drew himself across the ground a ways, pulled himself away from the hated, closed door.

Harrison came up through the clearing, leading his horse, walking slowly, his head lowered, as if he were humble. He tied the horse to a post and took a place near the door. He clasped his hands behind him, licked his lips to taste the sweat on them. He moved his feet to get a firm place to stand, and waited. After a while, when he heard no sound, he said, "How far's she along?"

Mooney said nothing, nor did he look at the man, but Fate spoke up, for his grandfather had been generous to help thus far and might be able to help now. "She screamed once," he said, and looked up at him, hoping to see a sign that told him it was over, or that it was going properly.

"Your mother's strong," Harrison said, "so she'll more'n likely bear up all right, though the baby might not. Connie ain't lost a mother in some years now. She lost a few women in Virginia when she got a notion in her head that they ought to sit up to bear."

"She—she's sitting up," Fate said.

"No, no," Harrison said easily, "she don't use that style no more; that was what she done in Virginia, I told you."

Fate choked on his effort to speak. "She—she's doing it now," he said.

Harrison squinted down at him, his eyes sharp and questioning. He saw that the boy was telling the truth. "Why, she shouldn't be," he said. "A birth is painful enough the other way." He looked up at the doorway, as if remembering how painful a birth was, as if he had been carried back abruptly and set squarely in the midst of an experience he had gone through before. "Connie, open up the door," he said suddenly. "Connie, you let her lie down."

The dog, tied at the back of the lambing shed, turned to the cabin now, sensing danger. It was not a danger she had known before. She could not smell it, she could not see it; she saw only the same cabin she lived in and knew was safe, but the danger was near, she knew that, and she howled suddenly, startlingly, in fear and frustration.

The sheep moved anxiously about in the pen. The horse moved about in her stall. The cow watched with raised head from near the dogwood tree at the top of the clearing, not far from Imy's grave, while the dog kept on howling.

"Hush that dog," a woman said.

Fate's confused mind cleared and he saw Mina coming up the spring path, hurrying, Jacob behind her, and Florence farther behind.

"Hush that dog up, don't just stand there like tree trunks," Mina said, and Mooney came out of the stupor he was in and spoke sharply to the dog, and the dog stared at him, even more perplexed now than before. Mina moved past Fate and pounded on the door.

There was no answer from inside. Mina turned to Mooney. "She won't let me in."

Mooney frowned. "Damn her," he said. He looked past Jacob to where Florence was coming along now. "Wait till she gets here," he said.

"Connie ain't a bad midwife," Harrison said apologetically.

When Florence got to the yard, she stopped to get her breath, then pushed at the door to open it. She stepped back, surprised. "Shouldn't lock a door on a birth," she said.

"I told them to tell her to open it," Mina said. She pounded on the door. "Two women is out here to get in," she said. "You open this here door."

There was no answer.

"Damn her," Mooney said.

Harrison spoke up, "Connie, open up the door."

"Connie," Fate shouted. He felt a hand on his shoulder restraining him, and knew it was his grandfather's.

"You open this here door," Harrison said.

Mina knocked at the door, then struck it with the palm of her hand.

"She's in there," Harrison said. "She wants to do it all herself. She's as proud as a riding horse, and she's old and set in her ways." He looked sharply at the door and shouted, "Connie, open this here door!"

There was no answer. Mooney moved to the door and kicked it. The door trembled in its bed, but it held. He had made it to hold against almost any blow. He kicked it again, then moved back from it and studied it. He looked up at the chimney, which was large enough to climb down; smoke was boiling from it. "If I have to knock that door in," he said to Harrison, his voice trembling and dangerous, so that it chilled Fate to hear it, "I'm going to lash her." He spoke loud enough for the midwife to hear him.

There was no answer.

He went to a pile of logs near the crib. He selected a log, pulled it toward the door. The dog began to howl again.

Jacob took one end of the log and Mooney took the other. Harrison went to the door and pounded on it with his fist. "Connie, now you listen, you open up this door."

Fate stared at the door, awed that a woman could withstand so many orders.

"They're going to knock the door in," Harrison said. He pounded on the door again, but there was no answer. He stepped back, wiping his brow with his hands. He shook his head wearily and got out of the way, and Jacob and Mooney moved toward the house, struck the door with the log. The door flew open, and in that instant Fate caught a glimpse of the old woman kneeling on the floor near the bed, her face held by her two hands. She was staring straight before her, and on the bed, open before her, was the Bible with the torn pages that she could not read. And he saw his mother on the bed, sitting there still, the wall of the cabin pressed against her back, stiff with pain.

Belle arrived soon after that. She said Grover had gone to inform the

Germans and the Plovers, and that she herself had called the news to Mildred and Amos across the river. She went into the cabin and shut the door firmly.

Soon Grover rode up, only a little while ahead of the cross-river people, who came trooping in, carrying guns and food, the children strung out along the valley road. "Is it borned yet?" Frank asked as he stalked up through the field.

"Well, look a here," Amos said, impressed by the work that had gone into Mooney's clearing. "You have a prosperous place started here."

Mooney, murmuring, walked over to one side and looked at the cabin door.

Charley Turpin tied his horse. "Lord, looks like everybody's here," he said. "Where's the women—inside the house?" He walked about, limbering up. "Is the baby going to live?"

"Lord knows," Harrison said.

"If it lives, it will be a good sign for Mooney Wright, won't it?" Charley said.

Harrison, frowning, glanced at Mooney. "And a bad sign for Lacey."

The Plovers arrived with their brood, and Inez went at once into the cabin.

Charley Turpin went around saying hello to everybody. He even shook hands with the children. Then he walked across the clearing and set up several pieces of gum bark on tree limbs. "Anybody want to try his hand at shooting?" he asked.

Amos answered at once that he did, and Ernest said he would, too. The three men made small wagers, then fired at the bark. "You want to try your hand at it, Mooney?" Charley Turpin called.

"No," Mooney said solemnly.

Every time a man would hit a piece of bark, he would let out a whoop. Belle opened the cabin door and said to make less noise out there, but the men didn't pay any attention to her. Tinkler Harrison walked up the hill and made a wager. He fired carefully and won his bet, for he splattered the piece of bark all over that part of the woods.

The men went on shooting, but Harrison's powder got low, so he came back to the cabin, for he was not one to borrow anything. "Is she about through?"

"Nobody appears to know," Mooney answered.

"If it don't live, most likely she'll be going back to Lacey. You know that don't you? It'll be God's will, clear and simple."

Charley took aim and fired at a chip of bark, and struck it dead center. He let out a cry. "Ain't that something?"

"It was the closest bark," Amos said dryly.

"That's all right. I hit it. You too nervous to try, Mooney?" Charley said.

The Germans arrived and Nicholas proved to be the best shot. This so irritated Charley Turpin that he suggested there be a change of sports to wrestling. Nicholas said he had never wrestled, but no excuse would do. There was a wrestling bout, which Charley won.

Nicholas' loss so irritated the young German, Felix, that he asked for a bout with Charley himself. Charley said he thought that was as funny as a story told by a woman, and he went to his horse and got some whiskey to wet his throat, to prepare, he said. He came back up the hill, calling for Felix to look to himself afore he got hurt. When he was close to Felix he suddenly spat whiskey in the boy's face. Before Felix could get his sight, Charley got a grip on him and tried to throw him to the ground.

The boy stayed on his feet. Charley jabbed his knee into Felix's groin, but the boy would not go down. Charley bit the boy's arm, but like a stout tree Felix stood there. "Damned Dutchman," Charley said.

Felix got a hold on him; his big arms closed around him. Charley's eyes got bigger and bigger as he tried to keep from crying out. Felix lifted him. Whiskey and dirt were in his eyes, were matted there, but he could see well enough to lift Charley from the ground and hurl him down, then fall on him. Charley bit him, but Felix held him down until Charley said he was whipped. Then a cry went up from Nicholas, and laughter went around.

Charley got up from the ground and walked about, angry and frustrated, claiming that Felix had cheated him. "I'll race ye and beat ye at that," he said, spitting dirt out of his mouth. "You big bastard, I'll beat ye at that."

"Here's ye the jug, boy," Frank said. Felix tilted it to his mouth and drank until tears formed in his eyes. It was one of the few drinks of whiskey he had ever had.

Fate had been amazed by the goings-on. How anyone could shoot and wrestle while a person was suffering was beyond him. He wished he didn't even know them, much less have to stay in the same settlement with them; he was so annoyed he went down to the spring and stayed off to himself until his worry about his mother made him come back.

He walked back to the cabin and was about to ask if there was news, when Mina stepped out of the cabin. The dog looked at her and growled, for the dog was confused beyond his own power to reason or to know friend from enemy. Mina let the door lean closed against the frame. "It certainly is taking a long time," she said. She smiled wanly. "That old woman ain't doing nothing except praying, talking in foreign tongues like a witch."

Mooney murmured a few words.

"What you say?" Mina asked.

"Damn her, I said."

"I say the same as you," Mina said. "If I was to have a baby, I expect I'd do it alone afore I'd listen to her. We made Lorry lie down, and that old witch got to complaining, but she let us do it. I said nothing mean to her, and Florence didn't neither, because you never know when you'll need doctoring your ownself. Anybody might catch an earache or a back suffering, and it don't do it to irritate her needlessly."

Fate didn't want to listen to them talk any more, for they seemed to believe it could all be understood. He walked up to where the dog was, and after a while he was able to pat her head without her snarling at him. "You see how it is?" he said to her.

He heard his grandfather talking to the other men, getting louder as he talked. "They sent for Connie once in Virginia to come help a woman bear, and it was a lightning storm that night, and she got on a horse and I mounted one, too, for I didn't know but that her horse would bolt. The storm was close above us, and the thunder would crash in our ears. The horse I rode would squat down and shake and tremble, then carry me on for a ways, but her'n never faltered, and she never fell from it, neither, though sometimes the horse moved faster'n the word o' God. She looked far off into the distance and sat it."

Jacob shook his head irritably. "It appears to be strange," he said.

"There are strangenesses to all we do in birthing." Harrison nodded knowingly. "She considers what she's about. Did you know that when a baby's born, it's best to hold it upward by its heels and shake it?"

"No, never heard tell that," Jacob said.

"Keeps the liver from growing to its side," Harrison said. "Did you know that when a baby won't come to life in birth, if you get a man other'n its father to blow into its mouth, it'll commence to squall and unblue?"

Jacob seemed to be none too impressed. "Imagine that," he said.

"She's got the knowledge," Harrison said. Even as he praised her, however, it was evident that he was annoyed. "She's so old, that's all, so set in her ways, and she don't know nothing in the world but doctoring."

"She burned a page of the Bible," Fate said suddenly. Harrison and Jacob turned and stared at him. Each man considered him as if from a long way off, then Jacob moved away, and Harrison turned slowly and looked at the cabin, both men ignoring what he had said, sensing the seriousness of his charges, and the boy felt a pang of wonder and fear at their strangeness.

All that day the men waited. They ate what food they could get and shared what they had, and some of them spent the afternoon throwing rocks and wrestling. Toward evening, Belle came to the cabin door and all the men looked down that way; they were tired now and ready for the baby to be born so that they could have their supper fixed. Belle stood in the open doorway for a moment, swaying there as if about to faint. She came on out and let the door shut.

Harrison said, "What's happening?"

"She's bearing yet." She leaned limply against the cabin.

"Is it turned wrong in her?"

Belle covered her mouth, but she was sick beyond controlling herself; her stomach threw up what it could, and she began to weep, she was so ashamed of being sick before so many men.

"Oh, for God sake," Harrison said, embarrassed. "Well, at least cover it up. If you're going to make a shame of yourself, at least throw dirt over it."

"Let me alone, will you?" she said. "I never saw the likes of a birth afore."

"Well, you would a saw it if you'd not been sterile of womb, for you've had enough seed put to you. To come to my old age childless by a young wife is disgrace enough without her throwing up what she's eat all over the yard. Fate, get that covered up." He turned away from her and stalked up to the cornfield and walked through the rows of corn, looking at the tassels, as if they mattered one whit to him.

Mooney stood apart, staring at the cabin door, and Fate sat off by himself watching Mooney, the men and the cabin, uncertain of what he might do or when he might get a chance to do anything at all. It was twilight when the door was opened again. This time Mina came out. She stood in the doorway for a little pause, looking at Mooney; then she nodded to him. He came forward quickly, as if she had called him. Fate heard him say, "Is it borned?"

"Yes," she said, "it's borned."

"Is it alive?"

"It is," she said.

Relief swept over Mooney. He turned to the men, and as he turned, old man Harrison took off his hat, threw it to the ground and stomped it. "Well, I'll be damned," Fate heard him say. Charley Turpin's grin widened. "Why I knowed it would come in due time."

"It's borned," Mooney said.

"What kind is it?" Jacob called.

"It's a girl," Mina said.

"I never heard of a girl taking so long," Charley said.

"It's borned," Mooney said again, assuring himself and them that it was so.

———

Florence pushed the heavy door open and let the fresh air come into the room. Fate stayed outside, but Charley and Amos went in at once.

Florence came outdoors and looked about at the failing light. "Don't you want to see your sister?"

Fate shook his head. He hadn't any need for her, he said.

"She got a head full of hair, but she'll lose it afore long. They always lose it afore they get their own."

He nodded as if he knew all about that.

The midwife came out, the shawl wadded up and held in her knotted hand. She was weary and upset. She stopped outside the door and looked spitefully at the house; then she went to her hitching place and mounted the horse. She sat there on the animal considering the day, and either with meaning or without, she spat toward the house.

She looked down at Fate, and a grim smile came to her face. "Did you learn what it's like?" she asked.

"Damn you," he said.

"It pains, don't it?" she said. "The sin pains getting out. A woman's birthright."

As she turned her horse to leave, he sprinted around in front and began to talk, words bubbling out. "Damn you," he said, "damn you, you don't care," he said. "You want it to pain, you witch! You're a witch!"

The horse reared; it jolted down and the woman almost fell off. Fate picked up a switch and beat at her, struck the horse with it. The horse again reared, and the woman shouted shrilly for Fate to stop. Fate charged the horse again, and the horse wheeled and started to run, the woman bouncing up and down on the saddle; Fate started after her, but somebody caught him and he flailed about helplessly to get free. The man held him and he saw that it was Jacob and he knew he could not get free from Jacob. He stopped fighting then and began to cry, and Jacob held him close and said, "Don't worry none about it, don't worry."

Fate didn't go into the house until his eyes were dry. Then everybody made way for him. He saw his grandfather watching him and his grandfather nodded, as if saying it was all right to scare his horse, and Florence turned away, as if she were about to cry, and he went to where his mother was, and the baby thing was sucking its supper, but he didn't look at it or think about it. His mother held out her hand to him and he put both his hands in hers. She drew him closer to her, and she said gently to him, "Why, Fate, you're all a tremble." She pressed his hand, she who was not trembling at all now. "Don't you know," she said softly, "that the pain a woman has when a baby is born is the easiest forgot in the world."

19

"W e going to dance?" Amos asked, coming down from the woods, weaving from drunkenness, belching and clutching at his stomach. "Play us a song, Ernest," he said. He set a jug of whiskey nearby.

They were over across the river now, where they could freely celebrate the birth.

Ernest took up the jug and drank from it, letting the whiskey gurgle down his throat for a long while. He picked up his fiddle and pressed it to his chest. "Now I'm getting prepared," he said.

Fancy was there, sitting on a stump talking with two of the little boys. Charley Turpin went over to her and asked her for a dance. Amos' wife, Mildred, came out of the house, and her brother-in-law, Frank, said he wanted to dance with somebody and winked at her. She winked back, then laughed in the hollow tones she had.

Frank's wife, Edith, got up from the log, where she had been resting. She was a tired-faced, frail woman with a faint beauty about her, and she smiled for the first time that evening. "You children stay back from the fire," she said. Two of her boys started throwing firebrands about. "You set these woods to burning and you'll get a hide-tanning."

Amos came up to her and bowed in courtly fashion. "You dancing?" he said.

She guessed she was, she said.

The music started, Ernest playing and singing in a forthright manner. The words and melody floated out, stirring the thoughts of the men, sending their feet to shuffling. The children went to dancing, or tried to dance, and moving shadows were thrown by the fire onto the trees and the walls of the cabin.

> As I come down the mountain
> I give me fiddle a bow

You ought to have heard those pretty little girls
Say, "Yonder comes my beau,
My proud and handsome beau."

One cold frosty morning
Amos trooped down the road;
He had no shoes upon his feet,
So the frost bit off his toes,
All eleven of his toes.

The children began laughing. Amos bowed to Ernest.

Charley, he's a nice young man,
Charley, he's a dandy;
Charley is the very man
To pull my Fancy's candy.
Or try to.

Fancy looked flustered at such a comment from her own father, and
Charley roared with laughter.

Over the river to feed his sheep,
Over the river to see Charley,
Over the river young Fancy went,
And fed the sheep on barley.

When one song was done, he started another, the dancing continuing
all the while.

Oh, I went down to Mildred's house.
She was standing in the door
With her shoes and stockings in her hand
And her feet all over the floor.

One of Mildred's sons fell on the ground laughing, and his back had
to be pounded to keep him from choking.

The dance was long and exhausting; the dancers, as Ernest stopped fiddling, flopped to the ground, no strength for mischief left in them. The men took a drink of whiskey, and there was storytelling for a time, and efforts to pleasure the children with yarns about goblins and spooks. During one ghost story, Frank's littlest boy got so scared he chattered his teeth; Amos' oldest sneaked up behind him, his mouth full of river water, which was of course cold as ice, and sprayed it over the smaller child, who let out a scream and wet his pants all in the same panicked instant. That set everybody to laughing. The little boy was so upset he went off behind a bush to hide himself, but the memories of spooks and witches brought him back to the fireside.

"There was a witch lived nigh Morganton," Amos said. "She was an old hag, had no kindness to her. She would go out of door on moon nights and bark at the moon like a fox, or ary other distraught creature. She would invite little youngins into her house and feed them food she had put evil in, and for days after that the youngins would go around getting into mischief. One of the Caldwell youngins eat a biscuit she give him, and he went out in the field and cut the tail off a cow. You never saw such a mess as them flies gathering on that cow's stub. Even a hornet landed there."

"God preserve us," Mildred said, cackling out. She had heard the story many times, but she had never heard about the hornet before.

Frank said, "I heard Henry Phillips, the old cuss that kept marrying whoever was standing nigh, got so aggravated with his wife one day he cut the tail off the cow and beat her with it."

"Flailed her, did he?" Amos asked.

"They said he could slash that tail through the air like a bullwhip, for it's got hair on the end to give it weight and presence."

"You women take care," Amos said. "Mildred, hand me that there jug, or I'll go get that cow's tail and beat hell out of you."

"Get it yourself," she said.

He reached for the jug, but he couldn't get it. All he did was break his pants belt. "Good lord. You hand me that there jug, Mildred." He was angry now. "When a man tells his wife to do something, she should do it, God damn it. Look a there, I busted my belt."

"You've busted it afore," Mildred said calmly.

"You hand me that jug, Mildred," he said.

One of the children came forward to get it for him, but he shoved the child back.

"You hand it here, Mildred."

Mildred stayed where she was. "It's a brave man that will order a woman around," she said, "even after the woman has bore him six youngins."

"Ay God, if that jug ain't in my hand afore I count to three, you'll know more'n the pains of birthing."

Mildred wiped snuff juice from the corners of her mouth. She calmly looked at Amos, then belched, and the belch seemed to defy him.

Amos leaped at her, but she bolted away. He landed in the dirt and the children set up a gale of laughter, but the laughter stopped short when Amos began to curse as he moved toward Mildred. She began to move cautiously around the fire, evading him.

Amos, seeing he couldn't catch her, leaped for a rifle, but even as he picked it up Frank grabbed him, pinned his arms to his side, and Charley Turpin took the rifle out of his hands. No matter how much Amos struggled, the two men held him until he was quiet and promised to stay that way.

Mildred walked to her place near the fire and sat down. "My, my," she said. She began fanning herself with a turkey wing. "Don't matter a mind in this world about him," she said to Ernest, who had watched the scuffle without moving from the fiddling log. "Whiskey makes him ornery, that's all."

Others arrived, attracted by the sounds of music; among them were Grover, Mina, Jacob, Nicholas Bentz, and his son, Felix. There was loud talking and gun firing, followed by a dance, which left everybody spent. Mina was so exhausted that she walked down through the brush to the riverbank and sat down with her feet dangling in the cold water. She couldn't see the campfire now, but she could hear some of what was said. Felix said something to Charley Turpin, and he made a reply. She heard Frank's boy come running to the fire, and she heard a call from upriver. It was all pleasant-sounding and lively, and a proper way to let pass on off the memory of Lorry's struggle.

Strong arms went around her all of a sudden; she gasped in surprise and squirmed, tried to break free. It was Nicholas Bentz, she suspected, getting hold of her, which he had tried before, daring to do so now that he was drunk. She was pushed roughly to the ground, and she heard a low voice laughing softly as she wiggled against him.

"You let me go, Nicholas," she whispered. "You hear?"

"Does Nicholas get you on the ground, too?" It was Charley Turpin, not Nicholas at all.

"You let me go," she said angrily. Her feet were in the water, and she was slipping down the bank into the water now, and he was letting her slip down. "Let go." She heard her father talking back at the fire.

"They'll hear you if you yell," Charley said. "Why don't you yell?"

"I don't want to alarm the whole place," she said bitterly. "Now you let me go."

One of his hands began to move alongside her waist and seek her breast. She half turned, but he held her. He got to kissing the back of her neck and shoulders, and when she squirmed, he made her slide down farther into the water, so she couldn't even squirm, and then he was holding her close to him and rubbing her shoulder with his chin and was talking gently to her and rocking her slightly, as if she were a baby, and once she whispered to him in spite of the way she disliked him.

They slid even farther into the water. "Law, I'm getting my tail wet," she said.

He kissed her neck, and when she turned her head, he kissed her cheek and tried to kiss her mouth. He turned her body around and got a tight grip on her. She saw a little stick nearby, a pointed one, and when he leaned over to kiss her face, she put the point of the stick against the back of his neck. "I'll knife you, Charley Turpin."

"You won't, either." He kissed her and the stick dropped out of her hands and there wasn't anything she could do, she guessed. She thought about that man in the blacksmith shop a long time ago in Virginia, but it seemed so far away now, and here she was with a man she liked next to nothing at all, and his hands were on her body and he was in the water with her, they were halfway in the water, and the bank earth was cold to her back, and he was whispering to her again.

Suddenly she brought her knee up sharply against him and wiggled free, leaped away from him, and waded out from him into the river.

"Come on now, Mina, what's that matter?" he said, astonished and angry. "You said you loved me."

"Law, listen to that," she said. "As if I meant a word I said to you while you was biting my ear. I just said what I thought would make you glad."

"You and me could beat the world, don't you know that? Now come on back here to this bank."

"You get a hold on a woman that she can't break, and then you say she loves you."

He started toward her, wading slowly, but she moved farther into the stream, toward where most of the mist was rising. His teeth got to chattering and he stopped. "When I catch you I'm going to teach you something," he said.

"I thought that was what you just tried."

He tried to run toward her, but she turned and swam downstream. He was chattering and murmuring threats, and was exasperated with the cold and the predicament he was in. "You devil," he said, and started for her again, but he slipped and fell into the water and a shout came out of him, one of surprise and cold-anguish, and the group back at the fire set up a questioning.

He was wading toward the bank when Grover and Felix Bentz reached the riverbank. Felix, who could see that Mina had been trying to flee Charley, let his jealousy of her and his dislike for Charley get the better of him. He leaped, caught hold of Charley, and carried him backward into the river with a splash and a cry. Nicholas arrived and moved at once to fight beside his son. Frank came into the water and began helping his friend Charley. Mina was amazed to see such a commotion; she had never before seen such solid hitting of blows.

Frank, with his staff, broke up the fight. He whacked Felix then turned on Charley, and broke it up completely in the way he would break up a hog fight in the road, and the men stumbled over to the bank and slumped against it, clung there exhausted. It seemed like the only ones who weren't all wet and soggy and club-beat were Amos, Ernest and the children, who were up on the bank looking down, confused smiles on their faces.

The men helped each other up the bank and back to the fire. Mina, water dripping from her hair and body, her clothes clinging to her, climbed out of the cold river and sank down on the bank. Grover came close to her, stooped over her and touched her face. She slapped at his hand. "Git away," she said, out of sorts with them all now.

Soon after Grover left she heard the sound of music at the fire and somebody said, "To hell with women," and a shout went up. Evidently all the men were friendly once more.

Disgruntled, she looked back toward the camp and saw Mooney, who must have just arrived, coming along the path. He saw her and came to stand over her, and she felt more comfortable all at once and was grateful to him. "How is Lorry feeling?" she said.

"She's well and better," he said. He sat down on the riverbank. "It's been right much of a night, I hear," he said.

She had to smile at that, and she felt friendly toward him and leaned over and put her chin against his shoulder and nudged him. "There's been a party going on," she said. It's like all the others, except there's been only two fights so far."

They listened to the music together; then he said, "Did he get to you, Mina?"

She touched his arm and squeezed it. "No," she said.

"He's a clever man, so I thought he might've, but he's not a steady one. He's not going to give a woman a place for her family, and you'll be wanting one of those afore long."

"I saw Lorry work the day through bearing, and if I thought I had to do that, I'd jump in that water and float away."

"You better leave Charley Turpin alone then," he said, smiling. "I expect he's got an attraction for women, with that head of curly hair and those big dark eyes."

She sniffed; it was chilly and she was catching cold sitting on that damp place; she ought to go to the fire, she knew, but she had rather talk like this. She could stay there all her life and have him close by to comfort her, for she was content to be with him. Maybe they could have made a life together if she hadn't got skittish in that cabin three years before. She wouldn't have been skittish, she guessed, except for that man who had tried to attack her in Virginia, and had hurt her so much. She supposed life went from one such moment to another, each one breaking open and showing itself, each one coming on a person in surprise and with freshness, yet each one a reminder of the others, so that they were the prints her life made as it had found its way through all the many plights of place and time and had come at last tonight to this river.

She caught a willow branch in her hand and ran her fingers along it, entwined her fingers in the twigs of it. "I used to think about you all the time," she said. "Even after you married Lorry, I would think about you."

"What did you think?"

"I thought I'd die, I did, for a long time. Then I forgot about you mostly."

He smiled. "You might get that young German for a mate. He's strong."

"Make sauerkraut all my life?"

"Yes, that may be, but you're not Charley's kind of woman, either, are you?"

"Sometimes I am," she said. "Sometimes I get to wanting to love somebody crazy."

"Uh huh," he said. "You better watch those kinds of days."

"It comes on me mostly at night," she said, and saw him smile, so she smiled, too, and suddenly she turned to him and said, "I think about Lacey Pollard of a time, too, but seems like ever man I like has got to travel."

He considered that. "I'm only telling you that Felix is the best one that's here now. You need to choose a strong one, for it's no pleasure farming a mountain place alone. It takes a will to do it. And there's a plenty that's not got it."

She turned to view the river and fell to wandering about Lacey Pollard and where he was now, and about herself and what she was to do, caught as she was. "You ever worry about me when—afore you married Lorry?"

"That's right," he said, his voice husky. "I worried afore. I've always been more'n average fond of you."

"Do you think about me now?"

"I do," he said. "I do. It's there yet. But a man has never had a better woman than Lorry."

She let the words settle into the river sounds; then she pressed her head against his arm, nudged her chin at his arm. "You're funny to hear talk," she said. "You and Lacey speak so well of Lorry."

A fiddle started playing another tune. She heard Charley let out a yell. "How many kinds of love are there?" she said.

"Oh," he said, "there's kinds I don't know."

"I love you so much, and I love Felix, and I love Grover, and I love my sisters, and I love Charley, but they're ever' one a different love. Maybe love is like collecting things, like collecting colored rocks to put at the bottom of a spring."

"It might be. I wouldn't be surprised," he said.

"And some people got so many they can't hardly use the spring. And some people got just the one. Or none at all."

"That older boy of mine, he thinks I don't have a fondness for him, but he don't know. 'Course, he's not like me, and I don't understand him, but I think as much of him as I do the other'n, and maybe think about him more, for I know I've not been able to help him as much. He looks to Jacob now more'n he does to me, for Jacob knows hunting, and I don't interfere, for it seems Jacob knows what that boy is after. If a boy don't want to plow and plant and harvest, I don't know what he's after. That's why I like Felix, and why I never have got to care for Charley Turpin, nor to think he's the one you need. And I don't know what to make of Lacey Pollard, except it seems to me after all he's done that he's not a proper sort."

He had not meant to say that, but it was said now. He got up, embarrassed by his frankness, and stared out over the shiny river.

She stood up, too. "I love you like a piece of colored stone," she said, and went up the path toward the fire.

The party got bigger as the night wore on. People came and went, the fight was forgotten, the whiskey was passed around again and again. Ernest played better than ordinarily; everybody got to singing so loud they got hoarse, and they danced until they were leg-weary. Ernest was the last to lose his powers and call a night of it. His arms were tired from playing; it seemed his arms had sapped the strength from the other parts of his body, and he was wobbly as he went down the trail that led away from Mildred's house, from the ashes of the fire, from the empty jugs and sleeping children.

Where is Mina, he wondered, and where is Fancy? The last he had seen of Fancy she had been running from Charley Turpin. Where had they got to?

The moon went behind a cloud. He stopped and tried to remember where he was. It was hard to keep track of a woods like this, of where one was in it, in the dark. The bench must be on down the trail.

Suddenly a figure loomed up out of the darkness. It rushed toward him, making strange sounds. He froze in his tracks, and it came on and brushed past him, and was gone all in one instant. As his terror lessened, his fuddled brain began to work. It had been a woman, he reasoned, a large woman. It must have been Mildred. And she had been sobbing and running back toward her house.

He waited. Not another sound, not a breath did he take that could be heard. He waited until the moonlight came out again, and he saw that the trail was empty.

It had all been a vision, he realized, and supported by confidence, he boldly walked on down the trail. He had not gone far, however, when the moon went behind another cloud and directly his foot struck something hard but yielding that sent him sprawling on the ground. Cursing, he groped around for his fiddle. His hand touched something warm. The moon came out again, and he looked down at the figure of a man lying still, his mouth open as if he were trying to speak or cry out. Amos, he thought, Amos dead drunk. But why wasn't he breathing?

Not so, not so, Ernest thought, turning away, shutting his mind to the sight and to his thoughts. Ah, he had seen so many sights that were not so.

He got up and stumbled away, seeking the bench, and found it before he was fully aware that he was there. He stopped at the edge of it, wondering how he was to cross a bridge so narrow. He moved onto it, driven by his fears of the place he was leaving, fleeing the ghost of the dead man who he knew was not dead, hurrying, until suddenly he stopped, sank down on the shaky bridge to save himself from tumbling headlong into the river, his confidence in both bench and reasoning leaving him at the same time. He held to the bench with both hands and stared down at the rushing water.

He began to inch his way forward, holding to the board, accepting unprotestingly such splinters as the board stuck into him, swearing an end to the curses of drink and nighttime travel.

20

Often Mina would go by and see Lorry's baby. It was as round-faced and pretty as any she had ever seen, and Mooney most often was hovering about, talking about every look and way the baby had. He said the baby, whom they had named Amarantha, could tell when Mina was singing. Mina knew a lot of songs babies liked, for she had sung a hundred to her own sisters.

> Bye, baby bunting,
> Daddy's gone a hunting
> To get a little rabbit skin
> To wrap the baby bunting in.

The baby would smile and laugh with Mina.

> Pitty patty poke,
> Shoe the wild colt.
> Here a nail, there a nail,
> Pitty patty poke.

Verlin and Fate learned to sing some of the songs. They were both timid at first, but singing soon became as natural with them as talking.

> I bought me a hen and my hen loved me
> I fed my hen under yonder tree.
> Hen said, "Fiddle I fee."
>
> I bought me a turkey and my turkey loved me,
> I fed my turkey under yonder tree.

Turkey said, "Gobble gobble,"
Hen said, "Fiddle I fee."

I bought me a duck and my duck loved me,
I fed my duck under yonder tree.
Duck said, "Quack quack,"
Turkey said, "Gobble gobble,"
Hen said, "Fiddle I fee."

The song went on and on. Sometimes it seemed to take up much of the afternoon, with the sheep saying, "Baa baa," and the horse saying, "Neigh neigh," and the guinea saying, "Potrack potrack." Mina made up many new verses for it.

I had my baby and my baby pleased me,
Had my baby in the crabapple tree;
Baby says, "Ba ba,"
Turkey says, "Gobble gobble,"
Guinea says, "Potrack potrack,"
Hen says, "Fiddle I fee."

She liked more than anything being there in the house, cuddling the baby and laughing with Lorry and the family. Often when she left there, she would go up to Jacob's place and fuss with him, for he liked fussing so well and seemed to want her company. One evening she was coming back from there and was almost to Mooney Wright's clearing, when she noticed the hoofprints of a big horse. She stopped and saw through the trees a black jacket hanging on a tree.

She moved up a small path and came upon Lacey Pollard sitting there.

He had been down to Morganton. He had been waiting, he said, but he didn't say for what. He had got restless, he said, and there was indeed a restlessness about him, Mina saw.

"I went to her clearing and I heard a babe cry," he said.

"Yes," Mina said. "It's borned. It's a girl."

"So it lived?"

"Yes. Did ye want it to die?"

He considered that, and without answering turned and went up past a stand of bushes, and stayed up there on the mountain until it was so dark Mina had to lead him and his horse down the trail to the cabin in Harrison's field, which he agreed to use that night.

———

When he awoke, it was morning, and she was there.

"I never saw anybody sleep so much in my life," she said. A fire was made and she crouched before it, heating water in a skillet she must have borrowed. "I was a telling myself a while ago that it looked like you wasn't going to wake up today at all, but would cuddle yourself to nightfall."

He watched her, suspicious of her kindness to him.

"I've been hoping the birds wouldn't out do theirselves a singing so loud. They're so noisy they seem to think they're part bobcat. There's a mockingbird not more'n a stone's throw from the spring that thinks it's a lawyer in a courtroom." She put more wood on the fire. "I talked to it a while ago and said you was sleeping and for it to quiet its singing. I said you was making enough noise your ownself. I never heard a man make so much noise sleeping. You was a moaning and groaning your soul away. You was a cradling your head and sighing like a heartsick sheep."

"Maybe we're not all cheerful as you," he said gravely. He put his feet over the edge of the bed.

"'Oh myyyyyyy,' you was moaning; then you would groan and then you would say, 'Loo-rrrrrrrrry.'"

"What was I saying to Lorry?"

"Not so much to her as to your own bed. You was hugging it and talking to it."

He grunted and went to the door, where he looked out at the weather and his father-in-law's cleared fields. Mina rested back on her heels and studied him thoughtfully. "I know how it is to be sad," she said.

"Do you now?" he said.

"I've been sad afore. Not many people lives to be as old as me and not get sad."

"That's so," he said.

"Many a time I've had disappointment stuck in me like a thorn, and it's not the sort of pain a cup of sour adder tea will cure." She smiled up at him. "Wouldn't it be better'n a creek full of sirup if there was a tea that would cure a person's sorrows?"

"Yes, I suppose it would," he said.

"I would have drunk my fill many a time. I'd a drowned myself with it, if the truth was known, that time three year ago when so much worry struck me all in a season."

"When was that?" he said, crouching beside her, watching appreciatively the quick, flowing changes of her expressions.

"I won't say who it was, nor who it wasn't, but a man left me for another, and it certainly did get the better of me. I expect I would a hugged my bed at night, myself, if I'd had a bed."

"Was it Grover?"

"Law no! I don't think he cares for me."

"Was it that German boy?"

"Who, Felix?" She laughed out loud. "You think I'd look more'n a second time at a German boy?"

"I've known good Germans back in the fighting places."

"I wouldn't any more go courting a German boy than I would turn over on my back on the floor and roll in the dirt. And that Felix is so fat in his legs that he looks like he's standing on gateposts."

"He's stout, strong for work, that's all."

"I'll have to say this for myself: I never have wanted to rob the cradle to get a boyfriend."

"Felix is old enough to court, seems to me."

"If he could bring his mama with him."

"No, he's old enough."

"He's got such a round face his wife'd wake up in the night and think the moon had got into the room, and he's got such a thick tongue on him that a body has to piece together what he says long after he's done with it."

He was about to tell her it didn't matter who had deserted her years before, when he realized all in a moment who it must have been. A pang of friendship instantly came over him. "I know now," he said gently. He touched her hair, brushed it back from her face. "I understand," he said. He felt a kinship, a nearness to her. "My, my," he said, then smiled. "You and me suffer for the same cause."

They ate for breakfast four hen eggs which Mina had brought with her, and she suggested he interest himself in what noon dinner might be. Instead of that he started talking about Lorry. "She cut me off from myself," he said, "and my boys will grow up to be like him, be mountain farmers, that's all. There's more to life than that, God knows, and they'll guess about it sometimes. They'll come across a new thought now and then when they're plowing. A voice inside them will ask if it's not strange how life is, how it goes on. Here you are out in a field; how did you get here, a voice will say."

She studied him curiously.

"A man might sometimes stop his ox or horse, and pinch himself to be sure he's real. Like now, here in this cabin with you, I might pinch myself to be certain I'm here and real, and not dreaming or caught up in some idea I had once, or a story somebody told me."

She tried her best to think of something reasonable to say. It had always been her nature to be polite to a person. "I don't go around pinching myself, trying to find out where the fields come from," she said.

"Then where do they come from?"

"Why, they was here when my papa came into this valley."

"How did they get here?"

"Why, they was put here."

"For you?"

"More'n likely put here for him." Lacey frowned at her so critically that she felt uncomfortable. "Well, I'm not accustomed to being asked such as that," she said defensively. "I come across that field this morning, gathering wood, and I never the one time asked myself how it come to be there."

"But a man will ask."

"My papa never has said one word—"

"But he has, inside his mind, he has asked."

"Law, my papa don't care one bit how that field got there—"

"He does, I tell you," he said, so intensely that Mina was halfway convinced of it in spite of her own true knowledge. "And my boys someday out plowing will stop their horses and be aware of themselves, strange creatures in a strange world."

"I'm not going to listen to a word you say," she said, looking at him suspiciously. "I never heard such talk afore."

"And later each boy will see others to be the strange creatures they be, and to see women meaningfully. That attraction will get hold of him so that he'll stop his life progress and go fleeing after a girl. And later he'll come to fear dying; that thought will come to him in middle age, and it will throw his mind into a cavern where all the echoes of his life are."

He was lonely himself, she saw. His head was drooped and his face was sad. She touched his face, his forehead, where small drops of sweat were.

He seemed to come out of his private thoughts. Slowly he smiled and took her hand and pressed it. "I'll shoot a deer later on this morning," he said, "or a whistle-pig."

"Maybe we can make us some bacon out of it," she said.

"It takes salt for that, and we've got none," he said.

"Law, when I think of how many possessions it takes to set up housekeeping, I wonder if I'll ever get a start."

"You will," he said. He was looking at her so tenderly, she drew back from him, almost frightened of him and of herself, wondering what the change was inside her which was drawing her so close to him. She felt not a body-longing for him so much as a meeting of herself as a person with him as a person, and it was stranger than a red pumpkin in a row of yellow pumpkins in a field.

Later that day while their dinner cooked, Lacey paced the cabin. He often asked questions about Lorry and Mooney, and he considered every answer thoughtfully. Toward evening he started to tell about the West. His mind seemed to be drawing him there again. He said all the exploring was opening up the country, and behind the explorers were the farmers moving in to make homesteads. Before long they would join into settlements. A country is being made, he said, more by the farmers than by anybody else. He told about a battle that had been fought at Kings Mountain, when the farmers had gathered at the foot of a ridge where a British army was. "We was all there, and all ready to start the fight and end it, and General Cleveland turned to us and shouted out over the big fire-dotted field, 'Every man is his own officer.' He said it twice and we passed that message back, then went up that hill and killed and captured ever' one."

"Ever' one?"

"There was a woman there, a pretty red-haired woman. Captured her, too. She was the mistress of the British general."

"What came of her?"

"We killed her."

"Not proper, seems to me."

"There's nothing proper about starting a country. Anything having to do with a birthing is bloody. A birthing pains. Even getting a homestead started pains, for nature doesn't allow births without suffering."

Late that afternoon, she decided to take him to the pool where three years before she had often taken Mooney, to the place far above Lorry's clearing. They walked along leisurely, and it was getting on late when she came to the pool and flopped down on the rocks. She watched a snake go curling away into the bushes. "This is where I come to bathe most often," she said.

He sat down nearby. "It's a pretty place," he said. "These mountains are full of surprises."

"Are they in Watauga, too?"

"They're not high there," he said.

"In the Cumberland how are they?"

"No mountains there," he said.

She couldn't easily imagine that. "I wish I could get out of these here mountains myself."

"No, you're part of them," he said. "You even talk like the mountains talk, bubble like the brooks, go running on like the river—"

"I never—"

"You coo like a dove, you whisper like a coon—"

"Why—"

"You weep like a wolf pup."

"I never do weep."

"Did you when that man left you alone?"

"Not even then."

"Have you never cried?"

"Not since I was a skirt-length girl."

"Why did you cry then?"

"I fell down on a cold morning and hit my hands flat on the frozen ground. I let out a cry that almost overturned the trees, and I remember my mama was so kind to me, and patted my back and comforted with me so much. I never have knowed her to be so tender."

"You never cried because your heart would break?"

"My heart's got nothing in the world to do with my eyes. My heart's down here and my eyes are up here."

"I've cried," he said. "Did you know that?"

"When?"

"The night after Lorry said nothing to me in that cabin of hers."

"Huh. Looks like a growed person wouldn't cry."

"I cried one time when I was foot-caught in rocks, too, way off from here, and buzzards gathered. They had big wings, Mina, and was so little in body, they was like Death, I thought. I watched Death sailing toward me, then turning aside when it saw I wasn't going to yield yet, I could see its hooked bill and round eyes. Death was coming in little bundles of feathers, I thought. I cursed them all and told them I wasn't going to die, that I hadn't yet made my mark, or even decided what my mark would be, that I had been searching for the place to make it."

"Have ye found it yet?"

"That stretch of land at the Cumberland is the best place I've found. But I'm not a farmer."

"What are ye then?"

"All I've ever liked to do is look," he said, suddenly smiling.

"You're a looker? Well, law, I never heard tell of one of those. I've knowed of smiths, potters, tinkers, farmers, shysters, judges, but I never met a looker afore now. What in the world does it amount to when you've done a day's work?"

He laughed. "You're a crazy little thing," he said.

"I'm not as crazy as I ought to be, or I'd run away from you. Anybody that is a looker is bound to be a danger to a person."

"Yes, that's so," he said, "I know that's so." He took her arm and turned it and kissed her elbow. "Can you kiss your own elbow?" he said.

"I reckon not."

"How do you know?"

"I've tried it afore. My papa told me when I was little that if I could kiss my elbow, I'd turn into a boy."

"So you tried?"

"I tried ever' way I could. I clamped my elbow in a tree crotch and tried to get my lips over to it, but I couldn't."

He kissed her elbow again. He kissed her arm. The deepest longing went through her, and she got up, left him aways, and began to examine her own reflection in the pool, wondering about the feelings she had. She had sung many a song about love, but she had never had personal encounter with it before, and she wasn't certain of its nature.

He was looking at her now, she saw, his eyes soft as a deer's.

He came up close to her. "We could go on out there to the West," he said, "if I could free myself from here, from what holds me. Maybe we could make a place out there, if you was able to go with me."

They were almost to the valley floor when they heard a shot. They heard yelling then and directly saw in the woods off to their right the slobbery great body of the big bear, carrying a pig in its arms. The bear moved on up the mountain, whoofing and puffing from the load. Almost at once they saw Mooney moving up from his clearing, shouting at the bear, hurrying after it.

Lorry began calling to him from down at the clearing. One of the boys, probably Verlin, began to call out, too—Lacey and Mina couldn't tell what. Soon Mooney called back that the bear had stopped and killed the pig and had gone on with most of it.

There was quiet; then Lorry after a time called out, "Are you coming back?"

There was no answer, even when she called again.

"I declare," they heard Lorry say, "he's gone on and it evening."

Mina and Lacey were staring at the path and listening to every sound. He turned to her, seemed to remember that she was there. He was strained and tired all of a sudden, she noticed, worry had come over him. "I'll be back directly, Mina," he said, and started up the mountain.

It seemed natural to her that he would go. Only as she walked back to the same valley cabin did she begin to wonder why he had gone.

21

I t was the second time in three days that this bear had raided the pig lot and done much damage both to stock and pens, breaking and destroying, doing damage the first visit which went beyond the taking of what it wanted for food, being more in the nature of an attack on the place itself.

As it happened, late this afternoon Lorry went to the spring for water. The dog followed her to the door; that was as far as the dog could go, being as heavy as she was with pups. Lorry walked on toward the spring alone.

It was quiet, she noticed. There was not a bird singing. Not even a boomer was chirping in the trees.

She filled the water pail and walked back up the hill. She was near the cabin when she heard a squeal, loud and frightening, from the pens. She ran as fast as she could back down the path, the pail still in her hand, and coming around the corner of the pens, she came face to face with the great bear. It was standing on its hind legs, and in its arms was a pig.

Lorry swung the full pail with all her might and struck the bear in the head. The bear growled and shook itself. She picked up a piece of cordwood and flung it. The bear turned, the pig still in his arms, and started on off. She saw the dog then, moving across the clearing; the dog caught hold of the bear's left back leg, bit into it. A gun fired somewhere near the house, and Lorry was near overcome by all the commotion. She called to the dog, but the dog held on. She saw the bear turn and, holding the pig with one arm, slash at the dog, and she heard the dog cry out in pain and saw her roll over and over on the ground.

Lorry closed her eyes, and when she next looked up, the bear was gone, and far off she heard Mooney call. She called to him, then picked up the dog, carried her to the cabin and laid her on the floor near the fire. She sat down on the floor near her and examined the tear down the length of the dog's belly. The dog whimpered and licked at her hand, wanting help.

The boys came to the door of the cabin and watched. She cut open the dog's womb and took out the pups and breathed into each one until it began breathing on its own, and then, because of the pain it was in, she killed the dog.

Toward nightfall they heard the sound of a gunshot. She and the boys hurried to the top of the clearing and waited for the second shot, Lorry counting to herself, her lips moving as she counted, as she stood tensely. But there was no other shot, and she came back at once to the cabin, hurrying so that the boys could not see the worry on her face.

When they had locked up the stock, she told them to cut firewood, but they found that the ax was gone; Mooney had it with him, Verlin said. So she had them bring what firewood there was and stack it inside the cabin. The pups were lying where the wood was usually kept, so she had it stacked near the ladder. Then she closed the cabin door and slid the locust posts across it, securing it.

After supper she had the boys feed the pups milk, using a cloth sugar tit she made. The room was busy now with activity; there was motion in it, and nervousness. She was afraid, and not of the unknown, either. She had seen the bear close enough, even the white slobbery bubbles that had formed around its teeth. "It was brown-haired," she said suddenly. The boys looked up from the hearth. "It wasn't black at all." It was a beast accustomed to killing and doing as it wanted to, she knew.

What if Mooney didn't come back, she thought, what would she do then? The man set the flavor and weather of the home, whether he was Ernest Plover or was her father or was Nicholas Bentz or was Jacob or was Mooney; the home took on the nature of the man, and there was nothing a woman could do about that, except comfort as she was able and prepare the food and make the cloth. If he did not come back, the farm would be a shell of itself. What might she do with the stock; what use could she make of them, or of the fields, or of the corn in the cribs?

Only one shot, she thought. One shot would not kill the bear.

She put the baby in the crib. "You can sleep down here tonight," she told the boys.

They got their pallets, brought them down and put them near the fire.

They lay down on their bellies at once and propped their heads in their hands. Nearby were the pups, and in the crib was the baby. The floor was covered over with her possessions, she thought.

She left on her dress and lay down on the bed, listening anxiously every minute to hear a shot from the mountainside.

"When is he coming back?" Verlin asked her.

"I don't know," she said.

The chickens began to cackle in their coop. A weasel, perhaps, had made a hole inside. She closed her eyes, but listened still. "Do the sparks go out the chimney top?" she asked the boys.

"Yes," Verlin said.

"He needs to see them to find his way." Let him come on home now, she thought. If he is ill, I'll cure him. If he is torn, I'll heal him. If he is broken, I'll mend him.

When morning came, she walked to the top of the clearing, hoping she might see him. She came back to the yard and let the sheep out. She told Fate to watch them carefully, for there was no grown dog about to scent a beast now. She let the pigs out to root and told Verlin to watch over them.

She went back to the top of the clearing and walked along the edge of the woods; she came to the bear path and followed it a short ways and called for Mooney, then went on until she came to the place where the pig had been killed.

She heard Fate call and she hurried back to the clearing. She saw him near the cabin, his hands on his hips, looking about, frightened.

"I'm here," she said to him, not at all reproachfully, grateful that he was frightened for her.

Verlin had come up the hill, too.

"I'll fire a shot," she said. "Maybe he'll hear me."

She carefully placed the gun against her shoulder and aimed into the air. She fired. They listened, but only the echo came back.

"He'll be along soon now," she said, and went down to the cabin and closed the door.

22

I t was Fate who ran the way to Jacob's house and told him what had
happened. Jacob and Florence straightway penned their stock and,
leading the horse and bringing Jacob's old dog, followed Fate home.

When they were close to the clearing, Jacob tied the horse, left it in
the woods. Florence hurried to the cabin, but he went down to the pens
and considered the bear's tracks and the damage that had been done.
"He seemed to want to tear it all down, didn't he?" he said.

"That's what he said," Fate answered, meaning Mooney, not knowing
how to call him by his name or call him as his father.

Jacob followed the tracks. He saw the place the dog had been cut and
the place Mooney's tracks had begun to follow. "Your father is barefoot
by now," he said. "You see there." He stooped over a footprint in the
ground and studied it. Fate studied it, too, but didn't know what was the
matter.

When they got back to the cabin, they found Harrison in the yard
talking with Lorry. He was scratching at his belly and darkly considering
what he heard. "Well, he's probably over in the next valley, if he's
hunting," Harrison said.

Fate saw the German coming up the path, his rifle resting on his
shoulder as he walked uphill. "Hallooo," he called, and waved, and Jacob
waved. "I heard shots," Nicholas said.

"Lorry was sounding out where Mooney is," Jacob said.

Fate waited near his mother, listening to the talk, which was too casual,
he thought. They let too much time go by, and he wondered what was in
their minds, for each man was different and each had a relationship with
Mooney that was different.

"I wouldn't mind tracking that bear myself," Jacob said after a pause.
"He's the big one."

"I wouldn't mind," Nicholas said quietly, glancing up to see what

Jacob thought about having company. Both men then paused politely to see what Harrison would decide.

"I've got bacon enough for us all," Jacob said, coaxing him.

Harrison said nothing.

"We could take that dog of mine with us," Jacob said.

Harrison said nothing even so, even though he had a pack of hounds.

Lorry stood nearby, but off to herself, as a woman most often stood apart from a group of men. Her arms were folded, her bonnet was on, her dress was buttoned close at her throat; she was looking at them and at the mountain, and Fate thought how pretty she was, and how firm, how unhurried she was, as she waited for the men to get their decisions in.

Harrison walked apart and looked down at the flock of sheep that Verlin was watching. He cleared his throat a time or two, but said nothing.

"We might meet Mooney up there," Jacob said quietly, and Fate looked up at him, studied his face. In nothing he or Nicholas had said had there been even a hint that Mooney might need help, or that Lorry need be beholden to them for going up there.

When silence had lengthened and nobody had said anything else, Jacob turned and walked straightway along the path past the sheep pen, and Nicholas went up the same path, almost in the same steps, following him. Suddenly Fate started up the same path, too, almost in the same footsteps, walking not running, as the men were doing, and he heard his grandfather say, "You're too young to go hunting, boy," but he went on, anxiously listening to see if his mother said anything. She didn't, so he went on, knowing she might even want him to go to help, for his eyes were sharp, sharper than the men's, and it was proper for a member of the family to go.

He caught up with them in the woods where the horse was tied. Jacob gave Nicholas the dog leash and led the horse himself. They said nothing to the boy. They led the way around the clearing, not through it.

They're going to bring him back on that horse, Fate thought; they don't want Mama to see that horse. The thought made him colder than the wind, for he had never known Mooney to need help of any kind, except that he might send Verlin to fetch an ax or to fetch a pail of water or to get the sheep, but never to do anything which Mooney couldn't do himself if he had the time and wanted to; never had he faced any task in which he needed to say to another man, Help me, and never had he said to any man, Protect me. He had even built the cabin by himself, he and the woman he had buried that first winter.

"There's where they went," Nicholas said, stopping on the hillside above the clearing. He patted the dog and watched as Henry sniffed about. Nicholas knelt by him and patted him again. "You want to let him go?" he said to Jacob.

"No, best to keep him with us," Jacob said. The dog was straining at the leash and once more bayed. "Henry don't smell nothing," Jacob said simply. "He sniffs, but he don't smell. If he got a scent, it'd be on the bushes, not on the ground; he's trying to fool us into thinking he can smell."

"We can follow the trail by sight," Nicholas said. He led the way up the path, the dog anxious in the leash, straining forward. The boy followed Jacob. It was not that they had told him he could go; it was that they knew he was there and had not told him he could not go. They had let him come along, he decided, not because they thought he was old enough to come, or even to make a decision about coming, but because they did not want to make it themselves and they knew the decision must have been made. They would not ask him if it had been made, for that would be unfeeling; the boy was old enough, they knew, to know if it had been made, though he was not old enough to make it.

Soon after Harrison left, Mina walked into the clearing. She asked about Mooney and seemed to be surprised that he wasn't home yet. She told about Lacey being up there, maybe being up there yet, and she let the meaning come to them slowly and tried not to look at Lorry's face.

Grover came by. This was some time later. He ate a bowl of food that Florence served up to him, and he and Mina talked. Lorry, whose worry was set on Mooney and Lacey, on each and on the two of them, went outdoors to get off to herself, went up to the top of the clearing and waited near the path Mooney and Fate had gone along. Soon she came back to the cornfield and pulled up corn stalks, working steadily. The energy which normally she expended in a day of work sought release now all at once.

Florence came up and stood nearby. Mina came up and stopped nearby, but soon she sneaked off into the woods. She went to the pond and sat down at the edge of it, letting the gentleness of the place soothe her. Far off she heard Florence calling her, but she didn't answer. She sat there as evening came on and watched the pool as it reflected the moving limbs of the trees and the wall of rock close by. She waited, still and quiet, thinking about being there the day before with Lacey.

Night deepened and she watched the pool as it reflected more gently and dimly the moving limbs of the trees.

At last she went back down the path, and she felt so lonely and afraid she wanted to weep for all that she had lost in her life and all that she had seen, and she began to sing softly to herself and was singing when she reached the clearing and saw Grover standing in the cornfield, looking for her.

Grover said he would walk her home, but she said she would stay the night. Verlin said he would bring down one of the pallets from the loft for her, but she said to leave it be. "It's no trouble for me to walk up a ladder to go to bed," she said.

Lorry gave her a bowl of food, and Grover ate, too, and said he was going home but would come back, and Lorry said they would be all right alone, that she had a gun. Grover said good-bye to Mina, and she, with her mouth full of food, said good-bye to him, and he said good-bye to Lorry at the door. "He'll be all right," he said.

"I know he will," she said.

"I'm going to come back tomorrow."

"Oh, that's all right, Grover."

"No, I want to. I'm going to bring that pack of hounds over here and set them on the trail."

"Papa won't let his dogs run up there," she said.

"What's he got them for then?" he said

She put her hand on his arm, the first time she had touched him in many years. "You'll get yourself in a world of trouble with him."

"I don't care," he said.

She watched him carefully and decided he was sure of himself, after all. "Well, then," she said, "do as you think best."

She locked the cabin door after him. The three women and Verlin sat by the fire. Florence began to yawn; she went over to the bed and stretched out on it, lying close to the wall. Soon she was breathing deeply. Lorry lay down on the bed, too.

Verlin sat by the fire, staring into it, not even looking at Mina. He went up to the loft soon, and Mina heard him undressing. She woke up one of the pups and played with it, then laid it back next to its kin. She gazed into the fire and poked at it and wondered where Lacey was. It was late when she climbed into the loft.

She crawled onto Fate's pallet and cradled her head on her arm.

She wished she were a man and on that mountain with Lacey and Mooney, with Jacob and Nicholas and Fate, instead of here, cabin-caught. She was lying there thinking about that when she heard a sniffing sound, which she knew was Verlin crying. He was such a big boy, so big-muscled, that it surprised her that he would cry.

She started to reach out, to comfort him, but she decided that would be unfeeling, so she started breathing deeply as if she were asleep. She breathed that way for a long time, and all the while she heard him sniffling. He's deeply caught, too, she thought, for if Mooney didn't come back, the boy would lose his own life hopes early, just as she would lose hers if Lacey didn't come back.

When Verlin stopped whimpering, she acted as if she were waking up. She stretched and yawned and sat up on the pallet. "Verlin, you awake?" she whispered.

He said nothing, but she knew he was listening. She shook him gently. "I just had the finest dream," she said. "I dreamed the men were on their way back now and would be here by morning."

"Did you," he said.

"I saw a white horse in the dream, riding through the air, its hoofs striking sparks of silver. That's a sign, I'm bound and certain, that the dream's so."

She lay back down, and soon she heard his heavy, regular breathing of sleep.

The dream's so, she told herself, repeating it to herself. The dream's so.

Fate lay by the campfire, his feet near the heat, his head in the coldness, and listened to Jacob and the German talk. It was solemn talk, for they were as weary as he. They had walked all that day, up the mountain and across into a broad valley, then around a range, and they had ended up on the side of the mountain, high above the settlement. They had come at nightfall to this bare-ground rocky place, where Jacob had tied the dog, and had flopped down on the ground, exhausted and hungry.

Nicholas was broiling chunks of pork on sticks held over the fire and Fate was watching them, worrying about his near-starved hunger and about the frustrations of the search.

"A bear can travel fifty mile in a day," Jacob was saying, "and like as not end up where he started."

Sparks leaped from the wood, leaped out to where Fate's head was resting on his arm.

"You ready to eat, boy?" Jacob asked.

"Yes," he said.

"You didn't care much for that slick, did you, boy?"

"No," he said.

"That was a big delay. A bear goes through one of those slicks fast as a gopher. How a bear as big around as a horse can go down those paths, I don't know."

"A bear can crawl on his belly for half a day," Nicholas said, "then go on as if he had been resting."

Jacob crouched before the fire and smelled of the bread. With a hooked stick he lifted the pone off the fire and broke it. "Go on and eat," he told the German.

Nicholas took a piece of bread in his hands and bit into it. He took a pork stick off the fire, too, and blew on the meat, and when it was cool, he began to pull it from the stick. Fate's eyes watered and he chewed on his tongue.

"You hungry, boy?" Jacob asked, not looking at him directly, only glancing at him. He gave Fate a piece of bread and the second pork stick. "Yes, we'll have bear worries till Christmas comes," Jacob said. "The mast is so slight this year they'll be on the prowl till they go to sleep."

"Where do they go?" Fate asked. He was feeling more interested in talk now that he had something to eat.

"Under bresh," Jacob said. "Or in a cave. It's a wonder how they live like that."

Nicholas grunted.

"The bearing-she will cub in February, like an old ewe, some'ers around February, and she nurses them from her tits. She does it all in a hole in the ground or in a cave, and she don't come out except for water."

"What she eat?" Fate asked.

"She don't. She has a layer of fat on her, and that supplies her for the winter. The he-bear don't move, don't come out at all. He lies still in a bed of ivy and twigs."

"You can see their tracks in the wintertime," Fate said. He had heard Jacob say as much.

"You see the sow tracks," Jacob said. "She's gone to get water, and maybe stretch her legs."

"I trailed a sow in one winter," Nicholas said, "and she went half a day's traveling, then ended up where she started, under the same pile of brush, and not a time had she stopped except twice for water. The rest of the distance she was strolling."

"Sleepwalking," Jacob said easily, and Fate blinked at him. "She had a bad dream and she was acting out."

"Must not of dreamed of much except walking," Fate said.

"Maybe she was trying to get away from worrying about her cubs," Jacob said, "and them so unpromising. Did you ever see a bear cub, boy?"

"No," Fate said.

"Little things. They got no hair on their hides, and they ain't much bigger'n that hunk of pork I'm roasting."

"I saw four in one litter once near the Yadkin," Nicholas said.

"Four?"

"I counted four."

"She must a had a time to feed that many."

Nicholas ate another piece of meat, then Fate ate again. His stomach was full by now and he was sleepy, but he was worried, too, and cold. He was worried about Mooney. Twice during the day Jacob had fired off two shots, and they had not got an answer.

Fate lay back on the ground. He didn't want to go to sleep, but he couldn't keep awake, so he fell between sleep and wakefulness. He could still hear the men talking. They were talking about how a bear could eat anything, whereas a cat could not, because the bear's teeth were different. Fate heard every word they were saying, but the voices faded sometimes, then they would come back again. It was as if he were on a ship, rolling on waves; the ship was rocking on the waves, but the waves were of sound, not of water.

Five toes on a bear, the German said. Left-handed, he said. Bears can't see well, he said, but can smell a long distance.

Jacob got to talking about how loyally a sow-bear protects its young. Somebody in Watauga had shot a sow-bear and her two cubs, he said. "That sow-bear and her cubs had been eating of a bear bait of horsemeat. The cubs died first, and she crawled with some of the meat over to where they was dead, and tried to make them eat. She was weak as could be herself, but she tried to raise them, and not being able to do it, she went past them, making cries so mournful, calling them to her, but the cubs couldn't hear."

Fate wished he could get warm. His feet were warm, but the rest of him was cold.

"Draw that fire away from that boy's feet," he heard Jacob say. "Did you ever see a boy crawl in his sleep afore?"

"I've seen men do it."

"He'll be on top of the fire coals if we don't watch him."

"Can he read tracks well enough to know about his father?"

"Which father is it you mean? They's two up here, if I can read tracks at all."

"About Mooney."

"No, he don't know. No need to worry him."

"It was that loose rock that took him off balance. He fell a ways, all right."

"I thought it was his left leg he hurt for a while, but it was the right one."

"Lost his powder, too."

"Must have happened soon after he fired that shot yesterday. Looks like he would a started back home for he's got no powder. He might have one shot left, if his rifle's loaded."

"He might a busted his rifle, too."

"He's still on the trail, anyhow. He's got a will as tough as that tree trunk. You can't bend him. He come into the woods to kill the bear, and he'll try to do it."

"He'll not kill him with an ax," Nicholas said.

"He might. He'll try anyway."

Fate was listening, but he didn't open his eyes. He heard Jacob grunt and poke around with a stick in the fire. "Lacey's been trailing him most of today," Jacob said. "He's often been close enough to watch him."

"Might a been," Nicholas said.

The dog began to bark, and the men were quiet. Then the dog stopped. "Must be a bear up there now," Jacob said.

"Or a deer."

"I wonder what ever happened to that bear that walked with Mina once up on that ridge. It was an old one and was reel-footed, like this one Mooney's after. I never could decide why the bear followed Mina, unless it was kindness."

"Waiting for her to die," Nicholas said. "He probably had chewed his teeth down to nothing, like an old cow. He had to wait for something to die."

"Well, that may be," Jacob said. "This could be the same bear, you know it?"

"You think he was heading back to the settlement tonight?" Nicholas asked.

"I don't know where he's going. He might a got so old his mind has froze on him. They get hateful then, get revengeful when they begin to scent their own days of weakness ahead. They get like an old man, like me, and want what they've not got, or want what used to be, and they're out of sorts generally."

They went on talking, and all the while, Fate knew Mooney was hurt, was out there on the mountain somewhere.

"A bear'll eat grass like a cow," Jacob was saying. "They eat potatoes. In the Watauga country, they dig them up from the ground and eat them, and they like corn. They eat fish, which they catch for themselves. One swat of a paw and they've knocked a fish out of water. They can strike faster than a fish can move. They eat all sorts of berries and fruits, dig up roots and eat them like they can't get enough, eat acorns and chinkapins and other nuts, tear open honey trees and eat the honey and bees both, eat grubs and bugs and insects, eat pigs and sheep; they'll knock a bull down with a blow and eat him; kill an ox and eat him; in fact, I don't know of nothing they don't eat."

Fate wished he were home and off that mountain. The bigness of the mountain was above him and below them, and the blackness of the valley was like a pit.

"Lacey tells of a white bear once in Watauga," Jacob said.

"White-haired?"

"I wisht I'd caught him as a cub. I'd a put him on a rope and tamed him, and inside of a month I'd been a king of the Cherokee."

Nicholas chuckled.

"I'd had all those Indian maidens around me, combing my beard and petting me, for the Indians come close to worshipping the bear. They even always pray before they slaughter one. I wonder why that's so with a bear more than anything else."

"The bears are tougher."

"I wonder; I wonder. A bear when he raises on his hind feet and looks at you, holds those two front paws of his up, ready to knock down anything that comes near him, he looks so proud and able, he looks sure of hisself, for I guess he never has seen a creature he couldn't kill. Even a panther he can kill. Then he looks away from you, seems to be looking off at the woods enjoying the weather and contemplating where he's going to go once he's knocked hell out of you. When you shoot him, he whoofs as if you've surprised him a mite, and then most likely he charges, moving faster than the word of God."

The dog began to growl low in his throat, but he grew quiet again.

They were all quiet for a while, and Fate faded off into deeper sleep. Far off he heard the German say, "If Mooney catches up with this one, he'll have his hands full."

He heard Jacob say, "I wonder what Lacey is waiting for," and Fate wondered what he meant. He faded off from them, and his mind dwelled on Indians and bears.

Before dawn they heard the dogs in the valley far off. The hound voices came up to them, a bellowing, howling music, hounds baying as they ran. Fate sat up and caught hold of Henry, who was straining at the leash to be off, and Jacob got up at once and told Henry to hush. He looked at the boy and Nicholas. "What the devil is it?" he said. But he knew what it was. Somebody had put dogs on the trail; even Fate knew that, and the dogs were racing along the mountain near its base. Fate could tell that they were traveling fast, probably near the Plovers' clearing, running toward the German house.

"Those are Harrison's hounds," Nicholas said.

"There are seven in all, sounds like," Jacob said.

The dogs made a fearful musical melody, yet the voice of each dog was distinct. Fate could count the voices, each one clear; there was nothing husky about any of them.

Jacob patted Henry, who was anxious to be gone. "You can't catch up with them, Henry," he said. "Those dogs are a long way off."

"Running up past the riverhead," Nicholas said. "Done gone past that."

"I think so," Jacob said. "But they're in that cove yet, and they're on a warm trail. That bear might a struck again this morning. Might a struck at Harrison's place, and Harrison let him have his pack."

"The bear's not in their sight yet, though," Nicholas said.

"That's so. The dogs ain't seen him yet."

Nicholas' eyes brightened as he stared into the valley. "Listen to it. You can't help listening to it. For a thousand years, men have followed that sound."

Baying, rising and falling, the sound went on, sweeping along the valley floor, starting up the mountain. Henry was so nervous he wouldn't lie down, and even Jacob got snapped at when he tried to quiet him. There was a loyalty in the dog that went back even further than his loyalty to Jacob.

"Henry, you ain't going to get in no fight this morning," Jacob told him sternly, but the dog pulled at the leash until he almost choked himself.

"They've crossed that oak-topped ridge," Nicholas said, "that little masty ridge."

"They ain't caught sight of him yet, but they're blazing ground, ain't they?"

The men watched as if they could see them over to their left, still making a big arc, for they had gone upriver past the headwaters, had kept bearing to the left, had kept coming around, had crossed the oak-topped ridge and had charged down into the shallow valley beyond. Now they were beyond the ridge of the mountain itself.

Jacob started throwing goods into his pack. "Hurry, boy," he said to Fate. "They're still coming around."

Henry was chewing on the leash and howling now and then. "Henry, shet up," Jacob said, but the dog snarled at him. "Damn you, I don't want you gone," Jacob said, and he tried to pat the dog, but the dog wouldn't allow it. The dog growled at him, and Jacob growled back; then Jacob shrugged and said all right, and the dog grew gentle.

Jacob took the leash off, and the dog licked his hand. The leash was off, but the dog lay there, his head between his paws. Jacob ran his hand over the dog's head and neck and spoke gently to him. "Now, don't do nothing crazy, Henry. Don't get yourself cut up or killed. You're getting on in years, damn you, so you slow down, you hear? Don't try nothing fancy out there. Them seven others are younger'n you, and they ain't got your experience, but they've got more strength left. You hear?"

The dog had got tired of listening to him. He cocked his ear toward the hound music and was ready to be off.

"All right, damn you, git," Jacob said, and the dog left in a burst of power, was gone before Fate knew he had left, was gone faster than any dog the boy had ever seen leave before, was gone like an arrow released from a strong bow, and not toward the hounds, either. Henry went up the side of the mountain, as if he knew where the hounds were going and would meet them.

Fate stood by the horse and watched the dog as long as he could see him. "He don't howl," he said, disappointed.

"What you mean?" Jacob said. "He'll howl when he gets on the trail."

"What's he gone up there for?" Fate asked, still critical.

"He's gone to meet him. He's got a notion that the bear is making an uphill circle."

"Which it is," Nicholas said. "But Henry might turn the bear, if he meets him head on."

"He'll tree him, more'n likely," Jacob said.

Nicholas looked up at the peak; then his gaze trailed to the right, to the gap that separated the peak from the ridge. "That's where Henry's headed," he said. "It might be that's where the bear's coming through, if he carries out a tight circle."

"There or at the gap the other side of the peak," Jacob said.

"That bear's running like a streak," Nicholas said. "Probably loped along easy for a time, but he knows now."

The dogs were over beyond the ridge, to Fate's right as he looked up the mountain. The hounds were over on the far side of that long ridge, in the far valley, where yesterday Fate had been. That was a long way off, and he didn't understand how they could be over there when only a while before they had been in the settlement.

The men without a word got up at the same time and started up the mountainside, leaving the horse for Fate to bring. They began to run, clambered upward. They made their own path; they went up the steep way, seemed to Fate, moving toward the east gap.

"They've swung in," Nicholas shouted back. Jacob stopped. Fate saw Jacob's face, saw that Jacob was breathing heavily, was gasping for breath, and Fate thought he saw pain there, but he could not be sure, for Jacob turned from him and started up the mountainside again.

The baying was loud now, coming along the far side of the ridge. "Damn, damn," Jacob said aloud. "Damn that, listen to that."

"They see the bear," Nicholas called, and leaped into the air. He began to run faster toward the gap, flailing one arm out as he ran to balance the weight of his rifle.

The howls of the hounds had grown more frantic; they were yapping now.

"Damn, damn," Jacob said, running upward, slipping on the rocks, finding his footing again, a shaft of pain crossing his face as he moved toward the gap. "Come on," he told Fate, who could not keep up. "Tie that horse, damn it, and keep up."

"He's coming through that gap," Nicholas called back, and swung around, ran upward again, yelling out in his excitement. They could not reach the gap in time, Fate knew. Nicholas might reach it, but not Jacob. Jacob was running toward a spot below the gap where doubtless a brook fell from the high place. Jacob was tearing through a thicket now which ripped at his clothes, was going forward powerfully, driving forward, his great legs beating against the thickets that tried to hold him, his powerful arms shoving back the bushes. The noise of the pack was close, was almost on them. The sound increased, and Fate knew the pack had reached the gap.

Above them they could see the gap, and below them was the brook bed, with brown and gray rocks and green ferns along it. The dogs were loud now. Fate heard a shot from above; Nicholas had fired. Almost at once he saw Jacob take aim. Fate heard the gun fire just as he saw the bear, a huge bundle of dark-brown fur moving like a flash of a prayer down that brook bed, tumbling, rolling and crashing through laurel, leaping, rolling again, running, tumbling, twisting himself around every obstacle, over rocks, through bushes with great blows and noise, hurtling forward, disappearing below, almost before Fate had seen him and well before he believed what he saw.

Henry appeared. "Get him, Henry," Jacob shouted, and began to run down along the top of the branch gorge, waving his leather hat at the racing dog, which was a streak of brown, and behind Henry came the pack, their voices loud, filling Fate's ears so that he could hear nothing except the noise they made as they moved without seeming to touch the ground, a pack of streaks of fur baying as they ran, and finally, behind them, running as best he could, waving his hat as he ran, came Nicholas, yelling out, "It's him, it's him, it's the big bear, by God, it's him!"

They found the horse and sat down on the rocks to get their breath. They were bleeding from hand and face cuts, but they didn't care. The hounds were in the valley now and were louder than before. It was restful to hear them now, to sit high on the mountain and listen to them without moving even so much as a finger.

"He went down that hill like a landslide," Jacob said. "He rolled. Did you see him, boy?"

Fate nodded.

"He left them dogs, once he hit that gap. A dog ain't been born yet that can match a bear going downhill."

"Have they got it to the valley yet?" Fate asked.

"The bear's turned," Nicholas said. "He's going along above the settlement. He's swinging on around the mountainside, finding new territory to lose them in. He's above your mama's clearing now."

"Did you see him tumble, boy?" Jacob asked. "Lord, they don't hurt themselves for some reason. He took those two gunshots and didn't even stop."

"I don't know that I hit him," Nicholas said.

"He don't care one way or the other," Jacob said.

They listened to the hounds awhile; then they ate a piece of cold bread and started walking along the side of the mountain in the direction the dogs had gone, moving to their own right as they faced the valley floor. They walked for an hour. Fate got tired, and once he mounted the horse and tried to ride, but the ground was rough, the horse could scarcely keep its footing, so he got off. He was tired to death, but he kept up, and the bear kept changing his course, switched around below them, came back this way, then went the other, uphill and down, until he and the dogs were at a place downriver. Toward afternoon the bear made its circle and started back, running along the river valley, then coming up the edge of the ridge moving slower, until at last it treed.

Fate could tell the difference in the voices of the hounds. The bear had treed to rest, and the dogs were barking at him to come down. At once Jacob and Nicholas started running, and Fate tied the horse and ran after them. He ran until his legs were shaky, so that he couldn't be sure of running much farther.

Nicholas stopped, waved them to be quiet.

They crept forward. The hound sounds were loud and were from close by now.

Fate was the first one to see the bear, and he pointed him out to Jacob. The bear was sitting high in a hickory tree, was gazing off unconcernedly across the valley, enjoying the breezes. When he looked down and saw them, he considered who they might be disinterestedly, watched them lazily, contentedly, as if he had been watching them all along.

Abruptly he started down the tree. Nicholas ran, Jacob following, Fate last in line. The boy broke through the thicket in time to see the bear reach the ground. Nicholas fired. The bear slapped down a dog, then caught another one in its paws and crushed it as if it had been a puff ball, threw it aside and started up the mountain. Dogs began biting at his heels as he ran.

Fate sank down to the ground, stunned by the show of strength he had seen and by the death of the dog.

The men stopped at the base of the tree where the bear had been. "I know I hit him that time," Nicholas said.

Jacob knelt beside the dead dog, one of Harrison's males.

Another dog was licking its wounds nearby. "That one's all right," Nicholas said. "Come on, girl," he said, clicking his fingers to her. The dog got up. He patted her head, and she wagged her tail. "Go on home, girl," he told her. He picked up a stick and threw it toward the settlement. "Go on, girl," he said.

She stood watching him, wondering what he meant.

"She'll get home," Jacob said, "or follow us," and he stared along the ridge to find the horse.

They had barely reached the horse when they heard the bear tree again, and at once Nicholas was off running uphill, but Jacob hesitated this time. He closed his eyes and stood near the horse, a grayness to his skin now; then he shook his head. "Come on, boy," he said, and started up the mountain.

They moved this time toward the northeast, toward the top of the east range. They went as fast as they could over the tearing, hard terrain, the sapling limbs scraping against their hands and faces and bruising their bodies. The urgency of the hounds pulled them on.

Nicholas was far in the lead. Jacob was too tired to stay near. Fate lingered with him.

They heard a gunshot and stopped, wondering if Nicholas had fired, but Jacob said it was not Nicholas' gun and that the bear was yet some distance from them. He began to run, and when he caught up with Nicholas, he found him confused about the shot, too. "Who you reckon fired it?" Jacob asked him.

"It might a been Lacey, or Mooney firing his last one."

"It's not likely old man Harrison or Grover, or them cross-river men, not on a hunt this tedious," Jacob said. He was panting for breath and holding a hand against his chest, as if his chest were trying to heave itself away from him.

They started moving in the direction of the hounds, but before they had gone half a mile, they heard the trail voices of the hounds again; the bear had left the tree and was off running.

"Whoever it was didn't kill him," Nicholas said.

Jacob stopped all of a sudden, stood listening. Fate asked him something, but Jacob waved him quiet. After a pause, a smile came over his face. "You hear that? You hear Henry?" he said.

Fate heard it then, a husky voice in the hound pack.

"That's Henry. He's with him yet," Jacob said.

They found the horse and came on around the south face of the mountain, above the settlement, even though the dogs were now on the far side. The men were too tired to talk, too tired to joke, even. Once Nicholas slipped on a loose rock. He caught a laurel bush and held himself, and Jacob and Fate helped him back onto the path, but even as they helped him, they said nothing. They were too tired to say a word.

They went on around the mountain toward the gap, and when they heard the dogs coming uphill, Nicholas and Jacob began to run again, and Fate began to run, trying to keep up.

But the bear changed course, so they stopped and sank to the ground and listened. "He's smart as a whip," Jacob said.

"Yes, he's cunning," Nicholas said.

The bear had crossed the ridge, but not at the gap. Now he was rolling and tumbling on toward the valley.

About two miles down, he treed, probably not far from where he had treed the time before, and Nicholas was off running at once. Jacob got up wearily. "Well, Fate, try to bring the horse far as you can," he said, and he started out, walking, then trotting. Fate led the horse and tried to keep up, gasping for breath, and all the while the dogs sent up their barks. The men got closer, and Fate saw Nicholas waving him back. He tied the horse and crept up on a big rock, where he could see.

He saw the bear. The bear was coming down a tree, moving swiftly from limb to limb, climbing as fast as a cat. The boy saw that Nicholas was hurrying to get near enough to shoot. The bear started off, but Henry caught him; then the others leaped on. The bear was covered with dogs hanging to him, and he flailed at them. He was weary now; Fate could see him well enough to know that, and could see Nicholas coming up behind him, but Nicholas couldn't fire because of the dogs covering him.

The bear threw off the dogs and began to run. Nicholas fired. The bear staggered, his legs went weak under him, and he whirled wrathfully, driven to the limits of his tolerance, achingly weary of the chase. He hurled a dog aside and moved toward Nicholas, who drew his knife. Then another man appeared, came up behind the bear and shouted. The bear turned. The other man had an ax in his hand and he dragged one leg as he walked. It was Mooney, Fate saw, now grimy and bloody, and the bear, dazed and uncertain, growling heavily, moved toward him.

A gun fired. It was Jacob's, Fate knew. The bear stopped, and his eyes closed, as if he could not clear his mind now for all the noise. The dogs were on him again. He opened his eyes and watched as Mooney came toward him, his hands bloody where he held the ax. The bear threw a dog aside and faced him, lifted his paws, waiting. Mooney came close, the ax lifted. The bear's paw flew out sharply, suddenly, but Mooney drove the ax downward with all his might.

The ax lodged in the bear's shoulder, and blood spurted out. The axhead was buried in the fur and flesh. The bear slapped at Mooney. Both of them were blinded by the bear's blood. The bear waddled close to Mooney, grasped him, hugged him close to his own bleeding fur. Mooney wrestled against him. The bear drew Mooney closer, until Fate heard the snapping of Mooney's ribs, which sounded like shots firing. Closer the bear drew him and blood gushed over them.

Fate stood there, horror-bound; his life swayed recklessly in the image of death that shadowed them all. He saw Jacob dive forward, grab a club from the ground. In the same instant he saw another man appear at the edge of the clearing, a rifle in hand. It was Lacey, and instantly he fired.

The head of the bear and the head of the man were close together; the sound of the gun was loud, reverberated sharply, and the bear released its hold and stepped back. The bullet had entered its head; blood started spouting from one of its eyes. The great beast turned to look at Lacey Pollard, and with a deep groan moved forward, caught Lacey and lifted him and held him high and hurled him away, as if disposing of him, as if Lacey were a dog that had annoyed him.

The boy saw Lacey's body bash against a tree trunk and fall to the ground, roll to the edge of a drop, and fall into the bushes and creek bed below.

The bear sank to the ground. It lay on its belly on the soppy ground. The ax still was in its shoulder and the hole in its head dripped a freshet of blood. Nearby, Mooney lay, moaning. Nearby, too, the dogs stood, silent, dismayed, awed by the shower of death they had helped bring about. They hovered back a ways and growled in frightened throat sounds.

Fate knelt near Mooney and touched his face. Mooney's eyes were open and the boy wanted to speak to him, but Jacob lifted the boy and turned him away. Jacob began treating Mooney for his breaks and ills, the two of them moaning as if they shared the pain.

The German took a dog and went down the mountainside to try to find Lacey. He came back later and said he had not found him, but that there was a bloody trail leading off from there that they could come back and follow, once they had Mooney home. Jacob grunted assent and went on working.

Nicholas worked the ax free of the bear's body; with his knife and the ax, he began to cut the hide free.

That night they carried Mooney home; they got the bearskin down to the valley, too, and tied it to the side of Mooney's cabin. The skin was thirteen feet long from the tip of the tail to the tip of the nose. Pretty soon everybody was coming to have a look at it, and there were pieces of bear meat for those who wanted a sliver to suck on.

To Mina, as she arrived, the celebration was a grim affair. A single yard fire was throwing dark shadow figures of the people against the cabin and crib and shed and hillside. Some faces were dark and corpselike; others were brightly lighted. Everybody moved slowly, wonderingly.

She saw that much of Mooney's body was wrapped with cloth; one of his legs was held from the hip down in saplings and vines. When he turned to face her, she saw that he had new lines in his face, and his eyes were in hollow sockets, yes, in bruised sockets which were black; his flesh had been torn by claws and rocks and thorns. She stood before him, stunned to see him in such a way, shocked to a stillness, except that her mind moved fast ahead to the chief point of her worry. "Where's Lacey?" she said.

The dark-socketed eyes stared at her. "He was up there."

"Where is he now?"

"He's up there yet," he said.

"Dead?" she said, whispering.

The eyes closed. "Not likely," he said.

There was no music here. The bear was dead, but the toll it had cost was not fully counted, so nobody sang or danced yet. On the wall of the cabin was the bear's hide, but the strength of the bear had not been evaluated yet. How long would it take Mooney to heal? they asked. Nobody could say. And where was Lacey? How many dogs were dead? they asked. Four were dead, and three more were torn and crushed and would not hunt any more.

There was one more loss, even more difficult to evaluate. That was the knowledge that Mooney's life had almost been lost, and had been saved through the actions of another man. Now Mooney was beholden for his own life's safety, was beholden to the husband of his wife, the father of his children. The man he could not accept into friendship was the man who had made it possible for him to continue living. How could he respond to that? Such a sacrifice was unnatural, yet it was an act of friendship.

Mooney walked from one group to the other, hobbling on his bound leg, breathing in slight puffs, for he could not bear to breathe deeply, moving slowly, his face the token of his body agony, the dimensions of his previous power never more clearly known than now in his near helplessness; wherever he went a silence followed.

He had been set free of the bear, and had been taken captive by the man. So quick had been the trade that he had not even made a decision in the matter. From the arms of the beast into the armless debt of Lacey Pollard, he had moved without deciding.

A sightless beast, he thought, had hold of him now. It was not to be seen, not to be tracked and followed. A most shadowy beast had crept over him, and hugged him closely to itself.

He had fallen into a trap that had not been set by hunters, nor set by beasts or the mountain or by anything natural, but set by the fateful invisible forces which moved through the air.

He picked up a sapling and broke off one end, and this he used as a staff. He walked heavily to Imy's grave, the rocky place he had dug out at a time when his spirit was no higher than it was tonight; at that other time he had lost his family; tonight he had a debt to pay which would be fully paid only with his family.

A twig broke not far away. He tried to swing swiftly and almost toppled to the ground. He stared into the darkness. It was Lacey Pollard, he suspected. Let him come out and ask for payment. Wounded of body let him ask, and let Mooney, wounded of body, answer. "Who's out there?" he said.

There was no answer. Angrily he hurled the staff. A small animal leaped toward the woods, darted to cover.

He sank down at the rock on Imy's grave and rested his head forward in his torn hands.

A while later Lorry came up the hill and sat down nearby. He knew it was she without looking up, for she walked so confidently always, yet softly. She walked between the way Mina walked, which was so softly it could not be heard, which was daintily, and the way a man walked; she walked almost like a boy walked if one judged the walk by sound alone.

She sat down near him on the rock. "It's like a dream, seeing them all standing around the fire, and not hearing a single note of celebration."

He looked down at the sight, the black figures in several groups, and over to one side the troupe of Plover girls.

"Jacob told me what went on up there today, and I said to him, 'I declare, Jacob, Lacey always was one to do what he did at the last minute.'"

Mooney turned to her.

"Jacob told me he had done a brave thing, and I said, 'Yes, it was brave, and Lacey usually decides the proper way; he always takes the proper course, given time, but he's most often too late.'"

"Don't you care that he's hurt, Lorry?"

"I do. I care. But after waiting for a person so long, a woman gets callous. In six absent years love gets to be a worry, that's all, a worry lest he come back and start the love again."

"You don't care now, even though he's back?"

"I worry, that's all," she said.

———

Mina hurried along now. Far behind her she could hear the men at Mooney Wright's house. An animal fled before her, a small beast, and she heard it splash across the branch and flee into the brush. She splashed across the branch, too, and welcomed a piece of moonlighted road, for she was tired of the dark.

She came to Harrison's field and approached the small cabin where she had gone earlier in the day to feed Lacey Pollard's horse and to sit by the fireside to wait for him. She saw that the door had opened on its own, and near the door a creature moved, then fled from her; a fox, she realized.

She pushed the door open, careful lest another fox be inside. The small fire was bright ashes now, and she stacked wood on it, for she was chilly, and she locked the door. She turned from the door and saw Lacey Pollard.

He was standing in the corner of the room, his shoulders pressed back against the walls, and he was breathing deeply, watching her.

Slowly, afraid to believe he stood there, she went to him. "Lacey?" she whispered.

"I been waiting for you," he said.

"You come lie down," she said, "for you look to be sick."

"No," he said. "I can't lie down."

"I'll help you."

"No," he said.

"You tore your clothes all to pieces. Look at that jacket. It's not worth making gate ties out of. And look at that shirt." She touched it and it was damp with blood. "I'll help ye," she said, her voice soft.

"I come a long way down the mountain to see you," he said.

"To take me on to the place you said, to the river?"

"Yes, we'll go to the Cumberland. That's our resting place, Pearlamina, with fields so broad and deep they can't be measured. We'll go there."

"I'd like it better'n anything."

"We'll make a cabin near a brook, build it tight and fire its hearth and drag up a baking rock."

"Yes," she said.

"And we ever want to roam from there, you and me, we'll walk down to the river, and I will say to you, Pearlamina, we can make us a raft someday and set it in the water and let the drift carry it down through all this wilderness. We'll see red men on a hundred banks, we'll see beasts come down to the water to drink, we'll lie on the raft and watch the stars and moon change and hold to one another to be safe with one another, and come at last to Frenchmen's country, to a town called New Orleans."

"I never heard tell of such a place."

"I'll tell you about it, though I've not seen it and most likely never will, for the river is the road we won't take, and New Orleans is the place we won't go. But when we want to roam out, you and me can go down to the river and talk about New Orleans, and make it what we want it to be."

"What will it be like?"

A pain came over him and he closed his eyes tightly; then it passed; it was like a pain in childbirth, Mina thought. Death was like a pain in birth, she thought.

"It will have golden streets," he said.

"You come lie down," she said.

"No," he said.

"You'd better be on a bed, if you're so sick."

"I lay on the rocks once, did I ever tell you?"

"And the birds come."

"I found if I sat up, they wouldn't come close, and if I stood up, they wouldn't come nigh at all."

"There are no birds here," she said.

"Oh, yes," he said, "the birds are here."

"I locked that door when I come in, and the smoke keeps birds out of the chimney."

"I feel their wings. Listen to them fly?"

She listened. "I hear the fire, that's all."

"Oh, no," he said, knowing he would die.

He lay down on the bed late at night. He breathed steadily for a while, and she sat on the floor beside him and in the little bit of light that reached the bed she saw to wash his face.

By dawn his face was cold to her touch. "We could a been partway to the Cumberland, if we had left yesterday evening," she said. She put her arm under his cold head and let his head rest against her breasts; she rocked him in her arms. We could a made a cabin, she thought, and peopled it with the handsome wild boys we could a had.

Later in the morning, after the fire was out, she began to weep, weeping without sound, the tears falling on his face.

1783

23

I t was Verlin, who more than anybody else, labored devotedly at Mooney's place. The boy was big-bodied and strong, and he could be seen of the morning driving the horse to harder labor, rolling rocks from the fields, cutting roots out of the way of his plow. He slashed and cut and dug and tore and dragged and burned and planted, and as he worked, Fate came to him and Lorry came to help him.

Mooney's leg still troubled him, but each day, it seemed, he worked a longer time, and after a while he was in the field at dawn and worked until light was gone, punching his staff into the ground to make beds for the seed, planting corn and sorghum, flax and potatoes and cabbages, then helping Verlin work the horse in the upper field, pulling more rock from the ground. He used locust posts and the chain, and he and the boys hauled the rock out of the planting places.

At nightfall he would eat his supper without speaking; then he would rise, a powerful figure, and holding to the staff would walk across the half-darkened room to the bed and would lie down clothed and sleep. And by the first light of morning, he would rise and tap the floor with his staff. "Get along, boys," he would say. And he would throw open the door to see what the weather offered, then would stalk out on clear mornings to count the pigs and the spring lambs, and he would come back for breakfast, then would join the boys for work, splitting boards and cutting holes with the auger, pegging together a springhouse door, for they had piled so many rocks near the spring that a springhouse could be made soon.

New life came back to him in the spring season, as always before, but this year found him older than by a year, and more anxious to break through the wall which separated him from success for his life. The toll of losses in this place had sapped his strength and confidence, had made him wary.

He filled his time with work, which is what he knew best. He covered up his hesitancy and doubt by work. He told himself he must keep working, that he somehow must work until autumn and then, after five autumns in this place, he must break free, and the place itself must break free.

The boys from across the river would sometimes come over to watch him, for they had not seen much good man-work in their lives. They squatted on their haunches like their fathers and stared about speculatively. After a while they would go bubbling down the road, enthusiastically talking to others about what they had seen, the marvels of new work at Mooney Wright's place.

Fate and Verlin would sometimes ask the dark-haired boy, Amos' oldest, if his father was over at the house. The boy would return their stares, but he would not answer. So they knew his father was not back. Amos had been gone since the day of Lorry's baby's birth.

Mooney, one afternoon, did the questioning. "I was wondering," he said, "if you've got a rifle at your place as pretty as mine." He showed him his rifle, which was well carved and polished on the stock.

The boy shook his head.

"Don't you have a rifle at home?"

"Got two," the boy said defensively.

"Your mama's and your papa's?"

"Yes."

"Got two now?"

"Yes."

Mooney nodded, accepting that without surprise. He shifted his gaze to the woods, then back to the boy. "I got a knife," he said, taking it out and holding it on his palm.

The boy studied it.

"Your papa's knife like that?"

"No. His'n is wood-handled."

"Have you got it on you?"

"No, it's to home."

Mooney put away his knife, and even yet no sign of surprise crossed his face.

Mooney said nothing to anybody about the matter. The time to worry about the disappearances of people and possible crimes was the time when the settlement tried to break through to the lowlands; that was when all things were counted, when all affairs were settled, when whatever hope they had as a community was either realized or thwarted. It was toward the drive that Mooney had set his mind and work, and almost every night he and Lorry and the boys discussed it.

Other than a member of the family, the first person he talked with about it was Jacob. Jacob had little to send on a drive, but he had a cart and an ox, which would be needed, and he was a strong man, unfearful of such an expedition. Mooney and Verlin encountered him and Fate on the path one day, the two of them having just got in from hunting, and Mooney brought up the subject.

"You planning a drive?" Jacob asked, knowing he was; Fate had told him all about it many times.

"I want to take my stock down there," Mooney said.

"How you plan to get so much stock across the streams?"

"A wagon. Rafts. Whatever floats."

"You have to carry right much corn if you drive a drove of hogs."

"I figure my horse can carry eight bushel of shelled corn."

"Eight bushels is not much. You can carry much more in a cart.

"That's so," Mooney said.

"You'll need a plenty. And you'll need to have enough men, too, to get the rafts over the river."

"I know," Mooney said.

"I'll risk my stock, if you get enough men. Fate and me can help you."

His bringing Fate into the situation gave Mooney and Verlin a start. There was a long quiet, then Verlin said he would like to go, too.

"There's room for two boys on a drive," Jacob said at once. "We'll need two drivers for fifty or sixty hogs."

"Somebody has to stay to help Lorry," Mooney said.

"Florence can stay with her."

"Florence might not want to be put out."

"She don't care, so long as I take her cow down to your place so she can milk it. So long as she can milk twice a day, she don't care about anything else. And Mina can stay at your place, if there's more need for a person. Mina can shoot as straight as a man."

"Mina can shoot?"

"I've taught her to shoot. And Florence can shoot. She's shot a plenty of things in the past, when they come after her stock."

There was quiet; then Mooney said, "I don't think too much of women's shooting."

There was quiet again and Verlin said, "I'd like to go, I'll say that."

Jacob said, "I told Fate he probably could go with me on my drive."

Mooney crouched on the path and drew the outline of a pig in the dirt, then brushed it off. "We'll take them both," he said.

Verlin sighed. Relief came to him, and he couldn't hide it. Jacob didn't move a muscle in his face, and Mooney was still bending over, working with the dirt; nobody could see his expression. Straightening, he said, "How much weight will the hogs lose, do you suppose?"

"Fifteen, twenty pounds apiece," Jacob said. "Those that ain't lost entirely."

"The last time I was in Morganton, cotton was seven cents a pound and hogs was half that. At such a price, if I had my hogs down there, I could get a hundred dollars for them right now; I could get enough to buy flour, sugar, coffee, powder, a candlemaker, lord knows what all. And next year I could make such progress that afore long this place would be finished. And more settlers will find us, if we open up the way. But we ought to make it now, for it won't come another time. If we don't make it now, we'll be more lean by this time next year than we can stand to be, and the cutting down of trees and clearing wasn't nothing and the rearing of houses wasn't nothing, and the birthing of the stock wasn't nothing, and the deaths of the people wasn't nothing, for it all passed for nothing, so we'll take both boys and your cart full of shelled corn, and take your drove and mine, and we'll go to Morganton. And by God we'll get to Morganton, too, for if we don't, we'll have nothing."

He had not spoken such a long speech before, and he was trembling when he stopped. He was close to tears, too, not of weakness but of a strong power trying to break through him. "You might not want to remember I said all that," he said. He cleared his throat. "Let's go home, boys," he said.

He talked with the German about what he planned. The German had nothing to take, he said. He couldn't take turkeys, and that was all he had. Mooney let him think about the matter, reason it out, come to see finally that he had to drive what he had, even if it was only a flock of turkeys.

The German woman was astounded at their decision; in a flurry of German words and gestures, she questioned it, and Nicholas, with a long-suffering kindness which had come to be his response to her, let her talk.

"I'll risk all I have," he told Mooney later.

Ernest Plover was fishing when Mooney and Verlin found him. He was sitting on the bank, whipping out a line and snagging a fish now and then. The idea of going to Morganton caught his imagination at once, and for a while it appeared that he took himself to be the leader of the enterprise. It was only when Mooney asked what stock he had that he grew quiet, became once more a poor man sitting on a riverbank. "I got not a thing," he said, "except half a dozen pigs."

"What about geese?" Mooney asked.

"There's a flock that Inez tends, hoping for a feather mattress."

"Can you take a share of them?"

Ernest decided he could take some of the geese and a few pigs. "I put one condition on my going, though," he said. "That Tinkler Harrison won't be permitted to join."

Proudly he made his terms. He put his few pigs and geese, and the slight strength he had for work, against the riches of Harrison.

"You better give me a few days to think that over," Mooney said quietly.

The only man across the river who had much stock was Frank. He told Mooney he realized the valley had to make the trek sometime, so might as well be soon as late. He had fifteen hogs he could bring, he said, and he and his oldest sons would come to help out. Charley Turpin would come, too, he supposed. "Charley will say he will, then will say he won't, then will say he will," Frank said. "It's going to be a matter of luck to have him say he will at the right time, but I know best how to handle him." He spoke of Charley as if he were a little boy who needed gentle care.

Tinkler Harrison was the last one to be contacted. Mooney rode to his house one mid-evening and found him gathering a few pigs to be altered. Harrison had heard about the drive from Grover, who had talked with Nicholas, and he was resentful because he had not been asked his opinion earlier.

"No," Harrison said, "I'm not going to send my horses and sheep down the road with a flock of geese; I'll not send a fine stand of cattle through the wild country with turkeys showing the way. The German is addled about them turkeys. My lord, it'll take two weeks to drive them all that distance."

"The German either gets his turkeys down there, or he'll be a pauper afore it's over," Mooney said.

"I don't much care what comes of him, for he's not doing nothing now but setting eggs," Harrison said.

"Each person ought to take what he has," Mooney said. "We can all get there if we go together, but no one of us can get there alone."

"I can," Harrison said.

"You can't build a settlement here if you go alone."

Harrison looked sharply at him, angered by him. "Somebody said you'd even gone across the river to them cross-river people. What they got to take down there?"

"Frank has about fifteen hogs."

"That's not worth thinking about."

"And they have two men and a boy to help us."

"Two men?"

"Charley Turpin and Frank."

"You taking Charley Turpin on a drive? My lord, I never thought you'd be so thoughty as to include him on a drive. What you think he'll do?"

"He's got some strength."

"I wonder about this settlement. I have since it started. Seems like nobody here has mind enough to build ary thing, except me and my folks, and now you're talking about taking them out into the lowlands. Well, that's work, a drive is work, did ye know it?"

"I know it."

"And it brings out weakness in a man who has weakness in him. No, I'd better go alone in my own time, take my own stock and my own men. I got precious little need for Charley Turpin and the German's turkeys."

Mooney let the argument rest there. He stood around, saying nothing for a while; then he said, "Not much of a settlement building up here, is there?"

"Let it go, let it all go. What can a man do?" Harrison's crafty eyes looked up at Mooney; then he closed them, as if hiding them from view.

"The German will lose out, Ernest Plover will lose out, Jacob's not farming anything to speak of, the cross-river people can't build anything to speak of. That leaves you and me."

"And we ain't working close," Tinkler said.

"You say you want to build a settlement, but you don't want one, seems to me. You want to make a single farm, and that yours. You would as soon see all the rest go down. If you plan to make a settlement here, you have to take part in it as a whole thing."

The old man abruptly started back to the house. Mooney followed, even though he knew there was no reasoning with him. Harrison stopped at the door and looked off across the fields. "Let it go," he said. "I'm too old and tired now."

"Then all the work goes. And Imy's death was for nothing. And Paul's. And whatever it was Lacey Pollard got killed for, that was for nothing."

"What did he get killed for?" Harrison said, watching Mooney.

"For his boys. That's what I see in it."

"Do ye?" he said, considering that. His eyes brightened. "You ain't going to let Ernest Plover go on your drive, air ye?"

"I plan to."

"And what's he to do?"

"Maybe he can drive the geese down."

"Maybe him and Charley Turpin can have a party at ever' river crossing. My Lord in Heaven, you got a team for yer drive. Ye got nerve to come to me and ask me for help."

"I'm asking, in any case," Mooney said.

"I'll do no more, nary nother bit," he said.

Belle was standing just beyond the door, trying to hear it all, Mooney saw.

"No, no," Tinkler said. "I'll stand out there by the river sometimes and see the flow go by and say that's the way all I ever saw goes by. My hopes for Grover is in the flow. My hopes for my two older sons is in the flow. My hopes for my first wife has gone by. My hopes for Lorry is all up on that hillside with the hogs and the bears. My hopes for Belle has all gone to the flow, for she don't bear and she don't serve as good company any more, except that her and Grover makes eyes across my own table, across her husband's and his father's table. My God, it clobbers my soul."

A pity, Mooney thought, that he had not died by now and cleared his head of his thoughts.

"All my hopes for this valley is in the flow. I thought maybe Lacey Pollard could set it right again, but he's dead; he got caught in the flow. And I come to see as I get old that life is too much for any of us, and all of us will end up in the flow."

He went into the house. He went on across the main room and opened his bedroom door; Mooney saw him lie down, fully clothed, and close his eyes.

Mooney was about to mount when Grover appeared beside him. "Belle sent me," he said. "I talked to her, and we'll go."

"You'll go? You and Belle?"

"No, not Belle. I'll go."

Mooney considered that. "To Morganton?"

"Yes. I'll take the men and stock down."

"You can't do that, can you?"

"Yes. We'll go." He turned to leave.

Mooney caught his arm. "I want him to go, too."

Grover shook his head angrily. "He's an enemy of all of it, afore it's done."

"I want him to go, too," Mooney said. "I want him and Ernest Plover and Charley Turpin and the German and you and Frank to go. There's nobody on that drive strong enough to go, but we'll all go."

"I don't know how to make him decide, for he won't change—"

"Yes, you know," Mooney said, "you and Belle. Talk to him, force him to consent. You can force him to consent as easy as you can work around him and take it all from him."

"No, I don't want to do it that way," Grover said.

"You'd rather tie him up and take it all from him, I know, but I'm telling you to make him go with us. That's harder, but you tell Belle, and the two of you make him go."

He and Lorry wrote on their cabin door the records for the coming drive.

| Jacob | 13 hog |
| Mooney W. | 39 hog |

Harrison	50 hog or mor
Frank	15 hog
Amos wife	4 hog
Ernest P.	6 hog
Mooney W.	19 sheep
Harrison	30 cattle or mor
Frank	4 sheep
Ernest P.	15 geese
German	200 turkey or mor
Harrison	30 sheep
Harrison	5 horses or mor

It was late summer when Mooney went cross-river to talk with Mildred. He found her watching over a small still, boiling mash. The steam from the mash went into a copper tube which was cooled by spring water, and drops of raw whiskey fell from the tube into a pot. She had heated the boiler so much that all the steam was not condensing; much of it was passing out of the tube and blowing away, an alcohol-laden mist. "It's that oak wood," she complained to Mooney. "If I had a red beech tree, I'd have a better fire."

"That's so," he said, sitting down nearby.

"I get so tired of doing this," she said.

"Is this the first or second run?"

"Second run," she said.

He put his finger under the spout of the copper tube and licked the whiskey. "Whose corn you using?"

"That German's. He brought over four bushel and I agreed to make him two of them in whiskey and charge him the other two for the doing of it. He'll get eight gallon out of his part, and that's enough, he said, to keep for medicine and snakebites." She wiped her face with the sleeve of her dress. She had smoke splotches on her face and sweat from the fire. "If that boiler was to give out, I reckon we'll starve to death, for I don't have nothing else to do with. My corn was eat by bears, and Frank can't seem to do much better, though he's got a few hogs in the woods, but his'n and mine and Charley's don't amount to so many when you think about three families having to make a curing. I don't know what's to become of us over here this side the river."

She spoke gently. She liked to talk, Mooney knew, and she was quiet-natured and, though she gossiped and liked to tell stories about others, or about herself, she didn't interfere in another's affairs or criticize others.

"How's your little baby girl?" she asked.

"She's loud," Mooney said, and smiled. "She's got a pretty face, as pretty as I ever saw on a little'n. Has a round face like a Lutheran preacher."

Mildred shook her head in wonder. "Ain't they nice?" she said. For a moment tears welled into her eyes; then she became brusque. "But they're all as mean as their pap underneath." She glowered at her own children, who had come close now. "Can't you youngins play to yerselves without hanging around me all the time?" she said sharply. They drew back a short ways.

"She got almost no nose at all yet," Mooney said. "A little button on her face is all it is. And her chin's not nothing yet; it wobbles when you put your finger agin it and shake it. But when she gets to bawling, it's time to go."

Mildred laughed.

"If a wild thing's young made as much racket as a human being's, they'd be discovered and killed off in a season. You couldn't keep a baby in a hole in the ground like a fox, or in a cave like a bear, or in a hidden nest like a bird. You have to build a house with thick walls to protect them. And they take so long to get grown, too. A bear takes a year and a half, two years. A baby takes more'n that to get ready to bark at you from the crib. A hog bears eight, then, twelve pigs, each one tiny, but they eat big and soon they sprout strength and end up a hundred and fifty, two hundred pound, and still they're not but a year, two years old. That's what I mean. It takes a baby fifteen, twenty years to get that big, if she ever gets that big. So it's strange."

"They live longer'n stock does," she said.

"That's so," he said.

She picked up a turkey wing and fanned the fire with it. The boiler was bubbling now, making protesting noises. She shook her head worriedly as she studied it. "There's that little mean man," she said, noticing Harrison across the river in his yard. "Never see his woman in the yard more'n once or twice a season. She must be white as a cotton sheet by now for lack of sun."

"Do you ever speak to her?" Mooney asked.

"Don't see her to speak to her. She used to have a flower in a clay pot, and she would set it in the doorway for sun and water it with a gourd dipper. But I ain't seen it here lately. Charley told me once she was Mina and Fancy's sister."

"That's so." He tested the whiskey again. "Charley Turpin wasn't home when I come by," he said.

"No, he's down the mountain some'ers."

"Gone to stay?"

"No. He goes and comes. I don't know where he is. He's always bobbing up in a surprise. He told me he plans to be back inside of a week, but he's been gone more'n that. They might have caught him for something and be holding him."

"Is he wanted for something?" Mooney asked.

"They's a plenty of husbands after him," she said.

Mooney smiled.

"He's got people that hates him, and people that loves him. They's just the two kinds, and he lives atween them all the time."

"When's your own man coming back?"

She didn't move for a moment. It was as if she hadn't heard him ask, but directly she said, "I've give up on him."

"He's not coming back?"

She leaned forward over the fire. "He left me with six youngins to tend."

"Just walked away one morning, I guess."

"Evening," she said.

He waited for her to go on, but she said nothing else. "Some of us are going to make the drive to Morganton," he said, "and I'll ask for him there."

She said nothing.

"People come in there from all over. We can find out where he is, if he's not changed his name."

She said nothing.

"I can send out letters to Virginia, if you think he might have gone north."

"He's not up there," she said.

"Uh huh," he said easily. The fire needed wood, and he put some on it, laying the pieces on carefully. "I expect you know there's people wondering about where he went, and the talk might mark the youngins, for he didn't take a horse and I've heard he didn't take a gun or a knife. You say he left of an evening, which is not a wise time to be leaving a settlement."

She looked up at him, and he saw the worry reflected in her face, the weariness with the work she had endured all her life in growing up, in marrying, in bearing, in chopping and cooking and cleaning up; it had been a burden to her, and now even the calamity of her husband not appearing around the house, even that, which was suffering in itself, was the cause for added complaints.

"I wouldn't say anything about it," he said, "but when it comes time for the drive, everybody totals up what they've got and what has to be done. If there's a man missing, they want him found, or looked for. You can't let a man disappear into the woods and not ask."

"Do they think I done it to him?" she said.

He studied the fire. "It's not often talked about," he said. "But since Charley's gone so much, they might believe Charley of it."

"No," she said, "he wouldn't do it. There's nobody more loyal to his friends. I wouldn't want it even said that he done it."

"Then tell me this—do you expect Charley to come back afore we get ready to make the drive?"

"When is that?" she said.

"Whenever we get the stock in order and the mast is on the ground. We need colder weather. The stock won't lose so much weight then, and the rivers are not so high in the fall."

"Well, I don't know where Charley is, or when he'll be back. He told me he'd be gone a fortnight, but it's been a month and he's not come home."

"Did he know where Amos went?"

"No, he don't know."

"Then he's not gone after him."

"He's not, no."

"Then he knows he's not down there to be found. If he knows he's not down there, it appears he might know where he is."

The words fell without hurry, and she didn't deny or turn from them, but slowly she sighed, a deep, longing sound, full of weariness. She rubbed her nose and gazed thoughtfully at the fire. "You better go on home now," she said.

He waited as if he hadn't noticed the solemn threat in her manner; then he got up slowly and went directly to his horse and mounted. He saw Frank coming along the path from downriver, and he waited until Frank was close. Frank stopped when he saw him, stood in the path trying to decide who he was. Evidently he couldn't see well at a distance. "Amos?" he said, and began to run forward. But when he saw who it was, he stopped on the path awkwardly, as if he had lost an idea he had had.

Mina wanted to go to Morganton in the worst way; she wanted to leave this place of heart losses. She talked with Mooney about it, and he said he feared she couldn't go. She talked with the young German about it, asked if she could help with the turkeys, and he said it wouldn't be fitting. He knew her going would cause a commotion in his family, that was the truth of it. He didn't want that, for he and his father and mother were getting along all right now.

She pestered Jacob into showing her how to cut a wood handle; she fastened a long leather strip to it and tied to the end a piece of bright-red cloth which Florence let her have. This made a fine turkey whip, and she learned to snap it. She could turn a turkey easily; she could make a turkey walk in a circle until it was dizzy and lay down. But Felix said she couldn't go.

So she made a hog whip and learned to crack it. She got so she could snap a leaf off a bush with it from ten paces. Mooney said he had never seen it done better, but he said she couldn't go. "You stay here and help tend the settlement," he said. "A drive's no place for a woman to be."

She was furious. She said she wanted to escape this lonesome place.

Jacob hated to encourage her to leave, for she was the brightest person anywhere around, but he knew she needed some experience to take her mind off of Lacey's death. "You would be safer with the women," he told her. "You wait until we try to get all this stock across that broad river; it's more dangerous than you think."

"I aim to be there to find out," she said. "There's nothing here for me but breezes, and the limbs all over everything."

They were up at Jacob's place, sitting in front of the door looking up the valley.

"It's time you got a man, all right," he said. "You'll dry up afore long, if you don't have one."

"What you mean?"

"Oh, women need to have loving, or they get crafty and dry-skinned. Get sharp of tongue."

"I never heard such talk."

"Only thing that keeps a woman from sliding to hell is that a man sometimes is willing to comfort her."

"Law, listen."

"You take a woman that gets much older than you without a man to tame her spirit, to help her along so she can stand herself, and you've sometimes got to tame her like a wild thing, for she gets clawing-mad at nothing, gets mean."

"You can't scare me with fool talk. I know when you're telling a lie."

"I've known women to jump off high places, crush themselves to escape their own meanness, when they didn't have a man to tend them."

"I thought they was in cages," she said.

"They're let out to feed," he said.

"If you don't let me go with you, when Charley Turpin gets back, I'm going to take my things and move to his cabin and marry with him."

"I wouldn't even joke that way."

"Or I'll marry Grover and get to be like Belle."

"No, no."

"No, no, you say, but who else is there in this valley?"

"Don't marry Grover."

"I'll marry that German boy then; is that what you want?"

"He's got a mean mama. She's a crow turned human, so keep away from him."

"Him and me can get us a pallet for the floor," she said, "and a cook pot, get a gun and an ax and a nest of turkey eggs."

"Lord, I never heard of such," he said. "It takes money to get a gun and an ax. Nothing's free in this world. A gun costs forty dollars; an axhead costs more. You ought'n to depend your life on one ax, either, for you need two, and need an auger and lots more. A man and woman could live in Philadelphia for less cost if they'd let our kind stay there."

"What's it like up there?" she said.

"You'll never know and it won't hurt you," he said. "They don't like our kind."

"Why not?"

"We don't take communion all the time. In Philadelphia they're allus kneeling at a bench. And you ought to see the men there, with their frills and collars on, wearing of perfume."

"Law, I'd die. Perfume?" She drew her knees close to her breast and hugged them to herself. "I declare, I'd go plum crazy over such pretty men as that."

"Wigs on, all powdery white, and sweat dripping out from under them like sulphur springs. Tight britches on so ever' woman in sight can see what they're hung with, as if somebody might be apt to deny they got nothing at all if it wasn't in evidence."

She shivered with laughter. "I want to see them," she said. "Maybe one of them would let me live with him. What do they raise?"

"Raise?"

"What stock?"

"House cats. That's all they got, and dogs that can't sniff beyond their own noses. You wouldn't want to live with one of them. Lord, he wouldn't know what to do with you anyhow, unless maybe he'd let you help perfume him of the morning."

She giggled. "How many times you ever been there?"

He cleared his throat uneasily. "Never heard tell of one of them plowing nor working. They sit there and collect the tariffs and talk kind about the English. Good God."

"Jacob, you ever been there?" she asked again, watching him carefully.

He fidgeted with his hands. "No," he said.

"Law, you talked like you'd been standing on the street corners all day, and you've not even saw it. I suspect those men are strong, have swords and hatchets to protect their women with."

"What the hell would I be doing up there, tell me that."

"I don't know, but you talked so grand, like you was a member of the parliament. You talked like you knowed what everybody was doing, so I expected to find that you had been a leader amongst them." She and Jacob talked this way often, fussing at each other, criticizing the ways of others and worrying about their own.

She even asked Grover if she could go with him. She stopped him on the road and talked with him about it. He said his father hadn't yet agreed to go, and if he did go, would have all the help he needed.

She crossed the bench one morning to Charley Turpin's place to see if he was back. He wasn't, so she came across the bench and went home, tossing stones at every bird she saw along the road. She was depressed, for a fact. If she could get to a settlement where there were stores and a church and school and order to daily life, she might find a place for herself.

She sat down by her father's fire and wondered what she was going to do. Ernest arrived directly carrying a mess of fish, and she asked him if she could help drive the geese to Morganton.

"Takes a man to do a man's work," he said.

The only work he could do, as she knew, was carry a bushel of corn across the bench to get Mildred to sprout it for him, for he wouldn't even sprout it for himself. He could carry anything across that bench if whiskey could be made from it, but that was all he could carry, that and a string of trout up from the river.

She took the fish down to the creek and cleaned them; then she and Inez laid them on a sapling rack over the fire, and the children gathered around to watch.

After supper Mina went down to the river and sat near a field of rushes and wished Charley were back and would sing with her. She felt lonely as could be in her life now. She needed somebody so much she sometimes cried to herself.

She might be able to trail after the drove, she knew, but she remembered the time she had tried to make her own way on that lonely high road.

She picked up a rock and tossed it into the stream. She watched as the ripples circled out from it on all sides. She was about to throw again, when another rock struck the water at about the same place.

She looked toward Charley's cabin. He wasn't in sight. She turned, and there was Mooney standing beside her, looking down at her. "Law, I thought it was a ghost a throwing rocks," she said.

He sat down near her on the ground. "Not many ghosts about here," he said. He threw another rock into the water. "I've been across the river, asking if they're getting their stock ready to go. Mildred says she's going with us."

"A woman is going with you?"

"Yes. She says she killed Amos."

Mina's mouth opened to speak, but she was too surprised to utter a sound. She sat there dumbly looking at him.

"She says she wants to be tried in a court. It ought to clean her sins and worries, she says."

"I wouldn't think she'd kill him. They was—"

"She says she got mad with him in a fight over near Charley's cabin, and she was so hasty she used a knife on him, more by chance than meaning."

"I want to go along to look after her," Mina said suddenly.

Mooney shook his head.

"You'll need help with her."

"That's maybe so," he said, "but not a man on—"

"I could watch after Mildred and the turkeys, too. It's not seemly for a woman like Mildred to be with such a drove of men, even on her way to a hanging, and not have another woman to protect her. And you and me has been in each other's way for a long time, and you know I have a right to be lonely, and a right to ask a favor of you."

He considered that. He sighed and took her hand, which was small in his hand as he looked down at it. It was almost as leathery and tough, too. He lifted it and rubbed her fingers against the stubble of his beard. "All right," he said, "you come along, too."

24

There were four yards of linsey left, and Lorry cut them into two parts and made shirts for the boys to take on the drive. She worked in secret, while they and Mooney were out of a morning.

She had a piece of ewe's wool, enough to make Mooney a shirt if she made it sleeveless. Under his hunting shirt, it wouldn't matter about its being sleeveless. She dyed the cloth brown and sewed it with linen thread.

She helped Mooney of a night make boots; she drove birch pegs into the thick sole leather. They made a supply of whips, too. The sound of the whips was all Lorry heard for several days, while the boys learned to crack them loud and aim accurately.

The knives were sharpened of a night. Lorry had a knife she said the boys could take, for Florence had a knife she would bring to the house with her. But the boys argued about which one of them could carry it, so Mooney and Lorry decided it would be better to leave it at home. The same problem came up with the gun. Lorry said they could take her gun, but the boys couldn't agree. "One can carry the gun and the other the knife," she said, but they got to arguing about that, too, and felt miserable, so she put her gun on the wall and told them to let it be. "Seems like brothers could be more friendly," she said.

"They don't have strength to carry a gun," Mooney said. "They're going to be running after stock all day. Going to be so tired they're going to go to sleep walking." He liked to joke with the boys sometimes. "Time you get them hogs to bed, you'll both be so thin your ribs will stick out so much a man can play music on them."

The boys would chuckle and carry on whenever he talked to them like that.

"Give Ernest a stick and he can make a skinny boy sound like a tune."

Fate began laughing.

"Get you two and get Frank's boy laid out down in Morganton and let the music flow, have a big party down there with boy-music for the show, and have cider and whiskey to drink. You laugh now, but you wait."

They laughed and made fun, and felt good because the drive was about to begin. Mooney was never more hopeful. He got so he would court Lorry often, joke about something, mention how good the meals were and how her dress was pretty-colored. He would ask what she planned for the cabin, ask if she wanted a new one. "We can use this place for a kitchen and build one to live in nearby," he said. It was as if now he were confident that they would win out before long.

The settlement was alive with excitement. Even the stock moved expectantly. The women stored firewood and rations, and practiced shooting; they could be found firing the gun often of a day, getting powder burns on their hands and faces.

Rain began to fall on the day before the drive; Mooney paced the cabin and told the boys it wouldn't rain for long. "It won't do more than settle the road dust," he told them. At mid-morning the rain stopped, but the day was overcast yet. He saddled the horse and led the way down to look at the river to see if it had risen much. Lorry watched them leave, quite willing to let them go, though she knew what they would decide. Nothing except a cloudburst would delay those men and boys now; they would go if they had to wade neck-deep in water, for there was no event they had looked forward to as much as this one. Everybody was expectant—except Mildred across the river, who was said to walk as if in a daydream, to speak of poor dead Amos in reverent tones and to testify often about how good a man he had been.

Lorry went up to the field and got a pumpkin from under the fodder pile. She brought it back to the house and cut it into chunks. She was dropping them into a pot when she heard the horse coming back. Then she realized it wasn't as heavy-hoofed a horse as Mooney's, and she went to the corner of the cabin to see whose it was.

Her father came into view. He was pale and frail, and his coat was buttoned tightly about him. He held to the saddle as if afraid he might fall off. He called to her as he dismounted.

She went back into the cabin and was dropping the remaining pieces of the pumpkin into the pot when he came to the threshold and stopped. She knew he was looking at her, but she paid no attention to him.

He sat down in a chair, gripped his small hands together; he rocked the cradle with his foot and touched the baby's chin where she had slobbered. He sucked his teeth and looked about sleepily, critically, fretfully. "Belle sent me," he said finally, and sat back in the chair and crossed his legs. "She wants you to come to the house and stay with her for this journey time."

"I'm used to this place, Papa, and don't want to leave."

"I told her you was set here." He sucked at his tooth. "I won't be there though, and I thought you might consent."

"You going on the drive?"

"I know you wouldn't come if I was there, but it'll only be Belle and the two servant women. I asked her this morning if she wanted company, and she said she wanted you or Mina, so I went to Inez's place and asked for Mina, and Inez said Mina was going on the drive, too."

"Yes, she'll help Mildred."

"I talked to Ernest, told him not to let her go, and he said if I didn't want her to go, she'd go in spite of all." Harrison pressed his lips tightly and shook his head irritably. "So I told Mina she'd have to go as a woman, not a drover, that I'd let her have a horse to ride, and she was to be a lady. She wasn't going to do Ernest's work for him, I told her."

Lorry tapped the cradle with her foot as she passed it. She took out the shirts she had made and laid them on the bed, hoping he would comment on them, for it was good work she had done.

"If you could come down and stay with Belle, she would be in better company than with Mina, anyway. Sisters argue and scratch at one another."

"Belle can come up here," Lorry said.

"No, she's got a big house and she's used to it. Belle's timid. I've got feed enough for your stock, too, got pens and everything that'll stand empty once I leave for Morganton. Why would you rather stay in such a place as this?"

Irritated, she turned from him and began stirring the pumpkin broth. Why, indeed, she thought. He had no sympathy, no appreciation for one's own, only for what he owned. He wouldn't understand that possessions matter to another, too. He could never know how after a few years a house becomes a part of the woman who tends it, so that her ways with the fireplace are old ways, and her pride in the springhouse, being built stone by stone, which she has wanted for so long, is a pride of ownership which owns her and holds her close to it. His will to own was never able to let him give himself to what he owned, as hers was. "I've got flax to break and weave," she said.

"Lord in Heaven," he said. "I'm not give many chances to do a thing for you, and you won't permit it when I try. I'm tired of offering to you and being turned down, do you hear me?"

"Then don't offer," she said bluntly. But at once she was sorry for him. "You want something to eat, Papa?" she said.

"I'll take a cup of coffee."

"I've got none. I've not had a coffee bean for months. We're not so rich up here, Papa."

"I see you're not."

She pulled hickory ashes under the pumpkin pot, for the pieces of pumpkin were soft now and could be boiled faster. She brought a chair up to the fire and began cracking grain for the bread. Her hands were strong. The tendons and muscles stood out; the veins were blue and prominent, toughened by the milking and milling, the cleaning and cooking, the hoeing and grubbing, the cold-water washing and the hot water of the outdoors when she washed clothes, by soap-making and thread-spinning and cloth-weaving, by wood-toting and skin-scraping, by stock-tending and the care of the family.

"Do you ever get through?" he asked her, speaking quietly now.

"No," she said

"I remember," he said. "Do you know it?"

"You don't get through at this season. We had two cribs to fill this year."

He sat back and closed his eyes. "It racks a person. It did your mama. You was a baby then, not even talking age. I had a place like this and nothing much on the wall pegs. I was as poor as Job's turkey, and a chance come to take fourteen hogs off a neighbor whose drove had gone in with mine. I was at the pig lot one morning getting mine ready to drive to market, and market wasn't but six mile—about a day's drive for hogs. Your mama and me was to do it, for we had no drivers. I didn't even have a horse for her to ride, though she was heavy with child. We was so poor we didn't have much to pray over of a night, and I saw those fourteen hogs. It seemed like Providence had put them there. Them hogs could mean the difference between having something and having nothing all my life, so your mama and me drove them in with mine; your mama and me drove them to market, sold them off, and their owner never could find them. Sometimes after that we heard him in the woods calling them, but they never come."

He kneaded his hands together and looked at her, stared at her anxiously. "Your mama and me was never the same to one another after that drive."

She gazed at him thoughtfully, then went back to stirring the pot. He went to the door and looked up at the mountain. "Lorry," he said. It was infrequently that he used her name when he addressed her. "You're showing your age, did you know it?"

The words shook and weakened her. She knew her age was telling on her; she could even see in the spring water that it was. She would sometimes take a pail of water and set it in the shade and look at herself, so she knew what he said was so.

"I told you afore. If you've got servants, you don't age so bad. Belle don't age. She looks like she did when I first took her home with me; she's as smooth and white of skin as ever."

Lorry snatched up the shirts and bundled them, put them under the bed. She was upset now, was angry, was afraid she might even strike him, for he hurt her severely with such talk. A woman knew when she was aging; she didn't need to be told. And it set up currents in her that washed back and forth like a twisting water storm. "You brought me to this place, Papa," she said firmly, "and I made the best bargain I could. There's work here, but I knew it then. We might not hold on; I know that, too. But he's holding now."

"If you had took Lacey back—"

"I lost him in Virginia, and that's healed. I don't think about him now."

"You don't?"

"I don't. We all lost something, but we go on. Now and agin we lost what's dear, and the wound is on us. We carry many a wound by the time we get to aging, but I'm not afraid of scars, and I'm not fireside-tied yet, needing warmth, neither. I'm not old yet."

"It's the work, I tell you, not the years or wounds, either. The work."

"I've got the work to do," she said firmly, finally, tired of talking wisply, not wanting to talk any more about it, wanting him to go and let her be. "Go on home, Papa," she said.

"I can't talk to you any more," he said, hurt.

"No, there's too much wounds atween us from the old days. Get on away and leave me be."

"I wish you'd come with me," he said. "I've got a place of ease in the valley, Lorry. I've worked and fought and even stole to get it, and I tell you something, it was done more for you than for myself, I tell you that's so, and now I've not got the ones with me that I done it for."

"No, I'm not coming to your place," she said. "Belle can come here if she wants to."

"I won't permit it, not to here."

"Then tell her that."

"I'll tell her you won't come."

"Tell her what you please. Now let me be."

He was standing at the doorway, the dreary daylight behind him, and he murmured to himself in his distress. It started to rain again, a fine rain; he didn't appear to notice. The rain made light noise on the roof boards, but he was wondering to himself about what he was to do. "This place'll be lost, Lorry, if he don't make the drive."

She watched him, her arms folded and her face set, but there was a tenderness in her for him in spite of knowing him so well. "You help him make it, Papa," she said. "If you and Grover and your men help him, he can do it."

"Uh huh," he said quietly, and he nodded. He cleared his throat and spat out into the damp black ground. "You come and stay with Belle," he said quietly.

She didn't move. She didn't ask of herself what he meant; there was no knowing what he meant. Whether he meant a threat she didn't know, but she knew that giving in to him was a weakness, an opening that he would force larger until every human life was open and bare before him. "Go on home, Papa," she said.

He nodded slowly, wearily. He sighed and stepped out into the rain and went to his horse. He stopped there and looked back at the place, this little hut perched on the low flank of a mountain, log on log, chinked with clay and stone-chimneyed, a gray-smoke plume rising from it. His daughter's home.

Lorry took a string of dried grapes and put them into the pumpkin sirup. She put in a handful of dried cherries. She laid chestnuts on the hearth to roast, and they were popping their shells by the time Fate came up from the road, singing a song Fancy Plover had taught him. He came in, sniffing the air appreciatively.

She put her arms around him and hugged him tightly. "Where the others?" she said.

"I don't know," he said. "I saw Mina and she began to talk so fast about the rain I rolled on the ground laughing." He crouched before the fire and stirred the ashes under the pumpkin pot. "I always did like her, you know it, Mama?" he said. "But she's more serious any more."

Lorry sat down on a chair near him. She took the comb out of her hair, let it fall long; she combed her hair and watched him. When he grew older, was of courting age, no doubt he would be a young knight, she thought, a shining danger in that valley to every young woman's heart, as his father had been in Virginia. There would be no worry about aging then, no looking for wrinkles in spring water for him, not for many years yet.

When she heard Mooney coming, she rolled her hair up quickly and went at once to the bed and changed her dress, put on her yellow dress, which was the only good piece of cloth she had left. She went outdoors and waited for him. The wetness from the ground seeped through the breaks in her shoes and around the edges of the straps which she had bound around them to hold them together. He came riding up through the clearing, a big man on a huge work horse, the horse's hoofs splattering mud.

Behind him Verlin loped along.

He rode up close, and the horse stomped the ground and mud and rain water swished out. "Be on our way by morning," he said. He gave the horse to Fate to unsaddle for him, and all the while he kept glancing at her yellow dress.

When the horse was put away, he and Verlin went inside, and she waited, holding her breath, wanting them to like what they found. She heard Verlin let out a shout, and Mooney got talking loud, and it was almost more joy than she had known before, to hear them.

She went inside; Mooney smiled at her, and a wave of tenderness and embarrassment came over her. At once she went to the bed, took out the shirts she had made, and laid them out. "Now, I didn't have time to do as well with these as I wanted to," she said. The men watched carefully what she was doing. "It's just a little piece of clothing to help keep the dampness away." She laid the last shirt out and stepped back, feeling awkward and out of place, even though she was at home showing what she had made.

"I declare to my soul," Mooney said, holding his up before him.

"I'd a made sleeves, but I didn't have the cloth ready."

"It's enough as it is," he said. The boys were putting on their shirts. "When did you get time to make a shirt for me?" he said.

"I did it now and then of a day," she said.

"I thought that piece of wool cloth was going to be for the girl."

"I'll make more cloth while you're away."

"But this wool is—"

"I declare, I don't think we're so short of cloth that you can't have a wool shirt when you're going on such a journey, and no telling who you'll meet on the road."

He put it on. He was obviously proud of himself in it. The boys had their shirts on, too, and she was so overcome with pleasure at the way the three of them acted, like children with colored presents, that she went at once to the fireplace and busied herself taking up the food. "You carry on so over nothing," she said.

When she called them, they came to the table, still talking loud, and as they ate they spoke confidently of the coming day, speaking with whipcrack sounds in their manner and voices. "First day's the hardest," Mooney told the boys. "Got to get the stock accustomed to the road."

The boys showed no fear of the work.

"Going to Morganton, boys. Going to get your mama a present and a half."

They were pleased as could be.

"Going to drive herds tomorrow," he said happily.

A joy, she thought, to have them happy. It had all been so hard and long, and now their life was coming to an opening. It would be rewarding now. The work of clearing had a meaning now, the planting and harvesting, the building of the cribs and pens, the nights of watching, the days of labor. It all had its meaning now, the bearing and the saving and the hunting down and the skinning, and she would be left to keep the cabin and the place for them, which had its meaning, too.

He kept glancing at her, at the clean dress and the way her hair was. "Get you a present," he told her again, and a wave of warmth went through her. It was a pleasure to be noticed, she would admit that. She remembered that first time he had seemed to notice her, in the cabin on her father's land, and she was even more thrilled now than she had been then. He kept glancing at her as they ate, and he talked about the food, how good it was.

They ate all she had made, then sat back in the chair and bragged on the dinner, and the boys beamed at him, and he said, "Verlin, you and Fate go down and count the drove; be sure they can all be found."

The boys appeared to be surprised, for they had counted stock that morning, but they went outdoors. Mooney sat across from her, listening to them as they went through the yard, looking at her with longing, and she got up and brushed her dress down in front of her, for there were bread crumbs on it. She glanced back at him and he was still looking at her. "I declare, a woman does a little something and surely gets praise around here," she said. She knelt to stir the fire, and she heard him get up and she saw the light on the floor close in on itself as the door was closed and latched. She stood, and suddenly a nervousness flooded through her, for it was as it had been a long while ago and she felt a youngness in herself. He came close to her, and she suddenly moved to him and put herself in his arms and put her face hard against his chest. Even in the darkened room she could see the outline of his face above her.

––––––––

The boys were up before dawn, cracking their whips and yelling, rounding up the drove and counting the sheep flock.

The family ate breakfast in the coolness, the fire burning low, and when they had finished, Mooney tested the sharpness of his knife, then tested the sharpness of his ax, then took his gun down from the wall. The boys crept past him and ran down toward the pens, calling back that Jacob's drove had arrived.

Lorry put a shawl around the baby and carried her down to where the drove was, where the boys were running about. The two droves mingled and mixed with a clashing of tusks and hoofs. Jacob's big boar easily won out for the lead, and Mooney threw corn to him and spoke roughly to him to get his attention. Jacob had his cart full of corn, and his ox was hitched to it and seemed none too satisfied. "Come along," he called to it, and the great ox lowered his shoulders and pulled, the old cart groaned and moved. "Lead them out," Jacob called. Mooney mounted at once and started down the trail, calling to the boar to follow, and behind the boar came the drove and sheep flock; then Jacob mounted, then the ox and creaky cart.

The women followed. They saw Inez coming from her clearing as they approached Harrison's big field, where most of the people of the settlement had already gathered. The men were sitting on horses, the boys were trying to keep the stock from bolting away. Mildred was there, sad-faced and dejected, astride a worn brown horse, her skirt pushed in tightly around her legs.

The cross-river boars began fighting with those of Jacob, Ernest and Harrison. Jacob waded in among them, began beating them with a club, fearless of their tusks, striking hard enough to addle them.

Harrison shouted to his men and rode partway across the field. His horses and cattle began to follow, the Negro flailing them with switches and cracking whips about their heads. Harrison's big fluffy ram followed the cattle, and the ewes and a few lambs followed the ram. Then Jacob and Mooney drove the lead boar into place. The drove moved, white and red and brown and spotted, big and small pigs, bobbing up and down as if riding on a sea.

Mina, mounted on a proud horse, came at the rear with the prisoner woman and Charley Turpin. Behind them came Frank, with two corn carts.

"Papa, you get them geese in the line," Mina shouted suddenly. She abandoned her ladylike ways and rode swiftly to where Ernest was pestering his flock. A turkey whip appeared as if by magic in her hand and she cracked it at the gander's head. "You take them geese along after them pigs," she said, "or you'll get left."

Ernest snorted at her defiantly, but one more crack of the whip sent his geese scurrying to take their places in the drive. "Papa, you keep up now," Mina said, starting back toward Mildred, who was staring ahead as if she could see a vision.

"You let my flock be, you hear?" Ernest shouted after her.

Mina rode over to where Inez and Lorry were. She sat there on her horse and looked down sadly at her mother and the children. "I'm going now, Mama."

"You're not coming back? Mina, why don't you come back?"

"Maybe I will when it's a settlement here and has more people in it."

"I can't stand to think of your living way off, with nobody to care for you."

"I'll take care of myself, Mama."

"And what'll I do for loneliness with you gone?"

"Mama, you got enough children to spare one. There's all them others." She leaned far forward and kissed her mother on the cheek, then touched Fancy's face, then, almost in tears, touched Lorry and the baby. She swung her horse and rode off, her hair shining in the sun, streaming out behind her.

The procession passed the German's place, and Lorry saw Nicholas and his woman waiting near their cabin, and Felix holding a long whip. She saw Mina turn in at their trail and ride up to where Felix stood, and together they went on through the clearing toward the turkey roosts.

Nicholas took corn from a leather bag and tossed it onto the ground, took out a whistle of wood and blew on it a shrill loud sound, and the woods above his clearing trembled, the trees seemed to shed a weight and to bob up and down in the air. A wave of turkeys came out of the woods and moved around the two horses and down past the pens. A great gobbler stepped to the lead, moving not fast, walking with high steps and pride, and the others fell in behind him. Nicholas threw out more corn and more yet as the turkey flock bobbed and bubbled as if in a broth, and he moved toward the road as he clucked his tongue at the master gobbler, which followed him. As the flock moved out, Mina and Felix worked slowly along the sides of it, clicking the red tips of their whips, encouraging the stragglers.

The master gobbler stopped at the edge of the valley road. "Come along, mister," Nicholas said, scattering corn before him. The gobbler looked at the road, at the long procession, then at the women and children waiting in the field. Behind him the mass of turkeys waited.

"Come along, mister," Nicholas said gently.

The master gobbler lifted his head higher, and seeing nothing dangerous immediately ahead, stepped out proudly onto the road.

The drove was stretched out for a long way now, pack horses and carts and stock. Lorry could not see the front of it from where she stood, but she knew it stretched on past the creeks which fed the river, and that it was moving toward the range road. Far off were the whip sounds and the cries of the boys and the deeper voices of the men, and the rumble and murmur of the herds.

She walked along with Florence and Inez. They passed Harrison's clearing, and she saw Belle out in the yard with the Negro women. Lorry waved and Belle waved back.

Inez said, "I want to come to see your place, see your springhouse that's forming."

"Come on now and we'll cook dinner," Lorry said.

"With all my youngins?" Inez said, pleased as could be.

"Bring them. We'll entertain each other," Lorry said.

The children jumped up and down, and Inez consented. "I don't have much to bring," she said.

"We'll find something at home," Lorry said.

That night she lay awake on the bed, lay beside Florence, who was asleep, and thought about the drive. She tried to decide in her mind how much stock was there, how many horses and carts. At the front rode her father, she remembered. Then came the horses and cattle, Grover following. Behind him came a Negro, leading the sheep, walking near the ram, a crook in his hand.

Behind the flock of sheep came four oxcarts loaded down with corn and supplies, a Negro man and two boys tending them, keeping them in line.

Then came Mooney, mounted, showing the way for the drove of swine. With the drove came Fate and Verlin and Frank's boy.

Then came the geese, with Ernest Plover in command.

Then came Mildred and Charley Turpin, then Frank and two oxcarts.

Behind them came Nicholas Bentz, and behind him came the master gobbler, leading the large, murmuring proud flock, and at the end came Felix on foot, leading a pack horse loaded with corn, and with him, mounted proudly, was Mina Plover.

Over and over in her mind Lorry recalled the order of the drove. It was the valley's fat and offering; it was the best they had of all they had made. From the shadow of the mountain moved now the valley's strength and wealth.

Be kind, she thought. "God, be kind," she murmured.

The valley waits, she thought. The mountain waits. There is no sound of the wind tonight. The mountain from far off can see the glimmer of their campfires on the ridge beyond the river. The house does not creak tonight.

Here all is well. Be well with them, she thought. The wood burning in the hearth is red ashes now; it glows on the wooden walls. The ewes and cow are quiet. The day is done.

Then sleep, she thought. The cradle rocks. The night has deeply come.

25

Lorry was down at the spring the next afternoon when she heard a horse coming from the valley road. She waited, watching anxiously, until a horse and rider came into the clearing. She saw that it was Fate, and he was riding Mooney's horse.

She put down the pail and ran up to the cabin. "Where's Mooney?" she asked as Fate dismounted. She was glad to see him but was worried, too.

"With the drive, still. They sent me back for corn for the stock."

He didn't look at her, and he fussed awkwardly with the bridle, she noticed. He and the horse were caked with dust and dirt. "Your grandfather took enough corn for everybody."

"He went on ahead," he said. "There was an argument last night. The German asked him for more corn for his turkeys, and he began talking about Germans he'd known in Virginia, said he didn't trust them." Fate was disgusted with the whole thing and didn't want to talk about it.

She was disturbed more than she wanted him to know. She went down to the spring and got water. When she came back, Fate had hitched the horse and was sitting on the ground, his back against the cabin. She put the pail down beside him and he took the dipper and drank thirstily.

"What happened then, Fate?" she asked.

He stared out at the fields, and finally he told her in a tired voice that Ernest Plover had sided with the German, making Harrison all the more angry, and Mina had sided with her father, and Harrison had tried to take her horse away from her. In the end Harrison had taken all the corn and moved his cattle, horses and sheep on ahead, making his own campsite. "The others sent me back for eight bushels of shelled corn," he said.

It was a bad omen for the drive on its first night out, Lorry knew, but she said nothing about that. She sent Fate to tell the news to the valley women, and to ask them to meet at Harrison's house.

By late afternoon they were there with their children, and they went to work shelling the sent-for corn. They used Harrison's cribs, thinking nothing of it, and even made baskets out of billets he had stored in his plunder room. When the work was done, they stayed around the place, speculating about the weather, which was cloudy, and about what progress the stock might have made that day, and they began asking Fate questions.

As best he could, Fate told them what he knew, how on the day before the stock had been resentful of the morning hours, had sought ways to turn back or to leave the wearying trail, but that by afternoon they had got trail-broken pretty well, and a fair amount of distance had been gained. He told them about the singing, with the drovers and drivers making up verses as they went along.

> Move on, boy.
> You ain't no chicken on a nest.
> You're a pig, boy,
> And got no right to rest.

And how some of the stock would step in time to the music.

> Called on a pig to tell me a tale,
> He told me the story of a boar named Martingale,
> Sou, boy, sou, boy, sou, boy, sou.
> He had more pigs born to his name
> Than he could count or the sows could tame,
> Sou, boy, sou, boy, sou, boy, sou,
> Go and try to do like Martingale.

The women looked askance at the song, and acted as if they were offended by it; Fate wasn't at all certain why they might be offended.

Two hours before dark, he told them, the stock had been driven into the woods, where they could look for mast. The carts and pack horses were brought up and somebody had to help Mildred to dismount, for she was even more dismal of manner now than she had been in the valley. The geese came wearily down the road, Fate said, and Ernest sang to them and made light with them.

It's been a dusty road
　　and a long hard day,
And you look plumb tan
　　though I know you're gray,
Down under, down under.

"Everything was as even-minded as you please," Fate said, "until the German asked Grandpa Harrison for the feed, and maybe Grandpa was tired, or maybe all along he hadn't planned to help with the drive—" Fate didn't know. He told them again about the argument, breaking off abruptly and with embarrassment, and everyone knew that there was more to the story than he had said, or wanted to say, and the women looked at each other uneasily.

Late in the day, when the corn was shelled and bagged, ready to be put on the horse, Fate wanted to go on back, for he said the corn would be needed the next morning. Lorry didn't want him to leave, though, and she dissuaded him from going right away. Several of the women made corn bread and poured milk, and they waited around hoping to hear more about the drive from Fate.

They stood in the yard or sat on the porches at Belle's house and ate what they could find. The children clambered over the sheds and played alongside the river, and at dusk they gathered in the main room of the house, the women standing around the walls and children sitting on the floor. Fate found himself once more called upon to tell about the day before. The women interrupted now and then, asked about this man and that, this boy and the other, asked even about certain pieces of the stock. Frank's wife asked about a certain boar and Inez Plover wondered about her geese flock. All of this was most casually done, but it was not casual, either, for it was a tense circumstance. They seemed to be resting, to be at ease and relaxed, but they were on nerves' ends, each aware that most of their next year's hopes, and maybe their life hopes, were on the range, somewhere high up beyond the river.

"What happened after the argument?" Frank's wife asked, after Fate had recalled again all he could think of.

He shrugged. "I don't know. I was off with the stock," he said, but he lied and he guessed they knew it.

"Was there more trouble?" she asked.

"No," he said quickly, and realized at once from the silence and their expressions that he should not have answered so quickly. He guessed he was trapped into having to tell about something when he didn't understand all of it, for it had to do with Mina and something Ernest had said, and Fate knew it was embarrassing and anger-causing without knowing what it was, or whether he should tell it or not. He glanced at his mother, and she seemed wary, suspicious of the idea of his continuing, but she didn't tell him to stop. It was as it had been when he had started to go on the bear hunt; she had not told him to go or not to go, and now, as then, he took the more adventuresome way.

"It was when Frank and the German was cooking supper," he said, "and we was looking for wood to burn and going after water. Mina's papa come into the camp and said he hoped we'd have a pig to eat, and somebody said for me and Verlin to go get one of his'n to kill, but he said not to go, and he fell out of sorts with the idea and with us and everybody. 'Go get his best 'un,' Frank told us, but we didn't go. Then Mina's papa got to fussing at Mina, talking about the horse she had to ride while he had none, and talking about Grandpa Harrison. This was after Grandpa was gone to his own camp. Mina's papa said he was glad he didn't have any of Grandpa's blood in his veins, and said he had allus wished his wife hadn't borne a child at all, and he didn't know how it was that they was all girls unless there had been some way that Mina's mama knowed to change the thing with a stick or some other way."

Inez Plover, who was standing at the back wall, groaned and shook her head angrily. "He's a vile man in his ways," she murmured.

Fate was embarrassed, for he hadn't told all that Ernest had said, about how he guessed his wife had long fingers and could reach into herself and yank the little boy's peckers off, which is exactly what he had said, and Mina had got angry and told him to hush such talk. Fate didn't dare say all of it.

"He's not got kindness in him for his own young," Inez said bitterly, and the German woman nodded, as if she had known such men and such evil before.

"He said Mina didn't respect him," Fate told the women, "or if she did, she would let him ride her horse the next day. He said he was an old man, too old to walk. The German boy said he couldn't take the horse, for Mina had been helping all day with the turkeys and needed a horse, and the German man said the same, and the German boy and the German man got to arguing about which one of them should protect Mina from her pa. 'Ye honor yer father,' her papa said, 'and yer days are going to be long. The Bible says it. Honor yer father and mother and your days will be long on the face of the earth. That's from the Bible word for word.'

"And Mina said, 'It don't say nothing in the Bible about riding horses.'

"And her father said he was going to ride her horse the next day. They went on fussing about it until the German boy told him to be quiet, and then he got to fussing at the German boy, asking him if he liked Mina and if him and Mina had ever—if him and Mina had ever gone off in the woods together—if—" He stared before him at the far wall of the room, and the women were like waxen statues waiting for him to say the words they knew Ernest Plover would have said, waiting for the words to give them the right to their full fury and anger, but Fate didn't say them. "And the German boy leaped across the fire, scattering the bean pots and dusting the bread, and he got ahold of Mina's papa's throat and choked him and bit him on the shoulder—"

Inez groaned. "I knowed he shouldn't a gone so far off."

"And it was all that the others could do to haul them apart and hold them off of one another, and Mina's papa got to crying and talking about both the Germans wanting Mina. Then the murder woman started talking, reciting a poem she must a made up in her head, and she sat there by the fire near the turned-over bean pots and said it all, telling in verses about how she had killed Amos and how now she had walked a lonely road ever since."

There was a pause. The women watched Fate; every eye was on him, for nobody dared look, even in a glance, at the German woman, or even at Inez Plover, or to see the reaction of anybody else. All the little Plover girls were silent, too. Only Lorry didn't look at Fate; she looked down at her lap, where her hands were folded tightly.

"Where was Grover at all this while?" Belle asked.

"He was with Grandpa," Fate said. "They was off at the other camp."

"Did anybody go to visit that camp that night?"

"Mooney did," he said. "And when he got back to where we was, he was upset, but he said nothing to any of us, and we had a party going then and singing going on, and everybody was having a time. Mina and the young German danced for a long time, and then they went off into the woods together, and the German's father went looking for them soon after that, and Mina's father went off to try to find Mina's horse and hide it for the night."

"Who was watching the stock?" Florence said. "Was Jacob caring for what went on?"

"Nobody was watching the stock so much as each other," Fate said honestly. "And Mooney told me to bring his horse back down here and get the pack saddle on it and get corn shelled, for he said Grandpa wouldn't give us another bit of corn or nothing, so when dawn come this morning I rode as fast as I could here, and I've been here ever since and ought to be going back now."

"If they was fighting so much last night," Florence said, "they might be warring all the more by now."

"They was tired, that's all," Belle said.

Lorry helped Fate lift the baskets into place and lash them to the pack saddle, the one which two winters before they had helped Mooney and Verlin make. "You take care," she told him.

He shrugged, as if he had no fear of that long road, of that darkness, though he did, he certainly had fear inside himself of all that way and what beasts might be on it, and also fear of what he would find when he reached the camp itself.

"You take this rifle," she said, handing it to him.

He took it, for he needed it, he knew. He felt better with it.

"It's loaded, so take care," she said.

"Yes," he said. They were standing there by the horse in the darkness, and he felt her hand on his arm, and then suddenly she was drawing him closer to her, so close he almost smothered, and he clutched at her, held to her, and then as suddenly she stepped away from him. "Help him and Verlin to come home safe," she said from out of the darkness.

"Yes," he said, his throat closing on him even as he spoke, and he turned the horse and started up the little trail toward the valley road. Some of the Plover girls, going home, had to make way for him, and Fancy said something to him, but he hurried on, and above him he saw that the moon was being covered up by clouds, and over to the west a bank of clouds was rising, maybe storm clouds, and even so, he thought, even now they were up there on the ridge, bedded down for the night, with a storm rising on them.

26

It was misty the next morning when Verlin awoke. He reached over to awaken Fate, for normally he had to awaken Fate of a morning; then he sat up, startled to find that Fate wasn't there. Then he remembered that Fate had gone on back to the settlement.

He yawned and stretched. He saw that Mina wasn't at the fire; neither was Felix. Maybe they were off watching stock, or maybe they were off in the woods together, for the night before he had come upon them standing close together, their arms round each other, on a rocky place which overlooked the east valley. He had started to speak to them and call them in to mind the stock, which they should have been doing, when he saw the German standing not far away, also watching them, so Verlin crept to the fire again and let them be.

He put new logs on the fire now to dry and burn, and went into the woods. The stock was moving about, dissatisfied with the strangeness of the place. A wind suddenly gushed in on them, fresh and stinging, and whipped the tree limbs. A thunderbolt broke and rolled in from the west valley, not loud, not sharp, either, but rumbling ominously, and Verlin saw Jacob loom up out of the fog as if the noise had called him. "Where's the lead boar?" he asked.

"Near the road," Verlin said. "He was nigh that far rock when night come."

"Go find him, boy. Don't let him bolt off."

"How do you hold him?" he said.

"Talk to him, act calm," Jacob said. "I'll come over and talk to him in a little while. Don't move fast amongst them, while this storm threatens."

Verlin went off looking for the boar, but he got lost in the fog. The fog was deceptive, was over everything and changed the size and appearance of everything. Another bolt of thunder rolled in from the west valley, and a tough wind followed, billowing the mist and whining against the rocks and trees. A flutter of protest went through the turkey flock, which was back a ways on the road.

Mooney and Nicholas appeared, and Verlin stopped nearby, wondering how serious the storm might be. He listened as the two men calmly talked, discussing if they should move out the drove now and leave the turkeys roosting, or if they should try to hold everything there in the same place for a while longer. "I don't want to be parted," Nicholas said.

"No," Mooney said, "but the drove will need to move now, or they might bolt down the hillside."

The crack of thunder sounded again, came in louder this time, and the drove began moving about, seeking the trail. It was as if the thunder had decided for the men what they would need to do, and at once Mooney told Verlin to go bring the stock to the road. As if in answer, the boar appeared, and two big sows waddled onto the road and sniffed at the air, which was heavy-misted. The ox began to move, pulling the cart. The flock of geese appeared, Ernest Plover not even with them, and began to walk down the road, mingling with the swine drove, and suddenly out of the valley came a flash of lightning, then a crack of thunder that startled them all, and the boar and the other members of the drove began to move away. Mooney ran fast through the mist to reach the boar, and he passed the place where Mildred was standing, her horse's reins in her hand, staring before her as if she were witnessing the end of the world.

Down the road a piece, Tinkler Harrison's stock was milling about, ready to bolt, so he gave the order to move out. He told the Negro men to take charge of the sheep and horses, and he took his customary place at the head of the beef herd. "We're not far from the Watauga road, air we?" he said to Grover.

"We're not nigh it yet," Grover said

"We'll move on anyhow," Harrison said, speaking over the rumblings of the storm. "I'll not wait for them others. Drive the steers atter me."

Grover pulled to one side of the trail and let the noisy, scared cattle pass. He fell in behind them, driving the laggards on. A steer bolted from the herd and went off through the woods; he let it go. It was better to lose one, or even a few, than the whole herd. Down the trail, moving toward the river, he and the herd and his father rode, moving dangerously fast, seemed to Grover, until as last they came to the bottom rim of the storm and he could see well ahead, and could even see the river valley far below with the river winding about in the forested country. The danger was over, or so he sensed at once, and he reined in.

"How ye doing with the sheep?" he called toward the rear. The Negroes had the harder task, he knew, for there were only two men and two boys of them, and they had sheep and horses and carts to bring. "Hello, back there," he called.

Doubtless they would need a hand to help, he thought, and certainly they would want to know the heavy mist did not control the road all the way to the river. He started riding back toward them.

He rode uphill for a long way, and, as he became more worried, he rode through the fog more recklessly, seeking the others. Suddenly the sheep were upon him. The ram was right before his horse, and terror came into the eyes of the ram and the ram bolted off the trail, went through the woods. "Hey, hey!" Grover shouted, but he only scared the ram all the more, and the flock followed, he could not block off the flock from following. "Damn you!" he shouted, and beat at them with his whip, but it did no good. One of the Negroes appeared, gasping for breath, for he had been running after the sheep, and he stared bewildered at the flock.

Rain splashed against them. "We got to fetch them," Grover said, and he spurred his horse and rode into the woods, the other man following.

The rain was slapping at the tree trunks and a wave of air came up from the valley floor and sent it hurling upward, sweeping up the side of the range. Then the rain began pelting downward again.

The horse abruptly stopped, reared up, and Grover saw that the trail he was on dropped there so steeply that the horse was balking. He could even see the valley now far below, so he was almost below the cloud. He dismounted and ran down the path anxiously. He came to the under edge of the cloud and saw clearly the valley floor where the rain was beating down on the treetops.

The Negro man stopped beside him. "Where the sheep?" he said.

"On down some'ers," Grover said. "There," he said, pointing.

The sheep appeared below, making their way over the face of the rock cliff, approaching the edge of the rock, running on toward it.

"My Lord help us," Grover said. He heard the Negro gasp, and at that moment saw the ram leap. It was leaping at a patch of cloud floating near the edge of the range. The ram leaped into the patch of cloud and fell through it, gracefully dropped toward the valley.

Each sheep leaped into the cloud, and each in turn appeared below the cloud, falling out of the cloud into clear space below, falling gracefully, not fast, falling rather slowly, all falling at the same speed, into the trees of the valley. All of this soundless; there was no crashing, no crying, no baaing, no bleating. There was only the leaping, as if inevitably they must leap, as if the sacrifice had been planned this way. Below him fell the white ram, the white ewes, each falling to the death of each, and there was nothing to be done.

Sometime later Grover rode onto the river valley and saw his father sitting on a big rock, sitting there with his horse and two steers grazing on river grass nearby. He knew Grover was approaching, but he didn't hail him. He gazed at the broad river, where the water was rushing along, filling the banks to the top so that for two days or more there could be no fording it.

Grover tied his horse near his father's and walked about a bit to limber up.

"Where's the remainder of the cattle, Grover?" the old man said.

"Scattered, Papa."

"Why are they scattered? Wasn't you driving from the rear?"

"Until the storm stopped."

"So you let them scatter. I see, I see."

"There's cattle all over that range," Grover said simply.

The old man nodded. "Where are the sheep?" he said.

"They're down in the valley already, Papa."

Harrison cocked his head to one side. "They didn't pass me."

"Yes, they did," Grover said. He didn't care now; he was beyond caring. Damn them and the valley and the settlement and himself for ever having cared, for ever taking part in such a calamity.

"How did they pass me when I occupied the trail?"

"They went down the side of the range partway," Grover said, "and jumped."

Harrison didn't move. Nothing moved except his white hair where the wind ruffled it. "Jumped?"

"They're in the valley some'ers," Grover said. "They rained down on the trees up that east cove. They're in a pile probably five foot deep, if you want to go see them. They're all over there some'ers."

The old man sat studying the river. "You lost them sheep?"

"I told ye," Grover said.

The old man made no reply. It was all beyond him now. God had done it, he supposed. God and Grover had lost both cattle and sheep, yes, and no doubt God and others had lost hogs and fowl, horses and oxen and carts. It wasn't the easiest matter in the world to believe, but a man did well to admit to what he had seen, and with his own ears heard.

Grover mounted and rode off up the trail, going somewhere—Harrison didn't know where or why, and didn't care. He had not thought the drive would prove successful; he had not expected disaster, but here it was; it had come and would need to be accommodated.

Off in the woods the wolf packs were moving, and there on the trail Mooney could see now and again a horse, an ox, or some other brute crossing, fleeing. Through the woods the creatures fled, as panic increased everywhere. All of it, as he saw it, was like the final judgment and was more awesome than judgment in a courtroom; it was judgment in a high place, and it must be God as the judge sitting behind the cloud up there, for who else would dare to give out so many sentences so swiftly? Or maybe it was that Tinkler Harrison was the judge, as he was the symbol of their disunity, which had played a part in all of this, or maybe he, Mooney Wright, was judge, for he had put this drive into motion but had not been able to keep it organized, so now he, standing alone on the trail, could witness the end of it, not in Old Fort or Morganton, but here in the highest part of the wilderness.

It was more mournful than death, he thought, for it was a living thing knowing of its own death. It was not that a living thing knew of the death of a dead thing; the living thing became aware of its own death.

He saw Verlin hurrying down the trail, two pigs scattering before him. In his face was fear more than anything else; not surprise so much as fear. He stopped nearby, and Mooney saw that tears were in his eyes. He asked nothing, but his expression was one of bafflement and asking, his body stance and all about him asked to know what had happened and what it meant.

Mooney couldn't bear to look at him. He shook his head and tried to indicate that the boy shouldn't feel so distraught, but even as they stood there, way off, somewhere in the valley judging from the sound, a brute began a shrill cry, that of a captured animal that is close to death, and the cry went on for a long while.

Mooney tried to make a fire, but the wood was wet. He used the last of his powder and, failing finally, he stretched out on the damp trail, tired beyond all thought, and rested his head on his hands. Up above him the clouds were parting and he could see the stars. At least, he could see a few stars.

Verlin sat nearby, hunched over. He was a steady boy, ordinarily; he counted on his plans working out properly. He had much confidence in work, and he believed that a man could do what he wanted to, what he planned to do. He had been ill prepared for such a catastrophe as this.

"We lost might nigh all of it, boy," Mooney said, "except the breed stock that's to home. Come way up here to lose it. Save it from the bears back home; drive it up here and lose it." The boy moaned, and Mooney guessed the boy had never known a soul pain as deep as this one. "What you going to tell your mama? Tell her how your real papa come home and offered to take you out west, to flat land, to rich soil, to a settlement; but we stayed back in here. Tell her how it was we chose wrong."

Verlin stopped moaning and listened. Way off they heard a pig squeal.

"That's how it was a long time ago," Mooney said. "Imy and me was coming into this country, and a pig got caught in the river and went washing off downstream. Sounded like that."

Before morning Grover arrived, too. He sat down and talked about the losses. He got a fire started, and all of them huddled around it. Pretty soon the Negro boy found them and warmed himself, too. He had been lost in the woods, he said and the stories he told were of killings he had seen, of carcasses left bleeding while wolves went on to some other butchering.

Soon after dawn Tinkler Harrison arrived. He was carrying a pack of personal possessions, and he was going home, he said. Nobody said anything to him. He went through the camp, and behind him the two Negro men came, each carrying a few cooking utensils, and behind them came three pigs and two horses that were following along, and a steer, and down the road came another steer. When the second steer had passed,

Mooney pushed himself up from the ground and stared down the hill, as if considering what he ought to do; then he turned and followed in the direction Harrison led.

A few pigs came out of the woods to follow along.

Up near the crest of the ridge, they came upon Fate. He was listening to Mina, who was standing beside her horse, calming it, and was watching the passing company. Fate joined Mooney, and Mina fell in beside Mildred, who rode toward home with the same forlorn and prophetic face she had shown on leaving it. Along the crest of the ridge they went, as sorrowful as a funeral procession, now and then somebody stopping and eating a piece of bread, or eating chestnuts.

It was sunny now; for the first time since the drive started, it was warm.

"There it is," the big Negro said toward nightfall. He was the first to see the valley, the cabins sending up columns of smoke, and to see the little river. "There it is," he said again. "We'll be home soon."

He and Harrison stopped partway down the ridge, near the lookoff that once Lacey Pollard had used, and waited for Grover to catch up with him. Then they went on. Mooney and the boys moved in the dust they created, and behind them, not far away, Mina walked, leading her horse, and near her a few pigs came along, and a steer, and behind her Mildred rode on her thin horse, and the Germans came along, and so it went on back up the line of walking ghosts, for each was a ghost, Mooney thought, and they were going into the ghost valley with the ghost stock and the ghost hopes and with the ghost stories from the drive.

Down past the webbed starting of the river, a dog was there; it had come out from the German's place to meet them. "The German'll be along," Mooney said to the dog. "He'll be along soon, for he has no stock to drive." They walked on past the German's house. His wife was at the door, her bonnet on even though it was evening, and she looked down at them wonderingly. They were dust-coated; they were gray and tan beasts walking, nothing else or more. She saw her husband coming along, tired out and dejected.

They went past the Plover place, and the little girls came out to line up alongside the road and stare perplexedly at so sad a company, which seemed so ridiculous now and had only a few days before seemed so powerful and grand. Harrison, without speaking, walked past them and led his men and the little bit of stock that had followed down his trail toward his own house; Belle came to the door of the house to watch him. "It's all over," he called to her gruffly. "We lost it all. It's all gone now."

Mooney was in the lead now of the diminishing company, and he walked slower than had Harrison. When he and the boys reached a branch, the one that separated his land from Ernest Plover's, he stopped and washed his hands and splashed water on his face. "I first saw the bear nigh here," he said, and he heard the boys stir, for they always perked up interest at the mention of the bear.

Fate came to the branch, knelt down and washed. Then Verlin came.

"It's not proper to come home so empty of goods," Mooney said. "I meant to come home with white sugar, as well as brown, with a candle mold, with cloth for a dress, with wheat flour. I saw myself coming home with all manner of kingly stuff, and what do we have? The same worn horse we left with."

The boys huddled nearby, quiet as sleep.

He roused himself at last. He crossed the branch and started along the trail. He came to the path that led to his cabin, and he was no sooner on the path than Lorry appeared, coming from the direction of the milking log. She saw him, and she stopped there, surprised, her hand shading her eyes from the low sun. She must have known then; she must have decided on seeing the three of them that they were there for a reason of defeat and losses, and maybe of tragedy. She started toward them, walking faster as she came, and Mooney walked faster to meet her, and they came together and embraced each other, each sensing loss and needing the other, and he said, the words choking him so that he could scarcely speak them, "We lost it all, Lorry, we lost it all, and never even come in sight of the river."

It was not that night; it was the next one when those who had been on the drive, or most of them, at least, for some reason began to gather at Mooney's house. Maybe it was to listen to Mooney and to Jacob, for he was usually there, or maybe it was to tell about their experiences, or maybe it was to find out who was leaving the valley and when they were going, and who was staying on in spite of poverty and the toughness of the life there.

Nobody said why they had come to the house, but they came to make company, of course, Jacob and Florence first, then Frank. The cabin was crowded enough; then Grover arrived; there was a bedful then, as well as the chairs full, and the boys were on the floor. There wasn't more than room to breathe in, as Florence said, but two more arrived before long—the German and his son, and everybody went outdoors.

A fire was made out there, and they stood around it, talking. They told stories about the drive, each one talking as if nobody had been present except himself, as if nobody had heard of the drive before. They told stories of surprise and danger and death and losses and terror such as they had not known before. They wanted all the happenings told, as if telling them to the fire would record them, or as if telling them to so many others would record them. Mina arrived, and she told mostly about her horse, about the courage of the horse, and then about its falling in the storm and spraining its leg, and about how she had helped it back home and wouldn't let it be shot, even though her father had wanted to shoot it.

The talk remained serious, as the drive had been serious. Somebody said the valley couldn't survive a year without lowland supplies, and nobody said anything different.

"It's easier by far to farm in the lowlands," Frank said, and everyone agreed.

"It might be better in the Cumberland," the German said.

"Be better to go on south to another valley," Grover said, "or leave the mountains entirely."

"Go out West," Frank said.

They formed a circle around the fire and talked about the drive and leaving, and nobody seemed to know when he was leaving. It was as if all of them knew they were leaving but were not certain yet, and hoped a miracle as meaningful as the miracle which made them want to leave were to happen to make them stay.

It was quite late when the women drew back from the circle. They went into the cabin and began to mix meal with water to make parting bread for the group. The men began to leave the circle, too, and shift about, walk along the edges of the field, and Mooney went on up into the field to the grave where Imy was, and from there he could see the others, and it was as it had been the night of the bear, when they had come to his house and had stood around a fire. Again they were severe, unsmiling, and again they were close, united, a people who had gone through dangers together.

He looked up at the mountain. It had a snow topping tonight, and the moon cast a warm light on it. There's no prettier sight, he thought, and no prettier place than this one. It traps a man into staying, into building here; then it shows him that he doesn't even possess his own cabin and fields. The valley is its own, he knew now. The valley and the beasts and the mountain and the snows and the water and the cliffs owned themselves yet. If he left here, in a few years there would be little sign that he had even come. The vines would cover the buildings and pull them down; they would pull over even the tombstone here at Imy's grave. The trees would spring up in the fields and gnarl again with roots the yielding land. The clearing he had made on the hill would become again part of the whole, as the bear had been part of the whole and now in its grave was part of the whole, unprotestingly.

He could hear the German talking. "If we could have got the stock to the river, we could a made rafts well enough..."

It was only man that was always moving, trying to get more than he had.

"With weather calm, it might not be so troublesome to make a drive," Jacob said.

That night Mooney lay awake in bed. He guessed Lorry was awake, too, and he spoke to her, and she made a soft, murmuring reply. He began to talk to her. They talked about what they would lose in leaving, mentioning the cabin and sheds and springhouse, the work already done, mentioning the plans they had had for other fields and for a mill and for a settlement.

"We'd have the graves to leave," he said, "there's that, too. I buried a woman, you've buried a man, and we buried Paul up there near what's Jacob's cabin now."

They talked that way, not yet seeing how they could stay, not yet willing to tear themselves free from the place they had made.

Grover came by several nights later and said his father was ill, had been sickly since the drive; maybe he had caught a sickness up on the ridge. Anyway, something was sapping his strength.

The family lighted torches and went down to Harrison's big house, where they were admitted by the younger of the Negro women. She told them Mr. Harrison was lying down.

They went quietly into his bedroom, and there he sat bolt upright in bed, fully clothed, with his hat on and a riding crop in his hand. He was tense and alert, but there was no sense of strength about him, and there was no more color in his face than there is in river water.

"Lie down, Papa," Belle said to him, but he would not. He sat there as if ready to go to his horse and ride out across his fields.

"Why did all of you come?" he demanded. "I sent fer Mooney only."

"Now, Papa," Belle said placatingly.

"Here, help me to my feet."

"No, you're too weak to stand," she said.

"Mooney, help me up."

Mooney helped him. He thought the old man ought to do what he wanted. He helped him up, and sensed at once the man's reliance on him, felt his hand tighten on his arm, holding to him desperately. "You carry that there split-bottom chair and come with me," he said, and he moved shakily across the room, the riding crop falling from his hand and he not knowing it.

He made his way slowly out of the cabin and across the yard. He went to the riverbank, where a casual wind was moving the willow branches, and he told Mooney to put the chair down. He sat down in it and for the first time realized he had lost his riding crop. Verlin brought it to him; he took it and chased Verlin away. "Git, git," he said, and the boy fled.

He held the crop firmly in his hand, as if it were the last authority left to him, and looked at the river, flowing so darkly and swiftly by. "I dreamed the other night an awful dream," he said.

Mooney was standing behind him, looking down at the back of his head and at the river beyond.

"A man's mind is a strange creature for a man to have to live with; God knows, it don't make sense most of the time. No telling what a man will dream, or what he will think, either." He stared down into the rushes of the river, and when he talked it was so softly that his words couldn't be heard distinctly. "I saw a hole in the ground, and I thought it was my own grave. I crawled into it and begun to dig into the ground, and I dug and made a narrow passageway, and I went on and dug my way into my wife's grave." He shook his head, aggravated by the thought. "I dug into the hole where she lay and clawed the pine boards away from her and made love to her remains."

Mooney stared sternly at him, sitting still in the straight chair.

"It was as real as if it happened in my own bed."

"I've dreamed strange," Mooney said.

"A man can dream anything. Years ago I dreamed I slept with Lorry. Does that surprise ye?"

"Yes, it does."

"A man dreams what he dreams, that's all, and might be anything at all, for he's all tied up with lies, anyhow, and worries. My Lord, we come out of a narrow opening in a woman and try to get our eyes to see something, not knowing at all what the world is, or our parents are, or we are. And now I'm nigh to old-age death and I don't know yet what the world is, or I am. I know it's been a pleasure to be alive for these years, though I don't know what being alive is. I might very well die in this chair afore I ever stop looking at that river, but I don't know what death is. Some say it's angels in Heaven, but I don't have any more use for angels than I have for a lame horse. Sometimes I hear tell about angel voices singing. What do they sing? Do they sing about work, about the plowing and planting? Do they sing about this valley when the blooms open out? Do they sing about that river? Can they sing better than that river can? Do they plant crops and watch it rain and watch growth come? Do they harrow the fields with a pine bough, like you, or use a harrow with locust teeth like me, or do they use a harrow with gold teeth, or some such foolish contraption, or turn soil with a gold-tipped plow?"

"No need to talk as if you're about to die, Mr. Harrison," Mooney said, for he felt he ought to say something like that.

"In one dream the other night, I was going back through the cord into the belly of my mama. That's a sign of coming death, ain't it?"

"I don't know what dreams mean."

"What I'm saying is that I'm dying, I'm going on out of here, and I've come to wondering what I'm leaving and who I'm leaving it to. A man likes to die in order, if he can, and I see now that all I got is here in this valley, and it was about this valley I used to have my dreams." He fidgeted with the riding crop. "They're not coming true, air they?"

"I believe not," Mooney said.

"There's no better river than that one, no better land than that you stand on now, no prettier sight than them hills over there, but something's wrong with it all. Is it me? I know it might be, for nothing I've ever done has been of the best quality."

"There's no road in or out, that's part of it."

"You can make a way, if you take control and drive on through, and have half luck with the weather."

"We tried it—"

"I know, but I didn't do so well, wasn't sold on it then. A drive takes working together, and so does a settlement. I tell you, a drive can be made, given time."

"It's still a long way up here. It's harder here than anywhere else."

"Then learn to make your own goods last longer."

"We're ragged now; we're nigh naked."

"Make more clothes, make more wool and cotton. You can grow cotton here, once the land gets wore out some."

It was so, Mooney knew, much of it was, but the old man needed to admit to the toughness of the situation, too. "Lacey Pollard left a section of flat land out West, and we're bound to go there and at least see if it suits us."

"Lacey's buried right over there beyond them willows, outside the root spread of them trees. I picked the place out myself. That damn fool Ernest Plover come down here and set about making a coffin, and I had to have it all done proper. His coffin wouldn't do fer a chicken coop. I had a hole dug as deep as a man is tall, and we put Lacey away in it. He's here in this valley now. He never cared one whit about the Cumberland, and neither do I, or you for that matter. I never cared one whit about Virginia, neither, or my farm there. But I care here, and that's what I'm saying. I know it's harder here, but I care more here. It takes more work here, it takes a man's life here, it asks all a man has to give and a man gains as well as loses by joining in with land like that. But now it's being deserted. Even whatever grave I have in it will be deserted, seems like. I don't want it that way. I want it peopled. I want a church here and a school and men and women on the trails; I want people out farming and women cooking meals. I don't want vines to cover over what we've made, or take away the best dream I ever had."

"Do you know what it takes to live up here, and how little it offers?"

"Yes, I know. But a settlement, afore it's started, is bound to be like that. Every new thing is unpromising at birth."

The water flashed behind, skitted over the rocks and rapids, and the clouds moved swiftly over the moon, there beyond the ridge across the river, and the ridge was shaded and was as dark as hemlock trees in summer.

"So I'm going to parcel out my possessions according to my wishes. My house will go to Belle; she's not earned it, for she's not bore a single time, is as empty of fruit as an elm tree, but I aim to give her the house and her choice of beds. These fields and most of my stock I'll leave to Grover. He can keep it unless he ever weds with Belle, in which case he loses ever' inheritance from me. I'll not have son and wife living together, do ye hear that?" He lifted the riding crop and whipped it through the air in a fierce and determined gesture. "As for the rest," he said, and once more he raised the riding crop, though now he used it as a pointer to indicate the valley, the mountain, the ridges on both sides of the river, indicating the land that lay as far as the eye could see. He turned partway around in the chair. "The rest I'll give to you. No, not to you, but to Lorry and the boys. I'll give you nary thing except whatever's left of my vision for this place. Do ye take it? Or do I go down plumb useless to the ground?"

His eyes flashed, as if moonlighted, and he sat there with his white hair blowing in the river breeze. His mouth was half open as he waited for an answer, and Mooney nodded curtly to him, felt sorry for him, gave him some assurance anyway, for Mooney knew, even before the old man had finished, that he was likely to stay here. The old man's dream was Mooney's dream as well, had been for a long time. He would not stay for that reason, or for the old man at all, or do anything else for him, but he would stay for the place itself, of which already he was a part, possessor of some of it and possessed by it. For five years he had dug himself into the land, and every death and loss had driven him deeper, every planting had made him more a part of his own fields, and he would not leave, could not leave, nor could Lorry. Maybe Fate could leave; maybe Fate ought to leave and seek out the property on the Cumberland. But poverty or not, lean years or not, suffering or not, Mooney would have to stay.

A person becomes part of what he does, he thought, grows into what grows around him, and if he works the land, he comes to be the land, and owner of and slave to it.

He looked away from Harrison, gazed at the far ridge across the river. Calmly he said, "That cow of mine, I been meaning to get a bull to breed her to, so's I can get the start of a herd that way."

Harrison's gaze sharpened. "How much is the service of a bull worth to ye?"

"And a bag of salt is needed at my place. I hate to travel all the way to Morganton for it, when I can borrow it from you and pay you back after next year's drive."

The eyes glistened sharper still. "Salt up here ought to be worth a sow a bushel."

"I'll give you two lambs for a bushel of salt and the use of the bull," Mooney said.

"Two sows is what I'm asking."

"I'll give you two lambs, and when I pay the salt back, you can give me one lamb in return."

"I'll not bargain for lambs. What do I want with mutton? I'll take two sows or nothing; now state your preference."

They stood out there in the moonlight, the old man trembling, Mooney being as adamant as he, and they argued the matter down to one lamb, one pig, and two hens from Lorry's chicken flock. It was the first trade the two of them had made together in some time.

He and Lorry and the boys were walking back up toward home, and they saw a fire burning in the woods between the Plovers' and the Germans' places. "Somebody camping," he said, and stopped to consider it. A hunter maybe, or new settlers who had stopped there for the night.

Then he heard a chopping sound. The sound went out across the valley and was echoed back from the far hills, and it reminded him of the time he and Imy had cut down the first trees long years before and had worked at night to bark and notch them in time to get a shelter up. "Who do ye suppose?" he said.

They walked along until they were near the fire. They moved quietly, feeling their way toward it. They were close by when he made out the figure of the young German, saw him lift the ax and bring it down with sureness. He made his way even closer, and was near him when Felix laid down the ax and wiped sweat from his face.

A girl got up from where she had been sitting, went to the ax and took it up. It was Mina, and as he watched she began to chop at the log, and his mind went trailing back in time to the earlier evenings, to when she had cut logs at Ernest Plover's place, and even back to when he and Imy had cut logs before that, at night, too, and when she had made a fire so he could see to cut logs, and from time to time had moved it.

"I thought I was done with cutting of trees a long time ago," Mina said. "I get so tired of trees I wisht a streak of lightning would come and set a blaze to ever' one that ever sprouted. The trees and the wolves is the curse of this country, and if I didn't know we'd have a cabin built afore winter, and if I didn't want to have a place to warm myself, I never would do such work again."

Felix looked at her fondly, watched her as she moved in the firelight, and now and then she would flash a smile at him.

It's all as it should be, Mooney thought, it's all right for her at last. Up on the ridge, in the days of the drive, she and Felix must have come to know each other; they had gone through dangers together and had suffered loss together. Now they would do very well.

It wasn't far, this place, from where he and Imy had first camped, he thought. Not far, either, from the place where the bear had come. A good starting place, he thought. It would take Mina and Felix only a few years to have children growing and stock ready for fall drives. They would start here their own clan to struggle with and be a part of the land.

He looked up at the dark mountain. Another small house and family will be set against it, he thought, close to the wildness of it, the merciless, the pitiless mind of it, there in the shadow of it.

1784

27

Spring must have intended to come in April that year, but coolness lingered at night in spite of the warm days, and it was May before the buds broke open and Mooney took from the rafters of the shed the handles of the plow which he had made. He fastened into place with hickory pegs the plowshare, and got out the horse. She seemed to know from many times past how to wait and what it was she waited for.

He fastened the harness, which he had cut from the bearskin, which he, Verlin and Fate had tanned. He flicked a switch and the old horse moved, and he and Verlin and Fate lifted the plow and carried it up the hill to the field. "Whoa, here," he said, and the horse stopped.

Lorry came to the door of the cabin and watched them. "How many rows you planning on making?" she asked.

"As many as we can fit in," he said, checking the harness. He and Verlin set the plow in place. He clicked his tongue at the horse, took the plow handles firmly in hand, and put his weight on the plow handles and weighted the blade, and the plow moved, the earth turned, the dark earth turned and the smell of the earth came into the air and the row opened to him and yielded to him and was ready.

TITLES IN SERIES

For a complete list of titles, visit www.nyrb.com or write to:
Catalog Requests, NYRB, 435 Hudson Street, New York, NY 10014

J.R. ACKERLEY Hindoo Holiday*
J.R. ACKERLEY My Dog Tulip*
J.R. ACKERLEY My Father and Myself*
J.R. ACKERLEY We Think the World of You*
HENRY ADAMS The Jeffersonian Transformation
RENATA ADLER Pitch Dark*
RENATA ADLER Speedboat*
CÉLESTE ALBARET Monsieur Proust
DANTE ALIGHIERI The Inferno
DANTE ALIGHIERI The New Life
KINGSLEY AMIS The Alteration*
KINGSLEY AMIS Girl, 20*
KINGSLEY AMIS The Green Man*
KINGSLEY AMIS Lucky Jim*
KINGSLEY AMIS The Old Devils*
KINGSLEY AMIS One Fat Englishman*
WILLIAM ATTAWAY Blood on the Forge
W.H. AUDEN (EDITOR) The Living Thoughts of Kierkegaard
W.H. AUDEN W.H. Auden's Book of Light Verse
ERICH AUERBACH Dante: Poet of the Secular World
DOROTHY BAKER Cassandra at the Wedding*
DOROTHY BAKER Young Man with a Horn*
J.A. BAKER The Peregrine
S. JOSEPHINE BAKER Fighting for Life*
HONORÉ DE BALZAC The Human Comedy: Selected Stories*
HONORÉ DE BALZAC The Unknown Masterpiece *and* Gambara*
MAX BEERBOHM Seven Men
STEPHEN BENATAR Wish Her Safe at Home*
FRANS G. BENGTSSON The Long Ships*
ALEXANDER BERKMAN Prison Memoirs of an Anarchist
GEORGES BERNANOS Mouchette
ADOLFO BIOY CASARES Asleep in the Sun
ADOLFO BIOY CASARES The Invention of Morel
CAROLINE BLACKWOOD Corrigan*
CAROLINE BLACKWOOD Great Granny Webster*
NICOLAS BOUVIER The Way of the World
MALCOLM BRALY On the Yard*
MILLEN BRAND The Outward Room*
SIR THOMAS BROWNE Religio Medici and Urne-Buriall*
JOHN HORNE BURNS The Gallery
ROBERT BURTON The Anatomy of Melancholy
CAMARA LAYE The Radiance of the King
GIROLAMO CARDANO The Book of My Life
DON CARPENTER Hard Rain Falling*
J.L. CARR A Month in the Country*
BLAISE CENDRARS Moravagine
EILEEN CHANG Love in a Fallen City

* *Also available as an electronic book.*